SIR ARTHUR'S LEGACY  BOOK 4

DEFYING ROGER

SARAH EDWARDS

Cover: Deranged Doctor Design
First Electronic Edition: October 2019
ISBN: 978-1-990731-09-9
ISBN: 978-1-990731-08-2

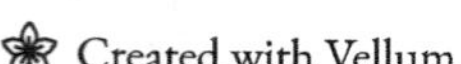 Created with Vellum

Chapter One

Roger would rather jab his dagger into his eye than sit in Anglesea's hall, like he currently was, and watch helplessly as his carefully laid plans went ass over head.

He despised failure, hated it, yet judging by his intended bride's reaction to his courtship performance, he and failure now shared a bed. Love and war, with a clear plan, a man could manage one in much the same manner as the other. Hadn't a lifetime under the guiding hand of Sir Arthur of Anglesea set this lesson into Roger's marrow?

Except, Roger's courtship had veered from the battle plan.

Lady Mathilda had accepted his flowers with her sweet, lovely smile and even moved her skirts to make a place for him beside her. Since then, his plan had moved from disarray into rout. Lady Mathilda should be sighing by now, at least peeping at him from beneath thick dark lashes. He'd watched William turn a woman sweet a hundred times.

In her haste to put distance between them, she inched her curvy hips down the bench, almost tipping onto her pert ass. She pressed a fluttering hand to her throat. "Five sons, Sir Roger?"

"Aye." He softened his tone. A woman would not enjoy being bellowed at like a man-at-arms. "My mother had four, and the two girls. I wager we could do better." He gave her a tiny nudge. "Aye?"

Agape, Lady Mathilda shook her head. Her nut-brown hair made a silky swish on the bench.

Too abrupt? Perhaps. He should have refrained from the nudge for certain, but more desperation crept through him with each passing moment. "Of course, that is if you are willing, my lady."

Gentle, his mother had urged. Woo her with sweet words and smiles.

Roger smiled.

She stared at him with huge eyes, dark like aged walnut, and gave him her flawless profile.

Mother had chosen well. Lady Mathilda boasted the sort of beauty that would make any man want to strut and crow like a barnyard cock.

"Your lips." He gave it another try. Please let the spirit of his brother, William, dwell within him now. "Are as ripe as...apples. Red apples, not green. Not the red and green ones either. All red, like..." Jesu, give him strength. Even he could do better than that. "I mean cherries."

"You are most kind." Her chest rose and fell with her quickened breathing, and while a man tried not to look, or get caught looking, she filled out the front of her bliaut with a tasty, ripe bounty.

Roger balled his hand into a fist, tempted to punch his own face with it. He made a dog's ballocks of this. Give him a keep to tear down, a young soldier to train, a horde of marauding Scots. Anything but this.

Still, he'd vowed to marry, and marry he would. Time to do his duty as the heir. At his feet, his favorite bitch peered at him and whined. She understood him, never needed pretty words from him. Why couldn't women be more like dogs? Only, with not quite so much fur and the bad breath. There must be something they could speak of. He waded into the oozing silence. "Dogs?"

Lady Mathilda clasped her hands in her lap, fingers white about the knuckles. "Dogs, Sir Roger?"

"Aye, dogs. Do you like them?"

"Nay."

He should talk about her. That last bit of counsel from older sister, Faye. "What do you like?"

"Me?" She started. A flush stained her peachy skin. Mother had certainly found him a girl to rival Faye in looks.

"Aye."

"I like flowers."

There, he had done one thing right. "Flowers are nice. And?"

"Um..." She stroked her skirts over her knees. "Silk. I like silk."

"Then I shall be sure to clothe you in silk for the rest of your days."

Her head snapped up and she went taut beside him. "The rest of my days?"

"Indeed." The rest of his life seemed to stretch in front of him like an endless road to nowhere. Did Lady Mathilda perhaps sense his reluctance to marry? "I am sure we will be very happy together."

Lady Mathilda sprang to her feet. "Aye." Retreat bellowed from every taut line of her as she scurried away.

Roger received the message clearly. Lady Mathilda did not favor his suit.

Her full hips rocked with the speed of her flight.

It was a pity for her, then, that Roger of Anglesea had decided he would wed Mathilda of Mandeville. Will she or nil she.

* * *

Kathryn stuck her head around the screens at one end of Anglesea's hall and tried to signal her sister. Matty charged straight into hell with all Kathryn's carefully conceived and executed plans. Why could a person not run a courtship like a battle? It would be so much simpler that way.

Matty stared at Sir Roger like the man had sprouted two heads. Blast! What ailed her sister? Sir Roger fit Kathryn's requirements to perfection. Not much for prayer, Kathryn had spent hours on her knees asking for just such a husband for Matty. They'd been at Anglesea for two days now, and Kathryn's relief when she met Sir Roger had made it easy to encourage Matty to welcome the match.

She could not fathom, why today of all days, the usually biddable Matty had taken one of her huffs into her head. Lord above knew, they did not happen often, but when Matty took one of her stands, there would be the devil's work to sway her. The wedding contracts remained unsigned, on Sir Arthur's behest, until Roger and Matty both agreed they would suit.

Sir Roger tugged at his tunic neck as he shifted on the bench beside Matty.

If only the man had a touch more address. To be fair, however, Kathryn had not aided his courtship because of his honeyed words and pretty gestures. She had explained all this to Matty.

Matty rose and near ran for the door.

Fists balled by his sides, wide shoulders taut, Sir Roger watched her go.

Matty rushed past and Kathryn dropped into step beside her. "What happened?"

With a shriek, Matty leaped away from her. "Kate?" She pressed her hands to her bosom. "You near scared the life out of me. I thought you were him."

"Father?"

"Nay, *him*." Matty jerked her head toward the hall. She glanced back. "Does he pursue me?"

Sir Roger stood, much as Matty had left him, with a tremendous frown on his handsome face.

"Nay." Kathryn lengthened her strides to keep up with Matty. "What happened?"

Matty stopped, one foot on the bottom stair. "Did you see him?"

"Aye, I did. Great comely fellow that he is." Kathryn suffused as much enthusiasm as she could into her words. Not as pretty as his brother, William, but Kathryn preferred Sir Roger's more rugged looks.

Matty shuddered. "He is a brute."

"Brute?" Kathryn followed her sister up the stairs. "Nay, Matty, but he is a warrior, which is why we agreed you should marry him."

Matty spun and glared. "We agreed to nothing. You and father said I should marry him."

"Matty." It was the first and last time Kathryn would probably agree with their father. "We spoke about this. Remember?"

Matty drooped. Her eyes filled with tears. "I cannot marry him."

"But why not?" Kathryn climbed closer to her sister. "He may be big and rough, but I enquired everywhere about him. They say he is tough but fair, and kind to his people. Men like that do not come about like the village peddler. We must snap him up while we can."

"I cannot." On a soft cry, Matty ran up the stairs.

"But you must," Kathryn whispered to the empty space. Desperation clouded her thoughts. Matty must marry Sir Roger. "How else am I to keep you safe?"

Chapter Two

Kathryn dug her heels into Striker's flank and urged him faster. The quintain sped closer, and Kathryn fixed her aim dead in the center. Her sword snug in her hand, she leaned to the side. Striker shifted his weight to accommodate her.

A hit! Dead center and the arm whirled around. Kathryn ducked low to Striker's neck to avoid the sandbag as it came about. She halted Striker before they plowed into the low wooden rail fence surrounding the practice yards.

After her failed conversation with Matty, she had gone straight to the stables and saddled Striker. Her intention to ride until she could formulate a new plan had been subverted by the Anglesea practice yards. Sir Arthur of Anglesea certainly kept a good yard for his men. Here amongst the predictable action of thrust and parry, the fine but exact joust against the quintain, she could think. Plan.

This marriage must happen. Everyone, from the stable hands to the village midwife loved Sir Roger, extolled his virtues. Could Matty have seen something in Sir Roger all Kathryn's clandestine enquiries had missed? She wiped her sweaty sword hand on her tunic. She would have preferred a lance against the quintain, but none lay about, so her sword would do.

"Get off that horse," Father bellowed.

Striker pranced to the side.

Father stomped across the practice yard toward her, ruddy with ill temper. His black stare bored holes straight through her tunic.

She'd disobeyed both parts of Father's decree. She hadn't stayed out of sight as much as possible, and even worse, she'd engaged in manly pursuits. Kathryn's belly tightened, but she hid her reaction behind a blank mask. Like a mad dog, her father sensed fear and fed on it.

She had last seen him happily ensconced in the armory with a mug in one hand and a buxom wench on his knee. It had augured well for a couple of hours out of his sharp notice.

She slid to the ground beside Striker. Sweat trickled down her sides.

"What did I tell you?" He grabbed her upper arm and yanked.

Kathryn stumbled forward.

His beefy hand engulfed her arm and tightened.

Searing pain shot up her arm. She refused to let the hurt show. Instead, she raised her chin and held his angry gaze. "There is nobody about. The men are all out."

"Lucky for you, you stupid girl." Spit dotted his thick lips and hit her face. "I warned you." He would leave bruises a mile wide on her arm. "You will not destroy your sister's chance at this match."

Matty's chance? His chance he meant. Her father was randy as a rutting buck for this alliance. Anglesea meant money and power, both of which the old cur would whore his soul for. Instead, he whored his youngest daughter.

"Forgive me, Father." She managed the words past her clamped jaw. "I will put Striker away and change before anyone is the wiser."

"Not this time." He shook her. The yard dipped and swirled

as her head jerked this way and that. "This time you will learn. I will have that horse carved into dog meat."

"Nay." Kathryn tried to step closer to Striker. She had raised him from a foal, trained him herself. Death would come before she lost him. "It will not happen again."

"You are right it will not." Her father pushed his face closer to hers. "Because when we return to Mandeville Castle, that horse will be dead."

A deep voice came from behind Father's heavy shoulder. "That would be a shame."

Tall as a tree and just as wide, Sir Roger stood with one booted foot on the bottom rail of the fence surrounding the practice yard. The wind toyed with his dark hair. "That is a fine animal."

"Sir Roger." Father gave a turd-sucking grin. "I did not see you there. Were you not whispering sweet nothings to our Mathilda?"

"Lady Mathilda was called away," he said.

Or ran away. Whatever the reason, he seemed disinclined to tattle on Matty. Another excellent quality in his favor. She would get Matty to see reason.

"What a pity." Father rubbed his hands together. "Such a fine pair you make."

"Speaking of fine pairs"—Sir Roger strode closer—"your daughter and that horse are as well-matched a pair as I have clapped eyes on. It would be a terrible shame to separate them."

"Separate them?" Father slapped Striker's withers. "As if I would. Nay, I am merely funning with the girl."

Relief made her dizzy. Father would never risk his displeasure. She wanted to fall at Sir Roger's feet and thank him.

"Is this your oldest daughter?" Sir Roger loomed above her, his direct gaze on her. Dark hair, blue eyes, and a pair of shoulders that looked as if they could swing a battle-axe with ease.

A flush crept over her cheeks. His intense scrutiny disconcerted her. She felt small and delicate before him and, for the first time in her life, she felt the girlish urge to giggle.

"Indeed." Father shoved in front of her. "This is Kathryn, but I beg you to pay her garb no mind." He sidled closer to Sir Roger. "She is a bit of a strange one. There is one in every keep, is there not?" Hearty laugher gushed from him as he nudged Sir Roger.

"Indeed." Sir Roger stepped away. "I taught my youngest sister to fight with a dagger. A woman should know how to defend herself."

Kathryn dropped her head to hide her surprise. Not many men thought as he did. He grew in her estimation.

"Aye." Father bobbed his head.

"I have never taught a woman to joust, however." Sir Roger smiled at her.

Kathryn's mind emptied. Her feet rooted to the spot. Handsome in repose, when he smiled...dear Lord. The man had a smile to bring the birds from the trees. It crinkled about his eyes and softened the stern lines of his mouth.

"Women do not joust." Father gaped at him.

"Come now, Sir Royce." Sir Roger clapped Father's back.

Father staggered two steps forward. A full head shorter than Sir Roger, but wide through the girth, her father bore considerable meat on his bones.

"You have two charming daughters. Allow a man the pleasure of both their companies." Sir Roger winked. "Let me get to know my sister by marriage, at least."

Father tugged his ear. "There will be time enough for that once you are wed to our Matty."

"You are right." Sir Roger threw his arm about Father's shoulders. "But an ally in Lady Mathilda's camp could not hurt."

Clever man, making the one argument that would weigh with her father. Was his intervention deliberate or merely a fortunate coincidence?

Father huffed, and shifted his feet. "I would not want her to cause offense. I have told her not to concern herself with men's matters." He shot a glare at her.

Her blood ran cold. Sir Roger's presence had merely delayed her punishment.

"I am not in the least offended," Sir Roger said. "I find it rather...endearing."

Endearing? That might just be enough to save her a beating. Sir Roger seemed a little more perceptive than she had suspected.

"Very well then." Father threw his hands wide and forced a chuckle. "Amuse yourself with our little Kate, whilst I go and find your bride."

"A splendid idea," Sir Roger said.

Her father shuffled across the practice yard sand toward the keep.

"So, you enjoy manly pursuits?" Sir Roger shifted closer to her.

Kathryn knew not what to make of him, and she trod carefully. "Aye."

"I have yet to see a woman joust," he said.

"That does not mean they cannot," she said.

Sir Roger crossed his arms over his wide chest. "Not very well."

"I hit the target dead center."

"Aye." He shoved his hands in his belt and shrugged. "But you hit a wooden shield with a sword. A lance is much longer and more unwieldy."

"I do not have a lance."

"And a man's chest is much denser to pierce and doesn't hang there like a ripe plum for you to skewer. The way you hung off your horse like a rag poppet would have seen your ass in the dust."

Father looked behind him before he entered the keep. Even from there, his scowl burned into her.

"I suppose you could do better," she said.

Sir Roger merely chuckled. "You know I could."

"Do it then."

He raised his brow. "Is that a challenge?"

"Maybe."

"Accepted." Sir Roger approached Striker, careful not to startle him. He stroked Striker's forelock, murmuring to him. "Will he bear me?"

"Of course he will." Striker was the best horse in the Kingdom. "Unless, of course, you do something stupid and then you will find your ass...I mean, yourself in the dust."

Sir Roger cantered Striker back to the far end of the yard. He drew his sword. "This is more difficult with a lance," he called.

Braggart. Kathryn sat on an overturned bucket.

"Hah!"

Striker shot forward, ears pricked, hooves beating a muted tattoo on the sand.

Sir Roger seemed part of the horse beneath him, smooth, fluid, and graceful. He had an excellent seat, controlling the horse with his thighs, making those tiny adjustments to keep his firm fit in the saddle.

He hit the quintain with a crack. It whirled in a blur, the swing arm heading straight for the back of his head.

Kathryn nearly shouted a warning, but he kept riding, sitting straight in the saddle, and the swing arm passed within a hair of him.

"Now"—he drew Striker in front of her and dismounted—"climb on this fine steed of yours and I will give you a fast lesson."

A real knight giving her instruction, an opportunity too good to be overlooked. "You will?"

"Up you go." Sir Roger clasped his hands for her to mount.

Kathryn sidestepped his hands and leaped into the saddle. Without touching the stirrup. Let him tell her any squire could best that.

"Good." He nodded, and ran a hand down Striker's shoulder. "You have a fine horse here."

"I trained him myself."

His harsh features softened as he caressed Striker's coat. "You did well, Lady Kate."

"Thank you." Kathryn grew breathless as he stared at her. "Kathryn. I do not like to be called Kate."

"Why?"

"I do not care for it."

"Kathryn it is then." His eyes, at first so cold, glowed warm and inviting. "You are not married?"

"Nay." She backed Striker up. "My sister is far more suited to make a wife. A man would be lucky to have her."

He looked at her, his expression inscrutable. "Your horse is not a tool. He is your partner, your helpmate, and together you enter the list."

His words warmed her heart, and she stroked Striker's neck. They were a pair, the two of them.

Sir Roger stepped back and crossed his arms. "Take your friend back there and show me what you can do."

"Aye, Sir Roger."

"And by all that is Holy, stop calling me Sir Roger. Roger will do nicely."

"Right you are..." It seemed so intimate to use his given name, but right somehow. He did not appear to be a man puffed up with his own importance. "Roger."

He grinned. "Now, ride!"

Kathryn rode Striker back and turned. She took aim and dug her heels into Striker.

Again, they hit the target square on. Let Roger tell her she foundered at this now. Why, the swing arm went round and round as if struck by the hand of God.

"Understand something first." He rested his elbows on the top rail of the fence behind him. "When you tilt, you ride fast, ride hard, and hit hard."

She already knew that and opened her mouth to tell him so.

"Which brings me to the second thing you need to understand. The force of your blow relates to how fast you ride and how much weight you put behind your blow." He pushed away from the fence. "As a woman, you are at a size disadvantage. One hit and you're in the dust."

"I would not be—"

"Your opponents will be bigger, but that does not mean you will always lose. You ride like a girl, however, and you will need to correct that."

"I—"

"Your timing and your aim need to be perfect as well, because everyone gets hit." He took hold of her bridle and stroked Striker's neck. "In your case, you need to mitigate against the force of that hit."

She still burned to correct him about the riding like a girl, but he had just voiced her biggest concern. "And you know how I can do that."

"I know it is not by sweeping across your target." He raised his brow. "Aim for the target, from the moment you begin your approach. The horse moves beneath you, and if you bring your sword down and then attempt to aim, your opponent will be past you before you can blink. Or have their weapon planted in your chest."

"Aim for the target?"

He patted Striker's shoulder. He had big hands, calloused from work, nails short and blunt. Capable hands. "Keep your eye on it."

Kathryn turned Striker and rode back again. "I do not ride like a girl."

His chuckle followed her. "Do not drop too early. On your approach, judge the speed of your mount and his. Bring your weapon down in one smooth motion, right on target."

Chapter Three

Kathryn skipped to Matty's chamber with an extra spring in her step. Her nethers ached from Sir Roger's instruction the evening before, but nothing could dim her happiness. They had stayed in the yards until Anglesea's Nurse called them in to get ready for dinner.

Nurse had not seen anything amiss with her mannish pursuits either, merely reminded her to get the smell of horse off her before she sat at table.

Roger had excused himself to bathe in the barracks. A hard taskmaster, but Roger rode like a dream, and he handled a sword as if it formed part of his arm.

Matty would marry the perfect man for her and finally be safe. She couldn't ask for better. With Matty safely tucked away in Anglesea, Kathryn need only concern herself with Mother. Still no apparent solution, short of burying the old cur ten feet under, had presented itself, but one step at a time. Matty's marriage represented a massive stride toward Kathryn's goal.

Perhaps Roger would allow Kathryn to spend time here at Anglesea with Matty. He had seemed to like her well enough yesterday, and she could make herself useful. She hunted well, tracked better than most men, and most assuredly did not ride like a girl. Indeed, she only need stay until he taught her how to handle a sword as he did. The world beckoned. Adventure. Freedom.

A serving maid smiled at her in passing. "Good morrow, Lady Kate."

"Kathryn." She softened the correction with a smile. "I prefer to be called Kathryn, and it is indeed a good morrow." Holding the girl's hands, she gave her a quick spin. "It is the very best of mornings."

Giggling, the girl danced away down the hall.

"Get up, Matty." She threw open the door to her sister's chamber. What a marvel Anglesea was, with its separate sleeping chambers. The views of the sea on three sides robbed her of breath every time she strode near a casement. Aye indeed, she would do her best to endear herself to the Anglesea folk. Perhaps she and Mother could spend the winter months here. Did the sea freeze like the lake beside Mandeville? "Matty?"

Matty must have risen already, and had left her linens in disarray. Matty despised mornings, but the prospect of her wonderful groom must have gotten her up and about early this morn.

They'd spoken long after dinner last night. Matty had proven surprisingly stubborn, but Kathryn had worn her down, made her see sense. She could not stay at Mandeville.

Kathryn picked up a discarded wimple. Matty should make an effort to keep her room tidier. Lady Mary had seen Matty and her housed in lovely chambers. Though small, the bright, cheery fabrics and gleam of fine wood furnishings made them feel like visiting princesses. Bright embroidered florals ran across Matty's bed hangings in a glorious tangle of green and yellow. At the foot of the bed stood Matty's clothes chest. Open and empty.

Thieves! Matty had been robbed, and right in the midst of one of the strongest keeps in the kingdom. A well-guarded stronghold that shut its gates at night and had men who walked the halls whilst the residents slept.

Kathryn paused before she opened the door and cried foul.

Matty's wedding bliaut hung from the clothes tree beside the casement. Morning sunlight glinted off the gems sewn across the bodice. Mother had labored for months, each gem stitched with care.

The bliaut stood ready, lonely for the absent bride to don it.

Warning prickled Kathryn's nape as she strode to the chest. What sort of thief took only the most common day raiment and left the gem-encrusted wedding bliaut?

The fabric alone could have kept a family fed for the year. The cost of the gems? Kathryn shuddered to consider. Father kept a tight fist about his coins, but even he would not send his daughter to one of the richest families in the land looking like a pauper.

Beside Matty's wedding gown, where her heavy traveling cloak should have hung, the clothes tree stretched an empty wooden arm into the room.

Kathryn's knees weakened, and she perched on the edge of Matty's bed. Matty was gone.

The door opened. Ella crept into the room and slammed it shut behind her. Matty's maid braced her slim back against the door and released a shuddering breath. "Lady Kathryn. I did hope it would be you."

"Where is Matty?"

Ella's pallor frightened Kathryn. She looked a breath away from crumpling into a heap on the floor.

"You must tell Sir Royce. Lady Matty said you would." Tears trickled down Ella's soft cheeks. Her hands twisted in her apron. "I cannot tell him, Lady Kathryn. I am afeared."

"Ella?"

With a cry, Ella tossed her apron over her head.

Kathryn wanted to shake the girl, but more than that, she wanted answers. "What has happened, Ella?"

"She is gone." Her apron muffled her voice.

"What do you mean, gone. Has someone taken her?"

Ella shook her head. She buried her covered head in her hands and wailed. "I cannot tell Sir Royce. You must not make me tell him, or I shall die."

"Never mind Sir Royce." Kathryn ripped the apron from her head, and gripped Ella by the shoulders. She towered over the smaller, frailer woman. "Tell me where my sister is."

"I do not know." Ella collapsed in a heap.

Dear God, grant her patience not to slap the girl into next year. "But you must know something."

"She begged me to help her." Ella hugged her knees to her chest. "I did not want to do it, but she cried so and I feared she would make herself ill. 'Save me, Ella. You are the only one that can help me,' she said."

"Help her? Why?" Kathryn needed to think, understand what the bedamned, blighted hell had happened. "Ella, if you do not stop crying, I will give you something to cry about."

Ella whimpered and scuttled to her feet. She edged toward the door.

Kathryn blocked her way.

"Dear God, help me!" Ella raised her hands to the sky. "God save me."

"Stop that! And do not move from there." Kathryn wrestled her temper down. She stood before Ella, and kept her tone gentle. "Ella, I need to know what happened."

"You will whip me."

"Nay, Ella, I will not whip you. I merely need to know where my sister is."

"You said you would make me cry." Ella sniffled.

Kathryn dug her nails into her palms. "I spoke in anger. Nobody is going to raise a hand to you."

"Your father will."

True enough. Father would beat the hell out of everybody if they did not find Matty and find her soon. "I will protect you from my father."

With a big sniff, Ella scrubbed her apron over her cheeks and peered at her. "She left, Lady Kathryn. Lady Mathilda said she could not marry that great oaf of a man and she took her bits and left."

"Left?" Her worst fear. Kathryn plopped onto her ass on the hard stone. "Why? Where did she go?"

"That is all I know." Ella stood and straightened her skirts. "She did not tell me more. You can try to beat it out of me, but I know nothing more."

"Oh, Matty." Kathryn dropped her head into her hands. "What have you done?"

* * *

Kathryn made sure to put herself between her mother seated at the casement and her father.

Sir Royce's anger seemed to build with each circle before the hearth. His wide chest rose and fell rapidly as he smacked his fist into his palm. "You know where she went."

"Nay, Father, I do not. I found her chamber empty this morning."

Sir Royce's cunning gaze fastened on her. Eyes as dark as hers and Matty's, but cold and merciless in their intent. "Are you lying to me, Kate?"

"Nay, Father."

Behind her, Mother gasped.

"Are you sure about that?" He lunged for her, wrenched her braid back, and forced Kathryn to look at him. Shaking a lock of dark hair out of his eyes, his voice went soft as silk. "It would be a big mistake if you were lying to me."

"I am not lying. I swear it. On my life." He would yank her hair out by the roots if he persisted. "On Mother's life."

He released her and stepped back. His stare swung to Mother, and he smiled. "Perhaps I am asking the wrong person."

Kathryn stepped into his path.

"You dare." His chest swelled on a growl. He lashed out, cuffing the side of her head.

Ears ringing, Kathryn stumbled across the room.

He pushed his face into Mother's, jowls quivering, and yelled, "Where is your bitch daughter?" Wider, taller, he loomed over Mother.

Mother shrank into the casement cushions. She shook her head, bringing her arms up to ward him off. Dark bruises already mottled the frail bones of Mother's wrists.

"She does not know either." Kathryn grabbed his arm.

Muscle tensed beneath his tunic and he shook her off. He yanked Mother to her feet. His huge hand engulfed Mother's delicate shoulder.

Mother immediately dropped her gaze to the floor. "I do not know, Sir Royce."

"I do not believe you." His knuckles whitened as he dug his thick fingers into her shoulder.

Mother whimpered and paled.

God, he would break her if he kept squeezing. Mother's health suffered with each year. A stiff wind could carry her away.

"She does not know." Kathryn raised her voice to get his attention. "Nobody does."

"She best not." With a snarl, he shoved Mother back into her seat. "How is it that you know so much about this?" Her ploy got her right back into his line of rage. He stalked her, boot heels clipping the flags.

"I told you." The note shook as she held it out to him. "I found this in her bedchamber."

Ella wouldn't stand a chance against Sir Royce's wrath. A hastily penned note saw the girl free from blame. Father could not read anyway.

Sir Royce knocked the parchment from her hand. "That could say anything."

"But it does not." Kathryn lunged for the note, careful to keep her eye on his boots. Sir Royce could be wickedly quick with a well-aimed kick. "It says 'Tell Mother and Father I am sorry, but

I could not marry.'" She smoothed the note. "Have the keep priest read it to you if you do not believe me."

Sir Royce went deathly still. His breath rasped. Through his snarling lips his mead-laden breath hit her face. He snapped his fist back and punched her. "God's Teeth!"

Kathryn flew across the room and landed with a hip-jarring crunch before the hearth.

"You did this." He stalked to where she lay. His legs, thick with riding muscle, blocked Mother from her. "You must have said something to her. Done something. Mathilda would never take it into her head to do this without someone whispering in her ear."

She raised her chin and met her father's glare. When she showed fear it only enraged him further. "I had naught to do with this. Matty did not seek my opinion, and if she had, I would have encouraged her to marry Sir Roger."

He sneered at her, nudging her with his boot.

"It is true, Father. I think you made an excellent choice."

"You approve, do you?" Fist in her hair, he dragged her to her feet. "Haughty Lady Kate approves of my choice." He shook her. "Proud, noble Lady Kate deigns to look down her nose and find favor in the action of her father."

Kathryn bit her tongue to keep from crying out. Ella he would have whipped until she told him something, anything, to get him to stop.

"Sir Roger is a fine choice." She prayed their presence at Anglesea would stay the worst of her father's hand.

Father laughed in her face. "Is that what this is about? You saw a man you wanted for yourself, did you? You decided you would have him and not your sister, and so you persuaded her to flee."

He had lost all reason. If Mother wasn't still cowering on the casement seat, she would have run by now. Grown slower and fatter with age, Sir Royce lacked the speed to catch her, and if she stayed away long enough, he invariably found one of his whores to pound his temper into.

"She does not want to marry, Sir Royce." Mother rose and stumbled toward them. "Kathryn would never do such a thing because she does not want to marry."

"Is that so?" he jeered.

"I have vowed to never marry."

"What a pity for you." He twisted his hand in her hair.

Kathryn's abused scalp screamed, and a moan escaped her.

He grinned. His teeth flashed yellow. "Because I will have this alliance with Anglesea, and one daughter is as good as another."

"What?"

"If your sister is not here to marry Sir Roger, you will marry him."

"Nay, Father. He does not want me. He wants Matty."

He laughed and flung her away from him. "One woman, another woman, what does it matter? He wants a wife, and he does not care who it is."

He slammed the door shut behind him.

Mother touched her gently on the shoulder. "Are you all right, Kathryn?"

"Nay." Kathryn shook her head. Her thoughts grew so jumbled she could not find the right words. "I cannot marry. I will not marry."

"Oh, sweeting." Mother cupped her face. "Surely a husband would be better than this."

No husband, not ever. Not for her. She shook her head because she would not wound her mother further with words she uttered. No man would own her, have dominion over her, and treat her as a convenient target for his ever-present rage. "I will fix this," she said.

"But how? Some things are not yours to fix."

God, that she could wipe that permanent sadness from her mother. "Have I ever failed you, Mother?"

Mother sighed. "Nay, Kathryn, you have not."

Chapter Four

Roger loved his mother, he really did, but the desire to bellow at her had his fists clenched as he stared into the bailey below. He blamed her and Father for this. With their infernal pressure for him to marry and beget sons. Oldest son, family name, Anglesea...*waffle, waffle, waffle.*

Now see this pretty pickle. Jilted at the altar. Nay, before he even reached the bloody altar. Failure tasted bitter on his tongue. Sir Arthur had picked a woman betrothed to another and still emerged victorious when he had come to marry.

"We should take Sir Royce's offer." Mother sat behind him in a pool of morning sunlight, golden head bent as she sewed some or other thing. Back straight, calm and poised, the perfect lady.

Easy. Swap one sister for the other and get the deed done. Except, Roger was not inclined to. "I had very specific requirements in a bride. If I meant to accept any girl, I would have married like William."

"Your brother is very happy." Lady Mary raised her chin. "He might not have married Alice for love, but it has certainly turned out that way."

Roger snorted and turned away. "You knew I did not want to marry yet."

"Aye, Roger." Lady Mary rose and stood beside him. "But you cannot take forever to choose a bride. Your father is not getting any younger, and I am tired. I want to play with my grandchildren, travel and see Faye and William. I want to hand over Anglesea to a younger woman. Your wife."

"You have met Lady Kathryn?" Somehow he could not picture his jousting hellion calmly becoming chatelaine to a keep such as Anglesea. If he could not have a woman he loved, then by hell, he would have one who would be a credit to his name.

Mother chuckled. "I have met her, and I find her...refreshingly delightful."

"You would." Roger shook his head. He should know Mother would like Kathryn. He was raised in the same household that had turned out Bea and Faye. Lady Mary had never held with a woman remaining in her place. His mother had never held with many of the ways other households raised their children.

"What do you care which sister it is?" Lady Mary tossed up her hands. "You cannot tell me you are in love with Mathilda."

"Nay, I am not in love with her, but she fit my list perfectly."

"Ah, your list." Mother shook her head. "Only you could come up with a list for a bride."

What else was he to do? With Henry on holy pilgrimage and William settled into fatherhood, he had run out of excuses. The real reason for his reticence sounded too pathetic to voice, so he had not. It would make him sound like an even greater disappointment. The great Sir Arthur of Anglesea had sired a weakling. A mewling sentimental baby who craved what his parents had. A loving partnership filled with laughter, passion, and joy.

Bea's voice rose from the corridor outside. "You cannot mean that."

Garrett stalked past the open doorway, shoulders rigid, fists clenched by his side.

Bea waddled into view. Heavily pregnant, she stood in the corridor outside Mother's sewing chamber and yelled after her husband. "You are just being stubborn. Nobody here thinks of you as a leech. You are married to me."

A big enough task for any man.

"We will discuss this later." Garrett's voice drifted up. "When you are prepared to be reasonable."

"Reasonable!" Beatrice reddened. "I am having a baby. I do not have to be reasonable." She suddenly looked to her left and caught them watching. "I am very reasonable," she said and burst into tears.

"There now, Sweet Bea." Mother bustled over and put her arm about Bea. "Calm yourself or you will upset the babe."

"H-he says he does not want to live at Anglesea anymore." Beatrice buried her face in her hands. Her shoulders heaved with sobs. "He says he is tired of living off scraps from Father's table."

Roger would not have thought Garrett capable of such stiff-necked pride. He kept his surprise to himself. He did not fancy ending up as the target of one of Bea's crying fits.

Mother pressed a hankie into Bea's hand. "Garrett has always fended for himself," she said. "His lack of purpose must weigh heavily on him."

"He has a purpose." Bea wailed into her hanky. "He is my husband and father of my children."

As heir to a mighty demesne Roger had always had his purpose, a preordained place in the world. Garrett, however, had risen from bastard blacksmith's apprentice to the husband of a powerful lord's daughter.

He winced as he opened his mouth, and hoped his mother could keep Bea calm. "What does he want to do?"

"Make his own way in the world." Beatrice raised her tear-stained face to him. "He says he feels like he is nothing more than a tick on father's back. Why would he say that?"

Beatrice collapsed onto Mother again, crying loud enough to scare the sun from the sky.

Mother looked pained and sighed. "A man has his pride, Bea," she said. "Now let me finish speaking with Roger and I will come to you directly."

"I did not realize you were busy." Bea raised her head and scrubbed her eyes with her fists, looking like she had as a tiny girl.

"Go and lie down, sweeting." Mother smoothed wisps of flaxen hair off Bea's face. "And I will be there before you know it."

"All right." Bea heaved to her feet. She trailed toward the door and drew level with him. The look of entreaty she gave him fisted in Roger's gut.

He waited until she had disappeared. "Has this happened before?"

"Aye." Mother folded her sewing into a neat square. "Garrett feels he has no place here. He wants to be able to support his own family."

"Doing what?" Roger stared at his mother. Anglesea already had a blacksmith.

"Anything." She shrugged.

"I could speak with Father."

"I have already." Mother rose and stretched her back. Sunlight caught the grey strands amongst her wheaten hair. "You are heir here, Roger. Marry and take up your duties."

Duty came before all, especially for Sir Arthur's heir. Aye, he had made a list, a damn-nigh impossible list to fill. Until Lady Mary had appeared with Mathilda of Mandeville. He had accepted with grace that he'd been bested. However, simply swapping one bride for another seemed a step too far. Anglesea demanded the right sort of chatelaine.

"Think on it, Roger." Mother patted his arm. "I am sure you will come to the right decision."

* * *

Roger batted at the insistent hand on his shoulder. A thump followed by a pained yelp wrenched him wide awake and looking for the threat.

"God's teeth!" A dark head poked over the edge of his bed. "You pack a sturdy wallop there."

"Lady Kathryn?" It certainly sounded like her.

"Aye." Using the edge of his bed, she pushed herself to standing. "You hit me," she said, sounding much more like an aggrieved woman.

"You shook me." This was his response? The best he could muster, given she invaded his chamber, in the middle of the night —Roger peered closer through the gloom—in her nightrail. "What are you doing?"

"I must speak with you." She motioned the bed. "May I sit?"

"Nay, you may not." Tension from her sister's disappearance had affected her mind. The jousting, he found rather endearing, but this, God's balls, or rather his, because he lay naked beneath the covers. "What you may do is march yourself right back to your chamber."

"I will." A flint struck and she lit the candle by his bedside. She plopped her ass onto his bed and wriggled until she settled into a comfortable position. "Once I have spoken with you."

She resembled her sister closely, the same dark hair and eyes in the delicate bones of their mother's face. Roger tried not to stare, but candlelight shone through her nightrail and outlined her full curves.

Kathryn made no such attempt not to stare. In fact, she cocked her head and studied him. "You do not wear a night shirt."

He hauled the linens up to his chin like a startled virgin. "Do you have any idea what would happen if you were discovered?"

"Never mind that." She flapped her hand close to his chest. "I have seen naked men scores of times."

"Scores?" Given Sir Royce, Roger had his doubts.

She squirmed and shrugged her slim shoulders. "Well, perhaps not scores, but a chest is a chest. I have one, too."

Where to start? Roger forced his gaze up. "You cannot stay here."

"It will not take long, and"—she leaned closer in a waft of

something sweet and flowery—"if you toss me out now, I will make enough noise to rouse the dead."

This entire family conspired to rob his affability. His pride still smarted over the vanishing Mathilda. "What do you want?"

"I think the question is more what I do not want." Her voice oozed like a hairpin peddler as she toyed with the end of her long, dark braid. Candlelight burnished her hair to bronze.

The sooner he got done with her, the sooner he could get her out of his chamber, and safely tucked into her bed. Unless the hour drifted closer to morning and the keep poised ready to stir. "What time is it?"

"Very late, or early." She tucked her long legs up beside her, as if she meant to stay for a while. Delicate feet peeped out of the end of her nightrail. "Not to worry, there is nobody about. I checked before I left my chamber. I also lurked outside your door for a goodly while just to make sure."

"Oh, good." Nay, not good. "There is always somebody about. Do you know what would happen if you were seen leaving this chamber?"

Smoothing her nightrail over her shapely thighs, she said, "I know very well what would happen. I would be forced to marry you, which is hardly any worse off than I already am. Now is it?"

"Nay." Clearly this sister giddily anticipated her nuptials to him as well. Next thing he knew the village whores would reject his advances. "Rest easy, I have not accepted you."

"I did not mean that the way it sounded." She took a deep breath. Her nipples formed dark circles beneath her nightrail. "Well, I did, but I did not, if you get my meaning."

"Not in the slightest."

"What I mean is, I do not want to marry. Anyone." She studied him. "As husbands go, you would not be a horrible choice, and were I inclined to marry, I would not be averse to you."

"I am humbled by your enthusiasm."

She chuckled, sweet and husky. "You are a very handsome man, Sir Roger. And a good one, which is why I am here."

Roger hid a smile behind his hand. She was an entertaining little thing, to be sure. "I also know how to use a sword."

"Aye. You most certainly do." She clasped her hands at her chest. Then she dropped them and squared her shoulders. "But that is what appeals to me and not Matty. And it is Matty I came about."

His good mood soured. "Lady Mathilda is no longer a consideration."

She tried to hide her smile behind her hand.

"Are you mocking me?"

"Nay. Indeed." Her eyes twinkled. "It is only that you sound so proper when you speak that way."

"My pardon."

This time she collapsed into a giggling heap, shaking his bed with her mirth. "Oh, I do like you. You will do very well." She cleared her throat and sat up. "For Matty. You will do excellently for Matty."

"Matty does not agree, it would appear." Her laugh tugged at him, and made him want to join in. How he could find any of this amusing escaped him.

"Matty is befuddled." She placed a slim hand on his knee. "She is rather timid, and something you said to her must have set her off. I know if we can find her, and you can reassure her, she will happily marry you."

Roger sat up straighter, the heat from her innocent touch scorched through the linens. "You are suggesting I go chasing after my escaped bride?"

"Now, now." She patted his knee with a coy smile. "It is not as bad as all that. We could not really call her an escaped bride at this point, could we? All we need do is get her to see reason."

"What would we call her?" The twisting of her mind almost distracted him as much as her hand.

"A frightened almost-betrothed, which is not the same thing

at all."

Lady Kathryn involved a lot of "we" in her discourse. "Where do you factor in all of this?"

"I am glad you asked, because it is vitally important." She shifted her hand up to his thigh. The girl had no clue as to men, not a whisper. "If we do not get Matty back, you and I will be forced to marry. My father is most insistent, and he can be rather unpleasant about it. I have already decided you are perfect for Matty, other than she does not care for dogs, and you appear to be never too far from one. Here is my plan."

Roger braced himself. She could take this wild flight anywhere.

"I am your best chance of finding Matty. I know her better than anyone. Without me, you would search in vain. We pretend to agree to this marriage between us, you take me on a betrothal tour of your lands, and we find Matty together."

He could ride his destrier through the numerous holes in her plan. "A betrothal tour would involve a retinue." He lifted her hand from its far too enjoyable sojourn on his thigh. "A man and his intended bride are not allowed to disappear alone."

"You will think of something to make them stay away." Her hand returned to his thigh, warm and delicious. In any other woman he would have suspected her of a little light seduction, but Kathryn had no such notion. She petted him as she would a favorite dog or horse.

"Nay, I will not." He placed her hand in her lap. "Because this is a ridiculous plan."

"But—"

"Go to bed, Lady Kathryn." He used his firmest tone, the one he reserved for squires assing around. "If you do not wish to marry me, then I will simply tell your father that it will not do."

"But—"

"I had no intention of accepting your father's offer, so you can sleep peaceful in the notion you are not going to marry me." Thank the Lord for his nearly impenetrable hide.

"You were not?"

"This conversation is done. Go to bed." He nudged her ass with his leg. "And stay there, before I run screaming into the hall."

* * *

Roger waited until the door shut on the dejected slump of her shoulders before he rose. The girl had one thing right. They would not suit. A jousting, planning, conniving wife would not suit him at all. He needed a docile girl, a calm force to counter his bluster. Not a hellion with a burgeoning sense of adventure. The name of Anglesea rested its almost crushing weight on his shoulders.

He found his chausses and yanked them on. There would be no more sleep tonight, not with his mind working as it was.

And what did she mean by not wanting to marry? Of course Lady Kathryn would marry, all girls did, but it would not be to him.

From his clothes chest, he pulled a handful of clean chemises and a spare pair of chausses. God alone knew how long this would take.

Mother had chosen well for him. Lady Mathilda, before her flight, had been exactly what he had requested. Beautiful as his sister, Faye, sweet as Beatrice, wise like Ivy, and with his mother's graciousness. Matty's wisdom appeared questionable, but a girl could learn, could she not? A few years beneath Mother's tutelage would see any girl right.

Anglesea. This castle, the entire demesne would be his. His father would leave him a legacy worth dying for. How did a man make ready for such a task?

Lady Mathilda was perfect. He did not want another bride. He had one already, and one he aimed to keep.

Lady Kathryn had given him a splendid idea. He would find his bride, woo her a bit more, and bring her back. Without Lady Kathryn hanging on his horse's tail.

Chapter Five

Kathryn dismounted. Her quarry stopped a little way ahead in front of a small inn.

She led Striker in between the trees and ducked behind a convenient juniper bush. "I see you, Sir Roger," she whispered.

The entire kingdom could see, and hear him, he charged around with so much fuss. His size negated any need for stealth she supposed. Whereas she...the ghost in the forest, the shadow on the road, and the girl who had followed Sir Roger from Anglesea for the past three days. He thought he had bested her, slipping out in the small hours before dawn. Kathryn of Mandeville did not give up so easily. Not when she hovered so close to her perfect solution.

Sir Roger dismounted and entered the tavern. His magnificent bay stallion pawed the ground, and a stable lad rushed to take his reins. The destrier stood a full hand higher than Striker. Kathryn patted an apology to Striker. He nuzzled her back and gave a soft *whuff*.

"At least you know how to be silent." She kissed his cheek. "Not like that big beastie."

Kathryn's belly growled, and she slipped deeper into the thicket. With Sir Roger's destrier being taken into the stables, she had time for a quick bite. Striker first though, and she slipped the nosebag over his head.

Anglesea's stables had been well supplied with what she needed. There'd been a momentary conscience wince as she filched the supplies for her and Striker, but a woman need do what she must. Shield-maidens of old would not have stopped at a few bags of grain, a nosebag, and a water bucket. Nay, they would have taken the entire stable, horses and all. Left only the wood intact enough to burn. Those had been grand times, when women could take their part as equals beside their men.

Not in England, however, but in the great frozen north many years ago. She had read all about it in the old scrolls at Mandeville. Those women had even owned property, become powerful *Jarls* in their own right. With her back against a graceful goat willow, Kathryn opened her pack.

Anglesea's larders had also been well stocked, and she ate a slice of jellied ham. After three days of following Sir Roger, she'd almost finished the ham, but she still had a bit of cheese, and some bread—if you did not mind gnawing it a trifle. She would have taken more, but a noise had interrupted her, and she'd had to leave with what she had. Still, the farms hereabouts appeared prosperous enough. They might not notice a little judicious raiding.

Kathryn closed her eyes and enjoyed the sun on her cheeks. Flickering light painted the inside of her eyelids. Life outside the keep was grand and filled with sounds and sights. Soon, she would have to announce her presence to Sir Roger, along with the unwelcome news that he searched in the wrong direction. First, she needed to make sure they were far enough from Anglesea for him not to send her back. A quickly penned note to her mother about retiring to the Abbey to pray before her marriage should give her time, but a girl could only pray for so long.

Matty would never have returned to Mandeville. Father kept

them confined to the keep and largely friendless. Nay, Matty would have headed east to the home of a girl who had fostered with them for a few years. Kathryn had been jealous of their friendship, as they had often left her alone. For a brief time, Kathryn had nursed the hope Matty would marry Cecily's brother, Ranulf. Until the day Ranulf beat his horse nigh to death when it unseated him. Stupid dolt! If he had ridden with any skill, the poor thing might have known he wanted to go left and not right.

"Ho!"

Kathryn opened her eyes.

"Bring me my horse." Sir Roger stood in the inn doorway. Sure and strong in partial armor, he shrunk the men around him to scuttling mice.

As she crawled forward, she stuck close to the juniper.

He mounted, tossed a coin to the boy and set off in a westerly direction.

Kathryn snorted as she stood and walked to where Striker waited. If he had taken her with him from the beginning, they would have Matty by now.

* * *

Roger kept Beast to an easy walk. Their journey soothed him, and he reveled in each mile he traveled. Out here, free of crying sisters and a disappointed mother, no expectations dragged him down. Here he could be Roger, and not Sir Arthur's heir.

Perhaps if he stayed out here for long enough, Sir Royce and his brood would make their way back to Mandeville. He shook his head at his unworthy thought. Lady Mathilda could be in grave danger, out in the world with no escort. Unlike her sister, Mathilda struck him as meek and gentle, a lamb amongst wolves.

Sir Royce's porcine eyes had lit up when Roger explained he would find Mathilda, and remained resolved to marry her. The man set his teeth on edge. Roger knew the type; brutal, uncouth bullies who picked only on those weaker than them. No wonder Lady Kathryn grew desperate to get her sister out from under his boot heel.

What would happen to Kathryn then? He did not like to think of sending her back to Mandeville. When he found Mathilda, he would invite Kathryn for a long stay at Anglesea. Other than her midnight wanderings, he enjoyed her. Kathryn had fire and spirit and did not deserve to have it crushed.

The sisters were of a height, which surprised him about Lady Kathryn. With her spirit, she seemed to stand taller than Mathilda, and broader. That night in his bedchamber, he'd noted the same pleasing curves as Mathilda. Pert, full breasts that would fit nicely in a man's palm, not to mention the way the fire behind her had clearly outlined her shapely hips.

Lady Kathryn would not make a terrible match. For another man. Nay, he did not need a harridan in his bedchamber. Chaste, mild-mannered, modest, meek—he sought these qualities in a wife.

Odd prickles sprang up along his nape, and he halted Beast. Not for the first time, he sensed eyes on him. A few times, he had circled about to confirm his instinct, but the path behind him remained clear. Still, the niggle persisted. Sir Arthur had taught him never to dismiss his instinct. Sometimes instinct alone stood between a man and hard steel.

He dismounted and fiddled with the buckle on his stirrup. Behind them, the road remained clear. He moved so he could see the bushes on either side. Breeze stirred though the leaves in a gentle wave. The sensation came from there.

Who in God's name would be following...ah, nay! He had best be wrong about that.

* * *

Kathryn approved of the rest place Sir Roger selected. Beside a stream, on higher ground and in the shelter of a large copse. As he'd taken the best spot, Kathryn made do at the bottom of the rise with a clear view of the road. Far enough away not to attract his notice, but close enough to keep her eye on him. Dense foliage aided her cause.

Nights proved the most difficult part of her adventure thus far. Whilst Sir Roger enjoyed peaceful slumber, she awoke every hour or so to ensure he had not left in the night without her. Her concealment made a fire impossible, and although the spring weather remained mild, the night could be long, chill, and jammed with strange noises.

Smoke drifted to her, followed by the belly-aching aroma of roasting fowl. Kathryn dug out the last of her ham and ate. Earlier in the day, he had taken a short break to bring down two fat pheasants. Roasting bird filled the air and her belly growled. She tortured herself with visions of fowl, cooked golden over a hearth, cooking fat glistening on their crisped skins.

For a moment, she considered sneaking into his camp once he slept and stealing the remains of his meal. A big man like Sir Roger would consume both pheasants. Also, following him for three days served as a chilling reminder of his competence. She dared not. A stiffening breeze renewed the torment and saliva flooded her mouth.

Kathryn leaped up, and busied herself with Striker.

He nudged her shoulder as she removed his saddle, greedy beggar looking for his feed.

The feed sack felt light in her hand. She would need to see about more food for Striker as well. Tomorrow her provisions would run out, and she would make herself known to Sir Roger. She certainly hoped he would prove more agreeable this time to her company.

She finished removing Striker's tack and fed and watered him. There was no need to hobble him, Striker would never leave her.

From the slight noises atop the rise, she guessed Sir Roger had settled for the night.

Kathryn huddled at the base of a large rowan. Through the trees the faint orange flicker of Sir Roger's fire gave her comfort and lessened the sense of alone. Above her, stars pitted the deep canopy of the sky. A waxing moon rose like a fat yellow cheese wheel and hung over her. Sir Roger's horse neighed, and Striker stamped in response. A fine night, to be sure. A huge yawn cracked her jaw, as she found a comfortable position. She would close her eyes for a bit, and then check on Sir Roger. Perhaps she would be fortunate and find half a pheasant sitting on the outskirts of his camp.

Kathryn closed her eyes. The sprightly chirp of the crickets faded away.

"Do you know what happens to little girls who are found where they are not supposed to be?"

Kathryn awoke with a gasp. Her heart thudded in her ears.

"I could slit your throat." Sir Roger's voice. Thank you, Lord.

"I wish you would not." Steel pressed against her pounding pulse. So close she dared not turn her head and look at him.

"You followed me," he said.

No point in denying the truth. Especially when she had bigger concerns. She did not believe he would cut her throat, but she had seen him sharpen his dagger often enough to know one slip and her blood would flow. "Do you think you could move your dagger?"

"I shall consider it," he said. "Best you start talking, little girl, before my desire to teach you a lesson you will never forget triumphs over my honor."

He sounded angry, not really surprising. "I came to help."

"Help?" He chuckled, jiggling the dagger at her throat. "What help can you be?"

"If you remove the dagger, I will tell you."

"You have stones for a girl with a knife pressed against her neck."

"I am wagering my life you will not use it."

The dagger vanished and Kathryn drew in a deep breath. She scrambled about to face him.

He crouched beside her, scowling. Night cast brooding shadows across him. His head and shoulders made a darker outline against the forest.

"My thanks." Kathryn touched her throat, just to be sure.

"Start talking." He played his thumb over the edge of his dagger.

"I followed you." She shuffled away from him. He had not seemed so large and fearsome within Anglesea's walls. "I aim to help you find Matty."

"I do not need your help." He slid his dagger into his boot and rested his elbows on his knees.

"Have you found her yet?"

He tensed and stood, casting his long shadow over her.

"And you will not find her either. That is where I can be invaluable."

The husky trill of a nightjar rolled through the trees.

A stiff breeze cooled her hot cheeks.

Roger shifted, hooking his thumbs in his belt. "You know where she is?"

"Nay, but I know enough not to be going in the wrong direction for three days."

Offering her his hand, he peered at her. "You should not be here."

"I am your best chance of finding Matty." She accepted his hand and he hauled her to her feet. "I know my sister, better than anybody else. I know where she went."

"You just said you did not."

"Well, I do not know...exactly, but I know the best place to start."

He caught her arm and dragged her closer. "And what did you mean the wrong direction?"

Ah, so he had caught that. "Matty would never return to

Mandeville. She knows that is the first place Sir Royce would seek her."

"Then where would she go?" Releasing her, he folded his brawny arms.

The beauty of his hauberk made her lose her train of thought. Finely wrought links that covered his wide chest and arms, but allowed for ease of movement. What she wouldn't give for one like it. Perhaps he would commission one for her, if she made herself extremely useful to him. Probably best not to wager on that, not with him glaring holes in her head.

"I cannot tell you that," she said.

He sneered. "Because you do not know."

"Nay, because the moment I do, you will cart me back to Anglesea and leave me there."

He dropped his hands to his sides and balled his fists. "I am going to do that anyway."

Blast! He intended to be stubborn. "Why would you do that when I can help you achieve your goal?"

He advanced on her, long legs halving the distance. "This is no place for you."

Kathryn leaped out of reach. "Just hear me out."

"Nay. You go back to Anglesea."

Her back hit the rowan's trunk. "And you will never find Matty."

"I will if I search long enough." He stepped closer until she had to tilt her head back to look at him.

"I am glad you have that much time at your disposal."

"Bedamned!" Spinning about, he scraped hard fingers through his hair until it stood up on end. "This is madness. I cannot be responsible for you."

"You need not be." Was he softening? She edged a step forward. "I have done fine by myself for three days."

"Up until the moment you woke with my dagger at your throat," he said and kept walking.

A direct hit, to be sure. "Up until then, aye."

Growling, he snatched up her provision sack. "Come along, then. We accomplish nothing by arguing in the dark. Bring your horse." He shouldered her saddle and strode up the rise.

Kathryn gathered her blanket and hurried after him, Striker at her heels. "Is there any pheasant left?"

Chapter Six

Capricious spring struck in a cold coating of frost the next morning. Roger woke and rolled out of his blankets. The fire had died down in the middle of the night and he blew on the embers until it caught again. Traveling at this time of year always proved uncertain and he drew a childish satisfaction from the white crust that covered Kathryn's blanket. The girl had no business being outside a keep on her own.

Should he put his blanket on her?

How she had managed to trail him for three days without getting into trouble escaped him. Last night, she had devoured the remains of his pheasant as if she hadn't eaten in days. He pulled out a small pouch of ingredients Cook mixed up for him, added water and stirred them together. He wrapped the dough about the end of a stick and placed it over the fire.

The smell of baking bannock bread had Lady Kathryn stirring. Her nose twitched over the edge of the blanket before her eyes opened. She caught sight of him and smiled. Lady Kathryn smiled with her entire being. It lit her from within and coaxed an answering smile from him.

Annoyed at himself, he dropped her gaze and dug out some salted ham and placed it on a stone beside the fire.

"Good morrow." She sat up and stretched like a sleek, hearth cat. Her hair tumbled around her shoulders in a dark cloud of walnut. Her tunic pulled taut across the swell of her breasts.

Roger snapped his stare back to his bannock bread.

Kathryn rolled out of her blankets. She stamped her feet and shook her hands. "It is cold this morning."

"Aye." He turned the ham for a crisp cook on both sides. Women had no business out in the elements like men. Let this morning's chill be a warning to her.

"I do like a little nip in the air," she said and disappeared into the thicket. He assumed to take care of necessities, but Roger kept an ear out in case.

After a few moments, she emerged with barely a sound. At the stream, she splashed the frigid, clear water over her face, rinsed her mouth and dug out a sprig of mint to chew. As he worked on breaking their fast, she moved to their mounts.

Try as he might, he could find no fault with her care for the animals.

"Who taught you to take care of yourself out here?" His plan to freeze her out notwithstanding, curiosity got the better of him.

"Oh, I do this all the time at home." She grinned and crouched across the fire from him. "The folk at Mandeville are quite used to me, and as long as I return before he has need of me, my father does not really care."

"You go out on your own all the time?" Roger could scarce credit his ears. Sir Arthur would rather have his fingernails drawn than allow his girls to risk themselves.

"I can take care of myself." Kathryn stuck her chin out.

That remained to be seen. Roger apportioned their meal and handed her a share.

After smiling her thanks, she tucked in.

She puzzled him, so many contradictions and unanswered questions. Sitting on a log in her soiled man's riding clothes, eating as neatly as a queen at court, sword strapped over her chausses. Fiercely determined to accompany him. "Why do you not wish to marry?"

She stilled, and dropped her head. "I have other dreams."

"Such as?"

She shrugged and tore a small portion of her ham and stuffed it into the bannock bread. "So, how are we to proceed?"

"I will return you to Anglesea."

"Nay." She jerked stiffer than a board. "I can help you find Matty, you know I can."

"I cannot be responsible for you."

"You do not have to be, I can take care of myself."

A few jousting skills, and a sword did not make her any more capable of that than a babe. "Why do you not want to marry?"

She huffed and rose to her feet. "I want to be a shield-maiden."

"A what?" He must have misheard.

"Like the north women." She crossed her arms and averted her gaze to the trees.

His history was not what he would wish it, but even he knew enough to recognize a culture long passed. "Umm...you do know—"

"Aye, aye." She flipped her braid over her shoulder. "Shield-maidens no longer exist, but I want to live by my sword, and roam the lands."

If her face were not so set and serious, Roger might have laughed. What a preposterous notion, worse than that. Women did not live by the sword, they remained in keeps, sheltered and nurtured by their menfolk. She'd be dead within the year, and the thought stopped him cold. There were female knights, aye, and Roger had even met one or two, but none of them looked like Lady Kathryn. Big women, large as any man, damaged by battle and life. The idea of Kathryn scarred from eye to mouth by a sword chilled him. Or her pretty eyes haunted and darkened by the cruelty of battle.

She had fire and heart, and the life she planned for herself would have that pulled from her and stamped into dust.

"Do not send me back to Anglesea." She came to stand before him. "I can help you find Matty and I can help you bring her round."

Roger had no idea why, but he nodded and rose. "Let us get started. The day looks to be turning cold."

* * *

Kathryn tugged her chemise sleeves over her hands. Dear God, she was cold. A nasty wind came in from the east and gusted for the entire day. Moisture streamed from her eyes and froze on her cheeks.

She rode in Roger's wake, her head ducked to keep out of the worst of the wind. If she uttered one complaint, she had no doubt he would turn south and see them back to Anglesea as fast as he could.

He kept them off the main roads, and stuck close to the trees. It took longer, but it did provide some shelter from the gnawing wind. Around midday he stopped and consulted with her on direction before they set off again. They kept to a walk so as not to tire the horses.

The long day slid into a frigid evening. By the time they stopped for the night, Kathryn's limbs had frozen in the saddle. Pressing her lips together to stop her groan, she tumbled off Striker. Icy shards of pain shot up her legs, and she took a moment to breathe deep, and breathe again.

Roger, preoccupied with his mount, blessedly did not notice.

She rubbed Striker's legs with her cloak and tethered him deeper into the trees to keep him out of the wind. Roger worked beside her, also caring for his beast first. Thank the Lord, she no longer hid from him and a warm fire would help them through the night.

While Roger unpacked their blankets, Kathryn gathered

wood for their fire. Clumsy and near frozen solid with the cold, her fingers scrabbled on the wood.

"Here." Roger frowned and took the wood from her hands. He dropped it and cradled her hands between his palms. Shaking his head, he chaffed her hands. "You should have said you were near ice."

Hot prickles shot through her hands as he worked. Through chattering teeth, she tried to form words.

Roger softened as he looked at her. The cold turned his cheeks ruddy. "You are a stubborn woman, Lady Kathryn."

"I am not a delic-c-cate f-flower."

He chuckled and blew hot breath onto her aching fingers. "Nay? But you are a frozen bloom." When color returned to her fingers he sat her on a fallen tree trunk, and got to work on the fire. Deft, efficient movements soon had small flames eating up the kindling and licking about the larger wood. He took a fur-lined traveling cloak and dropped it about her shoulders.

The cloak smelled of wool, horse, and the faint trace of mint and lemons that clung to Sir Roger. It enveloped her like a cloud of happy and Kathryn hunkered into the warmth.

He crouched by the far side of the fire and fed the flame. Once satisfied, he rose and came to her side.

"Keep your hair on," he muttered beside her ear. "I am going to warm you up again." With his back braced by her tree trunk, he tugged her to him.

Awkward with cold and exhaustion she allowed him to tuck her between his powerful legs, with her back to his chest. Her position was beyond immodest, and metal links pressed into her spine, but, Dear Father in Heaven, warmth. "Are you not cold?" She shivered hard enough to set her teeth clacking together.

"There is a lot more of me," he said. "And I have a gambeson on below my hauberk."

With the fire before her, and Sir Roger at her back, heat crept through Kathryn. With it came a sneaky lethargy that weighted her eyelids and turned her limbs to lead.

* * *

Roger's belly growled, but he stayed where he sat.

Kathryn's head rolled onto his shoulder, her pert nose pressed into the side of his neck as she slept. Stubborn wench would rather freeze solid to her saddle than tell him she was exhausted and cold.

He blamed himself. Irked that she had bested him and followed him despite telling her nay, he had pushed her harder today than he should have. Despite her pluck and spirit, she was a girl, a delicate flower. He chuckled softly, loath to wake her. She would have his ballocks for suggesting such a thing.

Trusting as a child, she slept in his arms. The subtle scent of lilacs clung to her hair, almost imperceptible beneath the pungent tang of horse. He could not recall, what if anything, Lady Mathilda smelled of. Of course, he had not managed to get close enough to Mathilda to know much.

Her desertion pricked his pride. Four days in the saddle, he had thought of it often, along with why in God's name he hared over the country after a woman who had run from him. Some wounded male pride had sent him out of Anglesea, but the burn had eased. Now, he mostly enjoyed the freedom being out of the keep afforded him.

With Beatrice married to Garrett and wrapped up in each other and their boys, Faye happily wed to Gregory and living at Calder, William ensconced with his bride in the north of England, and Henry off on some misguided holy pilgrimage, life at Anglesea seemed very different. The old keep echoed with the lack of their voices. Mother used the opportunity to press him to fill the castle with the sound of his children.

He would like that, too. Children brought life to a keep. Aye, Mathew remained, but the lad grew forlorn with just himself amidst all the adults. It had taken Roger these days of travel to name the empty feeling within him. He felt lonely.

Despite what he said, he wanted a wife. A warm body in his

bed, a sweet smile over his trencher, a light, feminine voice to answer him. But he did not want just any woman. He had grown to manhood seeing the way his father would light up from within when his mother entered a room. Heard their soft, quiet laughter when they thought all the children slept. Happiness wrapped about his parents. When Bea found her Garrett, she had the same look his mother wore when she glanced at her husband. Soft, gentle, loving. When a woman looked at a man in such a way, it filled his soul, and Roger's soul felt empty, bereft.

In his arms, Kathryn snuffled and pressed closer.

He tightened his arms about her, and she sighed. The sort of contented, feminine sound that made a man want to rip the moon from the sky to keep her safe.

Jesu, he was a stupid sod. One lovely woman curled up in his arms on a cold, clear spring night, and his head filled with ridiculous nonsense. Hunger trifled with his thoughts.

Best he make use of her and find Lady Mathilda. When he found his bride, he could put to rest this nonsense and see to the business of getting married. Lady Mathilda was a lady in the true sense of the word. She did not careen about on horseback, brandishing a sword and yelling like a lusty Scot.

What a sight Kathryn made on horseback. His sisters rode well, Father had seen to that, but Kathryn moved with her mount, as if they shared one mind and spirit. He'd never met a woman who could ride to unseat a knight. Come to think on it, he'd never met another person, man or woman, who could follow him for three days before he spotted them. If he hadn't obeyed his instinct and taken a very wide sweep last night, she would still be silently on his tail.

Kathryn stirred in his arms, her lashes tickling his neck as she opened her eyes. "Roger?"

"Aye?"

"Is there aught to eat?"

And, he laughed, she had a man's appetite to go with her man-sized spirit his Lady Kathryn.

Chapter Seven

Kathryn sat up straight in her saddle, excitement sparked along her spine. They had entered the quiet village through the far end, but as they approached the green it bustled with life.

She twisted in her saddle to speak to Roger who followed in her wake. "It is market day."

A group of shrieking boys ran past his horse and set the beast to dancing. He frowned and fought for control. "So it would appear."

From the middle of the green, pipe music floated their way, played by a small traveling band of minstrels. There would be dancing later, or she missed her guess. "We should stop."

"Indeed." He nudged his horse to the left, forcing Striker to alter his course.

"Look!" Kathryn pointed to a gaggle of girls decked out in their best bliauts, streamers floating from their gleaming loose hair. "They have a maypole."

Roger quirked his eyebrow at her and dismounted. "Have you ever danced around a maypole?"

"Aye." Kathryn tapped her fingers to the sprightly tune. "Every spring."

"You do?" He stared at her, arms braced on his horse's back.

"I love to dance." Kathryn pulled Striker up beside Roger's destrier and leaped to the ground. Roger's destrier was a truly beautiful, powerful beast. Tall and dark, muscle rippled beneath his gleaming coat. Like rider, like horse. She smirked at her forbidden thought and followed Roger's broad shoulders through the crowd.

After an unflattering inventory of her travel preparations, Roger had insisted they visit the nearest village.

"You know I have no coin to buy supplies." She lengthened her stride to keep up with him.

Roger grunted and gave a quick nod.

The sweet bite of roasting apples teased her nostrils and she turned like a hunting hound toward the smell.

"What is it?" Roger strode back to where she stood fixed to the spot.

"Pies." Merely saying the word made her salivate. "Apple." She took a deep sniff. "And peach."

"Come on." Roger tugged at her arm. "We have no time to linger. This cold weather may hold for a few days and we need to get you well-provisioned."

Kathryn bit back a sigh. Pies should never be gobbled, but left on the tongue and savored through every bite. They did not often have sweets at Mandeville because Father did not partake. But when they did, Kathryn and Matty perched themselves at the kitchen table and waited. Before the pies finished baking came spoons and bowls for licking, bits of leftover fruit stewed in treacle for shoveling up.

Roger took her hand and wove them through a throng of farmwives as the women gossiped and picked over the offerings of fruit and vegetables. Her hand disappeared in the warm, calloused clasp of his great paw. No wonder he could swing a sword with such power. Swordplay started with a firm grip and it helped to have hands big as a hambone. They also made a girl feel safe, if a girl was the sort who needed protecting.

"Here." He drew her to a cloth and garment merchant.

Good, serviceable clothing hung from pegs. More clothing, of lesser quality, dyed yellow and brown sat on the ground cloth.

The merchant eyed Roger as one would a plump partridge, all ready for the plucking.

"How much for that one?" Roger pointed at a fur-lined cloak of russet wool.

"My lord has a fine eye." The merchant smoothed back his thinning sandy hair and oozed closer. "It is my very finest wool. And the fur—"

"How much?" Kathryn stopped the merchant before he went into a frenzy of delight.

The merchant stiffened. Peering down his thin nose at her, he sniffed. "I could accept no less than one mark for it."

Roger nodded and went for the pouch at his waist.

"One mark?" Kathryn threw her head back and laughed. "You must be daft. Three shillings and nothing more."

The merchant planted his legs apart, chin jutting out. "Surely you jest? Three shillings for this?" His stroked the cloth with spindly fingers. "See the wool, russet it is. And fur lined. Thirteen shillings."

Kathryn snorted. "Four."

"My lord." The merchant held the cloak out to Roger. "Surely a man of your taste can see the value?"

Roger folded his arms. He looked at her with a wry grin. "The lady speaks for me."

With a deep breath, the merchant scowled at her. "Ten shillings."

"You are a funny man," Kathryn said. "But not that funny. Five."

"Nine."

"Five."

"Nine."

"Six," Roger said. "And I do not bash your head in for trying to cheat me."

Grumbling, the merchant snatched up the cloak and handed it to Roger.

Roger took it, paid the merchant and laid it over Kathryn's shoulders. His fingers brushed her chin as he tied the fastening.

"I could have got him down to five," Kathryn said as they walked away. "See how useful I am? I saved you seven shillings."

Roger snorted a laugh. "I am indebted to you."

"Indebted enough to buy me a pie?"

Turning on his heel, he shook his head.

Kathryn scrambled after him. Her step got an extra spring when she saw his direction. He stopped short and pressed some coins into her hand. "Go haggle yourself a hat."

"I do not need a hat," she said. "See, my cloak has a hood."

He rolled his eyes. "Pies it is then."

* * *

Roger tried not to grin, and lost the battle, as Kathryn worked her way through two apple pies and a peach one. Her look of abandoned delight dragged a smile out of the dour-faced baker.

Her pink tongue darted between her fingers as she caught the last sticky remnants. She ended by sucking on her fingers with a soft moan.

Not a clue. He glowered at a young yeoman caught wide-eyed in the innocent sensuality Kathryn employed. He would bash the little cur's head in for thoughts no decent man should be thinking. Like how her tongue could be better used.

"Are you done?" His voice came out a little brusquer than he intended.

She blinked at him. "I do like pie," she said with a flush.

"Here." The beaming baker nudged him with a cloth-wrapped bundle. "I will only have to toss them later, and it does a man good to see someone enjoy his wares like your pretty lady."

Roger opened his mouth to explain that Kathryn was not his lady, but shut it again. He accepted the parcel with a nod of thanks. As far as the village knew, Kathryn was his lady. For her sake, they needed to keep thinking that, because they travelled alone, her an innocent, and him an unmarried man. "Blast!"

Kathryn's head came up. "What is it?"

Clueless! He wanted to shake some sense into the damned girl. Had she even given the prudence of their traveling arrangements a thought? He'd wager not a one. "Sod it!" He spun on his heel and stomped to their horses.

Villagers cleared from his path. An apple-cheeked matron snatched her toddler to her bosom.

"What is it?" Kathryn trotted along in his wake.

The stupid girl had fixed them up tight. If they didn't find her sister, he would have no way of explaining their journey together. He could protest their innocence until cows sang mass, but the damage was done. No other man would touch Lady Kathryn when they discovered how she had spent the last few days. He did not care how much she protested she did not intend to marry. Women like Kathryn needed a man. A firm hand on her wayward nature, a guiding force to direct her spirit, and a warm body to soak up all the sensuality she exuded.

She had just volunteered him for the position. And he had let her. Out in the woods, sticking to back roads, the immodesty of their situation had not occurred to him. Add her father's eagerness for a match with Anglesea to the brew, and he might as well find a priest and be done with it. "Get on your horse, we are leaving."

"But there will be dancing later."

"Now."

* * *

Clearly, she had erred in some way because Roger appeared to be enjoying a fine sulk as they rode along. He had barely said a word to her since commanding her to get on her horse. Commanded?

More like bellowed. Even Striker had sidled away from him when he had done that.

They traveled southeast. She had given him the general direction, and with a grunt he had moved that way. He made no mention of Anglesea and on their current route they would slip past the keep to the north. The new cloak kept the sharp spring wind off her chest, and she snuggled into its warmth. The cloak must mean he had accepted her on this journey with him. Please God let it mean such because she could not go back to Anglesea and face Father without Matty. His rage over her actions made her shudder. Her only hope to pacify him would be in handing him the marriage he so dearly wanted.

Herds of cattle, released from their winter confinement, dotted the lands through which they traveled. Spring calves pressed weak-kneed and clumsy against their mother's bellies. In another month or so, they would be gamboling across the new green grass.

They passed a group of peasants turning the soil for spring planting. Their bent backs spots of color between the earth and the dull sky. Kathryn waved as she went by, and a few of them looked up and waved back. Riding out in the open was definitely easier than lurking around following Roger.

Her stomach reminded her that midday had come and gone, and still they rode in silence. She ate her leftover pie, and even offered Roger some.

He shook his head, jaw clamped shut.

The sharp wind freshened and blew brisk and icy at their backs. Another cold night on the way. At least her new cloak would keep the worst of the chill off. Or perhaps Roger would wrap his arms about her again, and share the heat of his big body with her. His embrace warmed her deep within, and brought a strange tingle to her skin. Heat quivered low in her belly. An odd sensation, not unlike the feeling when she fought with her sword, or galloped Striker over the fields.

With Matty's coming marriage, this year brought new

promise for Kathryn. Even in his present dark mood, Roger showed no signs of temper or cruelty. He would make Matty very happy.

"Shall we go for a gallop?" It always helped clear her fidgets and glooms.

"Nay. We need to spare the horses."

She grew tired of the back of his head. "Are you afraid I might win?"

A rude noise floated back to her.

"I will grant you, your mount has a longer stride and looks to be powerful, but Striker here has more heart than most horses I know, and I ride much lighter in the saddle than you."

"You ride like a sack of oats."

His rudeness sparked her ire. "I have an excellent seat."

"You have a reasonable seat for a woman."

"I am a woman!"

He tossed his head back on a bitter laugh. "Aye, and I know it, all too well."

Kathryn spurred Striker closer to Roger. "And what do you mean by that, anyway? I am the best rider at Mandeville, men included."

"Against a knight of even middling skill you would be unseated in a heartbeat." He dug his heels into his horse and widened the distance between them.

"Why are you so grumpy?" Kathryn called after him. She had the sense this had naught to do with her riding.

"Grumpy?" He whirled in his saddle, a dark cloud over his features. "I am not grumpy, my lady, I am angry."

"My mistake." She preferred when he called her Kathryn. All this "my lady" nonsense made him sound pompous and boring. "Why are you angry?"

"I do not wish to speak of it." Now, he sounded like a blasted monk.

"So you will merely sulk instead?"

He stopped his horse. His back went even more rigid.

Well, at least she had broken through some of the ice.

He turned to her. His scowl left scorch marks in her tunic. "Have you given no thought to the position in which we now find ourselves? A position that is in every way thanks to you."

Kathryn shrugged, because, nay she had not. Indeed, she knew not to what he referred. "What position?"

Wind ruffled his hair, a muscle jumped in his jaw. "You. Me. Alone on the road."

Was that the burr up his ass? "It does not mean anything. I trust you."

"You trust me?" He opened and closed his mouth, grew a little pink and puffed up his chest. "That is not the blasted point."

"Then what is the point?"

"The point is, Lady Kathryn." He dragged out her name as if it pained him to utter it. "You are an unmarried woman, presumably chaste—although anything is possible with you—alone with a man who is not related to you."

"What do you mean presumably chaste?" Kathryn dug her nails into her thigh before she smacked his smug face. How dare he even hint otherwise? Granted her manners could be a mite free at times, but that was no reason to assume she was a whore.

"Well, are you?"

"I refuse to answer that." Kathryn tried for a cool retort but she burned hot enough to bash him about the head.

"Very well." He nudged his horse closer. "Regardless of that, people will assume that you are no longer that way when this journey is over. It will ruin your chances of a good marriage."

"I told you, I do not intend to marry."

"Do not be simple." Jamming a fist on his hip, he frowned. "Of course you will marry, but not if word of this adventure gets out. Your future husband will want to be sure he marries a virgin bride."

"My future husband can go hang himself, and so can you for that matter."

He laughed, an ugly, grating sound. "Well, thanks to you,

Lady Kathryn, it looks like your future husband and I are one and the same man."

"Nonsense! You will marry Matty."

"What if we do not find Matty?"

"We will."

"What if we do not?"

"We will."

He growled and sneered at her.

Something unraveled in Kathryn's gut. A mist dropped over his features, and her breath grated loudly. "If that is what is worrying you, let me set your mind at rest. I will not marry, and I for certain will not marry you."

"You may not have left yourself any choice. Or me, for that matter."

"I do have a choice. I do." Kathryn heard herself shouting, but didn't seem able to stop it. She wanted to punch the smirk off him, and damn the consequences.

"Do not be a child."

Her father's voice rang in her ears. It lit a fire in her belly hotter than scalding and Kathryn planted her hands on Roger's chest and shoved with all her might.

Roger's eyes widened, moments before he toppled backwards off his horse with a shout.

Kathryn leaped off Striker, ducked around Roger's prancing destrier and pinned her tormentor to the ground. Blood pounded hard at her temples. All the years of her father's insults melted into this one inferno. "Do not call me names. I am not a whore or a child or a simple girl." Her fists scraped on the metal of his hauberk. "I will never be subject to another man. Never again. Not you, not my father, not anyone. Do you understand me?"

"Aye, Kathryn." He caught her fists in his and held on. "I hear you because you are sitting on me and bellowing it at me."

"Good Lord." She scrabbled off him and away. She hugged her knees to her chest and dropped her head onto them. Her loss of temper scalded her shamefully. Never had she behaved thus.

Not since she had been a child had she lost her temper so thoroughly. God, he must think her mad.

"Kathryn?" His voice came from right beside her. "Look at me."

She shook her head. She might never look at him again.

"Look at me," he said, firmer this time. Strong fingers gripped her chin and turned her to him. "I apologize for calling you names."

He apologized to her? Kathryn wanted to crawl inside herself and never come out.

"It was churlish of me." He stroked her cheek. "I was in a temper and I misspoke myself."

"I should not have done what I did." Her shame fit like too-tight armor.

"It was a mighty shove you gave me." With a rueful grimace, he chuckled. "It has been some time since I was unseated."

"Verily?"

"Verily." He winced. "But my ass remembers the pain well."

"I apologize for that." Her breathing grew labored with him so close. "And for the punching, and all of it. I cannot think what came over me."

"And I take back what I said about your riding. You ride better than most men I know."

Nobody had uttered a sweeter compliment to her. Ever. "You mean that?"

"I mean that." He winked, and then stood. Holding out one hand to her, he brushed off his chausses with the other. "Come on then. We need to find your sister."

Roger sat across the fire from Kathryn as they ate. The girl consisted of one puzzle piece within another, within another. She had surprised the piss out of him when she pushed him off his horse. He had seen men in rages like that before. He understood that heart-deep anger that flew well beyond any reason.

But what would cause such anger in Kathryn?

She brought to mind a cornered animal. The thought of Kathryn with that weight of fear within her sat sour in his belly. From her first wide, sunny smile, Kathryn breathed fire and light into the world about her. Truth be told, the first time he had seen her he had stood a moment, struck dumb by the sight of her charging across the bailey with her sword drawn. Braid streaming out behind her, her lovely face awash with the pure pleasure of riding at the quintain.

Matty possessed all the serenity and demureness of a lady born. Kathryn burned elemental, raw, and she drew him in an inexplicable way.

Now, she dug into her meal with gusto, biting off strips of dried meat as if eating the finest fowl. The girl threw her mighty spirit into every endeavor of her life, which is what made the darkness he had glimpsed today doubly disturbing. "May I ask you something?"

She glanced at him. One cheek bulged with her dinner.

"Is it just me you refuse to marry, or any man?"

She chewed and swallowed just ahead of a rich, throaty chuckle that took his head to a forbidden place. "Nay, it is just you."

Vixen! A man could never grow bored with this much spirit. "Anything particular about me?"

"Your great big feet." She gestured with her bread crust. "Never could abide a man with big paddles at the end of his legs."

He returned her smile. The moment hung sweet between them. "If you were to marry, what sort of man would that be?"

"What are you with all the questions, an old woman?" The wretch rolled her great, melting brown eyes at him.

"Just curious." He shrugged as if her answer held no importance. "I thought my sore ass had earned me an answer."

She gave that some thought and then nodded. Laying her

bread aside, she sighed. "It is not about the man, so much as it is about marriage."

He waited, a trick his mother employed to wicked effect.

"Marriage, for a woman is the end." She slashed the air. "Unless they marry a kind man, or one so besotted with her he allows her freedom, she becomes his chattel. To do with as he wills."

"And yet you want this for your sister?"

"Matty and I are very different." Firelight created dark pools of her eyes. "Matty is soft and delicate and fragile. She needs a man who can shelter her, and care for her."

Flattered she'd chosen him for the task he nodded. "And you do not?"

"Nay." She snorted and grabbed her bread. "When you marry Matty, and take my mother to live with you, I shall be off into the world to seek my fortune."

She had his future all planned for him. Not only had she selected his wife, she had his mother by marriage settled beside his hearth as well. He thought of asking how many children he could expect.

However, Kathryn's plan for her future made him go colder than death within. Kathryn out in the world, on her own, would dangle like bait for every sorry cur with an evil intent. He worked to keep his reaction concealed before he spoke. "Where will you go?'

"France." She wiped her fingers on her tunic. "I hear they have more tournaments there, and a person could earn their way through their winnings."

Dear God, her innocence terrified him. Men who lived by the sword stood only a small step higher than grave robbers. Between now and his marriage, he needed to find a way to change her mind. "You will need more training."

"Aye." She grimaced. Wood popped in the fire and threw a shower of sparks. "Only it is not easy to find someone to train me."

"I could train you." See that. His family thought William had the sharp mind.

She rocked forward and beamed. "You would?"

"Aye." He shrugged. "If you proved yourself worth training."

"Why would you do such a thing?" She stilled, and scrutinized him.

"I like you." He opted for the truth. "I want to see you well prepared." And while doing so, he would make damn certain he found the sort of man she could not resist. If he had to scour every keep in the land to do so. Kathryn deserved a man above others, one who would never seek to crush the light in her spirit or the fire in her veins. She needed a man who would understand and appreciate the precious gift Roger handed him.

Chapter Eight

Roger woke. Dark pressed in from all sides.

The horses whickered and shifted.

The total absence of sound rang like a bell.

Kathryn!

Where she had slept, her blanket lay crumpled on the ground.

"Now, we do not want no blood." A man stepped out of the forest, tall and unkempt. He kept a crossbow trained on Roger. "Get his sword."

Another man appeared to Roger's left. Wide through the shoulders, this one bore the stamp of the group muscle.

Blight! How had he not noticed a second man in the trees?

Then a third man stepped into the small ring of flickering light made by the fire. He darted forward and kicked Roger's sword beyond the firelight.

A fourth man slid into view, also armed with a crossbow pointed at Roger's chest.

This one looked as if he knew what to do with it. As ragged as the others, his posture keen and alert, but his eyes gave him away. The eyes of a man who had met death, and lost his fear of it.

That was the one to watch.

"What do you want?"

"We'll take your purse and them horses," the first man said.

Roger rose slowly, keeping his hands well in sight. He raised his voice until it carried into the dark. If Kathryn hid nearby, hopefully she would hear him. "You know the penalty for horse theft?"

The dangerous one snickered. Roger would wager he had more than horse theft to his name. A scar split the man's face in half across the bridge of his nose. Somebody had tried to top him like a boiled egg. He held his crossbow loosely, his finger poised, unlike their leader who had a stranglehold on his weapon. The other two stayed back, knives clutched in their fists.

Roger kept one hand high as he said, "I am going to untie my purse now. Nobody get nervous."

The scarred one stilled.

Roger shook his purse. The clank and jangle of coins drew all attention in that direction. Except the scarred one. He knew, first you eliminated the threat, and only then did you grab the spoils.

Something flew past Roger's nose.

A cry cut off in a wet strangled gurgle. The scarred one stared, dagger wedged deep in his throat. He listed and went over like a felled tree.

The leader loosed a crossbow bolt.

It missed Roger by a hair and thudded into a tree trunk behind him.

The two knifemen lunged for him.

Roger snatched the dagger from his boot. He was going to beat her ass black and blue, right after he thanked her for saving him.

Yelling, Kathryn leaped into the light. One lightning fast kick separated the leader from his cross bow.

The idiot dropped to his knees and scrabbled after it.

Kathryn dealt him a thundering blow across the back of the head with her sword hilt.

Roger's attackers paused, distracted by her shout.

Roger made short work of the first with a fist in his face that sent him wheeling into a sturdy elm. The last man stepped away from Roger, his gaze darting between him and Kathryn. His fist tightened around his dagger.

"Do not." Roger stepped closer. "I will snap your neck like a twig."

"Like a twig," Kathryn said and closed on the man.

Roger motioned her back.

She tossed him a mutinous glance.

"Turn about and leave." Roger told the remaining attacker. "And I might forget what your face looks like."

The man eyed him for a long moment. He whirled and darted into the trees.

Roger stood, his heart still banging like a drum, sweat breaking out all over him. "Of all the dangerous, unplanned, ill-timed..."

Kathryn knelt beside the dead man, the one with the scarred face. Pale and shaky, she touched the trickle of blood on the man's waxy cheek.

"Kathryn." Roger approached her.

"I killed him." She turned her white face up to him, silently pleading with him to tell her it was not so.

With his last breath, he wished he could do that for her. Roger crouched beside her. The first kill cut the deepest. No matter the situation, or how justified, taking a human life carved a trench through a person's soul. Would he could have spared his brave shield-maiden that.

"You did what you must." Clumsy words from a man who had no finesse in these matters.

"But he is dead." She frowned at her bloody finger.

"Aye, sweeting." Her pain eked from her. Taut enough to snap, she held herself rigid. Within he howled to hold her, take the bad thing from her. Yet he sensed he could not touch her. Like a wild thing, she might strike out. "Taking a life is never easy."

"I did not think." She hunched her shoulders. Her fingers dug into her thighs. "I just threw the knife, and I was glad it hit him, but now…"

"Now you are wondering if there is aught you could have done to keep him alive?"

She nodded, her hair making a silky whisper against her tunic.

"There is nothing you could have done, sweeting." He handed her a kerchief to wipe the blood from her hands. "Whatever the outcome here tonight, it would have involved death. His. Mine. Yours. The die was cast the moment they stepped into the clearing."

His kerchief bunched in her fingers. "But they only wanted the horses and the purse."

"Nay." He took the kerchief and cleaned her fingers. "They could not have left me alive. They knew the penalty for stealing from a lord. Those men came here tonight with murder in their hearts." His big hands seemed rough and too large against hers. "You saved me."

"I did?"

He would have perjured his immortal soul with a lie for her. "Aye, you did. This man is no stranger to violence."

Kathryn dragged in a ragged breath. Standing, she shook her head. "What do we do now? Bury them?"

"Nay." Roger rose. "Now we see if they have anything useful and worth keeping."

Kathryn shuddered and stepped away from the body. "You mean touch them?"

"Aye." A war waged within him. Not three hours past, she had sat here and blithely announced her plan to live a violent life. Now, after one swift death, she looked as if she might lose her dinner. Father would have given a sharp lesson and forced her to handle the bodies. "See to the horses, I will take care of this."

Chapter Nine

Kathryn woke well rested the next morning. Her fear the attack would haunt her into the remaining night proved groundless.

Roger let her lead the next day and they made Cecily's home, Castlereagh Manor, shortly before midday. At her insistence, they camped a little way from the manor and waited. Cecily took her walk in the afternoon, at the same time every day, prevented only by inclement weather. As the day had dawned clear and fair with only a trace of chill, Kathryn remained confident they would be able to intercept her.

Kathryn led a grumbling Roger from their camp closer to the manor gardens.

Roger drew his sword and thwacked at a grasping bramble. "Explain to me again why we are sneaking around like a pair of thieves instead of approaching the manor directly."

"Because if we enter the manor we will have to deal with Ranulf." If he knew Ranulf he wouldn't continue to blast her with questions. Ranulf kept a steady eye on his future wealth, wrapped up in his pretty sister. "And if Ranulf is about, Cecily will do nothing more than simper and giggle."

Roger grunted and thwacked at another leaf. "And you are certain this Cecily will know of your sister's whereabouts?"

"Nay, not certain." Kathryn prayed for patience. "But as sure as I can be. Cecily is the only friend Matty has. She trusts her. Matty would not return to Mandeville." She turned and presented her argument with a flourish. "Hence, she would come to Cecily."

Pausing mid-thwack, Roger frowned at her. "Lead on then."

An obliging hedgerow allowed them to enter Cecily's rose garden without detection from the manor.

"Where—"

Kathryn motioned Roger to silence. He would give up their position if he kept yammering like that.

Ranulf walked beside Cecily in the gardens behind Castlereagh Manor. Kathryn had not been entirely honest about her reasons for not wanting to run into Ranulf. Although with Roger by her side, she felt no fear. Still, yesterday's adventure had taught her avoiding a fight beat more blood-letting.

Roger covered her mouth and dragged her behind a large flowering hawthorn. The whole thing accomplished with breath-catching swiftness and no more sound than a robin fluttering through the branches.

"Now what?" He glowered at her. He did that a lot, or he laughed at her, which she rather liked. The glowering he needed to stop.

"I told you." She peered through the thinner branches at the edge of the hawthorn. Ranulf and Cecily kept at their slow procession like they partook of a death march. "We wait. He escorts her to this particular spot and then goes about his business."

Roger leaned over her, dwarfing her with his bulk. "How can you be sure?"

"Because neither of them has the imagination to do any differ-ent." Roger smelled like a warrior, of leather, horse, and old blood-infused chainmail. Kathryn drew shallow breaths. If her dearest wish came true, she imagined she would end up smelling that way before long. Best she get used to it. "If Matty was frightened and could not come to me, Cecily would be her next choice."

"Then let us go and ask her." Roger strode toward the garden.

Kathryn barely grabbed his arm in time and hauled him back behind the hawthorn. "Are you mad? Ranulf will see you."

"Ranulf is a man." He raised his brow at her. "I will simply explain our predicament and he will get his sister to tell me what she knows."

Kathryn hadn't factored that into her plan. Besides being a man, Ranulf would also squirm like a boot-licking cur at the idea of ingratiating himself with the powerful Angleseas. After all, there remained an unattached Anglesea brother for Ranulf to lust after for his sister. She steeled herself. "Ranulf must not see me."

"Ah." Roger smirked and folded his arms. "Now we get to the truth. And why must Ranulf not see you?"

Roger would stand there looking smug until she told him. "He does not approve of me. If he sees me, he will lock Cecily away and we will wait out here until Judgment Day."

Roger cocked his head. "What did you do?"

"What do you mean, what did I do?" Kathryn ducked her chin to her chest. Roger had leaped insultingly fast to the conclusion Ranulf based his dislike on her actions. It might have been any reason. Ranulf might be mad for all Roger knew. However, it had transpired that Ranulf possessed a touch more sensitivity than she had thought. Foolish man! It had been but a race, and Father had made her return the horse to him.

Roger shifted his weight and stared.

"There was a horse race," she said, fiddling with the lie of her tunic. "I won, Ranulf lost and had to give me his horse."

"Your father allowed you to enter a horserace with a man?"

Blast his perception! Kathryn peeked around at Cecily and Ranulf again. If Roger kept chatting their time away, they might lose their quarry. "Not exactly. I entered as a boy. I thought the entire thing a huge jest."

"Let me guess," Roger spoke right beside her ear, his breath warm on her neck. "Ranulf and whoever else saw the race did not share your sense of humor?"

"Aye." They had veered off topic and it would be best to return swiftly. "Cecily often spends the afternoon sewing beneath the trees. She says the light is good. Ranulf will leave her shortly and then we will slip closer."

"Where is the horse now?" Warmth surrounded her from Roger's proximity.

"My father made me return it. He said it was not fairly won, and I could not keep it."

Ranulf walked Cecily into the shade of an ancient elm, and assisted her as she sat. They spoke for a long moment, and then Ranulf handed Cecily a cloth sack. They chatted for a while longer. Surely, Ranulf did not intend to sit by her side and watch Cecily sew?

"Ah," Roger murmured, his breath stirring wisps of her hair. "It seems you were right. There he goes."

Ranulf strode back to the manor, his short legs giving him the jaunty strut of a bantam rooster. How could she have ever thought he might make a good match for Matty? She had nearly condemned her sister to a life of squat, bad-tempered children.

They waited until Ranulf disappeared behind the side of the manor into the stable yard beyond.

"Come." Kathryn threaded her way closer to Cecily. Still aware there could be watchers in the manor, they stuck to the hedgerow that bordered the formal gardens.

Motioning Roger to stop, she crouched behind a cluster of rose bushes Cecily tended like her own babes. "You stay here. If Matty has spoken of you, Cecily will be frightened of you, and she has about as much spirit as a pudding."

"Indeed." Roger clenched his fists on his thighs

"Never mind." Kathryn patted his hand. "I will set Cecily

straight. I will have to convince her you are not at all fearsome before she will tell me anything. But looking as you do, with your beard and your hair…" Which brought another thing to mind. "And when we do find Matty, you and I are going to have a long talk about your ham-handed approach to courtship."

He cupped her nape and growled her name. "Kathryn."

See there, he had neatly demonstrated the problem. Matty did not care to be growled at. Kathryn found it rather thrilling, but she and her sister were not woven from the same cloth. "Stay here."

Roger dropped into a waiting crouch behind the roses.

Kathryn crept as close as she could.

Cecily sang to herself as she plied her needle through the cloth. Good Lord, the girl mangled the tune almost beyond recognition. She would wager Ranulf kept his sister from singing when prospective suitors arrived. Pretty in a soft, plump way with her dusky cloud of hair and her rosy cheeks, Cecily held the key to Ranulf's ambitions, and he sought and discarded suitor after suitor. He saw his sister as the coin to purchase his better future.

"Psst."

Cecily started and stared at the rose bush. "Is anybody there?"

"It is me, Cecily."

She dropped her sewing and clasped a hand to her throat. "The rose bush?"

Not the brightest light in a summer sky. "Nay, Cecily, it is Kathryn."

Cecily frowned. "Who?"

"Kathryn of Mandeville."

"Oh." Fluttering her hands, Cecily giggled. "I thought the rose bush spoke to me." She chewed her lip as she studied the rose bush. "Are you a rose bush now?"

A snort made her whirl about. Roger, the conniving cur, had sneaked closer. Kathryn motioned him back to where she'd left him.

Roger tilted his head, and raised his brow.

"Nay, Cecily, I am not a rose bush. I am hiding in the rose bush."

As adorable as she was vacant, Cecily grew thoughtful. "Why?"

"So, Ranulf does not see me."

"Oh." Cecily's pink bow mouth formed an O. "Ranulf does not like you because you stole his horse."

Stole his horse! "I did not—"

Roger covered her mouth and dragged her ear to his lips. "Find out where your sister is."

With as much dignity as she could muster, Kathryn wriggled free. She would deal with his habit of hauling her about later.

"Cecily, I am looking for Matty." Kathryn crawled back to her former position. A rose thorn jabbed at her neck.

Roger snapped it off for her.

Cecily's shoulders drooped. "Nay." She shook her head, swishing her silky hair. "She is not here."

"Aye, but do you know where she is?"

"Nay." Cecily blushed prettily. "I did not see her."

"Are you certain, Cecily?"

Head tilted up, Cecily said, "I did not see her. She did not come here. I do not know where she is."

"She lies," Roger muttered.

Kathryn threw him a look that advised him to shut his pie-hole. "When did you not see her here, Cecily?"

"Three days ago." With a little squeal, Cecily jumped to her feet. "I did not see her. She did not come here. I do not know where she is." Her voice rose on each word.

"Of course you did not." Kathryn kept her voice soothing, whilst keeping a wary eye for Ranulf to appear. The man had the sense of a hunting hound when it came to his sister.

"Of course I did not." Cecily took her seat again, and patted her hair back into place. "Nobody can say that I saw her."

"Indeed." Kathryn forced a hearty chuckle. "You are the very best of friends to keep her secret so well."

"I am." Cecily flushed and giggled. "I have kept all her secrets."

"All her secrets?"

Cecily's expression grew guarded. "You should go before Ranulf returns."

"Surely you can tell me." Kathryn crawled closer. "I am Matty's sister. She tells me everything."

Cecily plopped her sewing in her lap, and smirked. "If Matty told you everything, you would not be here now."

Apparently, there did exist a trace of wit in that empty head. "Perhaps she did not find me in time to tell me."

"You cannot get around me." Cecily looked smug as she made a stitch. "I am the very best of friends, and I shall say no more."

"Cecily." Kathryn had almost reached the bench. She could not go much further without risk of being seen. "I am worried sick for my sister. I need to find her."

"She told me about you." Cecily tutted and placed another stitch. "She told me that you would force her to marry that awful man. He is big and hairy and he frightens her. He wants her to have hundreds of children." Cecily dropped her sewing into her lap and shuddered. "Hundreds."

"There was a misunderstanding." Something moved around the side of the manor. Kathryn slunk back. "You know I love Matty. I would never force her to marry a horrible man."

Cecily resumed her humming.

"Cecily—" A jab in her back nearly made Kathryn squeal. She whirled.

Grimacing, Roger motioned her to return to him.

Kathryn shook her head. She could get Cecily to spill her secrets. "She could be hurt, Cecily." She used her most cajoling voice. "In danger."

Poke went Roger with the stick in her back.

She grabbed the stick. "She could be exposed to all sorts of brigands and bad men."

Cecily shook her head. "She is fine."

Roger attempted another jab.

Kathryn yanked the stick. "You cannot be sure of that, Cecily."

Roger held on.

"But I am." Cecily drew her needle through the cloth. She glanced at Kathryn with a sly smile. "And if you do not go away, I will call Ranulf."

Roger nearly tugged her off her feet and Kathryn dropped the stick and conceded.

They retreated through the rose bushes, back to their hawthorn. Kathryn had been so sure she could get more out of Cecily. She stomped to Striker, needing to ride fast enough for the wind to snatch the curses from her mouth.

"Where are you going?" Roger trailed her.

"For a ride." Kathryn put her foot in the stirrup.

Roger grabbed her ankle. "Firstly, I have a fair idea of how wild you ran at Mandeville, but when you decided to follow me around the kingdom, you put yourself in my care." He held up a finger to forestall her argument. "And secondly, that was very informative and well worth getting pricked on the ass."

"She knows more." He could not have missed that.

"Of course she does." Roger nudged her ankle to the ground. "And now we know that she knows more and that gives us an advantage."

Hardly! Kathryn snorted. "What sort of advantage?"

"That is a most disagreeable habit," he said. "Snorting like a randy bull. Something else happened in that interaction that you are overlooking."

She nearly snorted again, but stopped herself. Randy bull, indeed. Did he not know he had no business speaking to a maiden of such matters? Not that she was a typical maiden, but still, a girl had to have some standards.

Roger rested his hand on Striker's pommel. "Cecily, although no deep thinker, also realizes she said too much. What would you do if you were keeping a secret for someone and you learned danger was heading their way?"

"Oh." He was right, brilliantly, blindingly, wonderfully right. "I would warn them, or try to send someone to warn them."

"Exactly." He winked at her. "Now unless I misjudge the situation, Cecily will not be going herself to warn your sister."

"Nay, indeed." Kathryn would pay good coin to see Ranulf if his precious sister jaunted off on her own. "But there could be hundreds of messengers leaving the manor."

"Hundreds?" Roger raised his brow at her.

One day she would get a nail and fix that thing to his head.

"At most, my father sends two or three messengers in the course of a normal day. We will have to pick the most likely suspect, and take the chance Cecily's intelligence does not extend to a deeper level of subterfuge." He tipped her chin up. "Now, would you rather go for a ride or have me find you something to eat?"

A brilliant smile birthed in her belly and spread. "Food."

Chapter Ten

Kathryn might have to make Roger her favorite knight as well as her brother by marriage. Other than a brief tussle over her entering an inn, they passed the lengthening spring afternoon in perfect accord.

By dint of threatening to tie her up, Roger entered the inn alone but returned laden with a bounty to make any girl's heart sing. Fresh meat pies with golden, flaky pastry that melted in her mouth, and perfectly seasoned pork that exploded on her tongue in a medley of herbs, meat, parsnip, carrot and peas. A wheel of pungent soft goat cheese that he spread over oven-hot bread for her. God bless the man, he'd even found sweet peaches, which he pared for her and placed on her knee. The inn's wine he judged as suspect, and so he added small beer to their feast.

Kathryn had never enjoyed a meal more. Seated beneath the shade of an ancient willow, her bare feet dangling in the icy cold waters of a chattering stream. From where they sat, on a hill above the manor, they had a perfect vantage point.

With her belly cheerfully full, she lay back and shut her eyes, and trusted Roger would keep watch. The chill of the past days had disappeared and the sun lay dappled warm on her. Matty would prattle about freckles, but Kathryn paid that no mind.

"Why did she run?" Roger's voice merged with the trill and chirp of a robin in the tree above her.

"Matty?" Kathryn cracked her eyes open.

Roger watched the manor, his harsh profile etched against a pale blue sky behind. "I lack William's charm, but women don't normally run from me."

"Matty is…" How to put a lifetime of knowledge into a few words that would not offend? "Delicate. Like a fragile flower. She is not made to weather harsh storms. My sister is a bloom to be sheltered in the protection of a mighty oak." She'd answered his question rather well.

Roger rested his elbows on his raised knees and chuckled. "The mighty oak being me?"

"Indeed." She grinned in response. "It is a perfect match."

"Other than the tiny detail that the lady fears me so much she risked the wrath of all by taking to the hills." Roger shook his head, as if he could not quite believe it. "I do not understand what I could have said or done differently."

"I do not think it was all you." The idea that Roger blamed himself twanged through her on a sharp sting. "Our father has a fearsome temper. It has made Matty timid."

"But not you." His gaze swept her from crown to toe. "It has made a fighter of you."

"I was born that way." She had always been thus. "Somebody has to shield my mother and sister from his anger."

"Why does that someone have to be you?"

She pushed herself onto her elbows. His line of questioning made her uncomfortable. Aye, there had been times when taking a beating for Matty had rankled, or when lying awake from the pain of having stepped between her father and mother she had whispered that question in the dark recesses of her mind. The answer remained the same. "Who else?"

Expression thoughtful, he cocked his head. "You are a woman of uncommon courage, Lady Kathryn of Mandeville."

Heat suffused her, even as the compliment pleased her. It

made her voice brusque as she dropped onto her back and hid her face with her arms. "Watch the manor."

A breeze danced through the willow strands. Water gurgled and splashed against the stones, and Kathryn drew deep on the crisp air.

"What makes you so certain I am the right man for your sister?"

Good Lord, he was garrulous today. "I just know."

"How?"

With a huge sigh, Kathryn sat up. "You are gentle."

"Eh?" He looked as if she had smacked him about the head.

"With your sisters and your mother, you have a softer way with them."

He laughed. "You only say that because Bea has not yet told you tales of me pushing her in the lake, or when William and I stole Faye's favorite poppet and hung it from the stable rafters."

"Those are boyish pranks." Kathryn waved his words away. "I watched you from the moment we arrived at Anglesea. Even when your mother is carping on at you about something, you listen and then keep your response gentle."

"Hmph!"

His disgruntlement made her smile. "And that day in the bailey when you stepped in and stopped my father from taking Striker from me. I was not your charge to protect and yet you did." A hug seemed too intimate, so she patted his hand where it lay on the grass between them. "Then you taught me how to correct my balance, and you were the first to do so. That all tells me you have a good heart and would treat my sister well."

Secret amusement lit him from within. "It sounds as if you should marry me after all."

"God nay!" His words struck her like a lance to the shoulder. "I never want to marry and besides you are for Matty."

"Matty does not want me, it seems."

"Matty does not always know what she wants. Not that she is tempestuous," she said, quickly before he got the idea her sister might make a difficult wife. Matty could be changeable and not always predictable, but with a bit of guidance from her, she felt certain Roger would grasp the knack of managing Matty. "When we find her, I will explain all of this to her. Then you will do your wooing thing, and all will be well."

He stared out at the manor, his profile rugged. "Your faith in my courtship skills may be misplaced."

"You worry for naught." Kathryn nudged him with her knee. She wanted to make him laugh away his dark mood. "You are a comely man, well formed, and not stupid. And your way with a sword." Kathryn thrilled at the image rising in her mind. "Sublime!"

* * *

His way with a sword! Roger swallowed his laughter. He clung to the tiny piece of driftwood she flung his way. Perhaps he could run some sword forms in front of Lady Mathilda and render her weak with admiration. God knows, his courting had not done the job. He could not even form a very clear picture of Lady Mathilda. She and Kathryn shared the same coloring, and basic form, but her features remained a blur.

Below them, the manor nestled in the waning spring sunlight. A groomsman released a small herd of horses into the meadow. Poor beasts that would benefit from the sort of beautiful bloodlines his brother by marriage, Gregory, worked on.

Like their conversation with hen-witted Cecily, his conversation with Kathryn had revealed much. He did not know much of Sir Royce, and what he knew hinted at a hard, brutal man. With no sons of his own, Sir Royce sought to keep his demesne in his bloodline through marriage. Rumor also had him fending off debtors and leaching his people for taxes.

Anglesea's deep coffers could persuade many a lord to see past the family's fragile relationship with the crown. The kingdom still waited to see how the young king would rule. Another disaster like King John could beggar them all.

Kathryn crossed one long, slim leg over the other and sighed. Those shapely appendages could never belong to a man, and the sooner he talked her into keeping them under a skirt, the better. Too often he found his gaze strayed to her legs, her rounded hip, the apple-pert roundness of her ass. She might have him pegged as harmless as a neutered monk, but she had no idea the thoughts he kept hidden from her.

In a different world, he might roll over and pin her beneath him. Kiss the elegant line of her throat where it emerged above her tunic, cup the full jut of her breasts in his hands. He needed to find her a man. A man who would have the right to do those things and more. His gut tightened around an angry roar of denial. He could not allow another man to befoul Lady Kathryn with his big, dirty hands.

A nun, then! He could have her join the holy sisters.

Except, she vibrated with raw, earthy life. To see that spirit cloistered away and hidden pained him near enough as much as another man.

What in God's name was he going to do with the blasted girl?

* * *

Roger nudged Kathryn's thigh. He'd left her to slumber most of the evening as he watched.

She came awake with a sweet little sigh and rolled onto her belly.

"Movement." He jerked his head at the manor.

Her gaze sharpened, and she scrambled to her hands and knees. Her ass beckoned as she peered at the manor. "Who is it?"

He pointed to a lone, cloaked figure scuttling down the road away from the manor.

"It looks like a woman." A post slumber flush still stained her cheeks, as if she woke in her lover's bed.

"Unless men have taken to wearing skirts with as much enthusiasm as you have taken to wearing chausses, it is a woman."

"Surely not Cecily." She shaded her eyes and studied the figure on the road.

"A maid would be my guess." He rose, limbs a little stiff from being seated for so long. "Best we move our asses and get down there."

Kathryn scrambled to her feet, and gathered their belongings. They'd left the horses ready to go, and she leaped into the saddle moments behind him.

He had yet to meet a woman with such a cool efficiency of manner. Even Beatrice would require a moment to straighten something or smooth another thing before she sprang into action. Kathryn moved as a trained man-at-arms would, but he had not sunk so far in self-deception as to believe he in any way confused her with a large, burly man.

Nay, Kathryn's femininity resided in her lack of affectation. The effortless grace she displayed in even the simplest gesture, like bending to pick up a sleeping blanket, held him annoyingly spellbound. The damnable snarl in his gut tightened.

They took a circuitous route to the village, traveling overland as opposed to alerting the woman on the road. If he had calculated correctly, they would arrive slightly ahead of their quarry.

Leaving their horses with a boy in exchange for a penny—which, of course, Kathryn deemed too much—they slipped into the village. Evening fell, leaving a few stragglers making their way home to their dinners. Overt hiding would merely attract attention so they stuck to the outside of a group of villagers who whiled away the pleasant evening outside the church. Again, Kathryn proved adept at being seen and not noticed.

She gripped his forearm. "There."

From the church end, the young woman from the manor hurried through the villagers. Her clumsy attempts at subterfuge made her easy to track though the milling people. Glancing left and right, and tugging her hood over her head, the girl ducked into a side street with enough flourish for a guild player.

Roger and Kathryn followed, staying far enough back not to alert her, but close enough to see her rap on the door to a house partway down the lane. The door opened and the girl slipped inside.

Roger ducked beneath the open window ledge, and pulled Kathryn beside him. From within the low murmur of voices proved impossible to catch. Roger slid around the side of the house.

A large mastiff darted around the corner. Large yellow teeth flashed as the dog snarled.

Roger backed off.

Kathryn tugged on his tunic as she slid beneath a large handcart.

It took him precious moments to wedge his larger form in behind her.

The tethered dog set up a warning to whoever lived in the house. Powerful jaws flashed large teeth as he let his displeasure at the intrusion be known.

A man's voice from within. "Blasted dog!"

"Who is it?" A female voice, filled with apprehension.

The door opened and a slim, dark haired man stepped out. He glanced about the yard, right past their hiding place. "There is nobody there. Stupid animal!"

He stalked to the dog.

The dog flattened his ears and cowered as the man drew nearer.

Kathryn tensed beside him. She jerked as the man kicked the dog in the ribs. A loud, pained yelp covered Kathryn's gasp. "Whoreson."

Roger agreed. Men who raised their hands to anything weaker constituted the worst sort of scum. He pressed her hand to keep her silent.

The door shut behind the man, and the voices grew distant.

After a few more moments, the woman emerged. She glanced about her, and then tugged her hood over her head. "Make sure you get a message to Lady Mathilda," she said.

The man tugged on his waistband and spat. "I will take it myself."

"See that you do." The girl made a pitiful attempt to sound fierce. "My lady pays you well."

They stayed put as the girl scuttled back the way she'd come.

The man turned back into his cottage, and slammed the door behind him.

"We should wait and follow him." Roger eased out from beneath the cart. The thrill of the hunt coursed through his blood. They had called it right, and Lady Mathilda hovered inches outside their grasp.

Kathryn stared at the dog. "Did you see what he did?"

The dog eyed him with suspicion. Roger dearly wanted to get away before the animal recovered his courage. "Aye. Some men are brutes."

"That poor puppy." Kathryn looked mournful.

It hit Roger in the gut like a kick. "Come, Kathryn." He crouched beside the cart. "We can do nothing for the dog, but we need to move before he comes out and catches us."

Fire kindled in her eyes as she wriggled out. "There is something we can do."

"Kath..."

Too late, he guessed her intention as Kathryn walked to the dog.

The animal crouched low and growled at her.

"Poor baby." She dropped to her haunches just out of tooth range. Holding her hand out, she cooed at the dog.

God's Bones. The beast looked ready to take a piece out of her.

"Stand back, Kathryn." He stepped nearer.

The dog's gaze flickered to him and his snarl grew more menacing.

Roger froze.

"He is frightened of you," Kathryn said.

"What precisely is your plan for this animal?"

"I am taking him with me."

Ballocks! He might have known she would say that. Any moment the man could appear, and they would have no explanation. "We cannot take someone's dog."

"We can if he does not treat it right." The intractable line of her jaw assured him she marked not a word he said.

"What will we do with a dog while we search for your sister?"

"I do not know yet." She dug in her waist pouch and took out a piece of meat. "But I am not leaving him here. So, you can either help me or stand there and glower."

Standing and glowering sounded about right to him.

She dropped the morsel a few inches from the dog.

The dog's lip quivered as if it had not yet decided what to do with the woman in front of him.

Roger shared the beast's pain.

"Come on, sweeting," Kathryn murmured.

The dog sniffed the piece of meat, snapped it up and retreated

Kathryn dropped another piece of meat.

He did not have time for this. Roger marched to the cottage door and hammered his fist against it.

Kathryn hissed at him. "What are you doing?"

The door yanked open. "What do you want?"

"Your dog." Roger jerked his chin toward the dog. "My lady has taken a powerful liking to him. How much for the dog?"

"He is not for sale." A calculating gleam entered the other man's gaze.

"One crown."

The man rubbed his chin. "He is a very good dog."

"Two crowns."

"You could get a good cow for that," Kathryn said, and came up beside him.

"But that dog was my sister's, and I am very fond of my sister."

"Five crowns." Roger wanted to pound their heads together. "Or we leave the miserable cur here."

"Done." Greed won out and the man held out his hand.

Roger dug in his pouch, and slapped five crowns into the outstretched palm. "Get your dog and let us go."

Roger stormed away and headed for the horses. Behind him Kathryn negotiated with the messenger about a stringy piece of rope to tie around the dog's neck. Roger needed to walk off some of his ire. He had just made damn sure they couldn't reveal themselves to Cecily's messenger again. All because Kathryn had those big, melting brown eyes that looked at him and silently begged him to make her world perfect for her.

Dullard! He'd never encountered a more capable woman than Kathryn and here he leaped into the fray on her behalf, and now had a dog to show for it.

Kathryn fell into step beside him shortly after. "See, Roger, he really is a very good dog."

The dog grinned at him, tongue lolling out of the side of his mouth. No dignity or pride, the beast was hopeless.

"Why are we running?" Her breath came out in pants.

Roger slowed his pace. "I want nothing more to do with that sorry animal."

"Indeed." Kathryn beamed at him. "You will not even know he is here."

Chapter Eleven

Of course, his destrier took exception to Kathryn's dog. It cost Roger precious time to introduce horse to dog and dog to horse. Fortunately, the dog appeared to have met horses before and desisted from barking at their mounts.

They rode out of the village to the open amusement of the boy who had watched their horses. Confused by the change in his fortunes, the dog sat in the middle of the road and watched as Kathryn rode away. Several times Kathryn had to backtrack, whistle to the dog and ride a few paces forward before the dog would stop, whine and stare over his shoulder at his former home.

Impatient to be hidden well within the treeline beside the crossroads before the messenger set off, Roger solved the problem with a steady trail of meat. The dog followed that happily enough.

He selected a denser pack of thicket and tethered the horses a little way from the road. From here, they would need to mark which direction the messenger took. Dog at their heels, they crept closer and watched as full dark fell.

Dog proved himself useful. One whiff on the breeze of his former master and he slid behind Kathryn's legs with a whine.

The man appeared on foot, so they stuck to leading the horses, and the bloody dog, from the safety of the trees.

The messenger took the lower road. He kept a swift pace, but stayed in the open and left an easy trail.

This escape of Lady Mathilda's nagged at Roger. Granted, his ire could very well be a result of his dented conceit, but he thought not. Cecily had spoken of 'all her secrets.' Roger had sisters, two of them, and knew feminine whispers and intrigues well, but this felt different. Even Cecily would surely not be employing this level of caution over some wounded female sensibilities or an aversion to his tunic.

Enamored of her new pet, Kathryn trotted on beside him. A large dog with a full, powerful chest and shoulders that tapered to a slim waist, he stuck to Kathryn's heels with a besotted grin. Roger had to concede the dog was a handsome, if smelly, beast.

Males of all species it seemed, bent to her will with a smile after a glance at those eyes.

"What will you call him?" The messenger remained far enough ahead to make conversation possible.

Kathryn glanced at her pet with a fond smile. "I have been thinking on it. Do you have any ideas?"

"Garrett." Roger couldn't resist a grin at the idea. "Garrett is a good name for a dog."

Kathryn stopped and jammed her hands on her hips. "I have never known a dog named Garrett."

"I have." He chuckled. Bea would kill him for sure, but it would be worth it.

"You're up to something." Alight with mischief, she resumed walking. "Which tells me that I for certain should not name him Garrett."

"Fluffy?"

She burst into a muted peal of laugher, throwing her head back. Her cheeks flushed pink in the rich cream of her skin. "What about King?"

Roger pulled a face. He preferred Dog if King was his option.

"Dagger!" A huge grin split her face. "Because he is strong, and dangerous. Aren't you, Dagger?"

Dagger grinned back at her.

"Dagger it is," Roger said. He kept his suspicions about Mathilda to himself. He did not have enough to share, and he could not ruin Kathryn's enjoyment of her adventure.

* * *

As the night grew chillier, Kathryn dug out her cloak and donned it. Three hours after moonrise, the messenger stopped at an inn and went inside.

They waited.

Laughter and chatter drifted from the inn. Pale yellow light from within cast long shadows over the dirt yard that flickered every time someone crossed before the casement.

"Do you think he stopped for the night?" Kathryn wished they dared go inside.

Roger propped his shoulder against a tree and crossed his arms. "I would be able to go in and find out, if you hadn't insisted on that cur."

"Pay him no mind, Dagger." Kathryn toyed with Dagger's silky ears. He smelled like a midden, and would need a bath when they arrived somewhere they could attend to the matter. Dagger would make a great companion on the road. Only, she first had to return to Mandeville with him. Her stomach dropped. "Roger?"

"Aye?"

"You know how you have dogs at Anglesea?"

He dropped his chin and frowned. "Aye, I like dogs."

"Me too."

"Roger?"

"Spit it out, Kathryn." He straightened from his tree. "What is it you want? I am guessing it has something to do with that."

"Dagger." Kathryn put her arm about her dog. "His name is Dagger...and it might."

He shifted his weight and waited.

"It is just that my father does not like dogs." She stroked

Dagger to be sure he understood that she liked dogs a lot. "I am not sure he will let me keep him at Mandeville."

Roger dropped his head and shook it. "Do you not think you should have thought of that before you made me buy him?"

Now he sounded like a nagging old woman, but he did make a fair point. "Perhaps."

"There is no perhaps about it." Roger sighed. "And aye, Kathryn, I will keep Dagger at Anglesea for you."

Such a good man. She gave him her sweetest smile, and hugged Dagger again. "Only until I come for him. Striker, Dagger, and I shall travel the world together."

Roger growled and stomped closer to the inn.

Braziers burned against the walls, lighting the way for any weary travelers. From within, warm, rich smells of good food rode the night air, and teased her growling belly.

"Wait here." He skirted the inn yard, and approached the stables.

Dagger pressed closer to her legs, and Kathryn dropped a hand to his large head. His presence helped ease the wait.

Roger slipped into the stables. He reappeared after a short time and eased his way back through the yard shadows to where she waited.

"He is staying for the night," he said. "The stable boy knew him, and told me he often passes this way and stays for the night."

"Should we make camp?"

Roger's teeth flashed white in the dark as he smiled. "I think I can do better than that. What say you, my lady, to a bath and a bed for the night?"

"In there?" A bath sounded temptation enough but the idea of sleeping on a soft pallet would be heavenly.

"Aye." Roger nodded. "The groom says the inn has a chamber for rent. I also promised him two crowns if he woke me before our friend leaves."

"Do you trust this groom?" They had come so far, to lose the messenger now would be awful.

"I trust his desire for two crowns," Roger said. "And even if he does not rouse me, we will wake early and there is only one road and we know which direction he is taking."

His reason nibbled at her objections. A bath! To wash the stink of travel from her. Even Dagger seemed to approve, his gaze locked on her in silent entreaty. "What if the messenger sees us?"

"He will not." Roger took up his destrier's reins. "He beds down in the common room, and the groom says he has a wench who beds down with him."

Kathryn blessed the dark that hid her blush. "Lead on."

They left their horses with Roger's stable boy, who winked broadly before pointing them to the back entrance to the inn.

The innkeeper, a man of middling height with a paunch and a thin dusting of hair, let them into the kitchen.

"We understand you have a room for the night?" Roger spoke.

The innkeeper's keen stare took in Roger, her, and Dagger. Then locked on the coin in Roger's palm. He canted forward. "I do, but that animal sleeps in the stable."

"Nay, he sleeps in the room." Roger dropped another coin into his palm.

With a smirk, the innkeeper stuffed the coins in his apron. "Well, when you put it that way, my lord. Follow me."

They crossed the stable yard to reach the room. Attached to the back of the inn, the room could only be entered from this side.

Dagger had to be persuaded not to eat the poultry.

Kathryn really needed to teach Roger the value of the coins in his pocket. He tossed them about like he had plenty to spare. Perhaps he did. She and mother spent most days wresting a meager existence for the residents of Mandeville from the amount Sir Royce provided. Some days they had gone to bed hungry so the keep children and infirm could eat. Gathering coin for Matty's bliauts for Anglesea had meant many nights of scant food. But a prospective bride must look her best. It must be a strange luxury to not think about where the coin came from or if there was enough.

"Here we are, my lord." The innkeeper threw open a rough door. Nudging Roger, he chuckled. "Nice and quiet. Nobody will disturb you here."

A small bed stood against the far wall, clearly meant for only one person, and not a Roger-sized person. The rest of the room held a wash stand with basin and ewer beneath a window placed high enough in the wall to prevent looking outside. A rough bench sat before the empty hearth, swallowing most of a wool rug that seemed in danger of unraveling. From the lingering smell, it might have served as an animal pen at some past point.

"Well." Roger placed their packs against the wall inside the door. "Rude, but better than the forest floor."

Indeed.

Dagger explored the room with his nose to the ground.

"My lady would care to bathe." Roger clapped the innkeeper's shoulder.

The innkeeper twitched and toed at a piece of straw. "That be extra."

Roger's knuckles whitened as he increased his grip.

The innkeeper paled and wriggled beneath the punishing hold.

Teeth bared in a far from convivial smile, Roger said, "I think not."

"Right you are, my lord." The innkeeper bowed himself out the door, nose almost smashing his knee. "Straight away and I will see if Cook can dig up a soup bone or some'at for the doggie."

"I have faith in your cook." Roger shut the door on the man. "You will take the bed. I will sleep beside the hearth." He pushed the hearth bench against the wall.

The air in the room seemed thicker somehow, awash with currents. She struggled to draw breath and Kathryn loosened the neck of her tunic. "Nay, you take the bed. I will be happy as a tick curled up beside the fire."

"Kathryn." Roger stripped his cloak and draped it over a peg near the door. "Please, give my knightly honor enough credence to believe I would not allow a lady to sleep on the floor whilst I occupied the bed."

"Oh. Indeed." Well, put that way, she really did not have an option. "I thank you."

"My pleasure." Head cocked, he studied her. "Are you well?"

"Marvelous." Her voice resounded off the bare walls, and she flinched.

Roger grinned. He bent to unlace his boots. "I feel sure I must be mistaken, but you, my lady Kathryn, seem a mite uncomfortable."

"Never." She waved her arms about in a manner as ridiculous as it was mortifying. Why could she not sound and behave like a sane person? It must have aught to do with the room. The room with its tiny bed, close walls, and big handsome knight who watched her with a smirk on his rugged face. "I am well accustomed to this sort of accommodation."

"Indeed." He dropped his boots by the door, and padded to her on his large, bare feet. "And how many times have you been thus alone with a man who was not your blood?"

Kathryn jammed her hands on her hips, which made her appear ridiculous she felt certain, and then shoved them into her pockets. "All the time. Many a time. Plenty." She needed to shut her pie-hole.

"A woman of vast experience indeed." Roger worked his sword belt lose and hung it over the cloak.

"You are laughing at me." She tried to glare, but her sense of the ridiculous sparked beneath her outrage.

"Just a mite." Bending at the waist, he wriggled out of his hauberk. It hit the floor with a clink of metal. "Be easy, Kathryn. I have, on occasion, been known to control my boorish lusts. I shall endeavor to do so now."

She sketched a curtsy. "I would be very grateful."

"You can curtsy?" He gaped at her.

"I will have you know I am very…" She marched to him and shoved his shoulder. "You are laughing at me again."

A fist pounded on the door. "Got your bath here, my lord."

Roger opened the door and admitted the innkeeper and two men who struggled with a linen-lined tub. They placed it before the hearth, and the innkeeper bent to light the fire. "Girls will be along shortly with your water."

The 'girls' had passed their middle years a while back, but they did bring in the water and poured it into the tub. One of them even opened a small vial of rosewater and added a few drops to the water.

The door shut behind them, and the air grew thick again.

"This is awkward." Kathryn blew out her breath to dispel the tension.

"Not at all." Roger's smile seemed a trifle tight. "I will wait outside until you are done, and then we can call for more water for me."

* * *

Roger let himself into the kitchen yard. Which stupid bastard had thought it would be a good idea to spend the night alone at an inn with Kathryn?

This stupid bastard. The same idiot whose braies grew suddenly tighter at the idea of her stripped naked as she climbed into her bath. Did the peach sun-blush on her face extend to the rest of her? Or was she pale as parchment beneath her mannish attire?

Not his bloody business.

Shouts from the common room dragged his attention away. He stuck closer to the shadows, out of the light that spilled from the casements.

The door hurtled open and two men tumbled out, locked on each other in a snarling, brawling tangle. From the casement and doors, men hung out and shouted encouragement.

Roger moved closer to the door that housed Kathryn. Normally, he would not have stayed at such a rough inn. Perhaps, and all things considered, he and Kathryn might have been better in the forest.

With a shout, one of the combatants rose, blood dripping from his nose. He spat more blood onto his opponent.

The other man stayed down. Head pressed into the dirt of the yard.

The innkeeper bustled out with a bucket of water and upended it on the grounded fighter.

The fallen fighter stirred, raised his head and shook it before he dropped it back into the dirt.

Two grooms grabbed him by the feet, dragged him onto the road, and left him there.

The winning fighter turned and wiped his nose with his fist. He caught sight of Roger and stiffened. "You want something, your lordship?"

Roger crossed his arms and leaned against Kathryn's door. "Nay."

"Bit lost are you not?" The man swaggered closer. "Not sure the king is within."

Loud guffaws greeted his sally from the common room.

"You do not want to fight me," Roger said.

The bully stepped within strike of Roger's fist. Bullies! One taste of power and it went straight to their heads.

"And why is that?" The man's breath reeked of mead.

Roger stretched his neck to ease the slight tension. He did not want to fight tonight, but his friend had that determined jut to his jaw that told Roger he needed more inducement to leave. Father had drilled it into them, a preemptive strike stopped a messy war. He fastened his hand about the bully's throat. Tightening his grip, he raised the man onto his toes.

The bully choked and clawed at Roger's hand, his eyes started out of his head.

Aye, you stupid sod. Roger squeezed, limiting airflow to a trickle. The man really should look before he issued a challenge. A warrior's most powerful weapon was observation. "Because." Roger kept his tone conversational, but loud enough for the silent watchers to hear. "I will snap you like a twig and piss on your bones."

Roger opened his fist and the man crumpled to the floor. The watchers dropped their gazes and stepped back into the tavern in a murmuring, muttering mass.

The bully crawled back and clambered to his feet. He dashed into the inn.

Roger kept his back against the door, a silent warning to anyone who rediscovered their ballocks. Inside the room, Kathryn splashed about in her bath. Naked.

Roger took a deep breath. *"Now to Enoch was born Irad, and Irad became the father of Mehujael, and Mehujael became the father of..."*

* * *

Even knowing Roger waited outside, could not quite persuade Kathryn to hurry her bath. It had been days since she'd felt clean. She lay back in the water and let it soak away the grime and ache of travel.

Noise from the inn permeated the walls in indecipherable snatches. She thought she heard Roger's voice, but the warm water persuaded her not to investigate further. Roger could take care of himself. She'd lay her last mark on it.

Why had Matty run from him?

Perhaps in his brusque forthrightness Matty had glimpsed their father and been afraid. The resemblance was fleeting at best. Sir Royce held none of the honor and nobility embedded in Roger. Or the sense of humor that peeked through his gruff exterior. Roger's size made him more intimidating. Unlike Matty, however, Kathryn liked his size. A big man to stand between Matty and the world. And their father.

Kathryn would like to see Sir Royce try to browbeat Roger. Unlikely!

Poor, timid Matty. Out in the world alone and frightened. Kathryn had to find her soon and allay her fears. Perhaps the rutting part of marriage had set Matty all atwitter. If only they explained it a bit more, it might not be so daunting. Bulls covered cows, stallions mounted mares, even roosters went about the entire business unabashed. Yet, they sent girls to their marriage beds with no more knowledge than that which they had gleaned from the home farm.

Roger, fierce and intent, rising behind Matty like a stallion on a mare. Kathryn's stomach lurched, and she shied away from the picture.

She would wager a man such as Roger would have lusty appetites. Warmth spread low in her belly. A peculiar, new sensation that seeped through her as honey running through the comb.

The peak of her breasts tightened, and between her thighs she grew restive.

She sat up and wrung the water from her hair. Her disordered senses disturbed her, and ruined the peace of her bath. For once she wished she had spent more time with the keep ladies. They might tell her what ailed her. Why the idea of Roger marrying Matty suddenly bothered her.

She stepped from the bath and snatched up a drying cloth. Applying the cloth to her skin with vigor, she attempted to scrub away the unwelcome sensitivity. Would that she could scour her mind so effectively.

Matty did not deserve Roger. The thought stopped Kathryn's leg drying. What a stupid thought. Of course Matty deserved a man like Roger. Who else could protect Matty so well? Shelter her, nurture her and keep her from Mandeville.

Except, Father did not treat Matty as he treated her and mother. Like Ranulf, he understood where lay his riches, and he seldom raised a hand to Matty. Matty also had this way about her of appeasing Father, wriggling around his anger and escaping unscathed.

Roger's question from when they lay on the hill echoed in her mind. Why did she protect Matty?

Kathryn resumed her drying. She protected Matty because Father's temper swung and twisted like a summer storm. One moment all seemed well, and the next, you faced the hard end of his fist. Only a horrible sister would think for a heartbeat that if Matty could not see her good fortune, that she did not deserve it.

"Kathryn?" Roger pounded on the door. "Are you done?"

Aye, she was done. Done with this line of thought. "Just a moment."

He grunted.

Kathryn hurried to dress and braid her hair before she opened the door.

Roger stepped through and stilled. His gaze took in her scrubbed face, and wet hair. A disquieting smile played about his firm mouth.

Her unruly flesh started up again. "I will wait outside."

"Nay." Roger shut the door with a firm thud. "The common room is full of thugs and louts. You will remain here." He grinned at her. "And promise not to peep."

"As if I would." Her face heated. "I will stick to the shadows outside."

"Nay." He spread his large fingers over the door. He grew deathly serious. "I mean it, Kathryn, you will stay here."

She could not stay here. Impossible! Already her skin grew too tight for her bones, and her breath came ragged as if she had been running. "I cannot—"

"You stay." Roger slid the bolt home. "Do not make me chase you, girl."

"Girl?" To whom did he think he spoke?

He jerked his chin toward the bed. "Sit there where I can keep an eye on you."

"I will not." She needed to escape him, and herself.

Roger clasped her by the elbow, marched her to the bed and pressed her to sit. "I will have your word, on your honor, that you will not move from this place. Otherwise I will tie your hands and feet."

Chapter Twelve

Kathryn nearly broke her word as Roger hauled his gambeson over his head. Now only his chemise stood between her gaze and his chest. Dear Lord, she did not think she could do this. She swallowed to ease the dryness of her throat. She was being ridiculous. Times past counting, she had seen the men of Mandeville stripped to their chausses in the summer heat.

Roger fisted the back of his chemise and pulled it off.

Those men did not look like Roger. She tucked her clammy hands beneath her thighs.

Broad, powerful shoulders blocked the fire from view. Strong, defined chest muscles gilded by the weak firelight tapered into a line of ridges that marched down his belly. Fine hair dusted the area between the flat, dark discs of his nipples, and then arrowed beneath his chausses.

His broad fingers worked at the drawstring of his chausses. "You are staring."

"Nay I am not." Kathryn glared at her knees. She forced her gaze to stay there, even as he shucked his chausses, then braies, and hair roughened calf muscles hovered within view. She concentrated on his feet.

Large and flat, with coarse dark hair across the toes, they were truly ugly feet, which vanished from sight as he walked to the tub. With a splash he upended a bucket of fresh, hot water into the tub before stepping in.

"It is safe to look now," he called, his voice full of laughter.

Kathryn risked a peek. Nay, not at all safe. Because now she had the back view of those shoulders and with his arms, easily the width of her thighs, laid over the tub sides. No wonder he had no difficulty swinging steel. Arms like that could wield a sword tirelessly for hour upon hour. Muscle surged and bunched as he pushed his hair back.

Arms! His arms struck her dumb. How to explain such a thing, or the intense desire to bite them? He had placed a dagger beside the bath and grabbed it now. First, he lathered soap on his jaw, and then he scraped away the growth of the past few days.

"I can feel your eyes burning a hole in me," he said. The knife scratched against his whiskers.

"Do you not grow a beard?"

"Nay." He raised his arm to shave the other side. Such a simple, practiced motion and so very male. "It itches too much."

Once he'd finished shaving, he rinsed the knife and placed it beside him again. He ducked beneath the water, knees poking out, and came up shaking his head like a big dog. Peering over his shoulder, he said, "You might want to close your eyes again."

His way of bathing differed so vastly from hers. Where she lingered and let the water soothe her, he kept it short and stuck to his purpose. A bit like he did most things.

Water swished as he stood.

Kathryn got a glimpse of taut buttocks before she shut her eyes. Her eyelids flickered in rebellion, and she jammed her palms against them to keep them closed. Dear God, what if his man parts resembled that of the dogs Father kept for breeding—all pink and glistening. Kathryn shuddered.

"You can look now."

Kathryn cracked open one eye.

Roger had donned his braies. She shoved the nasty man parts image away, and stared at the pleasing flesh in front of her. The men at home looked different. Some had a roll of belly that drooped over their braies, others had a pelt of coarse dark hair, and the younger ones seemed unfinished somehow. Roger looked...seasoned, tough...virile.

Perhaps when she accomplished her goal of being a lady knight, she could take a lover. A lover who looked exactly like Roger. One, who like Roger, did not constantly bellow and beat at her.

"We should sleep." Roger pulled a blanket from the pack and laid it before the fire. "We do not know when our friend will depart." Next he extinguished the taper and threw the room into near dark, lit only by the flickering firelight. "Sleep well."

He lay on his blanket and spread his arms beneath his head. Interesting shadows nestled into loving pockets across the fire-gilded expanse of his chest and belly.

"Are you not going to dress?"

With a smug grin he glanced at her. "I am dressed for how I normally sleep."

"Oh." Blast! She did need to do something about her constant flushing. Women who lived by the sword did not blush like sheltered maidens.

Still clothed, she crawled beneath the bed covers.

Noise from the common room swelled and grew softer again. A shout followed by a wave of raucous laughter startled her.

Roger's eyes closed. His chest rose and fell in a smooth motion.

She had nothing to fear from him, yet she could not sleep. His mere presence filled the room, and pressed against her awareness.

He rolled onto his side and faced the fire.

"Roger?"

"Aye."

"I cannot sleep."

He chuckled. "Close your eyes and think peaceful thoughts. That is what Nurse always said to me when I could not sleep."

"Nurse?"

"Aye," he said. Affection filled Roger's tone. "On my mother's marriage, Nurse came to Anglesea with her. And has ruled us all since we first appeared in the world."

"Is she still at Anglesea?"

Roger grunted. "Aye, even death is afraid of Nurse." He shifted onto his back. "I imagine she will have a hand in the raising of my children."

"Your and Matty's children." A curious emptiness happened in her chest, which was ridiculous because of course they would have children. Men and women married to beget heirs. "You and Matty will make beautiful children."

He sighed, and closed his eyes. "Sleep, Kathryn."

She tried, she really did, but what seemed like hours later she lay and stared at Roger's back as the steady huff of his breath rode the silence.

Even the common room had quieted enough for the sounds of the night to penetrate their room.

Framed by the high casement the moon hung as a half crescent in a star littered sky. Mother always said something about wishing on the moon. Father mocked her, called her stupid when he heard. Father did that a lot. At times he used his fists to make his point clearer. Over the years, Mother had grown more and more silent, until now she only spoke when father was not about. Even then she did so nervously, always glancing around for him.

Roger wanted to know why she would not marry. Was it really any wonder that she would never let herself be tied to a man like a horse harnessed to pull a plow? Treated no better than the lowliest servant.

Men like Ranulf hid their true face when they courted. If she had not watched for Matty, Ranulf would have succeeded in marrying her sister, and Matty would have become another Mother, a slow dying bloom that faded more every year. A word in Father's hearing here and there about Ranulf's pockets being shallow and the danger of Ranulf had been averted.

When the offer came from Anglesea, Kathryn had panicked at first. The ripe prize of a tie to Anglesea turned Father almost genial for a few weeks. She had accompanied her family to Anglesea determined to watch, wait, and see. Resolved to extract Matty by whatever means necessary if needed.

Now she found herself buried to the neck in a pig-swill of her own making. The still of the night would no longer allow her to deny what flit around the edges of her mind. Her girlish desires had woken in a shattering roar and aimed their useless selves at Roger.

Poor luck because they could not have him. Roger belonged to Matty. Matty could not protect herself, had no will nor means of escaping Mandeville other than marriage. Of course she could join a nunnery, but Matty was the sort of woman made to have children, and rule with gentle grace over a household. After growing up with father, Matty deserved to be happy.

As for herself? Kathryn sat up and rested her elbows on her knees. She would make her own way, and her own happiness. If she had found a Roger for Matty, surely somewhere in this vast kingdom there would be another one.

Her plan to install Mother at Anglesea would go forward. Father had no use for his wife in any case. He lifted every skirt at Mandeville he could, and keep gossip had him chasing a young widow in the village who proved to be rather resistant to his advances. Let him pursue his widow in peace, as long as Mother dwelled safe behind Sir Arthur's walls.

As a child she had heard rumors of Father having been in love with another woman before his marriage. They said the woman died before they could marry, and Father had never recovered from her death. For years, Kathryn had clung to that story, and had found in it a reason for his constant anger at Mother, and then her. As she grew older, she ran out of excuses for him. Her father took joy in behaving as a loutish brute.

Roger showed her daily that men could be different. In time, she would come to see Roger as her brother by marriage again. Her girlish crush would wither and die like a rose without water, and they could go back to being brother and sister.

Dull weight pressed against her chest. The moon blurred in the sky above her, and Kathryn touched her damp cheek. Tears dampened her fingertips. She hardly ever cried, and to do so now made her laughable. Pointless tears. She had stopped shedding them years ago. Another reason she stamped all those girlish emotions down deep and kept her boot on them.

At Mandeville when her feelings welled to an ache inside her, she would slip to the stables and talk to Striker. Her horse always understood her. He would stand still and let her pour her tale in his large, silky ears, her face pressed into his neck.

Roger said not to leave the room.

However, Roger slept like an innocent babe and the inn had fallen silent hours ago. She needed the peace Striker offered, and she slid out of bed. Using every bit of stealth she had learned from years of avoiding Father, she crept across the room and grabbed her boots from beside the door.

Dagger padded to her, and she motioned him back.

The door opened onto the silent night and Kathryn slipped into the yard. Just a few moments with Striker and she would sleep as peacefully as her companion.

Odors of greasy meat, dung, and burnt tallow tainted the fresh spring air as she picked her way through the unidentifiable shapes on the yard floor.

The shadows shifted. A heavy weight thrust her forward.

Kathryn stumbled.

A hand cut off her shout.

"Look what our lord was hiding away." A strange voice rasped in her ear.

Kathryn forced her mind to calm. She kicked back, but her assailant shifted. Her foot hit nothing, and she lost her balance.

As she struggled to regain her balance, he clamped her sword arm to her body.

Kathryn raked his face.

Her attacker ducked his head to the side. "Bitch!" Mead, onions, and rotting teeth surrounded her. His hand covered her mouth. Filthy fingers blocked her air. "Try that again and I'll rip your pretty face off."

He shoved her to the ground. Hard gravel skinned her knees as her hands tangled beneath her.

With his knees in her back, he pinned her with his greater weight.

Her legs were useless, her arms trapped. Dirt and stones ground into her cheek. He was too heavy. Too strong.

Something sharp pricked at the corner of her eye. "Will he like his pretty whore when I cut her up?"

She had to think. Fight. Get him off her. But the knife nicked her skin. A wet trickle slid down her cheek. Helpless. Kathryn fought the dark, sucking feeling. She refused to be helpless.

Except she could not move. The knife pressed a hairsbreadth from her eye.

Legs shoved her thighs apart. "I have never had a lord's leavings before." Hard flesh ground against her bottom. "Be sure to tell him how you like it rough."

His weight lifted. A boot connected her hip in a jarring thud and she rolled free. Two sets of legs churned up a choking cloud of dust.

An awful sharp crack, and a body hit the dirt beside her. Wide open eyes stared at her from a bearded face. The first time she had seen her attacker.

"Kathryn." Roger's voice reached her first and then he crouched beside her. "Are you all right?"

A scream caught in her chest and she clenched her teeth to keep it within her. Kathryn was never helpless and she did not scream like a frightened girl. She nodded.

With a harsh noise, Roger scooped her into his arms. He

carried her into their room and kicked the door shut behind them.

"I can walk." Only weak women got carried about like their legs didn't work. She refused to be weak. She would never be weak again.

He lowered her to her feet.

Her knees buckled. Kathryn fended off his hands stretched out to catch her. "Nay."

Back stiff, she sank onto the edge of the bed and dug her nails into her thighs. Bested, just like that, and with no recourse. If Roger had not come, she would have been at the whoreson's mercy. His to do with whatever he willed.

"Kathryn?"

Why did Roger speak to her as if she would break? She did not break. "Is he dead?"

"Aye." He approached her slowly. Strong emotion throbbed in his voice and he held his hands in plain sight as if he gentled a wild thing. "You are bleeding."

"Cur caught me with his knife." She swiped at her cheek. Her fingers came away streaked with her blood. She had sworn no man would ever make her bleed again. The blood on her fingers made a liar of her. A weakling. A failure. "Took me unawares." Her voice grated through her teeth. "Came at me out of the dark."

Roger sank to his knees in front of her, his gaze intent and searching. "Aye. We are all caught out at times."

"Not you." She shook her head. Her throat closed too tight to manage many words.

"Aye, me." He touched the torn fabric at her knees. It must have happened when she'd been shoved to the ground. "Nobody is infallible."

Why did he not shake her and bellow at her for leaving the room? Instead he stared at her, so full of compassion and she wanted to punch it away. His caring wriggled past her tightly held shields, and found the damned soft place inside her. The place that wanted to break down and cry. No more tears. Ever.

"You will have to show me how to deal with an attacker from behind."

"I can do that." He cupped her calves in his warm, strong hands. He broke her with his gentleness. "Kathryn?"

"I am well."

"Sweeting."

"Stop it."

"Nay." He leaned closer. "I would care for your wounds."

"I do not need it."

"Aye, sweeting, you do."

He wanted to break her, see her weep. Already she shook with the sobs that waged war to be released. "Get away from me."

"Never."

She opened her mouth to tell him she did not need him. A low keening wail broke from her, and she could not make it stop. Hunching, she tried to contain it inside her. The fear, the blasted fear that would not go away. It shook her so hard that her breath came in harsh sobs.

The bed dipped beside her, and Roger picked her up and laid her in his lap.

Her head found the dip in his shoulder and pushed into him. Strong arms came about her and held her there, held her together as she shattered.

His cheek pressed the top of her head, as he murmured words she could not decipher. Sweet words that were meant to comfort but made her cry harder.

* * *

She slayed him. Each sob clawed though Roger as he held her.

God's bones, he wanted to break the sod's neck all over again. Shake her for being so foolish as to leave the room. Hold her until the storm passed. Wipe the haunted look from her forever. Comfort her. Protect her.

Love her.

God's ballocks! Where, by all holies, had that thought come from? Barely a sennight ago Kathryn of Mandeville had cantered into his life. All these years of searching for what his father had, and in a wisp of time his thoughts turned to love.

Impossible!

Except Father had said it took him all of one glance to know he had met his love. Serving escort on the betrothal visit of another man to his mother, Sir Arthur had lost his heart to another man's promised bride. Somehow Lady Mary and Sir Arthur had made their way into marriage.

Kathryn's nails dug into his chest as she sobbed. Tiny pinpricks of pain versus the storm that raged through her. Her tears came from deep within her. Aye, the sod he had killed had frightened her, as such an experience would frighten anyone, but there lay more to this. In his gut he understood her hatred of being made to feel vulnerable, frail, like a woman.

His mother embodied the perfect lady, poised, gracious, lovely, serene, and he had never once thought of her as weak or fragile. His mother had steel through her backbone, but still able to bend with life's trails and not snap beneath the strain.

Kathryn calmed slightly and he stroked the elegant line of her back. This backbone that she hated bending like a curse. True strength lay not in the arm swinging a sword or the shoulder holding up the boulder. Nay, it lay instead in the ability to sway with the hardships, and arise again. The woman in his arms had that sort of strength. Strange, she sought to be strong like a man, when she was already so much more robust. She had a woman's strength to weather all storms.

Her sobs subsided to soft breaths that huffed against his neck. The tension in her eased until she melted against him. Her breathing deepened and slowed, and in typical Kathryn fashion between one breath and the other she fell asleep.

Roger laid her back on the bed.

Dagger whined softly and shoved his muzzle closer to her.

A mess of tears and streaks of blood from the small cut at the corner of her eye covered her pretty face. Tendrils of hair stuck to her cheeks. Paler than the linens beneath her, she slept like one exhausted. Roger tucked the blanket beneath her chin and rose.

Beside the bed, Dagger settled with a sigh. He laid his head on his great paws and glanced at Roger. Dagger had the next watch.

Outside, the body lay where he had left it. Gut heavy and flaccid, the body proved hard to lift. Roger hauled him to the far side of the road from the inn and dropped him three feet within the trees. A man such as this had to have made a multitude of enemies to account for this death.

On his way back, Roger peeked into the common room.

Their messenger lay on a bench against the wall, rolled in his cloak, head pillowed on his pack.

In the morning he would lead them to Lady Mathilda, and more decisions to be made.

He let himself back into the room and mended the fitful fire.

Dagger raised his head and watched him as Roger lay on his blanket.

Drifting halfway between sleep and wakefulness, Roger sensed Kathryn moments before she slipped onto the blanket beside him. He turned onto his side and tucked her back against his chest.

Chapter Thirteen

Kathryn woke to a low fire. A snoring Dagger shared her blanket. The strip of sky visible through the casement blushed the first touches of dawn. As she rose, an ache in her ribs awoke to greet her with a dull throb. Her knees stung, and one hip felt as if she'd been thrown from Striker. She'd had worse.

Glad for the privacy, she stumbled to the wash basin and splashed cold water over her swollen eyes. Last night she had wept like a weak, stupid girl in Roger's arms. Would that she could wash the shame away as easily as she cleaned the dried tears.

The door opened and Roger walked in. He left the door open a crack.

Dagger padded to him and nudged him for a greeting.

"Good, you are awake." Roger wore his hauberk already, with his cloak over his shoulder. "Our man is breaking his fast and will be on his way shortly." He held up a cloth bag. "Dagger and I have already tended to our meals. This is for you."

"Should we not be going?" Kathryn dodged his gaze. She could not face his condemnation, or even worse, his pity.

"We will see when he leaves." Roger jerked his head at the

door. "But it will not do to tarry." He moved about the room, preparing them for travel.

Kathryn ate quickly, her attention on the sliver of yard visible through the door.

"Here." Roger dropped a small earthen pot beside her. "You will want to clean your knees and put this on them."

Kathryn hid her flushed cheeks behind the business of studying the contents of the pot. A sharp, astringent scent rose from it. She poked her forefinger in it and found it cool. "What is it?"

"God alone knows," Roger said. "Nurse makes it for me and shoves it in my pack whenever I travel."

Roger knelt before her with a washcloth.

"What are you doing?"

"Cleaning your knees." He gripped her leg and applied the cloth to the scabs beneath.

Kathryn hissed in a breath. "I can do it."

"We need to be quick," he said. "Our man can leave at any moment, and I want these cleaned before we go any further."

Fine. If he chose not to mention her humiliating night, she could do the same. Blast it to hell. It hurt when he applied the cloth to her scrapes. She chewed her bread to keep from whimpering like a puppy.

Daggers ears perked, and he growled.

The messenger crossed the yard, his pack thrown over his shoulder.

"Time to go." She pushed Roger's hands aside and stood.

With a firm shove, he pressed her back to the bed. "He does not travel fast and we know his direction." He snatched up his pot of green salve. "First, this."

"Roger—"

"Stop wriggling, Kathryn, and stop looking at me like you stole my horse."

"Eh?"

"You cried," he said. Dark head bent, he spread salve over her scrapes. "The world did not end."

"Ouch!" The salve stung, and Kathryn tried to jerk her knee away.

His big hands tended her with heart-wrenching tenderness. "I have seen battle-hardened knights weep like babes over a dead horse. Men-at-arms cry themselves to sleep the night before a battle, and grown men piss their braies. A few tears are nothing."

Her heart constricted. If anywhere there lived a better man than this, she had yet to find him. "You are just trying to make me feel better."

He raised his head and grinned at her. "Is it working?

"Aye." Already the weight had lifted. "Have you really seen battle-hardened knights weep over a dead horse?"

"Kathryn." He rested his hands atop her knees. "We all get frightened, we all weep, and we all have a weak spot." He patted her knees and stood. "All except me, because I am better than most."

Kathryn laughed and tossed the washing cloth at him.

The horses stood ready and waiting as they left the room.

They rode to make up time.

Already, Dagger seemed to have learned the way of things, and trotted along beside Striker. Every time an interesting scent caught his nose, he took a short foray into the bushes beside the road, then returned. She had found a good dog in Dagger.

As the morning progressed, the events of last night replayed in her mind. The cur had caught her completely unawares. "Roger?"

"Aye."

"Could you really teach me how to fend off an attacker from behind?"

He glanced at her, breeze running through his hair. "For certain. There are ways to combat almost any attack. However"—he held up his hand—"even with the best preparation and training, there comes a moment in every battle where the plan falls away and the fighter must rely on instinct and individual strengths."

What he said went counter to everything she knew. "That is absurd. Are you saying training is a waste of time?"

"Not at all." He surveyed the land about them with a keen gaze. "Training is the foundation of a good warrior, but battle does not run according to the map we have in our minds. A warrior must adapt and react to the situation as it unfolds."

Kathryn mulled that over. "What sort of strengths?"

"You, for instance." He shrugged. "Chances are that unless your assailant is another woman, you are always going to be at a disadvantage in terms of raw strength and size." His grin dared her to argue.

She snapped her mouth shut.

"So, you need to rely on your advantages."

"Such as."

"Speed," he said. "Agility, and it would not hurt you to learn to fight dirty. It is all very impressive to perform a beautiful arc and thrust with a sword, but a knee to the ballocks will get a man on his knees just as fast."

The knights she had managed to coerce into teaching her at Mandeville had never told her any of this. Perhaps because they never expected her to use what they taught her. That Roger saw her as a warrior filled her with delight.

He stopped his horse and scanned the clear day about them. "We should spot him soon."

They slowed for a couple of men traveling with a handcart. Dagger warned the men off with a snarl in passing.

Last night raised another weakness in her plan. Men suffered from lusts. As much as she did not want it so, many would look at her and see a woman first, and a warrior only from the sharp end of her steel.

Naiveté could be allowed behind keep walls, indeed praised and encouraged in girls, but a woman who wanted to make her way in the world needed to face some of its harsher realities.

Someday, somewhere, a man might slip past her defenses and finish what that whoreson had started last night.

"Roger?"

"Aye."

"That man last night would have raped me." Her words made her cold inside.

"Aye." He motioned Dagger. "You have him to thank for your rescue. He woke me with his whining and pawing at the door."

Dagger had done that for her. She wanted to jump from Striker and hug him.

Dagger looked at her and lolled his tongue as if to say she was welcome. But she had a more important point to raise. "I do not want my first experience with a man to be that way."

Roger jerked in the saddle, and his gaze smoldered with an emotion she dared not name. "No woman does."

"I think I should rid myself of my virginity."

"What?" He yanked his reins so hard, his horse fought for its head.

Heat rushed to her cheeks and she kneed Striker forward of him. "I need to find the right man."

"This discussion is over." Roger's voice came cold as the grave from behind her.

"Perhaps you could help me."

"Over!"

Chapter Fourteen

They followed the messenger into the full light of day. Upon closing their distance to sight range, they dismounted and shadowed their prey with the edge of the woods as cover. Thus far Kathryn's adventure seemed to involve a lot of sneaking about, and although exciting, did not quite live up to her dreams of flashing swords and thundering hooves.

A short while after the bells of a nearby monastery tolled midday, the messenger veered off the road down a small earthen track.

Roger motioned her to halt. He drew close enough to stir the wisps of hair about her ears. "We should leave the horses here, and see where he goes. There is not much cover."

Kathryn nodded and they drew the horses into a small thicket away from the road. Her attempts to get Dagger to stay failed miserable, and so he joined them as they trotted after the messenger. They engaged in a thrilling game of dash and dart using small bushes and rocks for concealment.

The track opened into a yard in front of a humble, thatched cottage.

Three large boulders provided the perfect vantage point for

her, Roger, and Dagger. She took hold of the rope halter around Dagger's neck and held on tight.

The messenger approached the door and knocked. The door opened and admitted him.

A flock of hens pecked the unkempt yard. A hawk screamed from the clear blue sky, and sent a flurry of wrens into the gnarled branches of a huge oak shadowing the cottage.

Dagger grew bored and took the time to do some personal grooming. It would take a lot more than a bit of a lick to get him clean.

The cottage door opened and three people came out.

"Matty." Alive and apparently well. Relief was painfully sweet. Kathryn rose, but Roger yanked her behind her boulder.

"Wait."

They had found Matty and she slapped his hands away. "I have come all this way to find my sister."

"Then a few moments more will not hurt." He held her wrist. "Information is the best weapon at your disposal."

Matty wore a simple yellow gown Kathryn had seen her wear many times before. The differences lay in her bare feet and unbound hair. Matty never allowed herself to be seen in such dishabille.

The man beside her spoke earnestly with the messenger. Of middling height, slim and lean, he had a delicate, almost pretty face.

"He looks familiar to me." Kathryn had seen those features before, but she could not think where.

Roger grunted.

The pretty man put his arm about Matty's shoulders and drew her into him.

How dare he? Kathryn almost leaped to her feet. She would have if Roger had not tugged her down again.

"Who is he to be so familiar with my sister?" She shoved past a crouching Roger to better see the couple in front of the cottage.

Matty, who should have slapped the pretty man, gazed at him with open adoration.

Kathryn had seen enough. She stood, evaded Roger, and marched around the boulders and into the yard.

Pretty man spotted her first and froze.

Muttering curses to bring a blush to anyone's cheeks, Roger followed in Kathryn's wake.

Matty turned and saw her then. She squealed and ducked behind the man.

The messenger glanced at her, then Roger, and near ran from the yard.

Dagger pulled to give chase, but Kathryn tightened her grip. Her dog harbored no fond feelings for his former owner.

"Matty." Kathryn stopped in front of the man. "Who is this?"

Pretty man clenched the sides of his chausses. His gaze darted to Roger and back to her. "Lady Kathryn."

"I am not speaking to you. I wish to speak with my sister."

Matty poked her head over his shoulder. "How did you find me?" She paled and squeaked as she stared at Roger. "And you brought him."

"I followed you." Kathryn stepped around pretty man.

He moved into her path, one arm behind him keeping Matty away from her.

"How could you?" Matty wailed.

"How could I?" Kathryn would box Pretty man's ears if he stepped in front of her again. "I brought your betrothed."

"Um, Lady Kathryn." Pretty man swallowed hard. His chest swelled. "I am afraid he cannot be her betrothed because Matty is already married."

The yard dipped and swayed around Kathryn, Pretty man's large brown eyes the only sure point in her shifting world. "Married?"

"Aye." He raised his chin. "To me."

* * *

Roger nearly laughed. Kathryn's dumbfounded look stopped him. "Perhaps we should take this inside."

She turned and gaped at him. "She cannot be married."

He gestured the man by Lady Mathilda's side "Unless he lies, it appears that she is."

The man eyed him warily, as well he might. Roger topped him by a clear foot, and near dwarfed his slight build. "I am Roger of Anglesea."

Taking the proffered hand as if it were a viper, the man shook it. "Digory of..." He waved his free hand about the farm. "Here."

"I will not come back with you." Lady Mathilda tucked her arm through Digory's, a hint of Kathryn in the stubborn cast of her jaw.

"Inside." Roger hoped they had mead in their cottage. He was in sore need of a drink.

Stopping inside the door, Roger took his time to take it all in. The place looked as if it had been ransacked. Mugs, bowls and cutlery littered the table, and overflowed the wash bucket to the side of the hearth. Women's clothing spread across the rumpled bed, the table, the one bench and even hung from the rafters. Above the cooking hearth's dead ashes, a large black pot tipped and oozed its contents onto the hearthstones and then the floor.

Kathryn gasped. "What happened here?"

Digory flushed and unearthed a large hen from beneath the table. The fowl shrieked and clucked, dropping feathers in her haste to escape Digory's boot.

It proved too much temptation for Dagger who slipped his collar and gave chase with a happy growl. He dashed past Kathryn, nearly knocking her down, and lunged into the yard.

"Stop that awful dog!" Matty screamed.

A loud squawk died on a deep snarl. Silence.

"Oh, dear." Kathryn glanced out the door and back again. "I am afraid we owe you a hen."

Roger had to duck his head. Any more of this and he would lose his composure.

"Will you not sit?" Digory grabbed a handful of mugs from the table. He stood there, mugs in hand, and looked for somewhere to place them. "I am afraid we were not prepared for visitors."

Dirt coated the bench, and Roger wiped it clean before he assisted Kathryn to sit. She kept staring at Matty and shaking her head.

So relieved he wanted to dance a reel—and he never danced if he could avoid it—Roger took his seat beside Kathryn. The resemblance between Matty and Kathryn marked them clearly as sisters. The subtle differences lay in Matty's softer, more rounded edges. He supposed many would consider her the prettier sister, but give him Kathryn's delicate, angular features any time.

"Married?" Kathryn whispered, and there came the headshake again.

"Aye." Lady Mathilda smoothed her bliaut over her hips. "Digory and I have been married since last summer."

He had better pay attention to this conversation. "I beg your pardon?"

"Might I offer you some ale?" Digory's voice came unnaturally loud.

"I think you must." Kathryn looked even more confused than he felt.

Digory wiped a mug clean with the edge of his tunic and set it before them. Next he moved the chemise from atop a large stoppered jug beside the hearth and poured the ale into the mug. "I think we should explain."

"Aye." Kathryn took a long sip and offered Roger the mug.

Sharp and bitter, the excellent ale loosened his tongue from the roof of his mouth.

"We met on Whitsunday last," Digory said, cleaning a mug for himself.

"I loved him from the first." Lady Mathilda clasped her hands to her bosom. Tears sprang into her large brown eyes. Eyes so like Kathryn's, and yet so very different.

Kathryn's had a direct, honest gaze. Whereas Lady Mathilda…

He could not quite put his finger on it, but his nape prickled a warning.

"Indeed." Digory cleared his throat.

Dagger entered the kitchen, licking feathers and blood from his muzzle, tail giving the air a lazy stir.

"Get that horrible thing out of here." Lady Mathilda pointed imperiously, and then slid behind Digory.

"Oh, settle down, Matty." Kathryn clicked her fingers for Dagger. "He is only a dog, and not the most important issue to hand."

Roger could not have said it better. "So." His big, dumb soldier's brain needed clarity. "When you came to Anglesea to become betrothed to me, you were already married."

"Aye."

"You do not think you might have mentioned that?" Forgive him for his tone, but God's balls!

Kathryn put her hand on his arm. "You have been married for almost a year and you told nobody. Not even me?"

Mathilda glanced at Digory, who shrugged. "I told Cecily."

"Cecily?" Kathryn's voice rose. "You told that lack-witted peahen you were married and not your own sister?"

"How could I?" Mathilda held her hands out in entreaty. "You know what Father would have done had he known."

"And you thought I would tell him?" The hurt in Kathryn's voice cut through Roger. "You thought I would betray you?"

In mute appeal, Kathryn stared at him.

"I think you had better start at the beginning and tell us all." Roger spoke to Digory. He would like to hear this story without the declarations of love.

"We met at the festival near Mandeville." Digory proved himself a sensible man by refilling Roger's tankard before taking the seat opposite him. "I was immediately struck by Lady Mathilda, but never thought she would look at one such as me."

Roger nodded. Ladies did not, in his experience, look at men so laughably far beneath their station. Unless the lady bore the name Beatrice. "You are a farmer?"

"Aye." Digory nodded. "It is not much, but it is all mine."

"How did you meet?" Kathryn's hand tightened on his arm.

Roger took her hand in his and curled his fingers about hers.

Lady Mathilda peered at their hands and then stared at him with a smug smile.

Damn who saw the gesture, Kathryn needed the comfort.

"We danced," Digory said on a besotted sigh. "I was standing beside that large oak tree in the center of the green, and I found Matty right beside me."

"I asked him," Mathilda said.

Aye, she would have to. No small farmer would dare approach the lord's daughter, not even on festival day.

"I did not see you dance with anyone." Kathryn frowned at her sister.

"You were busy looking at swords." Mathilda gave Kathryn a fond smile.

"And where was Father?"

Mathilda sneered and crossed her arms. "Drunk and atop a whore."

"We danced all night." Digory got the sort of dreamy look that made Roger itch to cuff him. "And later we strolled in the forest beside the church. We talked and talked. We had so much to say to each other."

Talked? Roger raised his brow at Digory. A man did not waste time talking to a pretty girl in a forest in the middle of the night.

"I swear it." Digory placed his hand on his heart. "I did not touch her."

Roger believed the stupid fool.

"Then." Matty smirked and wriggled on the bench beside Digory. "You did not touch me then."

"Oh, dear God." Kathryn drained the tankard in three huge swallows. "My father will kill him."

Mathilda went deathly pale. "He cannot know." She leaned

forward, elbows on the table. "You must not tell him, Kathryn. You cannot."

"I came looking for you," Roger said. "How do I explain this?"

"Tell them you could not find me." Mathilda wrapped her arms around Digory's. "Tell them you looked but I had disappeared."

"You mean I should lie?" It sat ill with him to lie. If one of his sisters went missing, he would want to know where she was, and with whom she kept company. No matter how unsuitable. God's bones, none of them had celebrated the appearance of Garrett in Beatrice's life, but rather him than not knowing what had happened to her. "Your mother will be worried."

Digory's throat worked as he swallowed.

"You cannot tell her." Mathilda flushed, her eyes fever bright. "If she knows, it is only a matter of time before my father gets it out of her."

"She is right about that." Kathryn chewed her lip and frowned. "You could come back with us, Matty."

"I am afraid it is too late for that." Digory flushed scarlet. "Matters have proceeded apace. There might be...consequences."

"Nay, nobody knows yet, and...oh!" Kathryn's color rivaled Digory's.

"Please, Kathryn." Mathilda grabbed Kathryn's free hand. "I beg of you. Go away and pretend you never saw us. I love Digory." Tears welled and trickled down her cheeks. "He is my world, and I would rather die than see us ripped asunder. Please, Kathryn."

"I—"

"If you love me, then you will want to see me happy."

Kathryn's grip tightened on his, and Roger returned the pressure.

"I do love you, but Matty you have done a mad thing here," Kathryn said. "What made you think you could run away and marry where you pleased? You knew father had plans for your marriage."

"That you should say this to me." Mathilda reared back, and tossed her head. "You, who always do as you please, when you please. Why is it fine for you to choose your own fate, but I must meekly marry where Father says?"

"You know I would have made sure you were married well," Kathryn said.

"Married well by your choice." Mathilda laid her head on Digory's shoulder. "Married the man you judged right for me."

"Aye, well." Kathryn squeezed his hand as if to comfort him. Had they been alone, Roger would have told her he needed no such consideration. "I chose well for you. Roger is the very best sort of man. He would have kept you safe, protected you, taken care of you."

"I did not want Roger."

Good thing he possessed an impenetrable conceit. "I am sitting right here."

"I beg your pardon." Matty flushed and wriggled closer to a pale Digory.

Kathryn, the evil heifer, threw him a wicked grin. "I said you were the best of men."

"I am beyond flattered." How did a man resist a smile like that? Buggered if he knew. "I am unmanned by your praise, but we now have this situation to deal with."

"You marry him." Mathilda perked up. "You said yourself he was the very best of men. You marry him and both of you forget you ever saw me. Father will be happy, because he has the alliance he wants."

Kathryn gaped at her sister. A choked laugh escaped her. "You cannot be serious. I will never marry. I am going to make my way by the sword."

Mathilda snorted and rolled her eyes. "Oh, please, Kate. Nobody ever believed that. Not even you."

* * *

"She married a farmer," Kathryn said it for what must be the hundredth time, and still she battled to believe it.

Roger rode ahead of her. He shrugged like he had done the other hundred times she had said it. "You are supposed to be forgetting you found her."

"I cannot believe it."

"You had best believe it." He glanced over his shoulder at her. "Because you agreed to this lunacy."

"I know." They had left Matty arm-in-arm with her new husband, weeping with gratitude. "My father really will kill him if he ever finds out."

"And your sister?" Roger stared forward. "What would he do to her?"

Kathryn shuddered. Her father's rage would rip through them all for days and days. Mostly it would find a target in her mother, and Kathryn would not allow that. Mother did not have many beatings left in her to take. "It is for the best."

Roger drew rein. He gestured between them. "Have you thought what you will say about this?"

"He does not know I am with you. Nobody knows."

Roger raised a brow. "And you do not think us arriving back at Anglesea together will give the game away?"

"We will not arrive—"

"Do not even think I will let you travel alone."

"But—"

"Nay."

"Only when we draw close enough—"

"Never."

Kathryn bit back a growl. Roger could be the stubbornest man in Christendom. He conveniently forgot that she had followed him, without detection or mishap, for three days. However, the incident at the inn did not strengthen her argument. He wore that look now, the one that said he would tie her to his horse before he gave ground. "I told them that I was going to the Abbey to pray before our marriage," she said. "We could say that you stopped by the Abbey, saw me there, and escorted me home."

He glared.

"The Abbey is not even half a day's ride from Anglesea. It might be a little unexpected but nobody could suspect you of...*that*...in the middle of the day."

"What you know about *that*, I could write on the head of a nail." Roger shook his head at her and clucked his horse forward. "We will discuss this later."

Kathryn saw nothing to discuss. She had come up with a rather neat solution.

"We should reach Calder Castle by sunset." Roger squinted over the tops of a heavy stand of trees. "My sister and her husband reside there. They will provide us a bed for the night, and we can talk this through at a decent meal."

"But—"

He raised an imperious brow at her. It galled her, it really did but it also shut her up.

Chapter Fifteen

Roger led them west toward Calder Castle. It would cost them perhaps a day extra, but it would be worth it to persuade Kathryn to his plan before they reached Anglesea. From the stubborn set of her jaw as she rode beside him, he might need to stretch one day into two.

He could not fail in this. Before they left Calder, she would agree to be his wife. The tattered remnants of her reputation might still be salvaged, and after a few years of respectable marriage, nobody would even remember how Roger obtained his bride. Not to mention Sir Royce, and his now forever missing youngest daughter. Their best hope of keeping Mathilda's secret lay in giving Royce what the man wanted. Him.

Dagger darted back and forth as they left open farmland and entered the forest. Roger coveted the woodlands they rode through to reach the castle. So much wealth grew in these great stands of hardwoods. His nephew, Simon, already a young earl under Sir Gregory's guardianship, would grow into a wealthy man.

Anglesea had trees but nothing like this. Their coastal soils would not support the massive root systems that underpinned Calder's wealth. Last Christmas Gregory had spoken of rotating the tree harvesting, planting new saplings before they felled the grand old sentinels. Roger could not imagine Calder ever running thin on wood. These forests would stand forever.

Upper Mere bustled with the everyday business of a prosperous town. A few voices called out to him in greeting. Roger stopped a moment to chat with the midwife, Bess, as he caught her between house visits.

Dagger sat like a gentleman beside Bess and allowed his head to be patted.

"On your way to the castle?" Bess smiled at him and hefted her basket onto her hip. "Our lady will be pleased to see you."

"Aye." Roger made to dismount but Bess waved him to stay.

Adjusting her spotless wimple, she said, "Do not be clambering off that great beastie. I have but two breaths between young Gilbert sticking a bean up his nose and Black Peter's wife delivering."

The death of the former Earl of Calder had seen a change in Upper Mere. As if a fog had lifted, the town seemed lighter somehow. Townsfolk went about their business with bouncier steps and friendlier greetings.

"And who is this?" Bess cocked her head and stared at Kathryn.

"Bess, allow me to introduce Lady Kathryn of Mandeville."

Bess glanced from him to Kathryn. "Nice to meet you, Lady Kate."

"Lady Kathryn," Roger said. "Nobody calls her Lady Kate."

"Is that so?" Bess raised her brows. "And why is that?"

"I do not care for it," Kathryn said.

"Is your husband not with you, Lady Kathryn?"

Kathryn flushed to her hairline. "I do not have a husband."

"No husband." Hand on her hip, Bess glared at him. "What be you thinking, Sir Roger?"

"Oh, it was not his fault." Kathryn threw him an apologetic look. "He did not invite me on this journey. I invited myself."

"Invited yourself?"

"Aye." Kathryn nodded. "We have had quite the adventure."

Roger could have rescued her, but with Bess making his argument for him, he felt less inclined to do so.

"I feel sure you have." Bess tweaked her pristine apron. "All alone?"

"At first," Kathryn said. "But now we have Dagger with us. We rescued him."

"Indeed." Bess gave him a smug grin. "Fancy that." She patted her basket against her side. "Well, I best be getting on. Babies have a nasty habit of appearing when you least expect them." She tapped Roger's knee. "I am sure Lady Faye will be wanting a word with you, my lord."

* * *

Kathryn tried not to stare, she really did, but she had never seen a lovelier woman than Lady Faye. Hair the color of ripe wheat, eyes deeper blue than the sky above them and a complexion so creamy Kathryn's fingers itched to touch.

She had heard the ballads sung to Lady Faye, all of them, but who could guess that they would fail to do justice to the real woman. Of course, the furor over her marriage had transformed Lady Faye into a walking legend.

Sir Gregory, her grave and handsome husband, stood beside Lady Faye and provided a perfect dark foil to her bright beauty.

"Roger." Lady Faye stepped forward with a sun-bright smile. "We did not expect you."

Roger dismounted and hauled his sister off her feet in a huge hug. He put her down with a grimace. "Lord, Faye, what do they feed you."

Faye swatted him and turned to her. "Good day."

Kathryn scrambled from Striker's back, all too conscious of her chausses and stained tunic. She made an attempt to smooth her hair. "Good day to you."

Roger greeted Sir Gregory with a hearty handshake and a clap on the back that would have sent a smaller man to his knees.

"Welcome to Calder." Faye held her flawless white hand out to Kathryn. "I am Faye."

Kathryn winced at her filthy hand. "Forgive me, I am covered in travel dirt."

"I have two boys." Faye clasped her hand anyway. "I am no stranger to a bit of dirt."

"Faye." Roger strode to Kathryn's side, and she immediately felt bolstered. "I would like to make Lady Kathryn of Mandeville known to you."

"My pleasure." Kathryn made her curtsy, and flushed at how ungainly her chausses made her appear.

"Mandeville?" Frowning, Faye turned to Roger. "Is that not the name of...?"

"He was to marry my sister," Kathryn blurted out.

Faye stared.

Roger shifted.

"Welcome." Sir Gregory filled the silence with his rich, dark voice. "Welcome to Calder. I am sure you will want to refresh yourself."

A dunk in a horse trough might befit her appearance more, but Kathryn managed to return his smile.

"Ruth will show you to a chamber." Faye motioned a serving girl closer.

Ruth bobbed her head, and Kathryn dragged another rude stare away. A series of scars about Ruth's eyes and mouth marred what might once have been a pretty face.

"I will have a bath sent up." Faye thrust her arm through Roger's. "Take your time whilst I catch up with what my brother has been up to."

* * *

"Explain yourself."

Roger winced at the strident note in Faye's voice. His oldest sister very rarely allowed her temper to show, but it flew like a scarlet war banner now.

"Lady Kathryn is the sister to Lady Mathilda, to whom I was to be betrothed."

"You are betrothed to Lady Kathryn?" Gregory exhaled and smiled.

"Nay." Roger pushed a hand through his hair. He wanted a long soak himself, but first he had some explanations to wade through. He had known Faye and Gregory would have strong opinions about his appearance with Kathryn. He could not fault them their outrage. "I was almost betrothed to Lady Mathilda. Her father offered Lady Kathryn, but I refused."

Gregory squared off, his expression dark. "Best you explain then."

"This is not like you." However upset, Faye was always the gracious hostess and she settled him beside the hearth with a goblet of Anglesea's finest, and a platter of small pastries and cheese. "I would expect something like this from William, but not you."

"I did not plan it." Roger cursed the peevish note in his voice. "Lady Mathilda and her family came to Anglesea. She did not care for my wooing and ran away before I could ask."

"She ran away?" Faye dropped onto the seat opposite him, and gaped. "From you?"

"Aye." Roger's grin surprised him. "I managed to send a gentle maiden running to the hills to escape marriage to me."

Gregory chuckled and sipped his wine.

Faye looked murderous. "There is naught wrong with you. Why, the silly girl would be lucky to have you."

"Thank you, dear sister." Roger saluted her with his goblet. "But it has all turned out for the best."

Gregory grumbled and shifted in his seat.

"Let me make this short." Roger drained his goblet and accepted a refill. "On Kathryn's suggestion, I went after Mathilda.

Only, Kathryn followed me, and I did not know she was there until three days into my journey."

"She followed you?"

"You did not detect her for three days?"

Gregory and Faye spoke at once, then both sat back and stared at him in disbelief.

"She is something of a..." How to explain Kathryn to them? "She is a lady of singular resourcefulness."

"Indeed?" Faye rested her chin on her palm. Her eyes sparkled with interest.

"She rides better than a man," he said. "She wields a sword like a knight, can track me without me being aware of her, and cares nothing for being a woman."

"Roger." Faye snorted. "I feel sure that cannot be right. She is lovely."

"But she does not care for it." A smile came unbidden. "She has sworn never to marry and become a shield-maiden."

Gregory choked on a mouthful of wine. "Did you tell her it was a forgotten occupation?"

"She does not care." Roger laughed with Gregory. "She intends to recreate it, and my wager would be on her to get it right."

"I have no idea what a shield-maiden was or is." Faye tapped her slippered foot.

"A shield-maiden was a warrior from the north. North women owned land, could command armies—"

"I do not care." Faye prodded him with her foot. "What I want to know is why an unmarried maiden is journeying alone with a man who is not her family."

"I am getting to that." Roger should not still enjoy irking his sister, but once a brother, always a brother. "After I discovered her following me, she bribed me into letting her come along."

"Bribed?" Gregory raised a brow. "With what?"

"That is what I want to know." Faye crossed her arms.

"She knew where her sister was, and I didn't." Roger leaned forward. "I have not touched her, Faye. On my honor I have not."

Faye sat back in her seat. "Does she not appeal to you?"

He laughed at that. "Aye, she appeals to me. More than I can say, but there are some walls that you storm and other gates that you coax open."

"A keep that surrenders willingly makes for a warm home." Gregory nodded.

"Roger." Faye cocked her head. "Are you in love with this girl?"

His smile would not be denied. "I may very well be."

Chapter Sixteen

Kathryn gave her lilac-scented arm an appreciative sniff. She smelled like a girl again, from her clean toes all the way up to her freshly washed hair. Matty would scoff at the notion, but Kathryn had her moments of girlish enjoyment. Beneath her bare feet, the fur rug all but dared her to wiggle her toes in it.

A knocked sounded. "Kathryn, it is Faye, may I come in."

"Aye." Kathryn clutched the drying cloth around her breasts. It ended mid-thigh and exposed most of her legs. Never mind, she liked her legs and thought it rather a pity she could not display them more.

Faye floated into the room like she rested on her own cloud. "Feel better?"

"Aye. My thanks. Ruth was most...helpful." She could not lie outright.

Faye's expression grew pensive. "Ruth has been with me for a while."

Kathryn itched to ask about the scars Ruth bore, and the cold manner she had, but she did not know Faye well enough for that. In another woman, Kathryn might have judged Ruth's manner as sullen, but it didn't sit right. Ruth seemed to bear inner scars as noticeable as the ones on her face.

"I took a bit of a liberty." Faye smiled and indicated the cloth draped over her arm. The most glorious scarlet that Kathryn suspected might be actual silk. Nobody but Father wore silk at Mandeville. "I did not know that you had anything with you, and Ruth has taken your clothes to be washed."

"Is that for me?" Kathryn took half a step closer, and then stopped. She had never seen anything like the gown Faye held up, let alone worn one.

"It was mine from before I had children," Faye said. "Now I find it a little snug in the hip."

"Really?" As Faye's form appeared as lithe as a girl's, Kathryn found that hard to believe.

"Aye." Faye laughed, stroking the fabric. "Regardless of what I would like to believe, children do leave their mark."

The bliaut's fabric caught the light and shimmered as if woven by angels. "I do not think I can wear that."

Faye tilted her head. "You do not like the color. I have others in—"

"Nay." Kathryn touched the bliaut with one fingertip, afraid to leave smudges on it. Cool to the touch, and delicate as a cobweb. "I do not think I can wear something so fine."

Faye made a noise suspiciously like the snort Roger had teased Kathryn about. A lady like Faye would never snort however. There must be something caught in her throat.

"Let us get you dressed." Faye draped the bliaut across the bed, and held up a chemise. Also silk, with small red flowers embroidered on the sleeves. "Roger will bawl like an angry bull if we make him wait for his dinner."

Faye helped her dress, and then brushed out her hair before the fire.

"This color hair is glorious." Long, slow sweeps of the comb through her hair, lulled Kathryn. "It shines in the firelight."

"It is plain brown hair."

"Nay, there is nothing plain about this hair." Faye arranged a circlet over her forehead

"Matty's hair shines," Kathryn said. "My mother's hair is the same." Except now threaded with grey and lusterless as if it reflected the woman who bore it.

"There." Faye stepped back and grinned. "Now let us join our men."

Kathryn nearly tripped over the hem of her borrowed bliaut. She did not consider Roger to be her man. Not in the sense Faye meant it. Not in any sense, come to think on it.

The hall at Calder keep took her breath away. A setting sun caught behind the large stained glass window that dominated the western end of the hall and cast bejeweled beams over the occupants. Still early evening, people gathered in small, chatty groups before the meal.

Roger stood near the dais, wearing a tunic of deepest blue. Longer and more formal, the tunic clung to him like a happy limpet, broadening his shoulders, narrowing his waist and making his legs stretch on forever. Kathryn had never seen him so finely dressed. Not even when he wooed Matty. It made her want to giggle and blush like a silly girl. She stamped on the urge and returned his greeting with a smile.

He bowed low and took her hand as if he greeted the finest lady at court and led her to table.

He smelled of something spicy and robust. The sort of scent a girl wanted to roll around in like a dog. Speaking of which...

Dagger lay in regal splendor beside the hearth fire and surveyed the hall. He thumped his tail in greeting and went back to gnawing a large bone. His coat shone as if some kindly soul had taken pity on them all and bathed him.

"You look lovely," Roger murmured as he helped her sit.

Her cheeks heated and she bit back a curse. It did not seem right to curse in a bliaut as fine as this one. "So do you?"

Up went his eyebrow, a gleam in Roger's eye.

"Not lovely." She blushed hotter. "I meant you look handsome."

"Thank you, my lady."

Is this how he had wooed Matty? With that smooth, deep voice and the glimmer of admiration in his eye. Matty had made a poor choice of husband. She supposed Digory to be a pleasant sort, but he lacked Roger's height, his powerful shoulders, the stern set of his jaw offset by his smiling mouth. Could there be a man alive with eyes quite that shade of blue? Unlikely.

"My lady?" He cocked his head.

She flushed. Caught staring and they both knew it.

A clatter of running feet dragged her attention away. Two boys ran straight for Roger, yelling his name like a pair of marauders.

"Simon and Arthur." Sir Gregory took the seat to her left. "Our sons." Gregory claimed the late Earl's sons as his with pride. He went up another few notches in her esteem.

Simon and Arthur clustered about Roger, both of them telling their story at the top of their lungs.

Roger nodded and answered when appropriate. Although how he kept their stories straight, Kathryn couldn't fathom.

Ruth entered the hall with a small child in her arms, bearing a softer expression than Kathryn had seen her wear thus far.

"Ah." Gregory's smile blossomed from nowhere, like an unexpected sun through a rain shower. "And, of course, our sweet little Bess."

Ruth handed Bess to Faye.

Faye turned to Kathryn with the child and introduced her as if the child understood every word.

Kathryn guessed Bess's age at around a year or two and was as lovely as one would expect of the child of two such beautiful people.

An unexpected pang shot through Kathryn. Her chosen life would not bring her children, or a happy hearth such as this one. Up until this moment if you had told her she hankered for children, Kathryn would have laughed in your face. Suddenly the idea did not seem so ridiculous.

Bess blinked at her, and shoved her tiny, plump fist into her mouth.

"Would you like to hold her?" Faye held Bess to her.

Kathryn's arms shot out as if she had no control of them.

Bess pressed warm and soft against her breast, a surprisingly hefty little bundle with that unique scent of sweet milk. "She is beautiful."

"Aye." Faye touched Bess's dark silky hair. "My mother tells me she looks exactly like Roger and William did at this age."

Kathryn stopped her snort just in time. Picturing Roger as the delicate, sweet thing in her arms stretched her credulity too far.

"But not for long." Faye patted Roger's cheek. "Before Mother could finish cooing they turned into rotten boys."

"Oy." This, or a version thereof, from the four males present.

Kathryn enjoyed dinner. With the children in attendance it remained a relaxed, easy affair, mostly taken up with childish chatter and Roger's increasingly exaggerated and elaborate stories of feats in battle. At least, she hoped they were the rich brewing of his imagination. The idea of Roger taking on five men without a weapon chilled her. She would wager her last hair that dragons no longer existed however, but if they did...

Shaking her head, Kathryn chuckled at herself. She pictured Roger in the sort of fantastical acts that belonged in the minds of silly girls. In her imaginings she built him into the sort of sword-wielding hero of nauseatingly noble intentions that she'd known since a very early age did not exist.

Men did not put themselves in danger for their ladylove. Never mind putting themselves in danger, they would barely lift a finger to make themselves uncomfortable. It would never occur to a man to move from his customary place by the fire because his lady had a miserable sore head. Or allow her to take dinner in her room when her joints grew inflamed with winter cold. Instead they used her as a whipping post, a convenient target for their anger and frustration.

Roger's breath tickled her neck. "Dark thoughts?"

"Nay." Kathryn threw him a smile.

He quirked his brow, rose and offered her a hand. "Come. You look as if you could benefit from some fresh air."

"Where are we going?" Kathryn slid her hand into his.

"The view from the battlements of Calder is unequaled," Roger said. "A perfect cure for whatever worries you."

He kept her hand in his as they left the keep and crossed a small enclosed courtyard to a corner donjon. Steep stairs wound up through rock walls so narrow Roger's shoulders nearly brushed the sides. Perfect for defense, with no room to swing a sword or nock an arrow. Kathryn approved of the stairs twisting in a way that would advantage a right-handed swordsman descending. Calder's ancestors had built their keep to be defended from within as well as without.

They climbed until her legs ached. The air grew brisker as they rose. At the top, Roger stopped, and put his shoulder to a narrow door and pushed.

Wind whistled across the battlements and snatched Kathryn's gasp away. Below them spread the treetops in an eye-aching green tapestry.

"They built the donjon high enough to see above the trees." Roger led her to the crenellations that guarded the wall edge. "There is only one approach to Calder along that road." He pointed out a narrow road that wound past a small village. "That is Lower Mere."

The road disappeared amongst the trees.

"From there, the road winds through the forest until it cuts straight through the middle of Upper Mere." Roger indicated the bustling town at the foot of the castle walls. "The Earls of Calder were determined never to let anyone approach their keep in secret. And, of course, the mere itself guards the front entrance."

Upon the battlements the breeze, which would have been

gentle below, tugged at her skirts and whipped her hair about. Kathryn shivered as it cut through the thin silk.

Roger tucked her tight to his chest, and enfolded her from behind in his arms.

"What of the rear?" Grateful for the warmth, but still Kathryn's heart set up an erratic pattern. The heat from his chest crept through her back.

"Ah." Roger turned them until they faced the opposite side of the keep. "That is her weakness. You could hide an entire army inside those trees. Plenty of time for them to plot a way over these walls."

"They are very high. The walls."

"Indeed they are." Roger's voice rumbled through her. "And the reason for their height is to give the keep a fighting chance against their weakness."

"Would you clear the trees?"

"Nay." Roger chuckled. "They are too beautiful. From here it feels as if one were a bird, nestled in your aerie in the treetops."

Sentiment? From Roger? Kathryn half turned her head to see if he mocked her.

His gaze roamed the view, his expression quiet and contemplative. Perhaps even a little gentle.

He glanced at her. "What is it?"

"I did not judge you as one for romantic notions."

"Ah, Kathryn." He pressed his cheek against hers. "I have entire swathes of romantic notions."

Even a girl as inexperienced as she recognized the intimacy of their position. She should wriggle free of his hold. Instead she said, "Tell me of these notions."

"Swathes of notions." His chuckle rumbled through his chest. "And that is a conversation for another time. We must speak, my lady."

A warning prickled through her, along with the "my lady" it was enough to have her tense. For a moment she considered pretending not to know where he headed, but Roger would see through her too quickly. He was also right. They did need to have this out. Although she might care little for her reputation, the rest of the world did not share her opinion. She had marked Bess's shock, caught the significant glances between Roger and his sister.

Her entire argument for Roger being on this quest in the first place had collapsed with the discovery of Matty's marriage. Which left them where precisely?

"Clearly I can no longer marry your sister," he said.

Kathryn nodded.

"You know your father offered you as her replacement before we left Anglesea."

"Aye." Sir Royce would not happily forego a match with Anglesea, which was too bad for him. "I have also been thinking on that."

"You have?" He sounded surprised.

It irked her. Why would he think she had not considered her future? "Of course." She shoved aside the ache and spoke what she knew to be true. "It is obvious that I cannot return to Anglesea with you."

"Ah." Roger tightened his arms about her. "I might have known that would be your solution. You intend to disappear like your sister."

"Is there any other course?"

"Aye." He rested his chin against her temple. "You could marry me."

Shocked near speechless, Kathryn pulled herself from his hold. "Are you addled?"

"Nay." He gave a wry smile. "I am in deadly earnest."

She could see that.

His jaw locked in a firm line, his eyes intent.

"I have told you," she said. "I will not marry."

"And what then?" He growled at her. Aye, growled! "What will you do if I allow you to leave Calder and disappear amongst the trees?"

Allowed her? She rather thought not. No man allowed or disallowed her aught. "It is not your decision."

"Aye, it is." He grew stern. "Your father betrothed you to me and that makes it my decision."

* * *

God's Balls. Roger could bash his own brains out as Kathryn's shoulders went back and her stubborn chin jutted out. He had erred, and done exactly the opposite of what he had set out to do. "Look." Roger put some distance between them. His thoughts muddled when he touched her. "I said that all wrong. Let us start this conversation again."

"I do not care what my father did, or did not do." Her taut posture shrieked defiance. "And you refused my father's offer of me."

He wanted to shake her, so he stuck his hands behind his back and clasped them. "I understand. I misspoke." He needed a little of William's fancy footwork through her stubbornness. "Let us say you leave Calder. Alone." Over his stiff corpse. "What will you do then?"

"Whatever I like."

"Offer yourself as a sellsword?"

"I have the skill." A martial light lit her lovely eyes. "You said so yourself."

"Aye, but what baron would hire a female mercenary?"

Let her try to deny the truth of that. She chewed the lush pillow of her bottom lip as she concocted her next counter argument. "I will go to France."

"You have the coin to reach France?"

"Nay." Doubt peeked at him from beneath the bravado. "But you do."

She surprised a laugh out of him. "You think I will give you the coin to embark on a venture that will get you killed?"

"You cannot know that."

"Aye, I can." Roger strode to her and gripped her shoulders. "You must see reason in this, sweeting. The world we live in does not lend itself to your dream."

Her dejection made him want to lie to her, to tell her all that she wanted to hear. But broken dreams could be mended, put back together with new dreams. He knew no cure for death, or the fate that would find Kathryn if he let her leave here without him.

"Listen to me." He tightened his grip and drew her to him. "Listen with your heart and you will know what I say is true. Your dream was a fine one, a beautiful one, but it cannot come true."

"Why?"

God's bones, she killed him. "You know why. Because of men like that one at the inn, because of men like your father." He would rather hack his sword arm off than hurt her like this, but he saw no other option. "Do you think your father will let you and Matty go? Dust his hands and say good riddance to the pair of you?"

She hung her head, obscuring her expression in a cloud of walnut silk.

"You are the coin by which he secures his future, and he guards that coin like a dragon its gold."

Beneath his hands, her shoulders slumped. Unable to resist any longer, he tugged her back into his embrace. "If it were different, I would let you go." And chase after her the second she turned her back. "But you must be pragmatic, sweeting. There are often times in war, where logic must win over pride or desire."

She stayed resistant and tense against him.

Roger tried to soothe her pain and stroked the rigid line of her spine. "Think about this instead. You know me, Kathryn. I am not some brutish stranger your father foists on you. And I know you." She relaxed a mite and he wrapped her tighter. "I know you like to ride breakneck on that horse of yours, yelling like a savage as you wave your sword around." That earned him the tiniest of chuckles. "And it bothers me not one whit. Jesu, I will teach you how to yield that sword even better."

She stilled.

"I would never seek to change you, or stamp out your spirit. With me as your husband, you could be free to be who you are."

"Why?"

Roger weighted his answer carefully. He sensed the truth would set her running faster, so he said, "I need a wife, and I find you suit me very well."

With a soft snort she wriggled free and gazed at him. "I am not a lady. I would make a poor baroness."

"You would make the best baroness." He pulled her against him. Her clever wits would read him too easily. "Because you are the baroness I would choose for myself." This wooing was an exhausting business, even more so when a man's very soul hung on the outcome. "Anglesea is a large keep. Your mother could reside there with us."

"She could?"

Victory surged through him. He had her there. "Aye. She would be well cared for and happy amongst her grandchildren."

He cursed silently as she stiffened. "Children? You would want children?"

"Aye." He would not lie about this. "But not right away."

"Hmmm." The sound hummed through his chest as she pressed her head to his shoulder. "That would require rutting."

Roger nigh choked on his tongue. "Pigs rut, Kathryn. I am fairly certain I have never rutted in my life."

She snorted, the nuance clearly lost on his ladylove.

He would leave that for a day when he could show her the difference. "Does the...rutting frighten you?"

"Nay," she said, but her tone belied the word. "I do not believe I am a rutting sort of girl."

The conversation rapidly fled his control, as his unruly body demanded he show her how wrong she was. "Are you a kissing sort of girl?"

"Eh?" She glanced at him, and gave him the gap he needed.

"Shall we find out?" He closed the slight difference between their mouths. "Rutting and kissing are not so very far apart." Not for what he intended, in any case. "I propose an experiment."

Her gaze flickered to his mouth. At the very least, he had awakened her curiosity.

"Let us see how you feel about kissing first?"

"Are you going to kiss me?" Flushed, she peered at him.

Roger touched his mouth to hers.

She froze.

Roger feathered his lips over hers. This would go a lot easier if Kathryn would participate. Although she had not punched him yet, so he took that as encouragement.

Her lips were soft beneath his, succulent, and he sucked her bottom lip into his mouth.

"Oh." She parted her lips in surprise, and Roger slanted his mouth, and touched his tongue to the lip he'd just sucked.

"What are you doing?" At least that is what he thought she said, it was hard to speak and kiss at the same time.

Enough. Let him fail in a blaze of glory.

Roger cupped her cheeks, tilted her head, and slipped his tongue into the depths of her mouth.

Sweet Jesu, she tasted of honey and heaven. A heady taste that shot straight to his rod.

Shyly, tentatively, she moved her tongue against his. Her eyes drifted shut.

Reining in his desire, Roger kissed her slowly. He took his time exploring her mouth, coaxing a greater reaction from her.

His Kathryn learned quickly. Her hands clasped his wrists as if to keep him in place, and she opened her mouth, deepening the kiss.

For all her courage and bluster, the delicacy of her innocence rang in the back of his mind. He held back the need to cage her against the wall and press his body to hers. He longed to take his hands on a happy exploration of the curves that had taunted him for days. Instead he held her face, gently with all the reverence a girl deserved as she received her first kiss.

His control slipping, Roger ended the kiss and stepped back.

Kathryn opened her eyes slowly. Her lips glistened from his kiss and she gave a soft little sigh. "That was...not what I expected."

"Better or worse?" Her skin warmed by the pink sunset proved impossible to resist, and he stroked her cheek.

She pressed into his light caress. "I believe you know the answer to that." With a small shake of her head, she stepped back from him. "There will be more kissing if I marry you?"

"A lot more." Of that he could assure her.

"Hmm." She strode to the far end of the battlements. Hands on the parapet, she leaned forward and breathed in the night air. Her bliaut curved to the swell of her ass. "I will need a promise from you."

"Aye." He need tread carefully here. There could be no knowing what Kathryn would ask of him. "If it is in my power to make this promise, I will give it."

"My mother." Kathryn tilted over the edge at an angle that made him nervous. "I need my mother to be safe. She has to be."

Had he not said so already? "You have my word of honor. It shall be so."

She turned to him with a glittering smile. "Then, by all means, let us marry."

"Could you come away from the edge?" God's Balls, he'd become a mother hen, but she had leaned so far forward it would take but a breath of wind to send her hurtling to the ground hundreds of feet below them.

A cheeky grin greeted his demand. "Do I make you nervous?"

"In ways you cannot imagine." Marriage to Kathryn promised a lifetime of challenge. Good thing, he fed on challenge. The thought stopped him for a moment. Could his mother have known that when she invited the Mandeville family to Anglesea? Nay, impossible. How could Lady Mary have predicted Matty would run and he and Kathryn would end up chasing her? Then again, his mother was a wily one.

"Roger?"

"Aye."

"Did you kiss Matty?"

Her question shocked him. Did she think he went about kissing women willy-nilly? Perhaps when he and William were younger…"Nay."

"You should have." She strolled back toward him. "I am sure she would never have run had you kissed her." One hand to his chest, she peered at him. "You are powerfully good at the kissing."

And there you had Kathryn. A knee to the balls and a stroke to the pride, all in one blinding statement.

Chapter Seventeen

Kathryn accepted another bliaut from Faye the next morning. This one fine linen, and a deep blue that looked well with her hair. Normally she would not travel in skirts, but Roger looked at her differently in skirts. A similar look to his kissing look and she rather liked it.

Faye and Gregory insisted they accompany them to Anglesea. It seemed rather pointless as she and Roger had travelled alone for so many days, but Faye had a stubborn streak it appeared.

Kathryn stood in the bailey and chafed at the time it took to get the large party ready to travel. People darted this way and that, with Faye at the center of the storm. If it were just her and Roger, they would be partway to Anglesea already. The amount of food loaded onto the traveling wagon cheered Kathryn immensely. However, Faye insisted on what she called "proper" provisions. This meant tents joined the food, along with travel pallets and linens.

"I do not sleep on the ground," Faye said to Roger when he protested. "And neither does the future Baroness of Anglesea."

With a start, Kathryn realized Faye meant her. She was the future baroness of Anglesea. Of course, Lady Mary and Sir

Arthur appeared to have many healthy years ahead of them, but the title made it all the more real.

When Roger kissed her mind into silence, it did not seem so daunting. The children he spoke of would be heirs to a great demesne, and she would rule the mighty castle as chatelaine. Her father had never considered that she might aspire to such a lofty marriage. All his ambition centered on Matty.

"What is it?" Always sensitive to her thoughts, Roger slipped his arm about her waist. This too was new. Along with all the courteous touches he pressed on her throughout the morning as if he dealt with that sort of girl.

"I think you have made a poor choice of baroness."

He bowed over her hand. "I beg to disagree, my lady."

This "my lady" nonsense must end. On the road before she had been Kathryn or "you" or "girl". Her new status constricted like a badly fitting pair of braies.

The watch had called midday when they, finally, mounted and the party took to the road.

The folk of Upper Mere stopped and waved as they passed. Faye reined in time after time to share a word with a resident. The people of Upper Mere adored their lady, and she seemed to know the name of every person who spoke with her. Faye asked after children and oldsters, mentioned events in their lives as if she had a stock of information in her lovely head.

If a chatelaine did all of this, then Kathryn floundered in deep waters. Ask her to name any horse in the stables and she could tell you its dam and sire and also its strengths and weaknesses. But people, nay. They passed before her in a jumble of features and names.

Roger's gaze found her again, and she clicked her fingers at Dagger, and pretended to call the dog.

Matty had been raised for such a marriage. Matty could plan a menu, have the keep glistening from turret to trough, and still find time to visit with a sick baby. Her sister wore gowns like Faye, rode her palfrey at a sedate walk, and always kept her hands clean.

Except Matty had married her farmer, and left Kathryn to step into her part.

"Are you well, my lady?" Roger nudged his destrier closer to Striker. "When you are fatigued we can stop."

Fatigued after a paltry afternoon lolling along in the saddle? Kathryn stared at him. Who was this man in Roger's skin? When she had agreed to marry, it had not been to this courtly stranger.

"Cease!" She drew rein, and Roger stopped with her.

He blinked at her." What?"

"Stop with all this 'my lady.'" She waved her hands in the air as she imagined a lady would. "When have you ever asked me if I needed to stop because I was fatigued?"

He stiffened and looked affronted. "I thought my betrothed deserved the courtesy of her position."

Kathryn snorted.

He started.

She did it again for good measure. "You are marrying me, Sir Roger," she said. "Not some gentle lamb who needs petting and cosseting."

"You would prefer I treat you rough?"

"Nay." The man looked honestly confused, and she softened her strident tone. "I would prefer you treat me as me. I am not Matty."

He grinned.

Kathryn wanted to cheer. Here was the man she had spent time with. The one who put her fears over marriage to rest. For as long as she had this man by her side, she could do this.

"Nay." He winked at her. "You are certainly not Matty, and I am glad of it."

* * *

Kathryn liked Faye, she really did, but the woman insisted they stop for Vespers. They set up tents, said prayers and prepared a meal as best they could over an open fire. Kathryn approved of the meal, and demonstrated her appreciation to the best of her ability, which also involved a little pilfering from Roger's portion.

Gregory led them in Compline, and finally they retired for the night.

Kathryn to her tent, Roger to his, and Faye and Gregory to theirs.

Gregory set sentries. The soft tramp of their footsteps as they kept watch through the night accompanied her into sleep. Her offer to take a watch had been met with a quickly disguised grin from Roger, confusion from Gregory, and a horrified murmur from Faye.

As much as she had protested their addition, she did approve of the sleeping pallets, and woke the next morning in fine spirits.

The day stayed clear and crisp, new growth lifting fresh green fingers to the sky. Roger took her for a long gallop ahead of the group, which Dagger enjoyed nigh as much as she did, and the meal that evening kept her mood sunny.

By the end of the next day, however, her mood reflected the glowering storm that brewed above them.

Faye refused to travel in the sharp wind, and they camped earlier that night.

It took them three full days more to reach Anglesea. Three days for a journey she and Roger could have traversed in a night or two. By the time they sighted the tall battlements of Anglesea, Kathryn had to bite her cheek to keep the scream in.

Roger drew up beside her, pride and love shining from him. "There she is. Anglesea."

Square, grey stone towers soared above the curtain wall, clearly etched against the endless blue of sea meeting sky.

The sight of Anglesea brought Kathryn's adventure jolting to an end. Within those walls lay her real life, and it demanded she take up her part again. She had been away longer than she first intended. They trod forward. She had left with the excuse of seeking spiritual guidance from the Abbey, and now she returned with a party. Had her mother fared well in her absence?

With her father's anger appeased by her betrothal, she had judged it safe to leave. However, Sir Royce's rage lived and breathed, as capricious as a forest fire, and always simmering beneath the surface.

Being at Anglesea should have kept the worst of his temper in check.

Their slow pace rankled. She would know within a glance how her mother fared. Sir Royce would never mark her mother for others to see, but Kathryn knew well the broken look her mother wore.

"What is it?" Roger cocked his head and studied her.

"Are we starting that again?"

"Nay." He chuckled. "But you look as if you are sitting on briars."

"I am missing Matty," she said. What happened at Mandeville remained family business. She could not dishonor her mother by making her shame common gossip. "You cannot tell anyone you know where she is."

He set his hand on her rein. "I will not, Kathryn. I gave you and Matty my word that I would keep her secret."

A horn blasted a long, mournful wail from the walls. They had been spotted, and Anglesea welcomed them home. The doors to the great keep swung open.

News of their arrival filled the inner bailey with people. Lady Mary stood with Lady Beatrice and her children near the keep door. Sir Arthur strode forward to meet them with his son by marriage, Garrett.

To one side, his arms crossed, waited her father.

The weight on her chest lifted as her mother left the keep with a smile of welcome.

"What is this?" Sir Arthur clasped arms with Roger. His kindly smile warmed Kathryn. "You go off on your own and come back with half the kingdom?"

Sir Arthur turned to assist Faye from her horse. "Ah, my Faye." He tugged her into a hug. "Looking as lovely as ever."

Turning to Gregory, he clasped his arm and asked after the children.

"Kate." Her father strode toward her. He placed a chaste kiss on her forehead. "Well met."

Kathryn glanced at him.

Sir Royce's stare glittered hard as ice.

She went cold.

* * *

"Get in there." Her father dropped his pretense and shoved her into the chamber he shared with her mother.

Mother followed on behind, eyes downcast and shoulders slumped.

All through dinner Sir Royce had kept up the amiable pretense, but Kathryn's belly tightened on the certain knowledge that he knew something. He waited until Compline ended before he gripped her by the arm and dragged her here.

"Where were you?" Slowly, he circled her.

"I went to the Abbey to pray—"

Hard fingers dug into her hair and yanked her head back. "You lie."

Kathryn glanced at her mother.

A quick head shake. A warning.

Her father hauled her around.

Hot breath hit her face.

"I sent a messenger to the Abbey to fetch you two days ago. Imagine the monk's surprise when he asked for Lady Kate of Mandeville."

Cold gripped her belly. "I went to clear my head. My thinking grew muddled with the betrothal."

"Indeed." He gripped her throat. "Stop lying, Kate."

"I am not lying." Why would her father have sent a messenger to the Abbey? Normally he did not bother himself with her comings and goings.

Mother twisted her fingers in her lap, head bowed over them, shoulders taut as a bowstring.

Kathryn drew in a calming breath. If she showed fear he would be worse.

"Aye, Kate, you are." His grip tightened on her throat "Shall I tell you where I think you were?"

Kathryn remained dead still.

"I think you went to look for your sister." The gentleness of his tone terrified her more than a bellow. "I think you knew where to find her."

"I did not know where she was." Matty's life depended on her now. "You are right, I thought I might be able to find her."

"Where is she?"

"I could not find her."

The punch plowed into her stomach, snatching her breath away and making her want to be ill. "Where is she?"

"I did not find her."

The second blow landed higher, against her ribs and pain exploded through her trunk. Kathryn doubled over.

"You filthy little bitch." Fist in her hair, he yanked her head up. "You lie to me all the time. I know you know where your sister is."

"I swear to you, I do not know." The words came with difficulty as each breath sawed jagged through her. "You know I do not wish to marry, and I would have brought her back if I knew where she was."

"You will marry, girl." He released her hair so suddenly that she stumbled. "I do know you do not wish to marry. I also know you will do anything for your sister and that whore."

Kathryn cradled her ribs. "Not this."

Her father turned from her.

Dear God! Her mother!

Sir Royce stalked her mother. "Let us see if she can persuade you to tell the truth."

He wrenched her mother's arm behind her back.

Mother stifled a cry, her eyes beseeching Kathryn.

Kathryn ran at her father. "Get off her!"

"Or what?"

Kathryn gathered all her strength, and shoved. She pushed him hard enough to make him release her mother to catch his balance, and then she pushed him again, putting herself between them.

Time stopped. Her breath gasped in the dead still.

Anger built in Sir Royce, tensing through his muscles until it burst from him. Grabbing her by the nape he threw her onto the ground.

Hard stone bit into her knees and palms. Kathryn spat blood from where she'd bit her tongue.

"You dare!" His voice bounced off the walls.

Kathryn tried to crawl to safety but his boot connected with her ribs. A sickening crack burst on her left side.

"You miserable, misbegotten whore!" With his fist he drove into her back, pushing her to the floor where his boots lashed out again and again.

Dimly her mother's voice penetrated, crying and pleading with him to stop.

"Nay." Kathryn opened her mouth but she had no air to make words.

He rained kicks and punches on her. Making contact with whatever part of her he could. Except her face. Even in his fury, Sir Royce would not mark her where others could see.

Kathryn crawled for the door. If she could reach the passage he would be forced to stop.

"They will hear you," her mother shouted. "Stop, Royce, you will damage her and then there will be no wedding."

Her father's feet stilled. He landed another punch to the base of her spine and straightened. He loomed above her, his breath coming in harsh grunts.

Then he was gone, shutting the door softly.

"Dear God, Kathryn." Mother smoothed Kathryn's hair. "What did you do? I thought he would kill you for certain."

Every movement, every breath hurt as Kathryn pushed herself to her knees and then onto her seat. "I am all right, Mother."

"Nay, you are not." Mother, pale but dry eyed, shook her head. "Are your ribs broken?"

"I do not think so." Gingerly she touched her aching sides.

"I have a root powder for the pain." Mother stood and went to her traveling chest. She rummaged within until she unearthed her trusty leather satchel. Lady Mary insured her guests always had a flagon of wine in their chamber and Mother poured some into a goblet and mixed in the grey powder. She brought it back to Kathryn. "Here. It will help. We can bind your ribs for a day or two to make it easier to move."

How pitiful that she and her mother knew how to hide their injuries so well.

Kathryn drained the goblet. It hit her stomach and she retched. Clamping her jaw together she managed to hold the wine down.

"Come." Mother helped her to her feet. "You cannot protect us, Kathryn. Not at this cost."

She could not protect her mother at all if they were separated. Her father's reminder came just in time. This was what came of putting your fate in the hands of a man.

Chapter Eighteen

Roger lay awake and stared at his bed canopy, trying to force his jumbled thoughts into order. He had spoken with his father, and the marriage would take place as soon as Mother could decorate the hall and the chapel. Roger voted for an immediate wedding, but Lady Mary insisted the thing be done properly.

For his part, he did not care about flowers and ribbons, when he had already won the true prize. Kathryn.

His door creaked open and he propped himself on his elbows. He couldn't say the slim, shift-clad figure slipping into his room surprised him. More like a welcome midnight visitor.

"Kathryn," he greeted her.

"Oh." She stopped partway between his bed and the door. "You are awake."

"Indeed." He sat up. "Shut the door before somebody sees you."

Slowly she made her way to the bed, her gait slightly impaired. Had he made her nervous with his suggestion she close the door? How different to her last nocturnal visit. Then he had been concerned about ridding himself of his unwelcome visitor.

He patted the side of the bed. "Come and sit."

"Nay." Three feet away from the bed, she halted and folded her hands in front of her. "I do not plan to stay long."

Her voice sounded strange, strained and labored.

"Are you all right?" Keeping the sheet to preserve his modesty, he eased his legs over the side of the bed.

"I am fine." Her hand fluttered toward her ribs and then dropped by her side. "Fine," she said, louder this time. "What I have to say will not take long."

Roger did not like the sound of that, nor how still and contained she stayed. This did not bode well. He motioned her to continue.

"I cannot marry you. And I would beg that you tell my father we do not suit." She turned and limped toward the door.

"I beg your pardon." With Kathryn moving slower than usual, Roger had time to snatch up his sheet, hastily fasten it and still beat her to the door. Part of him wanted to shake the life out of her.

She stopped, swayed and placed her hand against her side. "You heard me."

Aye, he had bloody well heard her. The blighted words still shredded him inside. He did not trust his voice or the anger that whipped his reason back like a cur. "Why?"

"We do not suit."

"You are going to have to do better than that." Did she think she could rend his heart from his chest and leave without an explanation? Not bloody likely.

"I cannot be a baroness. You must know how bad I would be at it. Only, I am going to need you to tell my father you cannot marry me." Her breath caught on a gasp.

Reason glimmered through his anger. Something was amiss, badly amiss.

She dropped her hand and straightened. Soft, but ragged, a choked whimper filled the silence between them.

Roger really looked at his Kathryn. The dancing firelight hindered his cause but he dared not leave her long enough to light a taper. His nape tingled a warning he could not ignore. He propped his shoulders to the door and crossed his arms. She need not think she could leave him like that. "You cannot marry me but you need me to tell your father that it is I who cannot marry you?"

"Aye."

"Because you believe you will make a terrible baroness?"

"Aye."

Once more her body listed to the right, as if to protect itself. The action seemed instinctive, without intent, and his sense of foreboding grew.

"We do not suit," she said.

"I cannot agree with you," he said. "I believe we suit perfectly. We have remarkably similar interests, we enjoy time in each other's company, and your response to my kiss gives me great hope for our future as man and wife."

"Please." It came out more mewl than word. "I cannot marry you, and you must renounce me. Can you not just let it be at that?"

"Nay, Kathryn, I cannot, and you are mad to think I would. I have searched long and hard for a wife, and now I have found her. I will not merely step back and let you leave."

"You did for Matty."

"I never felt one quarter for Matty what I feel for you."

Her breath hitched on a sob. She winced and wrapped her arms about her trunk. "You must not say such things."

Firelight glanced off the single tear winding down her cheek. It broke through the last of his anger. "And why is that, sweeting?"

"How can I leave you if you say such pretty things to me?" She looked haunted.

Instinct warned him not to do what his heart urged and clasp her to him. "I was rather hoping you would not leave me at all."

She gave a larger sob, bent at the waist. "It is impossible."

Something was very, very wrong with Kathryn. Tears she

hated to shed leaked down her cheeks unstopped, and he grew certain she had hurt her ribs. As a lad in training, he'd fallen off his destrier onto a stone wall. He had pissed blood for two days, but nothing had hurt more than his ribs.

He cupped her elbow and took some of her weight. "Tell me why it is impossible."

"I cannot." She leaned into his clasp and he took a firmer grip on her forearm. Aye, she was hurt or he was the king's jester.

"Is it because you are afeared of me?"

She laughed, gasped and then doubled over.

"Enough, Kathryn. Where are you hurt?" He grasped her by the waist.

Kathryn yelped.

Roger leaped back from her, truly frightened to touch any part of her. "What happened?"

"I fell." She stared at her feet.

Something feral, untamed and pure burned through him. She lied to him, and he knew of only one reason a woman lied about her injuries. To protect the sod who had put them on her. Faye had lied for years to them about what her first husband, Calder, inflicted on her.

"You did not fall." His voice shook with the rage he barely contained.

Her head came up but she evaded his gaze. "I fell, I swear it."

"Tell me, Kathryn, or I will wake up your mother and father and find out."

She gasped. "You cannot."

"Where can I touch you?" He held his hands out to her. She looked as if she might crumple at any moment.

"Do not." Her jaw clenched.

Sweet Jesu. He could no more cut off his hands, than not touch her. "Sweeting." He approached as he would a wounded animal. "Let me take care of you. I need to."

"I...hurt." Her sob cut him deeper than the words.

Roger cupped her elbows. Too scared of hurting her by picking her up, he eased her across the chamber and onto his bed.

No marks on her face or neck, her arms as smooth and silky as always. The damage must be hidden from sight. He plucked the chemise ties at her neck. "May I?"

She nodded. Her unbound hair hid her face.

He loosened the ties, and eased the chemise from her shoulders.

She clutched the falling fabric to her breasts. It did not matter. For once, her breasts held no interest for him.

"Dear God!" Bile rose in his throat. Covered from below her neckline to her hips, her skin bore the mottled blue-black and red of recent bruising. If defied him that she could still stand. Her ribs had taken the brunt of the hits. "I need to get Nurse to look at these."

"Nay!" Cheeks flushed, she tugged her chemise over her shoulders again.

Ivy would have been preferable, but Ivy, now wedded to Tom, lived with him on their farm. Still, Nurse had eased more than her share of his bruises and hurts. "Sweeting, these are bad." He crouched at her feet. "We need to know if the hurt is only on the outside."

"You would parade my shame throughout Anglesea?" Her chin came up in a flash of the fire and steel of his Kathryn.

"Nay, my Kathryn, I would ease your pain, and ensure your wellbeing." He raised her hands to his lips and kissed one and then the other. "Nurse will say nothing, but she can make you more comfortable."

She stared at him, and finally gave him the nod he sought.

"You will wait here?"

"Aye." She gave him a tremulous smile. "Time was you did not want me in your bedchamber in the midst of the night."

"Seems I was mistaken." He touched her cheek.

Nurse kept her own room below the kitchens, down eerie, dark stairs that led to the cooler depths of the Anglesea cellars.

She awoke with a grumble, took one searching look at his face and hurried him out so she could dress. She emerged again with her bag of medicaments and followed him back to his chamber.

Nurse could chatter a man's head off when she took it into her head to do so, but she remained cool and competent when needed.

Shutting his bedchamber door on him, Nurse went to work.

* * *

The old woman shuffled toward her, a huge leather satchel banging at her hip. Mandeville had no resident healer, and her mother had nursed Matty and her. Roger seemed to trust the woman.

"Our lad tells me you have been hurt." The older woman's wimple pressed all the flesh of her cheeks forward like a bloated pig's bladder.

Kathryn affected a casual shrug, and her body bellowed its protest of even that light movement. "I will be fine."

"Aye, you will be." Nurse stopped right before her. "When you let old Nurse have a look at what's amiss."

Her manner drew Kathryn in, and held her there. *Trust me,* seemed to whisper from her.

And, just like that, she did. With some help from Nurse, Kathryn wriggled out of her chemise. "It looks worse than it feels."

Nurse stilled. "Oh, I doubt that, darling girl." Gentle as a butterfly, Nurse touched gnarled fingers to the worst of her bruises. "Just fists or boots as well?"

"Both."

"Men!" Nurse spat the word. "The times I would like to take some whoreson out to the woods and beat him to a wet heap of bloody mush."

Kathryn choked back a laugh, because it hurt too much.

Nurse dug in her bag and brought forth a small, earthen pot. "This will sting a mite."

A mite! Kathryn near jumped out of her skin at the burn of whatever foul smelling concoction Nurse spread over her ribs.

"Think of something else," Nurse said. "Like what you are doing in Roger's bedchamber when you should be in your own."

As a distraction it worked instantly. Kathryn had naught but the truth to offer. "I came to tell him I could not marry him."

"Oh, aye." Nurse carried on applying salve as if they discussed the weather. "And why is that?"

"I think he should know if I am not going to marry him."

Nurse chuckled. "You are a lively one, aren't you Lady Kate?"

"Kathryn." She winced as Nurse applied salve to her hip. "The one who did this calls me Kate."

After a searching stare, Nurse returned to her ministering. "Here." She mixed a red powder into a glass of wine. "This will ease the swelling and also the discomfort."

Kathryn sipped and nearly spat it out.

Nurse's hard stare made her swallow.

"What was that?"

"A little something I save for lively-lipped lasses." Nurse winked. "So, why is it that you cannot marry our lad? Seems to me you would be better off with him."

"My mother," Kathryn said. "If I am not there, he will do this to her."

"Ah." Nurse nodded. She stepped back and put her hands on her hips. "Talk to Roger, Lady Kathryn. He is a good lad, right down to his huge heart. Men like him are a rare find, and a clever girl holds onto one if she has him."

Kathryn did believe she was a clever girl, and she nodded.

Nurse helped her back into her chemise. "I will give you a moment or two with our Roger, then it is back to bed for you, my lady. Your bed. Alone."

Roger opened the door at her knock and Nurse bustled past him with a stern look. "A couple of minutes and then you walk her to her door." She wagged a finger. "You cannot lie to me, Roger-lad."

"And well I know it." Roger kissed her weathered cheek. "My thanks, Nurse. We will keep this amongst us."

"I can keep a secret." Nurse adjusted her satchel. "Not like that sister of yours."

Roger shut the door on Nurse's rotund figure retreating down the dim corridor. He came to sit beside her. "How are you?"

"Better." The ache in her ribs had subsided to a low grumble. That powder Nurse had given her made her not care nearly as much.

"Was it your father?"

"Aye."

"Why?'

"He wanted to know where Matty was."

"And you did not tell him." Roger rested his elbows on his knees, hands clasped.

"Of course I did not tell him."

"Of course." He sat up, his gaze searching. "This I swear to you on all that I hold dear, that man will never lift a finger to you or your mother ever again. Ever." The chaste kiss on her forehead tingled. "Marry me. Give me the right before God and man to keep my oath."

"Aye."

Chapter Nineteen

Roger left her at her bedchamber door. Once the door shut behind her, he let his mask drop. He slammed his fist into the wall, relishing the pain.

Fury clamored at him, demanding he wrench Sir Royce limb from limb.

He punched the wall again. The skin split over his knuckles.

"That's a stupid thing to do." Garrett appeared out of the gloomy corridor. He looked tired and rumpled.

"Sod off." Roger leaned against the wall and fought the rising tide of his anger.

Garrett propped his shoulder on the wall opposite. "How bad?"

"Bad enough." Roger balled his fists before he slammed them into the wall again. "How did you know?"

Garrett shrugged. "I watch." He leaned his back to the wall and pushed a hand through his rumpled hair. "And I spend a lot of time walking these corridors at night."

"Bea kicked you out?" The taunt came as more habit than aught else.

"Aye." Garrett shoved his hands in his pockets. "We do not see my future path the same way. She sees my need to make my own way as ingratitude."

They stood for a long moment, both of them lost in their own thoughts.

"I have never wanted to kill a man more," Roger said.

"Aye." Garrett nodded. "But that will not solve the problem."

"Aye, it would." Blood lust surged through Roger. "He can't lift a hand to her again if I rip them off him and shove them up his ass."

"You are lord of Anglesea first." Garrett pushed away from the wall. "You cannot afford to kill another of the king's barons. And nobody will openly condemn what they see as a father's right to discipline his daughter."

Roger wanted to punch the wall again.

"Do not." Garrett read his mind. He chuckled, a dark, evil sound that lifted the hair on Roger's nape. "You are so full of honor and nobility it does not occur to you that there is more than one way to make a man pay."

"You can see a way to make him pay?" Roger shook his head. Garrett and his twisted mind baffled him.

"Not yet." Garrett strolled away from him. "But I shall certainly give it some thought."

"You would help me?" Roger found that hard to believe.

"Nay." Garrett spoke over his shoulder. "I would help Lady Kathryn. No woman deserves that."

Roger took the opposite direction. His conversation with Garrett had calmed him enough to ensure the safety of the wall and his bruised knuckles.

His father had raised all three boys never to raise their hand to someone weaker, particularly not a woman. At seven years, Roger had pushed Faye over some minor childish squabble. The lesson taught him that day by Sir Arthur stayed with him into adulthood. His father, by not raising a finger, had managed to convey the inherent evil in allowing violence to win over reason, and using might against a lesser opponent.

Sir Arthur had taken him and William to the river, and demanded they drown a sack full of newly born puppies. Both he and William had begged and pleaded for the lives of the mewling, squirming pups. Father had been adamant—drown them! Crying all the while, Roger had taken the sack and approached the water. Only at the point his younger self felt certain the end was nigh, did Sir Arthur stop him and sit both boys by the river bank. Strength was a gift and a responsibility, he had said. The measure of a man's strength was not in the sword he wielded or the fist he made. It lay, instead, in his judgment and his humility.

Roger strode toward the stairs. He would not sleep anymore this night. Gregory had lived for seven years with the knowledge the woman he loved suffered under her husband's hands. How the hell had he stood it? How had Gregory looked at the marks on Faye and not wanted to rip the heavens asunder?

Anglesea lay quiet and sleeping about him as he descended into the hall. All this would one day be his, and he still had insufficient power to prevent Sir Royce from beating his daughter ragged. Anger grumbled and stirred within him. Roger breathed deep to quell it. If William still lived here, he would speak with his brother. William always saw the larger scheme at play. His younger brother had the ability to push aside the haze of emotion and use his reason.

Sir Arthur sat by the hall hearth, his favorite bitch resting her head on his knee. She pricked her ears and watched Roger as he drew nearer. "Father?"

"What are you doing awake?" Father leaned his head back.

"I could ask you the same thing." Roger took the seat beside him. It seemed the men of Anglesea all stood watch through the early hours.

With a chuckle, Father poured a goblet of wine from the table beside him and handed it to Roger. "I find it hard to sleep most nights."

"Is that because you sit on your ass all day?" Roger tried to lighten his father's mood. The old man looked burdened, his powerful shoulders wore a slight stoop that had not been there ten years afore.

"Still young enough to kick your ass." Father responded as Roger knew he would, and they shared a smile. "Nay." Arthur sighed. "I am weary, Roger."

"Then sleep." He sipped his wine.

"Too weary for sleep, you arrogant young cur." Father reached out with a half-hearted cuff that missed Roger's head altogether. "Do you know I have been lord here at Anglesea since my fifteenth year?"

"Aye."

"My father passed when I was young. For a couple of years, an uncle thought to rule in my stead, but I was like you. Young, fierce, full of piss and pride and I soon disabused him of that notion."

Roger would wager his sword arm on that.

"I sit here at night and count all the wars I have fought, all the battles waged—won or lost. It presses on me." Father rubbed his nape. "Like a yoke."

"What are you saying?" This new mood unsettled Roger. His father, impregnable and solid as the walls about them, did not grow fatigued.

"Your mother has been at me again." Father sipped his wine. "She wants to see her grandchildren. I am not much for children, but what my lady wants, my lady gets."

By all the saints, you would never guess Sir Arthur was not one for children by the way he played for hours with Bea's three boys and Faye's Simon and Arthur, or dandled Bess on his knee. Roger hid his grin behind his goblet.

"It is time," Father said.

Roger stilled and stared at him. "For what?"

"This." He waved a hand about him. "I never agreed with young men waiting for their elders to die before stepping into their roles." One craggy brow lifted. "Far too many fathers have an early demise that way."

"I have no immediate plans to kill you, old man."

Father threw his head back on a guffaw. "As if you could, you puny little runt." He refilled both their goblets and sat back. He stroked his dog's head.

Firelight flickered over her brindle coat.

"What are you really about?" Roger studied his father. "What is it that you want me to do?"

"Take over." Father rubbed his nape. "Take up the yoke of Anglesea as her lord. I will not get in your way. My lady wishes to travel and spend time with Faye and William. She is even nattering a hole in my head about France." Father snorted. "France! Nothing wrong with the place other than it is filled with Frenchmen."

Baron Anglesea. That had always been his father, and now it could be him. Of course, the title would not pass to him until Sir Arthur died, but to take up the role for which he had been raised. Right before him, the possibility danced and flickered, and Roger hesitated. "Am I ready?"

"Is any man?" Father pounded the arm of his chair. "Was I ready at fifteen? God's teeth, I was not. But it is your duty, your purpose, and I am weary."

"When?"

"Once we have seen you married." So soon? "Your mother has some wriggle in her drawers about seeing you happy and settled before we go. Wants this brangle between Bea and the bastard smoothed away. But she also wants to be up north for the birth of William's second."

Baron Anglesea. The weight of his title settled about his shoulders like a heavy, fur cape—both welcome and burdensome. "I am prepared."

"Nay you are not." Father drank his wine. "But I have done my best by you and you are a lot less stupid than most who take up their duties."

High praise indeed. Roger laughed.

"Now." Father slapped his palms against his armrests. "What has you up and about in the middle of the night?"

"A woman."

Father shook his head. "Is that not always the case with us worthless bastards? I hope you are speaking of the lovely Lady Kate."

"Kathryn." The correction came unbidden to him. "She likes to be called Kathryn."

"Are you as besotted with the girl as your mother claims?"

"Probably more so."

"Good." Father upended the flagon in Roger's goblet. "And God help you with that. It has certainly played merry hell with me for all these years."

Roger weighed his next words carefully. "I need something from you."

Father raised his brow in question.

"Kathryn came to me tonight, she wanted to break the engagement."

His brow rising even higher, Father sat back.

"Sir Royce is handy with his fists, and he does not spare his womenfolk."

On a large sigh, Father stroked his dog's ears. "There are too many such."

"Aye." Roger swallowed his raw rage. "Kathryn fears for her mother if she leaves."

"Ah." Father's expression darkened, and he rested his elbows on his knees. "Son, your name will protect Kathryn, but you know I cannot intercede between a husband and wife."

"You did it for Faye."

"Faye is my daughter." His head shot up, gaze burning. "Even then it took some fancy footwork by your uncles to get the king's favor on our venture."

"I know." Roger held his ground. "I gave her my word I would protect her mother."

"Jesu, Roger." Father sprang to his feet and paced into the

open. "Why would you make such a vow? How can you possibly keep it?"

"I intend to keep it." Roger rose and met his father in mid-stride. "With or without your help, but I was hoping you could assist me in some way."

"Is nothing ever simple with my children?" Arthur stared at the ceiling and pleaded with God.

"Why would it be?" Tension coiled in Roger's gut. He had not been naive enough to expect unconditional help, but this? "Naught with this family is simple, including you. You challenged King John, and I marched with you. Knowing it could mean the end of Anglesea, of all of us." Roger stood a half-foot taller than his father now. "You went to rescue Faye, and again, I did not ask if it could be done or should be done. You called and I answered. You are my father and my liege lord. I claim your protection for my wife and her mother."

Arthur growled at him and shook his head. "Settle down, you silly sod. I did not say I would not help you, but you cannot drop something like this on a man in the middle of the night and expect him to be happy about it."

"I do not much care how you feel about it. Are you with me or not?"

"I should beat you bloody for your arrogance and imperti-nence." Sir Arthur straightened, every inch the most feared warrior in the kingdom.

"If this was Faye." Roger refused to give ground. Kathryn was his everything and he had made her a promise. A man never broke his promises, particularly not to those whom he loved. This griz-zled old warrior before him had taught him that. "If this was Faye and we had a chance to do something before matters became dire with Calder, would we not have declared damn everyone and stepped in?"

Father dropped his gaze and spun back to the fire. "That was foul tactics, son. You know I would remove every trace of a mark that whoreson put on Faye if I could."

"What if you had a chance to prevent her from being in that position in the first place? Would you not take it?"

"In a twinkling." Sir Arthur sat heavily on his chair. The dog replaced her head on his knee. She gazed at him as if she would soothe. "We need a strategy."

Roger's shoulders lifted as if suddenly relieved of a heavy burden. "You will help me?"

"You are my son," Father said. "I would do no less for you than I would for a daughter. Sir Royce is a canny one. He is not a man to let go of an advantage without gaining something in return. Sit and cool your blood. We will need more than piss and pride to see this thing done."

* * *

Sitting still across the table from Sir Royce took an act of will Roger had not known he possessed. His fingers flexed to fasten about the man's flaccid, corpulent neck and squeeze the life out of him. Beside him lounged Garrett, toying with a goblet in his upraised hand. Father had raised merry hell about the addition of Garrett, but Roger stood firm. No man knew more about a well-plotted revenge than his brother by marriage.

Garrett twisted the goblet until the gems caught the sunlight that streamed through the armory casement.

Sir Royce's coarse, wiry-haired hands lay on the table before him, his knuckles split in places. Wounds gained by beating Kathryn black and blue.

As if sensing his mood, Garrett shot him a warning glance. Never reveal your weakness to an enemy. If Sir Royce even suspected how much Kathryn meant to him, they would lose valuable ground. Then he might be forced to beat the man bloody to keep his vow. The idea held limitless appeal.

They had discussed her dowry, and the wedding portion to be bestowed on Sir Royce once the marriage was concluded. The greedy bastard preened with satisfaction as Sir Arthur conceded ground. Royce needed coin and lots of it. He'd beggared his lands over the years, and now they could no longer support him. He also sought to make up for the loss of Matty, and any future income.

Sir Arthur had a simpler need. Land. A massive swathe of some of the richest pasture to be found between Anglesea's borders and London. Land, the plans for which, already littered father's chamber. Anglesea prospered, and with that came more mouths to feed.

Garrett grew restless sitting on his ass in Anglesea and taking Sir Arthur's coin. When Henry returned, he would serve as Roger's chamberlain. But Garrett needed a challenge of his own, and the new land would provide the perfect ground in which to sink his axe.

Brutish hands rubbing together, Sir Royce made to rise.

"There is one thing." Garrett spoke for the first time. He motioned Sir Royce to be seated again. "We have some concerns."

Father stiffened.

Roger pressed Father's foot with his own beneath the table.

"Concerns?" Sir Royce frowned and took his seat.

"Mere trifles, I am sure." Garrett motioned for a serving man to refill their wine and smiled. "Women! They are always more complicated than a man anticipates."

Sir Royce waved the serving man away. "I can assure you those complications are now over."

Sir Arthur shifted in his chair, his smoldering gaze locked on Garrett. It sat ill with Father to allow Garrett any control in this situation.

Roger pressed his father's foot, harder this time. Garrett had skills Sir Arthur had never thought to make use of.

"Indeed." Garrett savored a mouthful of wine. "William would love this. We must be sure to send him a few barrels," he said to Roger before he turned back to Sir Royce. "When you first proposed a marriage, we were offered Lady Mathilda."

Sir Royce flushed. He glared at Garrett and then Sir Arthur. "Does this bastard speak for you now?"

"He speaks for me." Roger slid in smoothly before Father could speak. "I will take charge of Anglesea upon my marriage."

Garrett twisted his goblet in the sunlight. "How is Lady Mathilda?"

"She left to join the holy sisters." Sir Royce threw the remaining wine in his goblet down his throat.

"How wonderful." Sir Arthur smirked. "Neither of my daughters chose to take up the veil. You and your good lady must be prodigious proud to have such a devout daughter."

Was his father spreading the shit too thick? Roger glanced at him and then at Sir Royce.

Sir Royce's eyes glittered malice, aimed at Mathilda or Father, Roger knew not. For the first time, he caught a glimpse of the animal that lay beneath the surface. The same animal who had laid his filthy paws on Kathryn. Roger quaffed his goblet. He could not find a calm voice right now. He did not have one in him.

"Anyway." Garrett placed his elbows on the table. "For whatever reason, we had no more Mathilda. Now we have Kathryn in her stead, and my good lady and I are so looking forward to welcoming her into the family."

Sir Royce's shoulders lost a little of the tension.

"However." Garrett tapped his fingertips on the table. "Lady Beatrice has observed that Kathryn is a rather...excitable girl. We think her spirit will suit Roger admirably, but she has not the serene nature of her sister."

"Aye." Father joined the fray. "Lady Mary noted the same."

"How interesting." Garrett steepled his fingers before his mouth.

"Kate will do as she is told." Sir Royce's expression hardened.

Roger dug his hands into the bench to keep from strangling the sod. Father stomped on his foot this time.

"Of that, I have no doubt," Garrett said. "But perhaps it helps a girl to have her mother with her, at a time of such great change. A mother's wisdom and guiding hand can provide the stability to which a girl of lively disposition may look as she makes the change to wife."

Sir Royce scowled. "You want me to leave her mother here?"

"I think it is a rather splendid idea." Sir Arthur beamed at him. "We have more than enough space for her, and I am sure, Kathryn would be so much easier."

Sir Royce considered him. "Are you making this a condition of the marriage?"

Roger showed his teeth, more snarl than smile. "I am afraid that I am."

Chapter Twenty

Kathryn's stare fixed on her wedding gown and refused to move. Her mouth went suddenly dry. Her. Wedding. Gown. As in the gown she would wear to get married.

Married.

Her heart leaped into her throat.

"Oh, Lady Mary, it is lovely." Mother clasped her hands to her bosom. Tears glistened and she dabbed at them.

"I wore it the day I married Sir Arthur." Lady Mary stroked the ice-blue samite encrusted with seed pearls. Lady Mary must have looked like a faerie princess in that gown.

Kathryn stood, her feet frozen to the spot as her mother, Lady Mary, Nurse, Faye, and Beatrice all grew misty-eyed. An interloper in the land of women. When the gown brought for Matty proved too short and gaped across the bosom, Lady Mary had made the offer to gown Kathryn.

The longer she stood, the more her body hurt, and she had trouble hiding her pain from the other women. Mother would not want the other women to see the marks on her and witness their shame.

Now they all expected her to don the gown, then follow them

to the chapel where Roger waited. Sweat broke out over her skin. After today she would be Roger's bride, his wife and chattel.

"Are you all right?" Beatrice sidled up beside her.

Not in the least. Her voice escaped her in a wobbly exhalation. "Aye."

Beatrice cocked her head. "You do not look all right." She stiffened and went scarlet. "Do you need me to explain the... um...tonight."

"Nay," Kathryn near shouted. That would be beyond awkward. "Nay. I mean, I believe I understand that part." The conversation with her mother yestereve had been even more excruciating than the act her mother described. It scrambled the mind that children came into the world at all if they got here that way.

"Good." Beatrice blew out a long breath. "Because I would, but with Roger being my brother, it seems a little odd."

"What maggot are you putting in her head?" Nurse bustled over, eyes narrowed like a ferret beneath her brow-squashing wimple. "She looks pale as a ghost."

Beatrice threw her arms up. "What? She looked that way before I got here."

"Looked what way?" Faye sidled up and peered at Kathryn.

"Terrified," said Beatrice.

Nurse pressed a goblet into her hand with a wink. "Drink this."

"What is that?" Beatrice peered at the goblet.

"Never you mind." Nurse stared at Kathryn until she drained the goblet. "It is just a little something to make the day go easier."

Faye and Beatrice exchanged glances.

Mother made herself busy, gathering up mugs and bowls from their shared meal and piling them by the door.

With a clap of her hands, Lady Mary drew all attention to her. "Might I have a word with Kathryn. Alone."

"Why?" Beatrice glanced about.

"Out." Lady Mary shooed them all toward the door, Mother

included. "I will have a quiet word with Kathryn and then you can all come back and we will see her dressed."

Faye gave her a look of concern and then the door shut behind the other women.

"There now." Lady Mary walked to the bed, sat and patted for Kathryn to join her. "It can get a bit overwhelming."

"I am not frightened." Kathryn did not think her legs could move.

"Indeed." Lady Mary laid her hands in her lap. "Perhaps it would be a little more convincing if you let go your stranglehold on your chemise."

Sure enough, Kathryn had the fabric bunched in her fists. She released it and tried to smooth out the wrinkles. Before the women came to dress her, she had made sure her chemise covered all the bruises. She could not subject Mother or herself to the inevitable questions.

"Tell me what it is you fear," Lady Mary said. "I suspect it is not your wedding night."

"Nay." Kathryn's face heated. "I mean, not entirely."

"When I married Sir Arthur, I vomited three times before I got to the chapel." Lady Mary sighed. "I had never set eyes on a more handsome or strongly made man. I picked him, and organized matters to my own liking. Still, the unknown is always a bit frightening. Is it marriage itself you fear?"

She barely knew Lady Mary, and she was Roger's mother. Yet she walked to the bed and sat beside her anyway. Lady Mary had this way of freeing a girl's tongue. "Marriage does not seem to hold a lot of advantage for the woman."

"There are children," Lady Mary said. "They bring huge joy."

"Aye." Kathryn tried to organize her thoughts, because the prospect of children caused a warm glow deep within her. "And it is not that I do not want children, for I do. But it is the other parts."

"Such as?" Lady Mary adjusted the lie of her bliaut sleeves.

"Like you become his property. His to command from the day you utter your vows."

"And this bothers you?"

"Aye." Kathryn released her breath. Her head swam with the relief of voicing this. "What if I do not care to be under a man's command?"

"Ah." Lady Mary smoothed her skirts. "It seems the lot of women that we are forever beneath the command of a man. First our father, then when they grow, our brothers, and eventually our husbands. It is hard for a woman of spirit to accept."

Kathryn stared at Lady Mary, the perfect lady in every way. "Did it bother you?"

"Aye." She pressed her fingertips to her lip. "I railed against it, but deep inside where nobody could see. My father betrothed me to a man I did not care for."

"But you said the first time you saw Sir Arthur—"

"It was not Sir Arthur to whom he betrothed me. Nay, it was another altogether. Sir Arthur was in the party when my betrothed came to my father's castle. I decided he would be the one I would marry, and I set about to make it so."

"How?"

Lady Mary blushed and patted her hand. "That is a story for another day, when we know each other a bit better. My point is that a woman of intelligence and will is never truly with no power over her fate. There are times when we have to use guile to gain our way, but there are ways. One of those ways lies in making a good choice of husband, and you have made the very best choice of husbands."

Of course Lady Mary would think thus.

Lady Mary laughed. "You are thinking I only say so because Roger is my son, and you are right. I had the raising of that man, and I raised him to adore women, respect and cherish them. You will not be some meaningless piece in a larger game to Roger."

Kathryn let her words sink in. Roger often asked her opinion on this matter or that. Even when wroth with her, he did not raise a hand to her.

"And if he does not treat you well, you come and see his mother. I will set him to rights." Lady Mary smoothed a lock of Kathryn's hair behind her shoulder. "Your marriage will be what you make of it, Kathryn. You will enter it as Roger's wife and partner, as his helpmate and his support. It is up to you what you do with that."

* * *

Roger forgot how to breathe.

Gliding into the chapel, candlelight catching her gown in myriad starbursts, Kathryn looked like an angel. Unbound hair streamed about her shoulders like poured treacle.

He hoped he didn't wear the idiotic grin inside him on his face.

His! Almost his. After the priest pronounced them wed, he would still have to win her. His lady came reluctantly to wife, frightened by the idea because of the smug whoreson who led her down the aisle.

Behind Roger, William cleared his throat. His brother had arrived with his new wife late yestereve, in time to stand up with him.

"You are a lucky dog," William whispered.

Roger grinned back at him. He most certainly was at that.

Cold to the touch, Kathryn placed her hand in his.

Tightening his grip about her icy fingers, he attempted to infuse some warmth into them. Never again would Royce have the power to hurt this woman.

The rest of the ceremony passed in a blur of Latin, and incense. Words exchanged, vows made that bound her to him. All his attention remained focused on the woman by his side. His bride.

After the service, he led her to the hall where a large banquet awaited them.

"You look beautiful," he whispered in her ear.

She gifted him a tight smile. "So do you. And it is your mother's gown."

"Mine is too."

She stopped. Then she giggled.

Not much of a laugh, but enough to encourage Roger. "I want to make you known to my brother, William."

"Is he the handsome one?"

"Nay." He affected a stern expression. "He is the tolerable one. I am the handsome brother."

"Ah." Color bled into her wan cheeks. "How foolish of me to forget."

"Would you like to meet him?"

"Aye." She peered past him at William. "Is that his wife? The lady with the red hair."

"Aye, that is Lady Alice."

She studied Alice for a long moment. "She is not what I would have expected for him."

"Perhaps not." Roger's sister by marriage tucked her tiny self into William. "But she makes him very happy, and he loves her."

"I can see that." Kathryn sighed.

Should he confess his love? He kept it to himself for fear of driving Kathryn even further into her shell. Every instinct warned to go slowly with his new bride. Woo her gently and carefully, one step at a time. Skittish like an unbroken filly, Kathryn might bolt at any moment. "They are expecting their second child."

Kathryn cocked her head, gaze still on Alice. "She is not pretty, precisely, but there is something about her that draws you to her."

"Wait," Roger said. "In time, Alice will grow to be lovelier and lovelier each time you see her."

"Hmm." She poked at their shared trencher. "I wish Matty were here."

"I beg your pardon?" Roger stilled, not certain what she meant.

Kathryn gasped and looked at him. "Not in that way." She crinkled her nose. "Not in my place, but by my side. Matty and I are close in age and this is the first time she was not with me for an important day in my life."

"Ah." Some of the tension crept out of his shoulders. "Come." He rose and offered her his hand. "Let me take you to meet William. He is guaranteed to bring a smile to anyone's lips."

Would that he could make her smile today, but his Kathryn had retreated. Roger wanted her back.

"Lady Kathryn." William stood as they approached. "Let me say what everybody is thinking." Mischief lit William's blue eyes. "You are far too good for Roger."

Kathryn laughed, and it warmed the cold place within him. This pale, silent ghost of Kathryn disturbed him.

Lady Alice let out a loud snort and came to stand beside Sir William. She barely reached William's shoulder. Mismatched, but still a perfect couple within their differences. "And let me tell you never to listen to William."

"I married a shrew." William winked at her. "I pray my brother did not."

Lady Alice smacked him on the arm, and he grinned at her. "Would you be terribly waspish if I took the bride to dance?"

"Nay," Lady Alice smiled back at him, and waved her hand over her huge belly. "I would be relieved, as my dancing days are clearly done for now."

"Lady Kathryn?" William held out his hand.

For a moment, Roger thought she might refuse William. But his brother was a clever man with women, and he grasped her fingers and led her to the center of the hall where the dancing commenced.

As if the men of Anglesea sensed her mood, William's place was taken over by Garrett—who made up for his lack of skill with enthusiasm. Sir Arthur followed Garrett, until Gregory relieved him.

Roger sat, content to watch her brittle demeanor melt and disappear altogether. Until he saw her grimace as the reel grew more boisterous. She made so little of her hurts, nobody in the hall would even guess what she concealed beneath that gown. A fierce wave of protectiveness shook him.

Into the churning bodies he charged, ignoring all overtures to join them.

"Come." He placed a gentle hand on her waist. "You are still injured."

"But it is the reel," she whispered back at him. "I do so enjoy dancing."

"Then I will have the minstrels play for you every night until you tire of it. For now, however, I must insist you sit."

Over her head, Gregory's sin-dark gaze tracked their conversation. He raised a questioning brow at Roger.

Roger shook his head. Not now. He would speak with Gregory later. If anyone would understand the overwhelming urge to protect his woman, Gregory would.

"I will ply you with strong drink, instead," Roger said.

"Good." Kathryn grinned at him, and he thought his heart might burst. Not the shy, polite smiles of earlier, nor the restrained smiles he had received since they had entered Calder, but a large, genuine beam of Kathryn as she was in the woods. His Kathryn.

Securing her arm in his, he led her to the table, and made good on his promise. Careful not to let her get too drunk. He had plans for his lady that did not include tucking her snoring self into bed.

* * *

A gaggle of chattering women swept Kathryn up the stairs to the baron's chamber.

Lady Mary and Sir Arthur had announced they would travel north with William and Alice to await the birth of their child. In all but name, Roger was now baron and Lady Mary insisted he took this chamber.

"You had everything changed." Beatrice entered first, and stopped in the doorway to speak with Lady Mary.

Lady Mary made an elegant sweeping gesture. "Indeed I did. A new day begins at Anglesea." She placed her arm about Kathryn's waist and led her into the chamber. "You may change anything you do not like."

Kathryn had not seen the chamber before, but this was too fine. Heavily embroidered bed curtains of deep blue swathed a bed large enough to accommodate all the women with her and more besides. Two large carved wooden chairs rested before the hearth with more cushions to ease the ache of hard wood from a person's ass. A cheery blaze filled the hearth and sent patterns dancing over the fine wood patina of the surrounding mantle. A beautiful room, richly appointed and ready to house a baron and his lady.

Kathryn walked to the double casement and parted the coverings. The Baron's chamber faced the sea. From here she had an eye-aching view of long, lazy ocean that stretched to meet a darkening sky. Beneath her, warm fur rugs kept the chill from the stones off her feet.

"Is that Roger?" Beatrice's voice pulled her away from the view.

Faye, Beatrice, and Lady Mary stood before a large tapestry that adorned the far wall.

"It is a knight who may or may not be Roger," Lady Mary said.

Beside the dark-haired knight stood a lady, who happened to have hair Kathryn's color.

"Roger will hate that," said Beatrice.

"Roger needs to accustom himself to his new position." Lady

Mary turned and spotted her. "But we are here for more important matters right now."

As to those matters, Kathryn would admit to a slight flutter of nerves. There would be kissing, which she really liked, and Roger had promised a whole lot more, which she had no idea about. The wine she had consumed at dinner went a long way to alleviating any nerves.

"I always thought this part was rather barbaric." Faye gave her a sympathetic grimace as she held out a linen nightrail so fine the firelight shone through it.

"That is because you married a pig the first time." Beatrice bustled to the bed with an armload of flowers. "And my brother may have many faults but he is not a pig, a lout, or a boor."

Nurse stomped through the door, red-faced and panting from her climb up the stairs. "Right!" She rubbed her hands together. "You lot." She jabbed a pudgy finger at Faye, Beatrice, and Alice. "Need to go and keep your husbands out of trouble."

Beatrice stuck her hip out. "But the wedding chamber isn't ready."

Nurse exchanged a speaking glance with Lady Mary.

"Sweet Bea." Lady Mary cupped her daughter's chin. "Kathryn is shy, let us not make this hard for her. You can come back in a moment."

Lady Alice tucked her arm through Beatrice's. "Come along." She threw her much taller sister by marriage a naughty grin. "It will give you five minutes to tell me how I mistreat your brother."

"You two." Faye rolled her eyes. She walked to Kathryn and kissed both cheeks. "Welcome to the family, dear Kathryn. Trust my idiot brother. He will take good care of you."

Nurse took the nightrail from Faye and herded her out. She leaned her back against the closed door. "I came as fast as I could. I did not think you would want them to see."

"Nurse?" Lady Mary latched the door. "What is this about?"

Nurse took Kathryn's hand, her gaze steady and reassuring. "You can trust my Mary. And she needs to know."

"I..." Kathryn took a step away from Nurse. She needed the distance to order her thoughts. Her bruises, her secret shame. She could not bear the looks of horror and pity.

Nurse followed her. "Shall I send her away, too?"

The idea of anyone sending Lady Mary away made Kathryn smile. In her gentle way, Lady Mary wielded a will of steel.

"If you are more comfortable with me leaving, I can go." Lady Mary stood, hands folded before her. "I could send your mother."

"Nay." Mother had left the feast early to rest. With Father still in the hall, his hand up some woman's skirt, Kathryn did not want to interrupt her peace. "It is just that..." The words wouldn't come and she turned to the casement. Brisk sea air cooled her cheeks.

"I will go," Lady Mary said.

"Nay." Kathryn sensed Nurse and Lady Mary were women she could rely on. In the days to come, she would have need of them. "Beneath my chemise. It is not pretty."

Lady Mary walked closer to her. "This is more than being modest, is it not?"

"Royce beat her." Nurse stiffened. "He left his mark all over her."

Kathryn took another bracing breath of sea air. She walked to where Nurse stood and turned her back.

Nurse made short work of the lacings.

Her bliaut pooled at her feet like flowing silver, and Nurse picked it up and lay it over the clothes tree. Next came her chemise. For a moment, white silk enshrouded her before Nurse took that away as well. Kathryn turned to face Lady Mary.

"Oh, Kathryn." Lady Mary pressed her hand to her mouth. "Did you not want to marry this much? You should have told me this morning, I did not—"

"It was not that."

Nurse slipped the nightrail over her head.

With her linen armor in place, Kathryn drew breath again. "My father thinks I know where Matty is," she said.

After removing the flower circlet, Nurse brushed her hair gently, mindful of the bruises on her back.

Lady Mary smoothed her skirts with shaking hands. "This is why you insisted your mother remain with us."

"Aye."

Nurse brought her a silk bed robe the same blue as Roger's eyes. She fussed with the folds and stepped back. "You are ready."

"Does Roger know?" Lady Mary stood beside Nurse.

"He knows," Nurse said.

Lady Mary took her hands. "Know this. From this day forth you have the might of Anglesea at your back. You are one of us, and we protect what is ours."

Tears clogged Kathryn's throat. A feeling unlike any other filled her. A feeling so unfamiliar she did not know what to name it, but it filled her near to bursting.

"Do not make her cry." Nurse elbowed Lady Mary. "Let us let the others in so we can finish getting the chamber ready."

Chapter Twenty-One

K athryn turned a slow circle. Alone in her wedding chamber.

Garlands tied with white ribbons fluttered from the top of the bed and draped over the open casement shutters. A platter of wine, fruits, cakes, and cheeses rested on the low table between the hearth chairs. Beatrice had scattered more flowers about the bed and the floor. Nurse had scented the pillows with lavender drops, and placed a honey cake beneath each one. Beside the bed rested a flagon of bride's broth.

Kathryn poured the potent brew into a heavily ornamented chalice. Mead, honey, and herbs hit her stomach with a wallop. A chalice or two of this and no bride would fear her wedding night.

Tugging the robe around her, she went back to the view. Mandeville lay inland, and she could quickly grow accustomed to the bounty outside her Anglesea casement. The sea had no fetters, no confines and no master. From here, all things seemed possible in a world larger than she had ever imagined.

Lady Mary's promise made her feel valued. For the first time in her life, she really mattered.

In all her imaginings of how it would be when she wriggled free of her father's grip about her life, marriage had never formed part of that. Yet, here she stood. Evening breezes carried the briny tang of the ocean up to her, and she drew it deep into her lungs. Life spread before her, new and unexplored, and completely uncharted. Matty, cozy with her farmer, and clear of their father's anger. Mother safe with her at Anglesea. And her future?

Kathryn leaned her head against the casement side. A lone gull winged back to the towering cliffs that fell away in a sheer drop beneath her. Its plaintive cry hung in the evening.

"Such deep thoughts." Roger's voice startled her. Large hands cupped her shoulders, slid down her arms and around her middle. He drew her back against him. "It is beautiful, is it not?"

"Aye." Kathryn rested against his warm strength.

"I grew up here, saw this every day and I never get tired of it." His chuckle hummed through her back. "Of course, my father saved the best view for himself."

They stayed in their simple embrace, breath drawing in and out in silent companionship, until the first stars winked awake and the night breeze bore a slight chill.

Kathryn shivered.

"Come." Roger drew her back from the casement. "Let us sit by the fire for a moment."

"Is this you putting me at my ease?" Kathryn accepted a goblet of wine from him, and took one of the carved chairs.

He poured himself wine with a wry grin. "Clearly, I am not too good at it."

"I am not afeared," she said. "And I think you are doing very well."

"My thanks." He toasted her with his goblet and propped a shoulder against the mantle. "I must confess to being at a loss how to proceed from here. I could simply hoist you over my shoulder and toss you on the bed."

Fool! Kathryn laughed and shook her head. "I would probably fight you."

"There is that." He grimaced and sipped his wine. "What do you suggest?"

Kathryn gave it some thought. They might as well begin at the part she liked. "You might begin by kissing me."

"An interesting notion." He stroked his cheek and frowned. "Why should we start there?"

His playful mood took any lingering trepidation away. "I believe it to be a good place to start."

"And why is that?"

"Because it is the part I like best."

"I am glad to hear it." His warm look caressed her. "How would you suggest I go about this kissing business?"

"Well." Kathryn held out her hands. "It might be best to make sure the target of your kissing was standing."

"So true." He took her hands and pulled her closer until his chest halted her forward movement. "And now what?"

"Now bring your head closer."

"Like so?" He bent until his mouth lay a mere breath away from hers. His voice roughened. "And then what?"

Her blood rose to meet the heated challenge in him, and it seemed easier to show him. Kathryn pressed her lips briefly against his. "Then you kiss me."

"And what do you do?" His lids hooded his eyes.

"I put my arms about your shoulders." She showed him. "Like so. And you put your arms about my waist."

"Tell me if I hurt you." He slid his arms gingerly about her.

"If I promise to tell you that, then you must promise not to be overly concerned about doing so."

"This I cannot promise." He sucked on her bottom lip and released it. "You are my lady now. Mine to nurture and protect. Shielding you from hurt has become my life's work."

Kathryn rose onto her toes and copied him, sucking his fuller bottom lip between hers. "And what has my life work become?"

He kissed the corner of her mouth. "Why do we not begin in this chamber and discover the rest as we go along."

Her breath came a little faster as Roger applied himself to the business of kissing her. More like taking ownership of her mouth.

Gentle pressure at her hips kept her flush against him while his kiss pulled her deeper and deeper into a heavy warmth.

His rod pressed against her belly, hard and demanding, and yet he kept his kiss gentle.

Kathryn learned from the motions of his lips and tongue, and sought to imitate him. She wanted to wrap him in the same heat that enveloped her. He had an essence, a taste uniquely his: cinnamon, sharp berries, and mint. It awoke a craving in her.

He broke away from her mouth. "Kathryn," he murmured. Trailing his lips to her jaw he pressed them against the pounding pulse in her throat. "My Kathryn."

His Kathryn? Aye, she was that.

His mouth moved hot down her neck. He buried his nose where her shoulder and neck met, and drew in a deep breath of her. His mouth continued its exploration. Her robe slid and Roger's lips burned against her exposed shoulder.

"What have we here?" The neck tie for her chemise dangled between his long fingers. "And what do you suppose it does?"

One pull and it would fall, leaving her exposed. Now her nerves made an appearance in a great big roar. She would be exposed to his gaze, naked and vulnerable. Would he like what he saw? "Roger, I..."

A half smile played around his mouth. "You are right, of course. It is rude of me to stand here still clothed."

First he pulled his tunic and then his chemise from him, and dropped them on the floor.

He was beautiful, male and fully formed in a thrilling melding of muscle and sinew. She had seen his chest before, but not so close. He differed from her in so many ways. She wanted to touch and see if his skin felt as hers did, or would it be rougher.

Hair spread between the raised slabs of his chest muscle and arrowed down the ridges of his belly, disappearing beneath his braies. With this body he would honor her, as she would cleave to him. Tonight they would become one flesh, and his body would be hers. His powerful male form, a warrior's body, and all hers.

She touched a small, blob-shaped scar across his ribs. "What is this from?"

"That would be William's first attempts at archery." Head bent to watch her touch him. His glance dared her to explore further.

Kathryn trailed her fingers down his flat, hard belly.

Roger sucked in a breath, the muscles tensing beneath her fingers.

She traced a diagonal scar running over the ridges of muscle. "This one."

"I did not get my shield up in time."

"Hmm." Smooth, silky and so warm his skin made her fingertips tingle. She trailed up the ladder of muscle on his belly to beneath his nipple, and stroked a raised, crescent-shaped scar. "And this?"

His breath came loud. He tensed beneath her touch. "A dagger I should have ducked."

A four-inch scar marred the perfection of his chest and Kathryn traced it. "This is very close to your heart."

"Too close." His voice took on a raspy note.

Emboldened, Kathryn traced the ridge of bone above his chest to his shoulder. Powerful muscle bunched beneath her fingers as she stroked his upper arm. She opened her fingers full width and still did not cover it all. "You are very strong."

"Right now, I am weaker than a kitten." A soft groan followed his words.

"Indeed?" She followed a thick, veined ridge to his forearm, and then journeyed back the way she had come. "Did you have too much wine at dinner?"

"Nay." His chest rose and fell on a deep breath. As she ghosted her fingers over them and down his chest, his nipples pebbled. "I have an inquisitive wench driving me out of my mind."

"Shall I stop?"

He growled and his hands tightened about her hips.

Kathryn giggled. She did this to him, and it was headier than the bride's broth. She did what he had done to her and placed her nose in the crook of his neck. Wood, leather, and musk, he smelled of Roger, and it stirred something deep in her belly. Following the strong column of his neck, she trailed her nose to beneath his chin, and risked a soft kiss to the pulse pounding beneath.

Her busy fingers stopped at his chausses. "What do you suppose I will find here?"

On a half-groan, half-laugh, he shook his head. "A mighty sword."

"Mighty?" Her laugh sounded wanton, thrilling. She undid his belt and dropped it to the floor. "I am sure all the knights say that."

"Knaves and liars. The lot of them." He clenched his jaw and dropped his head back.

Kathryn pressed her lips to his exposed throat. Then she pushed his chausses from his hips.

He exhaled harshly. "You issue a challenge, my lady."

Aye, and she rather liked it. Still, she lacked the courage to take her game further. Instead, Kathryn pressed more kisses along the straight edge of his jaw. She stopped at his mouth.

His stare burned into her, demanding she kiss him. Heart beating hard at her daring, Kathryn stood on her toes and kissed him. She swept her tongue between his parted lips to claim him as he had her.

With a groan that rumbled right through her, Roger wrested the kiss from her grasp. Kissing her until her breath ran out, and until she could no longer think past the taste of him, past the thrilling duel of his tongue with hers.

He pulled away from her, chest heaving as if he had run miles. "Now." He tugged on the ties to her chemise. "We are more than evenly matched."

Silk slithered over her sensitive skin on its path to the floor. It snagged for a moment on her sensitive nipples as it passed.

Roger stilled. His expression hardened.

Suddenly chilled, Kathryn drew her hands up to shield herself.

"Nay." He gentled and brushed her hands aside. "Never hide from me. You are beautiful. It is not that." Large, splayed fingers touched her skin. "Until now, I had not seen all of it."

Her bruises. Kathryn tried to bend and tug her chemise over herself again.

Roger raised her, then swung her into his arms. "There will be no hiding from me, my lady." He lay her on the bed, and came down beside her. With infinite care he made a thorough inspection of every mark on her trunk. Touching her lightly so as not to hurt her, he traced each bruise, welt, and mark.

His careful touch awakened a deeper need for him. One that went past the base urge to couple, and made her need to experience the desire between them.

Firelight played over the harsh planes of his face as he kept his gaze on his work.

"It does not hurt so much now," Kathryn said. The sensual mood of earlier had been overtaken by a tenderness that wriggled beneath her chest and made a warm place in her heart.

"I am the worst sort of lout to foist myself on you when you are wounded," he said.

"Nay, you are not." A lout would have taken from her what was his right by marriage. Instead Roger touched her as if he would commit each damaged place to memory. "And I wanted you to. I want you to."

"Kathryn." He cupped her cheeks and pressed his forehead to hers. "Bedding is a lusty, lively business."

"Then do it gently." She wrapped her arms about his neck and kissed him. "But make me your wife. Now. This night."

Indecision held him still.

Kathryn took matters into her own hands, kissing him with all the ferocity she could muster. Imparting with her kiss the message that he would not hear.

On a groan, Roger dropped onto his back, bringing her atop him. "If you insist, my lady." With a smug grin, he dropped his arms to the bed. "You may have your way with me."

Being atop him gave her the command. His big, beautiful form spread beneath her. Her breasts pressed into his chest in the most delicious manner. At her thigh juncture, his rod pressed hard and hot against her. Kathryn wriggled.

Roger shut his eyes and swore. Large hands spread over her bottom and held her still. He moved her against him, igniting a low burn in her woman's place. "Like this."

Sensation clouded her thinking, originating at the slow glide of his rod against her core.

Over her ass he slid his hand, and between her thighs.

Nobody had ever touched her there, and Kathryn gasped.

He parted the damp folds and slid his finger along. "Feel how wet you are," he whispered. "This tells me how much you want me."

"It does?" Kathryn ground down until she found the perfect press on a spot that demanded more attention.

"This is how you ready yourself for me."

She gasped as he slid a finger inside her. Shocked, she stilled and accustomed herself to the strange invasion. Not unpleasant, but peculiar and new.

Moving slowly, he allowed her time for the feeling to become enjoyable. "Aye, Kathryn," he murmured.

Heat built again inside her, driven by the dual attack on her senses of his finger inside her, and his rod rubbing her where she ached.

Another finger joined the first, filling her to slight discomfort before her body eased the passage.

"Sit up." His voice growled in her ear.

Kathryn obeyed.

He lay beneath her thighs like a beautiful carnal offering. With his hands firm on her hips, he raised her slightly.

His organ nudged her entrance, and she tensed.

Roger grimaced and lifted his hips while bringing her down onto him.

"It will not fit." Kathryn dug her nails into his chest.

"Aye, sweeting, it will." He eased a little more inside her.

It stung for a moment and then she stretched to accommodate his girth a bit more.

Sinew stood out in his throat from his clenched jaw. He slid further inside her. Sweat beaded on his forehead. "Be easy, sweetheart. Let me in."

For her, he kept command of his baser instincts, and Kathryn breathed deep and pressed his rod deeper within her. Her maidenhead ripped with a slight tearing sensation, but nothing close to what her mother had described. Inch by inch they went until he was fully seated within her.

He filled her in the wickedest of ways, and she rested atop him a moment and grew accustomed to him.

"Now you move." Roger showed her how with his grip on her hips.

Uncomfortable at first, Kathryn moved on him as directed.

He brought one hand to the place between her legs that still throbbed. That was what she needed, and she moved faster, racing for something her body craved.

Roger flexed his hips in time with hers.

Faster, deeper she moved on him, her being intent on him within her and where he touched her.

"Dear God, Kathryn." The taut ferocity of his face reflected her struggle. He needed the same thing she did. Sweat slicked his trunk to gleaming, flexing muscle. "Come for me, sweeting."

She had no idea what that meant, but she writhed on him, desperate to reach the end.

Her completion rose in a rush. Sweeping her along its path and tossing her over the edge into a throbbing, sated stillness.

Beneath her Roger thrust hard inside her, and then on a shout he tensed, his hands digging into her thighs.

Time stilled, and there was just her and Roger in a perfect joining of man and wife.

Kathryn collapsed against his chest, her breathing harsh, her heart racing.

In the still that followed, everything dropped away but them. She pressed into his chest, connected to him in a manner that touched every part of her.

After a time, he eased her to lie beside him with her head on his chest. His big arm wrapped about her waist and kept her close to him. "Are you well?"

"Aye." Kathryn burrowed into his warmth. Her heart slowed in time with the strong beat of his beneath her ear. She felt altered, complete, as if in this moment they had ceased to be separate beings. "But I am a little hungry."

Chapter Twenty-Two

Roger left Kathryn snuggled beneath the linens and clutching a pillow. Her hair snarled about her head in an unholy mess, but he would be back to help her untangle it before she awoke.

This wouldn't take long, but he could not rest until he acted. All night he had lain awake, committing every bruise and mark on her beautiful skin to memory. He was a knight, a warrior, a man of action, and his nature demanded its due.

He dressed and let himself out of their bedchamber. The first touch of sun made roseate streaks across a lightening sky. Within Roger, the weather raged from storm to tempest.

Rob, his father's youngest page, headed down the passage toward him with a welcoming grin on his freckled face. He started and faltered as he stared at Roger.

"Good morrow." Roger tried to arrange his features into more reassuring lines. "Have you seen Sir Royce?"

"Aye, my lord." Rob skirted him, keeping as much distance as he could between them. "I saw him in the stables a moment ago."

"My thanks." Roger quickened his pace.

Early morning chill still clung to the bailey as Roger strode across it. Two kitchen drudges staggered from the well with the massive black cauldron that would provide warm water to the keep. Roger waited impatiently whilst a goatherd moved his small flock out of the bailey to graze outside the walls. He wanted to run his quarry to ground before too many inquisitive eyes were about.

The rich, pungent smell of horse met him as he entered the stables. A soft whicker of greeting came from his favorite destrier. Roger would make it up to him with a greeting later. Beneath his feet, straw muffled his boot heels as he followed the murmur of voices deep within.

"Did you feed him the oats, as I instructed you?" Fabric straining over his gut, Sir Royce attempted to browbeat a stable boy.

Peter stood his ground, chin raised. "We did not receive that instruction, my lord. But if you would like me to add more oats to his feed—"

"Are you calling me a liar?" Sir Royce shoved Peter's shoulder.

It seemed Sir Royce did not confine himself to bullying women. Anybody in a weaker position would do. Roger's blood surged.

Peter caught sight of Roger, and nodded. "Nay, Sir Royce. I did not say you did not give the instruction. I said I did not receive it."

"Is this how you treat a guest at Anglesea? With impudence? I shall speak to Sir Arthur about this."

Sir Arthur did not treat his people as insects beneath his feet. They knew their place and their value.

"You are free to do so, Sir Royce. I will tell him the same thing I am telling you." Peter smirked and straightened his tunic. "Or better yet, tell Sir Roger. He is standing right behind you."

Sir Royce whirled, and flushed. "Ah, Roger, my lad."

Cold, deadly, the predator within him howled for blood. "Sir Royce."

He clapped Roger on the arm, and winked. "You are up early,

lad. And the stable is not where I would expect a newly married man to be."

"Nay," Roger said. "You can be about your work, Peter. I will sort this out."

"Thank you, my lord." Peter gave Sir Royce a respectful nod in passing. He grabbed his bucket from where it lay outside the stall and strolled into the main part of the stable.

Roger waited until Peter's footsteps blended with the gentle sounds of the stables. He motioned Sir Royce into an empty stall. "I would have a word with you."

Sir Royce thrust his shoulders back. "If Kathryn has displeased you in some manner, I will deal with her. But you should know, lad, I will not take her back."

"Nay, you will not." Roger stepped closer, crowding the man back into the stall. "You will not go near her again."

"Wha—" Sir Royce's words died in his throat, courtesy of Roger's hand about it.

The older man was shorter than him, but thick through the waist. Roger tightened his grip and slammed him into the back wall. Only his age protected him from Roger's fist.

Turning purple, Sir Royce stared.

Roger lifted him until his toes brushed the floor. "I saw what you did to my wife." He leaned close to Sir Royce's ear. "I counted each mark on her."

Sir Royce choked, his mouth working soundlessly.

"You miserable, cowardly piece of horse dung. Does it make you feel like a man to hurt women and children?" He slammed Sir Royce's head into the wall. "Do you think it makes you strong to raise your hand to those who cannot fight back." *Slam.* "I fight back, Sir Royce, and if you ever come near Kathryn again, I will rip your sodding head off and piss down your neck. Your welcome at Anglesea is over."

He opened his hand and stepped back.

Sir Royce dropped to the floor like a stone. He clasped his throat gagging and sucking in air.

"Lady Rose stays here."

* * *

Light prickling behind her eyelids woke Kathryn. She burrowed deeper into the pillow.

"Will you sleep the day away?" Roger's voice penetrated her sleepy fog and she opened her eyes.

He sprawled beside her on the bed, already clothed, his head propped on his hand. He smelled of crisp morning air and…the stables? Had he been riding?

Kathryn pulled the covers over her head to hide her blush. The things they had done last night fanned her flaming cheeks hotter.

"Nay, my lady." The bedclothes muffled Roger's voice. Then they were ripped out of her hands.

Kathryn shrieked and made a grab for them. The cold of the room stung her warm, naked flesh.

Roger, the tormenting cur, laughed and tossed the covers to the floor. He paused, and surveyed her with a wicked glint.

She knew what that look meant, and her blood stirred.

"I am rethinking my plan for our day." Roger spread his hand over her belly. "I had planned a day out of doors."

If it meant more time beneath the covers, Kathryn fully supported the notion. Making sure to put an extra arch in her back, she stretched her arms above her.

His gaze went straight to her upthrust breasts. "Woman." Roger slid his hand up to cup her breast and stopped. "I see your evil plan to lure me back to bed."

"Is it working?" Kathryn blew a strand of hair out of her face.

Roger's jaw clenched, his gaze hot on her nakedness. "Nay." He shoved his hands into his belt. "I will not be turned from my course."

"Are you sure?" Kathryn rose to her knees and moved toward him.

"Nay." Roger hauled his chemise off and tossed it aside. "I am not at all sure." Grabbing her by the hips, he pressed her back onto the bed. "You asked for this, wench."

"Indeed, I did." Kathryn wrapped her arms about his neck. "Now what are you going to do about it?"

"Why, my lady." Roger leered at her. "I am going to honor my lady's wishes."

"Get on with it then."

"Brazen." Roger bit her shoulder, and settled his hips between her thighs.

His hard rod pressed against her woman's place, and Kathryn writhed beneath him. "I am now."

"Now." His hot gaze caressed her breasts, her belly and the place between her thighs that already responded to him. "Where to begin?"

Roger's plan for their day seemed abandoned, as he made love to her with slow, sure languor. Wringing pleasure from her until he reduced her to a sobbing, begging mound of need in his arms.

After, he flung himself onto his back beside her, his breath coming hard.

Kathryn lay her head on his chest, and his arm came about her to keep her close. His palm drifted lower, caressed her bottom.

It appeared Kathryn enjoyed the kissing as much as ever, but she craved what it led to.

Roger stirred and patted her ass. "Come, your plan has failed. I am resolved."

"All right, then." Kathryn rolled to her feet beside the bed. She did not mind so much, now.

They helped each other dress, and Roger led her out of the keep.

In the bailey, his destrier and Striker stood ready.

Dagger leaped up and charged over to her, tail whipping his body from side to side.

Kathryn crouched and ruffled his fur, letting him know she was as pleased to see him.

"He has been causing havoc with the hunting hounds," Roger said. "I thought they could do with a break from him for the day."

"And this is your consuming quest?" Kathryn couldn't resist returning his smile. Wind ruffling his hair, wearing a broad smile, Roger looked younger and more carefree than she had ever seen him.

"I thought you might need a break for the day, as well." He cupped his hand for her to mount. "Before you know it my mother and sisters will be awake and then you will be fair game."

Striker stamped as she mounted. He fought the rein to be going.

Roger led them through the outer bailey and into the meadow beyond. Through a beech thicket, the branches already bustling and thick with life, they meandered and emerged on the outskirts of the village of Anglesea. Unlike Mandeville, Anglesea teemed with life. Villagers called out a greeting to Roger. A group of children stopped playing and openly stared at her. Kathryn waved, and was paid back in smiles and nods. A couple calls of "welcome, my lady" dispelled her lingering shyness. Neat, thatched cottages lined a central road that led past the church green and through huge sand dunes covered in wispy fronds of grass.

Dunes gave way to rough, pebbled beach. Here, the sea breeze pulled at her hair and flapped her skirts about her ankles. Pipers strutted up and down amongst the pebbles, dipping their beaks for food.

"Where are we going?" She had to shout against the wind carrying her words away.

Roger turned and grinned. "To a secret place."

Closer to the water's edge, the pebbles gave way to firm sand, and Roger dug his heels into his horse's flanks.

This was more like it. With a whoop that would have made her mother stare, Kathryn took off after him.

Striker stretched his long legs into a gallop. Beside her Dagger barked and ran, ears back, tongue lolling. Kathryn knew how he felt. She dropped her head close to Striker's neck. His mane tickled her face. Freedom. It drummed through her body with every beat of her heart, it rushed beneath her skin. Her laughter tore free and was snatched away by the wind and borne out over the sea.

Inside, the tight knot of her emotions unfurled and was whipped away and pounded into the ground beneath Striker's hooves. Until the weight lifted, she had no idea she was wound so tight. Matty, marriage, being a baroness all got left far behind the galloping horses. Like this, she was just Kathryn, with a handsome, wild man who made her heart beat faster.

Roger slowed his horse to a canter, and then into a walk. Both horses blew hard, and Dagger dropped into the wet sand, panting.

Roger turned to her with a boyish grin.

Their gazes met in a silent communion. They had both needed the release.

From the beach, Roger followed a small footpath over the dunes, and through a thicket that opened onto a large, wild meadow. Spring flowers lifted their colorful heads between the dancing blades of fresh, new grass. Above her stretched a clear sky, which housed the gentle morning sun.

Meadowlarks sang out from trees dotted about the meadow edges. A flock of robins darted past, busily chattering and paying them no heed as the horses brushed through the high grass. At the far end of the meadow, they entered a wood. Giant birches rose to shade them, new leaves quivering in the breeze.

The woods lay quiet after the meadow, hooves muffled by the leaf strewn damp ground. "What is this place?" Kathryn whispered. It seemed wrong to break the serene still with loud noise.

"These woods are believed to be ancient," Roger said. Rising up between the birches, aged oak trees spread their gnarled and twisted branches. "Anglesea folk say they are haunted by the spirits of the old ones."

"The old ones?" Kathryn glanced about her. She did not

believe in ghosts, but if she did, this would be the sort of place they would dwell.

"People from long ago." Roger stared at the thick tree canopy. "Folk who practiced all sorts of strange and lost magic. They believed the oak sacred, the king of trees."

"They certainly are big." Kathryn twisted in her saddle as they passed an oak whose trunk was thicker than three, nay, four of her. "Do you believe these woods are haunted?"

"Nay." Roger tossed her a grin. "And William, Henry and I certainly spent enough time here as lads trying to see a ghost."

"Henry is your younger brother?"

"Aye." Roger's expression grew serious. "He has gone on holy pilgrimage. We can only pray the sodding fool comes back in one piece."

Not knowing what to say to that, Kathryn kept her peace.

"See that tree?" Roger pointed to a large birch, the trunk nearly smooth. "We tied Bea to that tree one day because she followed us into our woods."

"What did she do?" The Lady Beatrice Kathryn had met would never have taken kindly to that.

"She told my father, and we were clearing the midden for weeks after that." Roger threw back his head and laughed. "And she hid all our boots, so we had to do it barefoot. Father said it served us right."

His clear love for his family made her heart ache a little for Matty. Not that they were ever permitted to play wild or unruly games, but since they could walk, it had been her and Matty. A brother might have been nice.

"Not much longer now." Roger dismounted and led his horse.

Dagger burst out of a patch of undergrowth he had been carefully examining, and wagged his tail.

Roger held his arms out and Kathryn dropped into them.

Warm and hard, his chest pressed against her as she slid to the ground. A few short weeks ago, she would have scoffed at the notion of accepting help to dismount. Now she could see the clear advantages. "Will I like this place?"

"I do." Roger held her to him, his hands on her hips. "I regard it as my secret place. Of course, so do my brothers, but they're not here now."

Hands clasped, leading their horses they wound through the trees until they came upon a stream. Roger tied his horse to a fallen log, leaving enough rein for the animal to drink. Kathryn did the same.

Grabbing her hand again, he ducked beneath the heavy branches that obscured their way. Bent nearly double, twigs snagging her hair and dress, Kathryn tried to peer ahead of them.

The thicket opened suddenly and she stood entranced.

"See." Roger held his arms out.

"Oh." Kathryn had no words.

Roger's secret place seemed apart from the world about it. Sheltered by the heavy trees and undergrowth, they were trapped in their own green cave. Water cascaded down a small fall that twisted to make its way between two tree trunks, and tumbled over the rocks into a deep, still pool.

Kathryn turned in a circle. "It is beautiful," she said. "No wonder you keep it as your secret place."

Roger tugged her into his arms. "Here I am not Sir Roger of Anglesea, son to the great Sir Arthur. I thought you might need a break from all the newness that besets you."

He understood and it made her want to bawl like a babe. Aye, they both had responsibilities and duties. In the world outside they were still Sir Roger and his Lady Kathryn. But here, they could just be themselves.

Kathryn pressed her face into his throat. "Now it will be our secret place."

Chapter Twenty-Three

The gloaming lay over Anglesea as they made their way back to the castle. Wind chilled the damp hair at her nape, but a rare feeling of happiness filled Kathryn. They had spent the day swimming, and making love in their private bower.

Roger had been all that was attentive and loving throughout their day. If this continued, marriage might not be such a bad business.

Dagger trotted along beside them, as happy with his outing as the rest of them.

Braziers flickered along the ramparts as the watch moved about their duties. Anglesea rose against the changing sky and declared to all who saw her that she watched over these lands spread at her feet.

They spoke little as they rode, wrapped in a golden day and each other.

The stream of folk entering the outer bailey had slowed to a trickle this late in the evening. Most occupied their own hearths or were already within the castle getting ready for the evening meal.

Kathryn's stomach grumbled. She had certainly eaten well at Anglesea. Lady Mary kept a generous table.

Roger helped her from Striker. Holding onto her a moment, he placed a sweet kiss on her lips. "It was a perfect day."

"Aye." Kathryn stayed a moment, content to be in his arms.

Hand in hand, Dagger at their heels, they entered the keep and took the stairs to the hall.

The hall lay quiet. Trestles half-set for the evening meal.

Sir Arthur paced before the nearest hearth. As they entered, he looked up, wearing a fierce frown. "Where have you been?"

Roger slid his arm about her waist and tugged her against him. "I took my new bride on an outing."

"We have bad news." Sir Arthur straightened his shoulders, bracing his legs like a man expected a bad storm.

Had they found her sister? "Matty?"

"Your sister?" Sir Arthur rubbed the back of his neck. "Nay, the news is not of your sister."

Roger's hand tightened about her waist. "What is it?"

Sir Arthur took a deep breath. "Sir Royce left, shortly after breaking his fast. He took Lady Rose with him."

Kathryn froze, her stare locked on Sir Arthur. Her mother would stay here at Anglesea. Roger had promised her. "Nay," she said.

"And you let him go?" Roger's voice cracked across the hall.

"I had no choice." Sir Arthur thrust his shoulders back. "He did it while we were away from the keep, and she is his wife."

"Nay." Her voice whispered from her tight throat. Roger and Sir Arthur glared at each other, while she stood there, her world shifting in a sickening swirl of sound and sight.

"We had an agreement," Roger yelled.

"Well, he broke it," Sir Arthur bellowed back. "He had his party out the gates before we knew what he was about."

"Did you go after him?" Roger stood toe-to-toe with his father.

"Of course I sodding went after him." Sir Arthur went ruddy.

"He pointed out that the girl is wedded and bedded, and how she went off quite happily with you for the day. He saw no reason for her mother to remain here."

Without her at Mandeville, who would step in when her father's rages grew too hot?

"I vowed to my wife that her mother would be safe."

"It was a stupid vow, son." Sir Arthur dropped his gaze. "How could you hope to keep it? We have no rights here. None. Kathryn is yours now, yours to protect, but Lady Rose belongs to her husband."

Aye, Mother belonged to her husband. Like a work beast. Fit to bear his children, bear his needs and his anger. Oh, God. She might be sick. Kathryn covered her mouth and ran from the hall.

Someone called after her. On the top floor she went first to the guest chamber, hoping against hope that Sir Arthur had not let her father take Mother.

The bare chamber mocked her. Already put to rights, it looked as if nobody had been there at all.

Kathryn clung to the doorjamb. All her life, she had lived for the moment when she could know they were safe. Every action she had taken since she grew old enough to understand what went on in her home had been fixed on the day when Matty and Mother would no longer need her.

"Kathryn." Roger's voice came from right behind her. "Do not despair. We can make this right."

"How?" Kathryn whirled to face him. She wanted to lash out and make him hurt the way she did. "You promised me she would be safe. You vowed if I married you, you would make it so."

"And I will." He pushed his hand through his hair. "Your father has her for now, but give me time and I will fix this."

"More promises?" A distant voice whispered she was not being fair, but she refused to heed it. She had married to protect her mother, and now mother stood in even more danger than ever. "Will you break those to me, too?"

"Kathryn." He reared back. "I believed I had secured Lady

Rose's future. I could not know your father would do this. You go too far."

"Really." How dare he get angry with her. "You saw the marks on me, you know how he is. How could you let this happen?"

"Kath—"

"No more of your empty words." The monster had her mother. She needed action not words. "I believe I do not go far enough. I kept my side of the bargain. I married you."

He flinched. A tiny movement but there nonetheless. "Indeed, my lady." His formal bow was as a slap in the face. "I see I have overstepped to believe more tender motives could have contributed to your decision." Beautiful blue eyes that had stared at her with open affection all day, now grew cold and distant. "Allow me to withdraw."

Suddenly her anger did not feel so just or so right. She had wounded him, and her chest ached with it. "Where are you going?"

He stopped, turning only his head. "You are quite correct, my lady. We struck a bargain. You have adequately performed your part. It remains for me to fulfill mine."

"What will you do?" Kathryn trailed him toward the staircase. This Roger she had glimpsed along the journey, but aimed at others and never her. Cold, ruthless, and intent, he resembled his father. A man who never let a slight go unpunished. A knight who waged war with the ferocity of the northmen she admired so much.

"I will do what I must." He took the stairs at a fast jog.

"Roger." She snatched up her skirts and ran after him. She wanted to undo the last five minutes and take them back. Her words had been uttered in haste. "I did not mean it."

"Which part?" He stopped at the bottom of the stairs. His manner so forbidding, she stopped partway down. "The part where I did not keep my vow?"

"Nay, but—"

"Quite so." He tilted his head at her. "Or did you mean the

part where you married me to ensure the safety of your mother and sister?"

"Nay, I did marry—"

"I thought not." He stared at her, locking them in a breathless bubble of fast-running emotion. "You spoke the truth, my lady. The only person who misconstrued appears to be me. I thank you for setting me to rights."

His heels rang on the flags as he strode away. She wanted to call out to him, run after him, make him stay. He left while she stood there in warring indecision. Kathryn sunk onto the step. It hurt, this being at odds with your husband. It nagged worse than the pain in her ribs, but deeper inside near her chest.

She brought her knees up to her chest, and hugged them tight. Dropping her face onto her knees, she wished she could jump back to the secret place they'd spent their afternoon and be that Roger and Kathryn.

"Kathryn?" Soft footfalls sounded on the stair treads. Lady Mary sat beside her in a waft of rosewater and lemon. "I would ask if you were all right, but as Roger stormed out mere moments ago, and you are hunched on the stairs, I think the question unnecessary."

"We had a fight," Kathryn said to her knees.

"Ah, well." Gentle hands soothed her back. "And, no doubt you will have many more in the years to come."

"Not like this."

"Nay." Lady Mary chuckled. "Some will be small, and others will be so large you will wonder how you will ever find your way back together again. And even others, you will not care to."

"He took my mother." Tears threatened and she pressed her eyes into her knees.

"I know, sweeting." The soothing strokes really did help. "We did everything we could to stop him, but we failed. We will make it right." Lady Mary's arm slid all the way about her shoulders. "My Arthur will do anything for one of his girls."

"I am not—"

"You most certainly are one of his girls." Lady Mary hugged her close. "Anglesea is your family now, Kathryn. You are as much ours to love, honor, and cherish as you are Roger's."

Blast! Why did Lady Mary have to say that, because tears threatened in earnest now? Lady Mary would not profess such sweet things if she knew how Kathryn had treated her beloved son. "I told Roger he had broken his vow to me."

"Ah." Lady Mary sighed. "With a man such as Roger, that would cut deep. His honor is the foundation on which he is built."

"And I said some other nasty things."

Lady Mary laughed. Laughed? Kathryn raised her head and gaped at her.

"What?" She raised her brow at Kathryn. A look so like her son, it made Kathryn's chest ache all over again. "Do you think you are the only woman to fling barbed words at her man? Come." She rose and held out her hand to Kathryn. "Let me set your heart at rest. You are not the first woman to flay her husband with her tongue, and neither will you be the last. Also, and as much as you are not going to want to hear this, neither will this be the last time you will do so."

Kathryn took her hand and stood.

"You are married now," Lady Mary said as they climbed. "You may not have wanted to be a wife, but I do not think you are all that unhappy with your choice of husband."

"I am worried for my mother."

"Aye." Lady Mary squeezed her hand. "And I believe you have just cause to be. Allow me to speak as a mother for a moment."

Kathryn nodded.

"From the day they put that babe to your breast, that child is yours. Yours to protect, love, nurture, and comfort. I am sure your mother draws great comfort from knowing you are safe."

"My mother is not like you," Kathryn said. "She is fragile and her health suffers."

"I understand," Lady Mary said. "And you are born with a

warrior's spirit in a woman's body. You have made it your labor to protect those who are weaker. In this, you and Roger are the same."

"There was nobody else." No servant at Mandeville would dare gainsay their liege lord. Not another family member to stand for them.

"You have borne a heavy burden for a long while now, Kathryn." Lady Mary stopped walking and turned to her. "But you do not bear it alone anymore. It is not weakness to allow those who can to help you. Right now, you are upset, and sick with worry. You spoke harshly in your grief, and when he calms, Roger will realize that." Warm hands cupped Kathryn's face. "You are not fighting alone anymore, sweeting. Think on that."

* * *

Kathryn waited for Roger to join her after dinner. She had thought much on her conversation with Lady Mary, and come to the conclusion Lady Mary knew best. Her concern for her mother had caused her to speak harshly to Roger.

The flash of hurt on his face rose to taunt her. Well, when a person did something wrong, she apologized. Fighting and flinging insults set a bad beginning to her married life.

The watch called midnight and still she waited.

Dinner was long since over, prayers said. What could be keeping him in the hall?

A murmur rose in the passage outside their chamber. Kathryn cracked the door and peered through.

Garrett and Beatrice walked arm-in-arm toward their chamber. Garrett spoke to Beatrice. Grave-faced, Beatrice pressed her head to her husband's shoulder.

Kathryn shut the door, sole witness to the turmoil on Garrett's face. An expression so similar to the one Roger had worn.

Newly wed and all alone. Kathryn paced to the casement. She

blinked away her tears. Feeling sorry for yourself got you a short trip into nowhere.

At times like these she wished she'd taken more interest in embroidery or some other womanly art. She unpacked her weapons from her clothes chest, and laid them beside the hearth. She checked her dagger for nicks on the blade. When she didn't find any, she cleaned it and lay it beside her sword.

Sir Royce had laughed when she had asked him for a sword. So, this one she had rescued from the pile of scrap behind the blacksmith's forge. Deemed not suitable, it had been tossed there to be melted down and remade.

She had added layers of sacking to make the pommel fit her hand, and if you stared down the blade you could see the imperfection, but she loved it anyway. Her sword, like an extension of her arm, proof of her fighting spirit. Kathryn dug out her whetstone and spat on it. The dull scrape of metal on stone soothed her. From her casement came the gentle suck and hiss of the sea. After honing her sword, she checked her bow, and counted her arrows. All appeared as it should, and she put her weapons away.

She gave in to the lure of the view and went back to the casement. Moonlight wavered across the swell and dip of the water beneath her. A clear, crisp night with a slight hint of chill hanging onto it.

Footsteps tramped over the battlement and the watch called the hour.

She knew Roger had not left Anglesea because he had sat beside her at dinner. More interested in his wine than his meal, they had barely said a word to each other.

Enough! Kathryn snatched up her bed robe and pulled it about her. She was not the sort of girl to sit about waiting and pining. Kathryn strode out of their chamber, and into the corridor beyond. Low tapers lit the way of any nocturnal wanderer.

Down the stairs she went into the hall.

Roger sat before the great hearth, his feet stretched out before him, eyes shut.

His eyes opened as she approached. Giving her a wobbly smile, he raised his goblet in a toast. "My lady."

"What are you doing?" She suspected the answer to her question lay in the overturned flagon by Roger's feet. Her belly gave an uneasy turn. Men and strong drink made a nasty brew.

"Thinking," he said.

"Thinking or drinking?" Good Lord, did that shrewish tone escape her?

Roger chuckled and laid his head back. "I find the wine oils my thoughts."

Her father's temper grew more unpredictable when he drank, and Kathryn kept a safe distance behind the empty chair that faced Roger.

"Have a seat." Roger waved at the chair. His eyes glittered and his cheeks were flushed. If he had been drinking since dinner, then he was well gone.

"I think I will return to our chamber." She would wait until morning to apologize.

Roger pointed, his voice hard. "Sit."

She had speed and could make it up the stairs and into their chamber if this was her father. Younger and lighter on his feet, Roger might prove abler. Experience taught her never to assume drunk meant sluggish. Kathryn touched her finger to a small scar beneath her chin. When a man tackled a running girl, the floor met her chin in a mighty knock. She took a slow step back, gauging his reaction.

"Where are you going?" Roger frowned, looking more confused than angry. "Did you not come down for a drink?"

"Nay." Kathryn edged a little further back. "When you did not come to bed, I came to look for you."

Roger chuckled. "Ah, the dutiful wife. Well, here I am." He held his arms wide. Wine spilled out of his goblet onto the floor. "Would you like a drink?"

"Thank you but nay," Kathryn said. "I will bid you good night and see you in the morning."

"Are you running from me, Kathryn?" His voice stopped her as she strode for the stairs. A goblet clattered to the floor.

"Nay." She increased her pace. Once in her chamber, she might bar the door. "I am merely seeking my bed."

Her foot hit the bottom step when a hand about her arm stopped her. "Stop."

Blast! He was so much quicker than Sir Royce. Kathryn braced herself, carefully hiding any traces of fear.

Roger cupped her face. Warm, wine-soaked breath hit her. "My beautiful Kathryn." His words held the careful enunciation of a drunken man. "I have a confession to make."

Ready for rough treatment, Kathryn struggled to find her feet on this new ground. "Indeed."

Roger nodded slowly. "I have been drinking."

"Aye."

His gaze lingered on her lips. "I fear I am quite drunk."

"Are you?"

He chuckled, stroking her bottom lip. "I have been sitting here, drinking, and pretending that I am not too afeared to enter my bedchamber."

Roger, afeared? The notion drew a snort from her.

"I did not know my welcome in your chamber." With a lurch, he rested his forehead against hers. His wine breath made her wince, but the simple gesture kept her there.

"I was waiting for you," she said.

"To stab me?"

Kathryn laughed. "Nay, I thought I might beg your pardon."

"Eh?" He reared back, went too far and lost his balance.

Kathryn grabbed his tunic and righted him. "I was sorry for my cross words today and wanted to beg your pardon."

"Hmph?" He pursed his lips and studied her. "Go on then."

"What?"

"Beg my pardon." His grin was sloppy. "Only make it good because my feathers are truly ruffled."

"You are drunk." Kathryn's last vestiges of fear slithered away. This was no Sir Royce she dealt with.

"I am," he said.

"Shall I help you to bed?"

He leered at her. "Aye."

"Come along then." Kathryn placed his arm about her waist.

He walked reasonably straight for a drunk man. Only leaning the veriest bit on her for support. She got him up the stairs and into their chamber.

With a groan, he dropped onto his back on the bed. "Now you have me where you wanted me, my lady. Do your worst."

Kathryn dodged his hands as she tugged off his boots. His tunic involved a lot more wrestling.

Roger used her proximity to cup her breasts and stroke her ass. Apparently, her husband was an amorous drunk. Kathryn removed his chausses. The tenting in his braies offered further proof of his eagerness.

Cupping his rod, he grinned at her. "I am ready."

Truth be told, so was she. Her body responded to his drunken fumbling in a mortifying manner. A sot should not appeal to her, yet he did.

Roger lay back, his broad, sculpted chest displayed for her pleasure, and Kathryn looked her fill.

Roger snored.

Stupid man! Here she stood prepared to apologize and he slept. Kathryn tugged the linens from beneath him and covered him.

She dropped her bed robe and crawled in beside him.

He grabbed her about the waist and hauled her into the cradle of his body. Wine laden breath stirred the hair at her nape, but she did not mind so very much.

Roger was not the same as her father when drunk. He was not

the same as her father in many, many ways, and each day seemed to bring a new discovery.

* * *

Roger slid out of bed, and worked his parched tongue off the roof of his mouth. God in heaven! His mouth tasted as if he'd been licking a dog's ass.

Kathryn lay on her stomach, face buried in the pillows, arms flung out. She brought him to his knees, and she had no idea.

He swilled water to clean his mouth, and then chewed a mint leaf left beside the basin and ewer.

Last night he'd drowned his lacerated feelings at the bottom of a flagon, and the sour belly and pounding head served him right. He could go about his day, and let her sleep. Or he could slide back beside his delicious bride and sample the tempting creamy shoulder that poked above the bed furs.

As if it were really a decision.

Roger slipped back into bed.

She'd come to find him last night. Forgoing a sulk, Kathryn had come to the hall with a sweet apology.

He slid his arms about her and shifted her into the cradle of his thighs. She smelled of sleepy woman, and something light and flowery that seemed embedded in her skin. The bruises on her trunk had faded to an interesting mottling of green and yellow.

Next time Sir Royce crossed his path, Roger would not grant him the courtesy of age. The cur had used their absence to slip away with Lady Rose. A fist raised in challenge, Roger would definitely accept. But he needed to think on his answering sally. King Henry's England in no way resembled King John's. Bit by bit, the boy king brought order to his barons, law to the lawless.

Kathryn stirred, burrowing her head further into the pillow. Not one to wake bright and cheery, but more of a bed wallower.

The tender arch of her nape beckoned and Roger pressed his

mouth to that sweet, vulnerable spot. Her hair clung to his morning growth and enveloped him in a sweet cloud of silk.

"Roger?" she murmured. Her eyelids flickered open.

"Aye." He traced the line of her shoulder with his lips. Such soft skin begged a man to taste. "You were expecting someone else?"

Her deep raspy chuckle vibrated through his ribs, and he smiled. He loved that he could make her laugh. There had not been enough laughter in Kathryn's life.

"How is your head?" She tilted her head to give him better access.

Roger gave her wicked shoulder a light bite. "As sore as I deserve."

"You were very drunk."

"Stop nagging, wench." He sucked her ear lobe. "You are in danger of becoming a shrew."

"Hmph!" Her outrage ended on a gasp. "Then we shall be a shrew and a sot."

"Or." Roger rose over her, keeping his weight on his elbows and off her sore ribs. "We could make up in the best way possible."

Brown eyes, so deep a man could lose himself, gazed at him. "Are you still wroth with me?"

"I was never wroth with you, sweeting." Roger held her still. It was important she understood this. "I was wroth with myself. I made you a vow and I broke it."

"It was an impossible vow to keep."

"Perhaps." Roger tossed away his resistance and nibbled her plump bottom lip. "I beg your pardon for yesterday. I will find a way to right this."

She wrapped her arms about his neck and kept him close. "Is this part of how you make things right?"

The sly wench pressed her hips against his rod, bringing him fully and achingly hard. "Partly." His wits retreated further with each voluptuous undulation she made. There was more to last night that he needed to tell her. "I want you to know, Kathryn, that there is never enough wine to cause you to fear me."

"I do not fear you." Out went her stubborn chin, eyes flashing defiance at him.

"Aye, you did." He stroked her hair back. "When you thought I was drunk, you became afeared and tried to run from me."

She snorted. "You imagine things."

"Nay." He kissed her forehead. "I am guessing your father became violent when he drank. But I want you to know that I would never hurt you. Not in anger, not in battle rage, and not in wine."

She softened for an instant, and glared another challenge at him. "I would break your head if you tried."

"And I would deserve it." He had made his point and he lowered himself between her thighs. "I also have a vague memory of an apology from you."

"I never." But her lovely smile spread.

"Perhaps you should remind me." He kissed her neck, right over the pulse, where she liked his touch.

She dug her nails into his hair and gave him more of her neck. "I feel sure you are mistaken." Her thighs tightened about his hips. "I would never have said how much I regretted the words I spoke in anger."

"Aye." He nibbled his way back to her mouth. "That does not sound like you."

"Or say that I had spoken hastily out of fear for my mother." Her voice faded into a low moan.

"My mistake." He halted, mouth poised over hers. "Then there is no need for me to tell you that I understand, and I hold no grudge."

"Nay," she whispered. "No need at all. But there is a dire need that you kiss me."

With that Roger happily complied, and being a man who liked to do a thorough job, a whole lot more as well.

Chapter Twenty-Four

Disliking his brother by marriage had become more of a habit than anything else. Roger could not remember the last time he had experienced the genuine desire to plow his fist into Garrett's face.

Beatrice had married far, far, far beneath her, picking a blacksmith's apprentice and a bastard at that. No matter how good the blood on his father's side, Garrett's mother had been a leman in her earlier years, and later a common whore.

For a prize like Beatrice, Father might have sought a groom from the highest families in the kingdom. Of course, Beatrice being Beatrice, had destroyed that plan and run off to London with Garrett. His youngest sister did not understand duty, and their doting father allowed her that ignorance. An heir had no such privilege. Roger made the ongoing tension between Beatrice and Garret his first act in taking charge of Anglesea.

Garrett followed the page Roger had sent to fetch him into the armory. No matter that he now wore a tunic of finest linen, the man always looked like a street rough. It lay in the way he walked, always alert for the next snatch-purse to leap out of a dark alley. William had endeavored to teach him to fight like a knight instead of a common thug. Garrett could now wield a sword like one born to it. But William had learned from Garrett as well, and now knew how to fight his way out of a tavern brawl by biting, ball-kicking, scratching, and pulling hair.

"You wanted to see me?" Garrett crossed his arms.

The man did not even stand like a nobleman. Chest puffed up, chin thrust out, he looked ready to wrestle Roger down.

"Aye." Roger indicated the seat beside him.

"Will this take long?" Garrett stuck his hands into his belt.

"You have something better to do?" If Garrett accepted his proposition, there would be nobody else to snipe and growl at. He might even miss that. A little.

"Bea is uncomfortable," Garrett said. "I do not like to leave her alone."

Then there was that. He couldn't completely dislike a man whose existence rose and set on his sister. For all his many faults, Garrett loved Bea to distraction, and in a manner Roger only now understood.

"If Bea is uncomfortable, then she should stop having so many babies." His sister's fourth in as many years.

Garrett's gaze hardened to black ice. "You overreach."

"My apologies." Ballocks to that. "Forgive that I do not want my sister worn down by childbirth."

"And you think I do?" Garrett balled his fists and stepped nearer. "She wants all these babies."

"She does?"

"Aye." Garrett ran an impatient hand through his dark hair and made it stick up. A street tough through to his marrow. "Damned if I can persuade her different. And double-damned that I cannot say nay to her."

A couple of weeks ago, Roger would have jeered. Not today however. An inkling of how that might be snaked through his mind. "Perhaps if we provide her with another outlet for her vigor."

Garrett glowered at him.

Aye, Roger surprised himself with his instant empathy. "God's bones, you stubborn bastard, sit down."

Garrett smirked but took the seat anyway. "What did you have in mind?"

Roger poured them both a mug of mead. Garrett preferred it over wine. "Sir Arthur and my mother intend to leave Anglesea," he said. "Their plan is to spend time with William first and then Faye, and return here occasionally. That leaves the running of Anglesea to me."

"How fortunate." Garrett curled his lip up. "Most men have to wait for their father to die."

Roger clenched his hand around the armrest. He did not have to rise to the bait every time. "When Henry returns, he will function as my chamberlain."

"What about the old chamberlain?"

"He has a cottage by the sea all picked out for himself. He will step down when my father leaves."

"Did you call me here for my approval?" Garrett sipped his mead, and wiped his mouth with the back of his hand. He followed that up with a hearty belch. The bastard knew how to behave. Garrett did it purely to gall him.

"Strangely enough your approval matters about as much to me as a pair of dog's ballocks," he said.

"Aye, and you would know, being well acquainted with the ass end of a dog." Garrett grinned.

The man did appreciate a good insult. Where others might be reaching for their sword, Garrett merely dredged up an even worse insult to return. Damn! He would miss him. "Nay. Even you might have noticed that I have recently married."

"Lady Kathryn has my deepest sympathies."

Roger fought his grin and lost. "What you may not know is that in marrying her, Anglesea has added to its northern border."

"Does the king know you own almost as much land as him now?"

Roger chuckled. Of course, Garrett knew. He probably knew

to an acre how much land and where it lay. It made his task that much easier. "I had not planned on sharing that with the king," he said. "It is good land, very fertile, but has been allowed to run wild for years now."

Garrett's shifted in his seat.

"There is a manor on the eastern edge of the land, mostly a ruin now, but it could benefit from a lord. The entire demesne could do with someone overseeing it."

Garrett drained his mead and set the cup on his armrest. "Your mother has been speaking out of turn."

"The entire keep has heard you and Bea going at it."

"The keep should mind its own business." Garrett clenched his hand around the armrests.

Just like the blighted man to get his back up over that. "I trust you do not include my mother in that statement." Roger sneered. "God knows why, but she seems fond of you. She wants to see the two of you happy."

"I do not want any charity from Anglesea."

"Good." Roger refilled Garrett's mug. "Because this is a sod's job. It will be years before she yields anything."

"And you thought I might be just the sod for the job?"

"I know what a sod you are," Roger said. "I thought you might want to make yourself useful."

Garrett rose, jaw jutting, fists clenched. "I will make my own way."

"Indeed." Roger kept an eye on Garrett's fists. The bastard had a wicked left hook. "And do you see my sister and your children making their way in a hovel right alongside you."

"Damn you."

"Nay, Garrett." Roger stood and went toe-to-toe with him. "Damn you and your stupid pride. You married an Anglesea, and now you would have her reduced to beggary because you cannot swallow your pride enough to take this opportunity."

"Beatrice will never suffer. Not as long as I breathe."

"Or I." Roger met his stare and held it. "I need this land

managed, and you need a way to be a man for your family." He softened his tone. "You will pour your sweat into that land before you make it profitable. I offer you a mixed blessing."

"With you and Henry interfering every step of the way."

"Nay." Roger sensed Garrett weakening and went for the kill. "The land is yours, all decisions will be yours. I will be your liege lord, aye, but I will treat you as I do any other vassal. Your land, your way. Of course, once you are yielding a good crop, you will owe me scuttage."

"Of course." Garrett thrust his hands into his belt. "And I can rely on your protection?"

"Aye." Roger held out his arm. "Do this for Bea, Garrett. Anglesea will provide assistance until you are able to support yourselves."

"Nay." Garrett stared at Roger's outstretched arm. "I do this alone. From the beginning, and I will pay scuttage as any other vassal."

Roger wanted to punch some sense into the bastard. "You expect my sister to live in a ruin?"

"It will be our ruin," Garrett said. "And you know better than to think I would ever put Bea in any danger or discomfort.

Roger did know it, and he nodded. "On your own then."

"No interference."

"None."

"No little gifts for Bea."

"Not from me." Roger smiled. "But I cannot control my mother, or my father, if they choose to do otherwise."

Garrett stared at him with narrowed eyes for a long, long while and then took his arm. "Show me the map."

* * *

Kathryn discussed with Roger and Sir Arthur how to get her mother to Anglesea. Four days of discussion and still they went in circles. Thus far, they could devise no good plan. Sir Arthur grew impatient. Roger counseled a considered approach. The tension between father and son grew apace their mutual frustration.

She tried not to fret, and her life certainly provided enough distractions to help her, but in the back of her mind persisted the concern. Keep life settled into a daily routine after the last of the wedding guests left. Sir Arthur and Lady Mary decided to delay their trip north. They never said so, but Kathryn knew they did it because of her mother. Kathryn's only comfort lay in the knowledge that her mother had considerable experience at staying out of Sir Royce's way.

Roger spent his days with Sir Arthur, as his father handed Anglesea over to his charge.

Sir Arthur showed her a different way of being a father, and somehow her father became Sir Royce even in the privacy of her thoughts. With his family, Sir Arthur could be loving, sweet, firm and even gruff, but he never raised a hand to any member or to anyone in his household staff. He did not need to. His power lay like a mantle on Sir Arthur's shoulders, but did not suffocate those around him. Instead, it sheltered them, keeping them safe and cherished.

This morning he invited her to the practice yards to "teach her a thing or two that Roger does not know." How could a girl resist such an offer?

Dagger lay on the edge of the practice yards, head on his paws, keen brown eyes watching every move.

"First off." Sir Arthur took the sword from her hands. "Let us get you some decent steel."

Kathryn tried to take it back. "But—"

"The stability is wrong." Sir Arthur sneered at the blade in his hand. "It will throw your balance at what could be a critical moment."

"I know that." Kathryn loved her sword. It might not be beautiful but it was hers. "I shift my weight to compensate."

Sir Arthur growled and motioned his page over.

Rob shuffled forward and took the sword from him.

"Do you have it?" Sir Arthur glared at Rob from beneath his unruly brows.

"Aye, my lord." Rob's freckled face broke into a grin as he handed Sir Arthur a wrapped sword.

"Right then." Sir Arthur pulled the sacking from the blade. "It seems that everyone but me has welcomed you to Anglesea."

"You do not need to—"

"Beautiful," Sir Arthur murmured. Sunlight blazed along the gleaming blade length. Jade stones encrusted the pommel, which appeared far too small for Sir Arthur's huge paws. "Our new smith knows his steel."

Raising it to eye level, Sir Arthur held the length of the blade straight before him. "See how she curves from the middle to the outside?"

Kathryn looked down the sword's length. "Aye."

"It means her heart is sound, and her edges are wickedly sharp." He flipped the pommel in his hand and held it out to her. "Welcome to my family, lovely Kathryn."

"Eh?" Kathryn stared at the gleaming metal. "For me?"

"Aye." Sir Arthur beamed and nudged the sword toward her. "I asked Roger what you would like best, and he suggested her."

"My own sword." Tears welled and she tried to blink them away.

Into her limp hand, Sir Arthur pressed the pommel. Her fingers curled about it.

"How does it feel?"

"Perfect." Kathryn ducked her head as more blasted tears welled. When had she become such a bedamned leaky pot? "Like it was bespoke just for me."

"And so it was." Sir Arthur tipped her chin up. "Any daughter of mine deserves her own blade."

Kathryn lost her words. Her throat too tight for them in any case, she pressed her forehead to his shoulder and managed a quick. "Thank you."

"There now." Sir Arthur cleared his throat. "None of that. Your tears will rust the blade."

A sob-choked giggle escaped her.

"You should name her," Sir Arthur said.

"Should I?" She stepped back and raised the sword. The grip molded to her hand. She cut down and left. And the balance! Sublime.

"All the best swords have names." Sir Arthur braced his legs akimbo and studied her form. "You are throwing your weight to the left."

Kathryn corrected her stance. "What is your sword called?"

Sir Arthur held his sword hilt. "Fate." He grinned. "When I was full of piss and pride, I would invite my opponents to meet their fate."

On a bark, Dagger got to his feet. Alert, he stared at the entrance to the outer bailey.

"What is it, boy?" Kathryn patted his head.

Someone entered the bailey, shrouded in a hood despite the hot day.

"Is it someone you know?" Sir Arthur stood beside her.

The way the person walked seemed familiar. "I am not sure."

"They seem to know you," Sir Arthur said. "Because they are coming this way."

Dagger pressed closer. Sir Arthur moved his shoulder in front of her. Protecting her. Kathryn almost embarrassed herself with more tears.

The figure pushed her hood back.

"Matty?" Kathryn drank in the familiar features. It really was who she thought it was. "It is Matty."

"Matty?" Sir Arthur frowned at her.

"My sister, Mathilda." Kathryn broke into a run. She had missed Matty so much.

Matty ran toward her, and they met in a tangle of arms and tears. "Oh, Kate." Matty sagged against her. "Thank God, I have found you. I am saved."

Chapter Twenty-Five

Kathryn handed her sister the soft, rose-scented soap Lady Mary made for bathing. "What do you mean he treats you cruelly?"

With a sob, Matty crumpled in her bath.

They had come here almost directly from the bailey. Matty had ridden with a swineherd and his family all the way from Digory's farm. The smell lingered on her clothes and hair, strong enough to have Kathryn call for bathing water to be brought to her chamber.

"I married in haste." Matty wiped away a tear. "I should never have done it."

Well, Kathryn might have told her that. In fact, she had told her that. "How is he cruel to you?"

"He shouts at me." Matty's breath hitched on another sob. "All the time. Naught that I do is good enough for him."

"Does he hurt you?" Nobody would raise their hand to Matty, not as long as she drew breath. She had made sure the harsh voices and raised fists of Mandeville had rarely come near Matty. Probably the only person at Mandeville whom Sir Royce truly valued, and if she believed him capable of such an emotion, Kathryn might even have said he loved Matty.

"He shook me." Face buried in her hands, Matty's words were almost indecipherable.

"Why?"

"I forgot to close the gate to the chicken coop." Matty trembled. "How was I to know that beastly fox was lurking there waiting to eat the chickens?" Fresh tears welled and spilled down Matty's cheeks. "We were not raised that way, Kate. I was raised to be a lady, not a farmer. He picks at me all the time. Looming and shouting about what I do wrong."

"But, Matty." Kathryn tiptoed carefully around her words. "Is it not possible that you and Digory need only to become more accustomed to one another?"

"You are taking his side?" Matty sniffed.

"Nay, Matty. I am on your side. Always. It is only that I was thinking the loss of all a farm's chickens is a heavy loss to bear." Matty's bottom lip pushed out, a sure sign she took one of her pets. Kathryn gentled her tone. "Perhaps he spoke in haste and regretted his words after?"

Matty turned her shoulder on Kathryn. "That is easy for you to say. You have all this." Water sprayed as Matty swept her hand to encompass the chamber. "You married a knight, and a future baron. Nobody will yell at you about chickens and plowing, and dishes."

Aye, but "all this" had been Matty's for the taking. In fact, Kathryn had tracked her down with Roger to try to ensure Matty took it. Nobody had forced Matty to marry Digory.

"I know what you are thinking." Matty heaved a massive sigh. "You are thinking I brought this on myself."

"Nay." Well, only partly.

"And you are right." Voice quivering, Matty buried her face in her hands. "But I believed myself in love. You cannot know, Kate, the agony of loving a man you may not have."

Kathryn had never known what it was to love a man, agony or no. "What will you do?"

"I cannot go back." Another sigh rippled through the chamber. "I will die if you make me."

"I would not make you go back." Where had Matty gotten such a notion? Kathryn always looked after her.

Matty peeped at her through her fingers. "But Sir Roger might not like it."

"I will explain it to him." She would not allow Roger to send Matty away.

"Perhaps while you are explaining, you might explain this." Matty rose from her bath. Water sluiced down her naked flanks. Dark bruises marred her thighs and buttocks.

"What happened?" Katherine went cold.

"I do not like to speak of it." Matty glanced at the marks. "Do not make me speak of it, Kate. But most of all do not force me back, where I may suffer worse. Just as Father did to you."

Kathryn stared at the marks mottling her sister's ivory skin. How dare someone mark her Matty in this manner? All the years of protecting and nurturing, and it all came to naught as one ham-fisted peasant put his hands on her sister.

"Kathryn." The door opened and Roger stepped inside. He gawped at Matty, went bright red and ducked back into the corridor. "I beg your pardon."

Matty lowered herself back into the water.

Kathryn's cheeks heated on her behalf as she hurried to join Roger. How mortifying for Matty. She blamed herself. She had not barred the door and, of course, Roger would not knock to enter their chamber.

Roger's color remained high as she joined him. "I beg your pardon," he said. "I did not know—"

"Nay, of course you did not." Kathryn took his hand. "I am at fault. I should have barred the door." Roger had been horrified, and Kathryn tried to stifle a giggle.

He gave her a stern look, but his lips twitched. "Are you laughing at me?"

"Your face." Kathryn held onto him as she laughed.

"Aye, well." He slid his arms about her waist and eased her closer. "It was not what I was expecting. Now"—he nuzzled into her neck—"if I had found you naked in your bath, I would have had an entirely different reaction."

Matty had always been the beautiful sister, and as wrong as it was, Kathryn reveled in his words. She did not begrudge Matty her beauty, but that Roger saw her beauty first made her want to strut like a proud peacock. "She has left Digory."

"Ah." Roger tucked her beneath his chin. "That is what I came to ask. I heard your sister was here. Did she say why?"

"He beat her." Digory had hurt one of hers, and she tightened her arms about Roger. "She is covered in bruises."

"He beat her?" Roger's surprised tone made her look at him. "I would not have judged him the sort. That he loved her, I did not doubt."

"Aye." Kathryn pressed her cheek to the comfort of Roger's chest. "I should never have left her there."

"Kathryn." Putting her from him, Roger's somber gaze fixed on her. "The choice was not yours. Short of you tying her up and slinging her over Striker, your sister was not leaving."

"Aye." Kathryn burrowed into him again. His gaze always stripped past her defenses and saw right into her heart. "But I could have persuaded her to come with me. If I had known."

Roger grunted. "Anyway, you did not know and here she is. What is to be done with her?"

"She cannot go back." Kathryn would not make the same mistake with Digory twice. "I will not allow you to send her back."

Roger raised a brow.

"I will not." Kathryn thumped his chest. "She is to stay here where she is safe."

Cocking his head, Roger smiled at her. Did she imagine the regret in his gaze? "Such a fierce warrior, my lady Kathryn. So loyal to those you love."

She did not know what he meant. "Matty stays here."

"Matty stays here." He kissed the tip of her nose. "Does my lady think I could deny her anything?"

Kathryn giggled. A sound she thought never to hear coming out of her. "Your father gave me a sword today."

"Did he now?" The man actually looked convincingly surprised. Kathryn squeezed his waist. "He said you gave him the idea."

Roger blushed. "He lies. The man is old. His mind is wandering."

"Perhaps, but I love my sword. He said I should name it."

"And?"

"What is your sword named?"

He blinked at her. "Roger's sword."

Kathryn laughed and tucked herself beneath his chin. "Thank you."

"Anything." His voice deepened. "If it is within my power, it is yours."

"Sir Roger." Matty appeared in the chamber doorway in a bathing sheet. Damp hair clung to her naked neck and shoulders. Rather a lot of bosom spilled out the top of Matty's clenched sheet.

"Lady Mathilda." Roger bowed, expressionless.

That particular careful lack of emotion gave Kathryn pause. Roger showed his thoughts and feelings, sometimes loudly, sometimes a little more subtly, but always there. Did he not like Matty? Impossible. He had wanted to marry Matty, followed Matty for days to find her and bring her back. Something akin to jealousy nipped at her.

Matty lounged against the doorjamb. The drying sheet slipped further.

Kathryn motioned with her head, trying to warn her sister of the danger of revealing her bosom. But Matty's gaze locked on Roger with an unsettling glitter.

"I trust you are comfortable," Roger said. His voice lacked any warmth, as if he spoke to a complete stranger.

"Very." Matty chewed her bottom lip.

"Good." Roger bowed. He pressed a soft kiss to Kathryn's cheek. "I will see you at dinner."

* * *

Roger's nape prickled as he took the stairs two at a time. The same battle instincts that had kept him alive many a time whispered to him now, which made no sense. Still, he had learned at his peril not to ignore them.

Matty did not look like a woman seeking refuge. She looked like trouble.

How had he not felt that warning when he courted her? Perhaps because his courtship had been a perfunctory effort to appease his mother. Beside Kathryn's willowy grace, Matty's more buxom looks appeared like a rose gone past its bloom.

"Roger." His father strode across the hall toward him. "Tell me of Lady Mathilda."

"She says her husband was cruel to her, and she seeks refuge here," Roger said.

Father studied Roger. "You knew she was married."

"Aye." Roger pushed a hand through his hair. Sir Arthur might get stirred up over this. "Kathryn and I found her on our search. It seems Mathilda was married all along, in secret."

"What sort of shady marriage is that?" Sir Arthur puffed out his chest.

"You know what Royce did to Kathryn?"

Sir Arthur nodded.

"When we discovered Mathilda had married a farmer, Kathryn begged me not to tell their father."

Sir Arthur shook his head. "And you made another vow."

"I am afraid I did."

Ramming his hands on his hips, Sir Arthur growled. "Women. They will twist the most sensible fellow into knots."

"Aye." What was the point in disagreeing?

"What do you make of Lady Mathilda?" Sir Arthur jerked his head at the stairs.

"I am not sure, yet."

"Can I expect an outraged farmer at my door?"

"I thought it was my door now?"

Sir Arthur shoved him. "Watch yourself, pup."

* * *

At dinner, Kathryn seated Matty beside her. Roger sat on her other side, a warm, solid presence she enjoyed.

Matty wore one of the new gowns Lady Mary had gifted Kathryn, a deep red silk that clung to her sister's fuller curves. Her hair worn loose and flowing down her back shocked Kathryn a little. Only a maiden wore her hair thus. But it seemed petty to say something, and Matty had much bigger concerns.

Matty giggled at something Garrett said to her, and turned sparkling eyes on him. It did Kathryn good to see her sister happy. Or perhaps Matty was merely putting on a brave front. Kathryn squeezed Matty's hand. She did not need to be brave anymore. Kathryn would protect her.

Matty shot her a quizzical glance and returned to her conversation with Garrett.

Over Garrett's shoulder, Beatrice watched Matty with a hard look.

Perhaps Matty should not lay her hand on Garrett's arm each time she spoke with him, or laughed. Also, must she lean in and display her bosom quite so much? Kathryn would have a word with her after dinner.

Beatrice caught her eye, and smiled.

It must be in her mind, after all. Beatrice did not seem wroth in the least. Or perhaps Beatrice and Garrett had argued again.

Roger spoke little during dinner. He too watched Matty.

Kathryn picked at her dinner, her stomach too tight for food. In the air about them hovered a tension that robbed her appetite.

"Are you well?" Roger glanced meaningfully at the slices of meat she had left on their trencher.

"Aye." Kathryn could not put her finger on what bothered her. She should be delighted to have Matty with her again. All their lives, it had been Kathryn and Matty against the world. And yet, she could not like the way Matty kept flicking her hair over her shoulder. The gesture seemed too coy for a married woman, too studied.

"Do you fret over Mathilda's husband coming here? Or perhaps your father?" Roger took her hand in his and kissed her knuckles. "Do not. I will make sure she is safe."

That was probably what niggled, and the weight lifted a bit from Kathryn.

Matty laughed again, low and intimate, and her discomfort returned.

"Come, Mathilda." Lady Mary rose with her lovely gracious smile. "I am afraid we are being selfish, keeping you amongst us when you must be so fatigued from your fraught journey."

"Nay, I—"

"Sweeting." Lady Mary approached Matty with her hands held out. "Such a brave girl to bear up so splendidly under your present trials."

Matty dropped her gaze to the table, and when she looked up again tears shimmered. "I do not like to make my troubles known."

"Of course you do not." Lady Mary cupped her chin. "What true lady would? Now come, and I will show you where you are to sleep tonight."

"Will I not sleep with Kathryn?"

Roger stiffened.

With a light laugh, Lady Mary waved. "Goodness me, nay, dear girl. Kathryn is wed now, and I do not think Roger can bear to be parted from her."

"Not for an entire night." Roger slid his arm about her shoulders.

Beatrice stood. "I will come along and make sure you are settled."

Kathryn rose to follow them, but Roger held her back. "My mother can see to Matty. I believe it is time for us to retire."

She liked the sound of that much better. This might be her favorite part of being married.

Chapter Twenty-Six

Roger suppressed the urge to wrestle his father down, and sit on him until the old dog saw sense. Sir Arthur had mentally strapped into his armor rendering him deaf to reason. Sir Arthur of Anglesea, god of war, had taken over his father.

From beside Sir Arthur, Garrett watched, ever calm, taking everything in and rolling it about the mystery of his mind. Roger had invited him to join the conversation in the hall.

"You say you will handle this, and you do nothing. You sit on your ass and think." Sir Arthur paced to the far side of the hearth. "I did not raise you to allow insult to pass."

"Nay." Roger dug his fingers into the armrests of his chair. His father had taken Kathryn beneath his wing, which in Sir Arthur's world, made her a woman worth fighting for. "You raised me to think before I acted, and that is with I am doing."

Look where his last thoughtless act had ended. Indeed, it lay at the heart of their current dilemma.

"And while you think, Royce could be beating Lady Rose to a pulp." Sir Arthur pounded his hand on the mantel. Soot and ash drifted down. "What are you waiting for? You have the other girl here at Anglesea. All you need do is get the mother."

Roger stood, refusing to have his father loom over him. "Kathryn is my wife and I will handle this."

"How?"

"If I might?" Garrett stretched his legs out to the blaze. "I have something in mind."

"You have something in mind?" Sir Arthur scowled at Garrett before cursing and stomping away.

"You do?" Roger looked forward to this. Garrett had a mind forged in the battle for survival.

Garrett shrugged. "It is not fully formed yet. I am gathering more information. All you have to do is keep that old warhorse from stomping everything to pieces."

"Old warhorse!" Sir Arthur's hearing had suffered none. He stormed over, towering above Garrett. "Get up, gutter rat, and this old warhorse will teach you a thing or two about your betters."

Roger's head ached. "Is this helping?"

He looked from his father to Garrett and back again.

Father threw himself into his chair, still glaring at Garrett.

Garrett smirked and crossed his ankles.

"While Garrett hatches his no doubt foul schemes, I have sent for William," Roger said.

"William?" Sir Arthur's eyes bulged. "What, in the name of all that is holy, is he going to do that you and I cannot?"

"Speak. Negotiate." Roger handed his father a tankard. "Use his smooth address to get us what we want. We cannot risk war with Sir Royce, not with the king finally looking with favor on us."

Sir Arthur grabbed the tankard. "This is not how I am accustomed to doing things."

"Aye, but this is a different time."

"Foul schemes for a foul man." Garrett yawned and stretched. "If you want to catch a pig, it helps to climb into the sty with it."

"And this is what your life in the sty has taught you?" Sir Arthur snorted.

Garrett grinned. "Nay, this is what I learned when I set a trap for you."

Sir Arthur flushed, fists clenched, ready to do battle.

Rob sidled into the hall and cleared his throat. "Begging your pardon, my lords. I would not interrupt unless it—"

"Get on with it." Sir Arthur drew a hefty draught of his tankard.

"There is a...person at the gates. Says he is known to Sir Roger. Refuses to leave until he sees him." Rob smoothed his hair back.

"Who is it?" Roger waved his father to silence.

"He says his name is Digory." Rob sniffed and rolled his eyes. "Smells of cow turd."

"Digory? You are sure?"

"Aye, Sir Roger. We do not get many farmers demanding to see Baron Anglesea."

That lippyness of Rob's would have to be dealt with, but later, when Roger discovered what Digory wanted. He exchanged a quick glance with Garrett.

Garrett shrugged.

Digory most likely did what any other man would do if his wife stepped out for a breath of fresh air and never came back. His promise to Kathryn uppermost in his mind, he told Rob to show Digory in.

Roger turned to his father. "I will handle this."

"Then handle it." Sir Arthur sat rigid in his chair.

Digory walked in with his chin raised, gaze flickering between the door and the men-at-arms flanking him. He spotted him, and looked relieved. "Sir Roger." He gave a clumsy bow. "I was just telling these men that I was known to you."

"What do you want?" Roger crossed his arms.

Rob sidled up beside him. "Shall I have the men toss him out?"

"I must speak with you." Digory stepped forward.

The guard at his side palmed his sword hilt.

With a whimper, Digory leaped back.

"Let him come." Roger motioned the men to stand aside. "I will hear what he has to say."

Digory edged past the guards and trotted to them. "I came for my wife."

There you had it, as Roger suspected. "What makes you think she is here?"

"Her sister is here." Digory glanced about him. "She would not return to her father. Or that limp...Lady Cecily. Is she here?"

"Tell me, my man." Sir Arthur of Anglesea squared his wide shoulders, every inch of him a wealthy, powerful baron. "Are you in the habit of bursting into castles and demanding people?"

Roger grit his teeth. He needed to have a word with Mother about when she planned to drag Father away from Anglesea.

"Nay, sir...my lord...Sir Arthur." Digory snatched his woven coif from his head and twisted it in his hands. "It is just that Matty...Lady Mathilda is my wife."

God's teeth, his father excelled at the whole lordly thing. Roger would have to grow that invisible shield of power about himself. And he would, if the old man stepped back far enough to let him handle this.

"Your wife?" Sir Arthur stood and approached Digory with measured steps. "Given into your care by her father?"

Roger exchanged glances with Garrett. The old man could not resist getting the bit between his teeth.

"Um...nay, my lord." Pale as parchment, Digory shook his head.

"Then I can only surmise that you took her." Sir Arthur stared down his nose at Digory.

Swallowing hard, Digory put his shoulders back. "I did not take her. She came with me willingly enough. Please, my lord."

Roger gave the man grudging respect for the ballocks on him. Not many men faced Sir Arthur and kept their composure. Still, time for the old man to step back and Roger stood.

Digory sidled away from Sir Arthur. "Will you at least tell me if she is here? She took off with a pig breeder, and I am concerned something might have befallen her."

"She is here," Sir Arthur said.

Digory's shoulders slumped. "Thank the Lord."

"I think the more interesting question is why she is here." Roger stepped closer to Digory, towering a good foot above him.

"She left me," Digory said. "When I was out working the back fields near the stream. I came back and she was gone."

"Aye, but why."

"I think that is a matter for my wife and me." Digory held his ground.

Sir Arthur growled.

Roger raised his hand and moved in front of his father. "A happy woman does not leave her husband."

"Nay." Dropping his head, Digory sighed. "My Matty was not raised to farm life. It does not sit well with her."

Digory had a point. Combining this with his niggle around Matty, Roger's gut whispered.

Sir Arthur frowned slightly, as if he were trying to piece Digory together.

Keen gaze taking in Digory, Garrett sauntered up to join them.

Roger would like to hear what Garrett made of this. Granted, Roger did not know Digory well, but the man he had seen on the farm did not seem the sort to beat on his adored wife. The way Digory said *my Matty* struck something in Roger. It was much like the way he called his wife *my Kathryn.*

"I think you should tell us why she left," Garrett said.

With a deep breath, Digory raised his chin. "I would rather speak to my wife."

"Nay," Roger said. "You will not go near Lady Mathilda until I judge it safe for her."

"Safe for her?" Digory's mouth dropped open. "Why would it not be safe for her?"

"That is what we would like to know." Unless he completely misjudged the man, Digory seemed confounded by the notion.

Frowning, Digory glanced between them. "Did Matty...nay. She would not say that I...beat her?"

"Not only does she say so." Roger got closer, and forced the smaller man back a step. "My wife tells me she bears the bruises to prove it."

"Bruises?" Digory paled. "She was fine when she left. If she is marked, then that blasted pig—"

"The bruises are older than that." Roger had no idea, having never seen the bruises. But he wanted to throw the man off balance and see what would shake free.

"Bruises?" Digory's frown deepened. "I have not—she fell." He threw his hands aloft. "A sennight ago, she was milking the cow and it butted her and she fell."

"Indeed." Sir Arthur glowered, a truly intimidating sight. The sort of look that would, and often had, sent Roger running for his mother as a boy.

Garrett circled Digory. "Your wife is marked because she fell. What an interesting story."

"'Tis not a story." Digory waved his arms. "She did. She fell. I tried to tell her she need not fear old Dewdrop, but she..." He shrugged. "Matty does not take to the farm well."

The two guards stared, fascinated by every word.

"You keep saying that." Roger needed a drink. "You should explain what that means."

He turned, trusting the others would follow.

Taking a seat by the hearth, with Sir Arthur and Garrett taking the others, he motioned for Rob to bring Digory a chair. This conversation could take a while, especially with Digory squaring his shoulders in that annoying manner.

Rob looked askance at Roger, then glanced at Sir Arthur for confirmation of the order.

"Did you hear me, Rob?" Perhaps the lad needed a gentle reminder right this moment. A boot up his ass would do the trick.

"Aye, Sir Roger, but—"

"Then do it. Now."

With a massive sigh, Rob dragged a bench from the wall. Wooden legs screeched on stone, preventing any further conversation.

"You had best take that squire with you," Garrett told Sir Arthur, "lest Roger break his head."

Digory looked at the bench as if it might bite him.

"Oh, sit." Sir Arthur gestured at the bench. "None of us are going anywhere until we get some answers."

"I just want my wife, and then I will leave you in peace." Digory crossed his hands in front of him.

Garrett stood, grabbed Digory by the shoulder, and pushed him onto the bench. "Sit."

For a moment, Digory looked like he might stand again. Garrett hovered above him. Wisely, he chose to remain seated.

"You cannot have your wife until I am sure you did not put those bruises on her," Roger said. "Rob, get our guest some ale."

"I told you how they happened."

"Aye, but we don't believe you." Roger glared at Rob's back as the boy dragged his feet out of the hall. "Rob," he called. "If I have to get up, you will not be sitting a horse for a week."

Rob scurried out of the hall.

"I did not touch her." Digory flushed. "In that way. I did not harm her."

"So says nearly every man when faced with a woman's angry relatives." Garrett took his time tasting his wine before swallowing.

With a groan, Digory half-rose, and sat again. "I am not a fancy lord. I do not have any way to make you believe me. I cannot swear by my sword or my honor. All I have is a simple man's truth and I give you that."

"Tell me again, about the cow and Matty's fall." Roger motioned him to speak.

Digory breathed deep. "Part of Matty's duties is to milk the cow in the morn. Only she does not care for the cow. She says it frightens her." He twisted his hands together. "But I cannot be out in the fields before it grows too hot to plant, and milk the cow and collect the eggs, and—"

"I believe we get the point." Roger silently thanked God he was not a farmer. "So, you insisted she milk the cow."

"We need the milk for butter and cheese," Digory said. "Matty is still learning to make those, but if she milks the cow I can get to them once I have finished in the fields and taken care of the rest of the animals."

Sounded to Roger like Digory worked harder than three men.

"And, aye, I did raise my voice to her and insist that she do it." Digory shook his head. "But I never knew she would fall and hurt herself."

"What happened?"

"Well, Dewdrop, that's the cow, has a habit of stepping around a bit when she's milked. I showed Matty how to bind her back legs so she would not kick the bucket over. But Matty felt it was cruel and did not do it. Dewdrop stepped to the side, Matty thought she might kick her or bite her or something, and she fell over the milking stool."

"And the milk?" Garrett spoke.

"It was spilled." Digory reflected Roger's confusion at the interruption.

Garrett cocked his head. "Did that make you angry?"

Digory wiped his hands on his thighs. "Well, aye, because we only have the one milk cow."

"How angry?"

Digory blanched. "Not that angry, not angry enough to do what you are thinking."

His father glanced at him, and Roger shrugged.

"The decision is yours." Sir Arthur sat back and crossed his ankles.

Digory told a believable tale. As much as he wanted to paint him villain and beat the life out of him, Roger could not do it.

"Digory, at this stage, I do not know what to believe. Your wife tells one story and you tell another. I need some time to find the truth."

"I told you the truth." Digory leaped up. "I did not hurt my Matty. I could never do such a thing."

"That I will decide in time," Roger said. "You may return to your farm or stay nearby while I consider all sides of this."

"I want my wife."

"You may not have your wife. Yet, if ever."

Digory stood there, clenching and unclenching his fists. "I will wait nearby." He stalked from the hall.

Sir Arthur spoke. "What will you tell Kathryn?"

"The truth. That I do not know what to believe."

Garrett chuckled and shook his head. "I wish you luck with that. In the meantime, I will ask around a bit."

* * *

"You did what?" Kathryn stared at her husband and tried to make sense of what he had just said.

Bent, Roger continued to unfasten his cross braces. "I told Digory he could remain at Anglesea until I discovered the truth."

"But you know the truth." Had she not told him what Matty said?

"I know what Mathilda says, and I have heard what Digory says, and their stories do not match." Roger sat up.

"You think my sister lied to you?"

"I did not say that."

He believed Digory over her and Matty. Of course he did. Digory was a man. Once more Roger had broken his vow to her. "You will let him take her back?"

"I never said that either."

"Nay you did not." Tears threatened, thickening her voice. She would not cry, refused to. Now she needed to remain strong.

"That you would even consider Matty lied to you tells me all I need to know."

"Kathryn." He approached her, hands outstretched.

"Do not touch me." She ducked around him and wrenched open the door.

The door slammed shut. Palms flat to the door, Roger caged her between his arms. "We will discuss this reasonably."

"There is nothing to discuss." Pulling at the handle proved futile. She could not budge him, but Kathryn kept trying. "You promised me my sister would be safe."

"And she will be." His breath tickled her ear. "I will not let her go back with him if I judge it not safe for her."

"You vowed to me."

"I know that." He pressed closer, his strong chest against her back.

Kathryn steeled herself to resist his warmth and comfort.

"I will keep that vow. But Digory…" He took a deep breath. "He does not seem the sort to hurt any woman, let alone a woman he clearly adores."

"You do not even know him."

"Neither do you." He folded his arms about her, drawing her to him. "I know Matty is your sister, sweeting, but meet with the man. Ask him your questions and then we will speak further."

Kathryn wanted to lean into him, to have him shoulder all her worries. Her weakness sickened her. Had she not learned never to put her fate in a man's hands? All her years as Sir Royce's daughter should have impressed that lesson into the deepest part of her. She wrenched free of Roger's hold. "I will never speak to that man."

"Kathryn." This time Roger let her open the door fully. "Where are you going?"

"Away from here. Away from you."

He folded his arms. "Think before you leave this chamber, Kathryn. You are drawing a battle line that need not be drawn between us."

His calm reason pressed at her and demanded she hear him. "The lines are already drawn."

"Very well." Roger stepped away from the door. "If you are resolved in this, I will not stop you."

Head raised, Kathryn stepped into the passage.

True to his word, Roger stood and watched her.

Indecision tore at her. Where was her pride? Kathryn raised her chin. Before she could dissuade herself from her course, she strode away from him.

The door slammed behind her, loud enough to startle her.

Where to go?

Well past the watch's call of midnight, the keep lay still and quiet about her. If she slept in the hall, the entire Anglesea would know she refused to lie with her husband. Such a blow would strike Roger's pride. Why she cared after his betrayal she knew not, but somehow she did.

Matty. She would go to Matty.

Kathryn retraced her steps past the bedchamber she had shared with Roger. The closed door stared at her in condemnation. It would be so easy to open that door, step inside and take her place where she belonged. Belonged? Kathryn straightened her spine. She refused to be any man's chattel. She strode to the smaller chambers at the east end of the keep, where guests were housed.

Matty looked up from where she sat by the fire. "Kate?"

She had told Matty she hated that name too many times to count, and each time Matty laughed and called her silly.

"What are you doing here?" Matty put her embroidery aside and rose.

Somehow she did not want to tell Matty of her argument with Roger. Bad enough that she need worry about Roger's doubts. Matty would react badly to the news of Digory being so close, and Kathryn sought some peace to make sense of all the emotions at war within her. "Might I sleep here tonight?"

Matty frowned. "There is only the one bed."

"Aye, but it is large enough for both of us."

"I suppose." Matty pulled a face. "But I am a light sleeper, so you must not disturb me."

Kathryn pressed her annoyance down, hard. Matty did not know she was upset from her fight with Roger. Light sleeper, though. That could make her fall about laughing. Matty would sleep through a band of traveling minstrels playing right beside her ear. "I will sleep quietly."

"What does your husband think of you spending the night with me?" Matty studied her.

"He did not say much."

"Hmph!" Matty sat and resumed her embroidery. "Digory would never let me sleep alone."

Matty seemed awfully smug for someone who sat in her sister's keep without her husband. "I did not ask Roger's opinion."

Matty smirked. "Are you tangling with the man already, Kate?"

"Do not call me that." Kathryn grabbed the frayed ends of her patience. "And I merely came to spend some time with you. If that is a problem, I can return to my husband." Aye, she did labor the words my husband a touch.

Matty held her hands out. "Not at all, Kathryn. It is lovely you are here. I have missed you."

Kathryn melted. This was her Matty. "I have missed you, too."

Chapter Twenty-Seven

Roger came awake instantly.

"Get up." Father dropped Roger's discarded chausses onto the bed. He wore a grim harried expression. "You need to come now."

The door slammed behind his father.

Roger had never seen him wear that look before. He hauled on his chausses and a tunic, then he grabbed his boots and ran to the hall.

Lady Mary sat before the hearth, wrapped in a blanket. Nurse stood beside her, patting her shoulder and murmuring in her ear.

"What is it?" Roger sought his father's gaze.

Sir Arthur stopped pacing and approached him. "There is trouble."

"Sir Royce?"

"Nay." Father's shoulders slumped and he dropped his head. In that instant he looked every year of his age.

Despite what he called him, Sir Arthur had more vigor than a man half his age. Roger should know because Father could still hold him in a sword fight. "What is it?"

Mother's tear-stained face turned his way. Her haunted eyes chilled him to the bone.

"What is it?" His voice rang loud and strange through the still hall.

Nurse limped to him, her hands outstretched. "It is Henry."

"Henry?" Roger clutched at the chair back. Henry had left on holy pilgrimage almost three full years ago. News of him came rarely, if at all. Dear God! Roger could not voice the dread. "Is he...?"

"Nay." Sir Arthur pounded his fist into the wall. "Do not say that word."

"We do not know." Nurse took his hands in hers. "Newt drove himself near death to get here. He saw Henry go down in battle, pulled off his horse."

Henry! The ripping through his chest made breathing impossible. His little brother. Such a pompous pain in his ass. Rife for teasing with that stick wedged firmly up him.

"They did not find a body." Nurse grabbed him by the shoulders. "Newt searched, and found his horse dead, but they did not find a body."

"Where is Newt?" Roger needed to hear the story for himself. He would not believe it true until he heard it.

"He is in the kitchen, Roger." Nurse grabbed his arm. "The lad is exhausted. He near killed himself and his horse to get to us."

Mother sobbed, and Father stood beside her, patting her shoulder. They both looked defeated by the news. He wanted to shake them, and demand like a small, impetuous lad that they not believe the worst. He needed not to believe the worst himself.

Roger had to get out. He ran to the kitchen.

Newt had changed so much, Roger barely recognized him. When Newt had run afoul of the king's game warden, Sir Arthur made good on the favors owed Newt and sent the boy to join Henry as a squire.

He rose, no longer a boy, but a man. Easily as tall as Roger and filling in his lanky frame.

Newt swayed with exhaustion. Lines of strain bracketed his

mouth, deep shadows beneath his eyes. His hollowed cheeks spoke of many a missed meal. "You want to hear it."

"Aye."

Roger motioned him to sit before Newt fell. He took the seat opposite. Perhaps he would find some missing part of the story they could cling to.

"I was supposed to be by his side." Newt dropped his head into his hands. "He told me to be back, but I was..." Newt's shoulders bunched, and when he spoke again, he had control of his voice. "I got to the battle late. I could not reach him. There were so many of them, and Henry was right in the thick of it. Where he always is. Was."

Streaks had made runnels in the dirt on his haggard face. Newt pushed the heel of his hand against his nose and sniffed. "You know Henry." He shrugged. "Always off to raise his sword for God."

Roger would have punched him, but the affection rang in Newt's tone. An unlikely partnership, Newt and Henry, the gutter rat and the saint, but somehow they had forged a bond thicker than steel. Newt grieved for Henry in a way that cut deeper perhaps than any of them. The connection he understood. If you stood arm-to-arm with a man in battle, he became the brother of your soul.

"They surrounded his horse." Newt gripped his hands together so tightly the knuckles turned white. "I saw the whoresons doing it. I shouted, but the noise..." He cleared his throat. "There were too many. He went down."

"You found no body?" Roger had trouble forcing the word body out of his mouth.

Newt shook his head. "And I looked. I swear to you."

Roger nodded. He got to his feet like he had aged fifty years in the last minutes. Every muscle ached as if he'd been pummeled. "Get some rest. We will speak later."

He left the kitchen and went back to the hall.

Beatrice had been woken and cried in Garrett's arms.

Roger ached to have Kathryn by his side. To feel her wrap herself around him and share his pain.

"Roger?" Beatrice raised her head from Garrett's shoulders. Her eyes were red and swollen.

She ran to him and he held her.

The dead pain inside throbbed, but unlike Bea, the tears to relieve the building pressure would not come. He handed her back to Garrett and went to his father.

Sir Arthur looked like a man broken. Heads bowed, he and Lady Mary clung to each other.

Why had Henry gone on this stupid pilgrimage? The need to pound something wrenched through him. They had all told Henry not to go. Not to fight a fool's war in a strange land. Bloody, bloody, bedamned, accursed Henry.

Roger gripped the mantle so hard his fingers throbbed. The pain felt good. A real connection in a world gone mad.

"We must go to London." Father ran his hand over his eyes. "They will know more."

"I will do it." He had to do something. Anything. Roger wanted to strike out and strike out until blood coated his fist. "You stay here, and take care of mother."

"I can go." Garrett glanced up.

"Nay." This task fell to him. Son and heir, oldest sibling, and the one who needed to hold them all together before they shattered. This was his duty. "Bea needs you."

"What of Kathryn?"

A good question. He did not even know where his wife slept. He knew that she did not stand beside him. "You will watch her for me?"

"Aye." Garrett led Bea to her mother and approached him. "I will make sure the rest of the family know. Leave matters here with me and go with God, Roger." He dropped his voice until only Roger could hear. "If they found no body, there is still hope. Go and see if you can find it. Bring the truth back as fast as you can."

Roger's words jammed in his throat. He thumped Garrett on the shoulder.

"As for Lady Rose, I have a plan." Garrett drew him further away from the others. "I will send Newt about it once he is rested. The lad needs something to keep him busy, and I do not want to leave Bea while she is so close to having her baby."

Life stopped for nobody. Trouble did not wait to arrive on their doorstep in neat turns. The weight of his responsibilities pressed heavy on his shoulders as he gathered a few things he would need and made his way to the stable.

Even the stables lay quiet, as if the horses somehow sensed the pall that hung over Anglesea. Roger took Beast out and saddled him.

"Roger?" A woman came out of the shadows.

Kathryn! Seeing her walk toward him made the pain unravel enough for him to draw his first clear breath. She drew nearer. He craved the scent of wildflowers that clung to her skin, the way her hands carried the calluses from too much riding and sword wielding, the innate grace, and indomitable strength of her. Inside, he cried out for her. Comfort.

Nay, not Kathryn but Mathilda and looking enough like Kathryn in her nightrail for him to mistake them.

"What are you doing here?" He did not have it in him to watch his words. Disappointment made them even brusquer.

"Cook told me what has happened." Matty held out her hands to him. "I am so very sorry."

"You should not be here." He did not want the touch of her soft, gentle hands. Releasing her grasp, he shrugged and turned back to Beast. He did not want her here. He wanted Matty to change into Kathryn, so he could share his grief over his brother. Henry was missing, believed dead.

"You should not be alone," she whispered. "Not when you have lost a brother."

He staggered under the force of the emotion inside him, leaning against Beast to right himself.

Henry, the only brother born flaxen haired. So like their mother that they had teased him about his "girl" face and "pretty" eyes. Roger pressed his forehead into Beast. To never hear the droning lectures on piety and temperance. Never again to see the way Henry's lips pursed in disapproval. God, how he had railed at those parts of his brother. Now, he would give his sword arm to have them back again.

Beast shifted, nudging his shoulder.

Henry with the light of battle shining from him. Passionate about some wrong he needed to right or slight he felt compelled to avenge. Henry and his blasted, sodding honor. An example to every lesser man around him. All gone.

Matty touched his back. "I will tell Kathryn when she wakes." Her arms slid around him from behind, and she pressed into him. "I will pray for you and Henry."

He throbbed for the soft touch of a woman, and Roger stayed like that. Letting the press of her breasts against his back soothe him in some elemental way.

She smelled wrong.

He did not ache for any women. He ached for his woman.

Roger loosened her arms. "Tell Kathryn where I have gone."

* * *

Kathryn had barely fallen asleep before Matty shook her awake. "Kathryn, wake up. You must get up."

A bright day made her snap her eyes shut again.

Matty shook harder. "Kate, you dare not sleep any longer. Roger has already left without you."

"Roger has left." Sleep vanished and she sat up. "Where has Roger gone?"

"Now you ask." Matty shook her head and put her hands on her hips. "You should have been at your husband's side, and now it is too late."

Kathryn dragged her thoughts into order. "Why should I have been at Roger's side?"

Matty rose, adjusted her skirts—another of Kathryn's new dresses—and sighed. "Get up and dressed, Kate."

Kathryn scrambled out of bed, but Matty left, closing the door behind her.

She had no clothes in this room. After snatching up her bed robe, she pelted down the corridor to her and Roger's chamber. Surely, she had not understood Matty correctly and she would find Roger still abed, or readying himself for the day.

Nurse rose from her seat by the fire.

"Where is Roger?" Kathryn searched the chamber, knowing he was not in there, but hoping all the same.

"There you are." Nurse straightened her back. As she drew nearer, Nurse's red-rimmed eyes and tear-stained cheeks made Kathryn's heart stop.

"What is it?"

"I came to bring you some more salve for your bruises." Nurse shuffled closer with a pot held out. "When I did not find you here, I thought I might wait."

"What has happened?" Kathryn wanted to wrap the older woman in her arms, but Nurse seemed remote in her strong emotion.

"Why were you not in this chamber?" Nurse uncapped the pot with her gnarled fingers.

Kathryn shed her robe and nightrail. "Roger and I had cross words last night. I slept with Matty."

"Silly wench." Nurse rubbed salve onto her bruised ribs. "You should never let your bedchamber become a battleground."

"Matty said Roger left." The cold salve caused her breath to hitch.

Nurse moved to her other side. Her voice heavy, she said, "Aye, he rides for London to see if he can discover more."

"Nurse." Kathryn caught her hands. "Please tell me what has happened. I woke moments ago to the news Roger has left."

"And you thought he left you? Not our Roger." Nurse clucked her tongue, but returned Kathryn's grip with a squeeze. "We have had some sad news. Faye and Gregory will be arriving soon I would guess, and William and Alice not far behind them. The family gathers." Tears streamed down Nurse's cheeks.

"Nurse." Distance be damned. Kathryn wrapped her arms about Nurse's stout shoulders. "Tell me."

"It is my Henry." Nurse's voice hitched on a sob. "They say he fell in battle, and now he cannot be found."

Kathryn burned to ask if he lived, but it did not seem kind, so she waited.

"At best, we can hope they will ransom him. At worst..." Nurse eased out of her clasp. She shook her head and sniffed. Using her apron, she wiped her eyes and cheeks. "As long as there is hope, however slim, I will pray for a miracle."

"Roger goes to see if there is more news?" Roger had not left her, but she should have been by his side as he received this awful news. Had she not heard him speak of Henry with such love? Along with the rest of the kingdom, she had heard of the conditions captured men on pilgrimage suffered. Seen the scars from horrendous wounds earned both in battle and in prisons. "You said they did not find him?"

"They did not find the body." Nurse finished with her and recapped her pot.

"Then that could mean he escaped," Kathryn said.

Nurse straightened her shoulders. "It could mean many things, my girl. Some of them good, some of them awful, but until we know more there is no purpose to making stories in our heads." She grabbed Kathryn's chemise and shook it at her. "Come, get dressed and go to the hall. My lady needs all her family about her now."

Chapter Twenty-Eight

Kathryn slipped into the hall and stood near the door.

Lady Mary, dressed and outwardly composed, sat by the fire, her needlework on her lap, and stared at the fire. Sir Arthur sat beside her and murmured to her, his hand clasped about hers.

Opposite them, Beatrice huddled with her head on Garrett's shoulder and listened to Sir Arthur.

Despite what Nurse said, Kathryn hated to intrude on their grief. She hesitated, not sure of her place.

"Lady Kathryn." A tall, broad, flaxen-haired man approached her. "I am Tom. Ivy and I came as soon as we received word. We attended your wedding."

Kathryn nodded and took his outstretched hand. She did not remember the man, or the Ivy of whom he spoke, but then her wedding day still blurred in her mind.

A beautiful woman with dark hair pressed a mug of something into Lady Mary's hand.

Lady Mary smiled her thanks and placed the mug against her armrest.

"That is Ivy," Tom said. "She is doing what she can."

Lady Mary caught sight of her, and held out her hand. "Kathryn. Dear girl, come and join us."

Pale as parchment, Lady Mary remained as serene as ever. She smiled as Kathryn walked toward her, but her smile stopped short of her grieving eyes.

Obeying her instinct, Kathryn hugged her. Lady Mary felt fragile in her arms. "I am so sorry."

"We retain our hope." Sir Arthur rose and kissed her cheek. The ravages of grief were much clearer on him.

Beatrice stood. "I must see to the children."

"Let me go." Kathryn jumped at the chance to do something. "You stay here with your mother and father. I can take them out to play, if you would like."

Garrett gave her a grateful smile. "Our thanks. That is very kind."

Kathryn found the boys upstairs. The youngest, Edward, slept. So she left him and led the two older boys out of the grim, silent keep. Even young Adam stayed quiet in her arms.

Richard took her hand and walked beside her. He stared at her. "Is it true? Is my Uncle Henry gone?"

Kathryn had little to no experience with children. She opted for the truth. "So, they say." Hand-in-hand they crossed the bailey to the postern gate. "They are not sure...where he has gone, and they fear for him."

Richard nodded, and slipped through the postern gate.

Briny air brushed their cheeks as they followed the path from the postern gate to the shore below.

"I don't remember Henry very well," Richard said. He kicked at pebbles in his path and sent them skittering along the beach. "I do remember he makes good dragon noises."

Adam stirred to get down, and Kathryn placed him on his feet beside his brother.

"I do not know how to make dragon noises, but perhaps we can build a tower from these stones." The sea spread out in a calm, deep blue, breaking over the beach in a languid soothing swish and suck. She steered the boys back from the water's edge and showed them a good flat stone to start their tower.

Richard took control, instructing Adam on finding the right sort of stones. Adam chattered away, his piping voice cutting through the sibilant wash of the tide.

A man called, "Lady Kathryn."

She turned.

Digory picked across the pebbled ground toward her.

What the hell could he want from her? She had naught to say to the cur.

"Who is that?" Richard shaded his eyes, and Adam copied him.

"A man." And one she did not want to see today, if ever.

Digory stopped out of sword reach from her. "I heard the news in the village. People have been called to prayers for your brother by marriage."

Kathryn nodded, not trusting her voice. So much grief for a man she had never met, and yet he felt real to her through the people about her. "What do you want, Digory?"

"I wanted to speak with you." He shoved his hands into his belt. "I did not want to disturb the keep."

"Go away." She turned her back on him. How dare he approach her now, with the keep reeling under bad tidings.

Richard and Adam stopped stacking rocks and moved further along the rocky shore. They squatted beside a small tidal pool.

"Allow me just a moment of your time." Digory clambered crablike over the rocks to her side. "I shall not keep you long."

Alone, Kathryn might have given her anger free rein, but the boys could hear them. She crouched beside Richard and Adam. "What do you see?"

"Mussels." Richard pointed out a cluster of black, shiny shells clinging to the sides of the pool. "They make good eating."

"I love your sister." Digory panted closer, slipping on the slick stone. "I would never hurt her."

He went too far. Kathryn closed the distance between them.

"I am minding the children. I have nothing to say to you. Now, go away."

"One moment." Digory stood his ground. "One short moment of your time."

Wind ruffled his brown hair, his gaze held hers, calm and steady. His chin stuck out at a determined angle

She had not the strength to fight him. One of the last things Roger had asked of her was to speak with Digory. "One moment." She turned to keep watch on the boys. "But I doubt anything you say could change my mind."

"Thank you." Digory moved closer to her and lowered his voice. "You know Matty better than I do. You know she was not raised to work on a farm."

Kathryn shrugged. No Matty had not been raised to be farmer's wife. Their father had groomed Matty, his chance at a great alliance, to take her place beside the most powerful men in the kingdom. Not some ham-handed lout.

"She was not happy on the farm," Digory said.

Adam had a stick and poked it into the pool.

"Be careful," Kathryn called. "You do not want to hurt something."

With a gasp, Adam dropped his stick.

Richard tugged on his tunic and led his brother to another tide pool.

"Do not go too near." Kathryn trailed them.

Richard crossed his arms, strongly resembling his father in the stubborn tautness of his shoulders. "I know how to swim."

"Does Adam?"

"Aye." Richard scuffed the rock. "A little."

Kathryn let the matter rest there, and Richard returned to tormenting sea creatures.

"Matty did not like the work on the farm. The animals, the land, the house. She did not know how to do any of it." Digory stayed his course. She would give him that much. "I tried to teach her but she missed her needlework, and most days, she sat by the window."

"Matty hates needlework." Kathryn glared at Digory. He need not think to lie to her.

He shrugged. "I only know what she told me."

"You should never have married her." They drew closer to the boys and Kathryn lowered her voice. "You had no right to marry her and carry her away to your farm."

"You are right." Digory rubbed the back of her neck. "She is as far above me as the angels."

If he spouted poetry now, Kathryn could not keep her silent promise to Roger. "Get on with it."

Digory reddened. "Aye, well, she is, and I should not have thought to take her away from her life. But I loved her. I love her." He cleared his throat. "And when she told me how matters were, at the keep, with your father. I wanted to save my angel."

"What did Matty tell you?" The idea of Digory knowing of her shame sickened her.

Digory averted his gaze and cleared his throat. "That he beat her. Sometimes so badly she could not rise from her bed."

Father seldom raised a hand to Matty. Not since she had shown signs of blossoming into her current beauty anyway. Nay, he saved his blows for her and Mother. But Digory did not deserve to know that, so she clamped her mouth shut.

"I believed she would be safer with me. I still believe that."

"I saw the marks on her." Kathryn fisted her hands. With the boys playing nearby, perhaps it was fortunate she had left her sword in the keep.

Richard and Adam worked on a new tower just to her left. This one higher than the one before.

"I did not put them there." Digory spread his hands in front of him. "May God strike me down if I lie. I did not put them there. She fell while milking Dewdrop."

Kathryn snorted. A likely story.

Digory took a deep breath and launched into a tale of Matty

and a cow. She wanted to ignore him, but the more he spoke, the more difficult it became. She could picture Matty refusing to milk the cow. And Matty would object to tying its legs together. Even the words he used sounded like they came straight from Matty's mouth.

"I raised my voice to her." Digory dug his fingers into his scalp. "I wish I had not because she is too fragile, and too delicate for a man to speak so to her. But I raised my voice, and then left her. When I came back, she was gone."

Adam tottered over and tugged at her skirts. He raised chubby arms to be lifted.

"Your moment is done." Kathryn scooped the boy up.

"We are hungry." Richard joined her.

"I will wait in the village," Digory said. "For as long as it takes. I will swear before a priest if you want me to. I never harmed your sister. She is my wife. I love her and I want her back."

"I am returning to the keep. This is not the time for this." Kathryn turned her back on Digory and picked her way across the rocks. "Go home."

"I will wait."

When she reached the top of the rise, Digory still stood on the rocks, watching her.

She had done her part, listened to him. "Let us go to the kitchens."

Why would Matty tell Digory that their father struck her? Why would any woman lie about something like that? Except, Matty did fit the truth to her means at times. Her disloyalty to Matty writhed inside her.

A kitchen drudge stood aside as she and the boys entered the kitchen.

If Matty lied to Digory, she must have good reason. And Matty feared their father with a terror that choked her at times. Time and time she had begged Kathryn to save her from the results of her actions. Kathryn did, because as the older sister, it fell to her to protect the younger.

She seated the boys at the table, then found a cloth and washed their faces and hands.

Adam tried to wriggle away.

Richard sat still, but pulled faces that drew chuckles from the kitchen workers.

Cook placed honey cakes and beakers of milk before the boys.

Richard guided Adam's hands around the beaker and helped him to drink.

As she had done for Matty when they were younger.

"There you are." Matty appeared in the kitchen doorway, one hand pressed against the frame, the other clasped to her bosom. "How could you be absent at a time like this?"

"I took the boys out." Matty's overdeveloped sensibilities in these situations chafed. By contrast, Kathryn struggled to express her emotions, and kept them deep inside. Perhaps if she could be more like Matty, the ache might not gnaw quite so much. The only person who had seen her cry freely was Roger. Dear God, she wanted to start this day again, by his side.

"Oh." Matty dabbed at her tears. "You poor little sweetings." She descended on the boys in a cloud of rosewater and flung her arms about their shoulders. "How you must weep and long for your Uncle Henry. He was the very best of uncles."

"You did not know Uncle Henry." Richard blinked at her, while Adam stuffed another honey cake in his mouth.

Undeterred, Matty pressed their heads to her chest. "Such brave little boys to keep your strength at a time like this."

"We are hungry." Richard wriggled free and shuffled down the bench.

"Kathryn." Matty straightened and thrust her shoulders back. "We must bear the burden of daily tasks for our new family. I will instruct the laundresses to die all our wimples black. They must also find black cloth to drape over all the casements."

Had Matty been at the mead already? She meant well, but only Lady Mary should give that instruction, and that would not happen until they had proof Henry had died. "Nay." She wiped

Adam's sticky hands. "That is not our place. If you want to help, I would suggest you make yourself available for Lady Mary's instruction."

Matty's mouth drooped. "Lady Mary is beside herself. She stares into the flames hour upon hour. Will not eat, will take no rest. I fear for her health. They say her health suffered with the birth of Mathew. This could kill her."

Richard paled and glanced from her to Matty.

"Matty, you go too far. The news reached us only a few hours ago. The most sensible thing we can do is remain calm, and help where we can."

"You are always so sensible." Matty stomped to the table and flung herself onto the bench. "I have feelings, and they need to come out."

"Is my grandmama sick?" Richard tugged on Kathryn's skirt.

"Nay." Kathryn crouched to his level. Why could Matty not guard her tongue? "But she is very sad and very worried. And she will need all the cuddles you can give her."

"Indeed." Garrett entered the kitchen. "Did you have a good time with Lady Kathryn?"

"Garrett!" Matty sprang to her feet. She ran to him, and cupped his face in her palms. "How do you fare?"

"He fares as well as he can." Beatrice entered on Garrett's heels. "But your concern is noted." She glared until Matty dropped her hands. "Thank you for taking the boys, Kathryn. It's not good for them to be cooped up with a bunch of weeping adults."

"My pleasure." Kathryn managed to formulate the words, but Matty's behavior left her dumbfounded. Matty barely knew Garrett. What was her sister about?

Chapter Twenty-Nine

Kathryn sat in her casement while the moonlight played hide and seek with the waves. As the days dragged into a fortnight she spent most of her nights here. With no news yet from Roger, Anglesea hung suspended between hope and despair.

Sleep evaded her, and when she did sleep, her worries chased her into her dreams. The silence from Roger stretched everyone's nerves to breaking. Anglesea folk went about their business, but remained tense and waiting. Any sound from the gates brought the entire keep to a halt as all eyes swung in that direction, only to suffer disappointment time and time again.

She missed Roger so much she had taken to wearing his chemise to bed. His scent clung to the fabric and she wrapped her arms about herself. All alone in London, on a task that must be tearing him apart.

Mother wedged into a secret place in her mind. At Mandeville, her mother lived with that monster and Kathryn could not reach her, and protect her. Anglesea had enough heartache right now, and she shared her worry with nobody. She had tried to speak with Matty about it, but Matty dismissed her fears. With a toss of her head, she had declared Mother to be fine.

Matty provided another niggling concern. Not as large as the other worries, but there all the same. From Calder, Faye, Gregory and their children had arrived two days hence. William sent word that Alice's confinement made travel too risky, but they would come when they could. God knows what Matty would have made of William. Already, she divided her time between comforting Garrett and Gregory. She'd even cozied up to Sir Arthur a time or two.

When Kathryn had suggested Matty speak with her own husband, who still lurked in the village, Matty had burst into tears, accused her of betraying her and taken to her bed for the remainder of the day.

A stiff breeze ruffled Kathryn's hair, cool on her face. She had left Matty to fend for herself that day, and she still felt like a bad sister. Matty had emerged for dinner, wan and listless, and sent her reproachful glances all through the meal.

The lightening sky marked the hour as close to dawn. As a child she had believed the moon granted wishes, and sent countless of them up to her.

"Please let Henry be alive," she whispered, her voice loud in the still chamber. "And guard over my mother." Her whimsy embarrassed her, but she sent another quick prayer anyway. "I know I ask much, but could you bring Roger back to me, too? And if it is not too much to ask, could you...do something about Matty?" The moon beamed down, cold and aloof. "I am not sure what, but Matty is accustomed to being the darling of the keep, and she..."

What? Matty liked all attention on her, and ensured it stayed on her. At times, Kathryn believed she and Matty had grown up in entirely different households. How could the same father treat two daughters in such a different manner?

She shifted her numb ass on the cushion. Her body urged sleep, but her mind would not allow it. Tomorrow would bring more of the same and she needed her rest. Over the last fortnight she had become the unofficial nurse to Beatrice and Faye's children.

Beatrice's time to deliver her fourth child also drew close, and she needed to rest more and more.

In search of warmed mead to help her sleep, Kathryn crept through the still keep. By the deep shadows beneath Lady Mary's eyes, she would guess if she knocked on Lady Mary's door, she would find her mother by marriage keeping vigil with her.

She entered the hall, and won her wager. Lady Mary sat beside Sir Arthur at the hearth fire.

"Kathryn." Lady Mary held out her hand. "I see we are not the only ones keeping watch through the night."

Sir Arthur rose and fetched her a goblet. "My lady had the uncanniest sense that we would receive news." He touched Lady Mary's cheek. "I have learned never to ignore her sense of these things."

"What he means is that when I cannot sleep, he cannot sleep."

Handing her the goblet, Sir Arthur motioned to his seat. "Take it." He pressed her gently into the chair. "I find I am too restless to sit for long."

Sir Arthur paced to the far casement and stared into the night.

"He finds the waiting hard." Lady Mary watched her husband. "He would be happier if I put a sword in his hand and sent him to fight something."

Kathryn nodded. In that way she resembled Sir Arthur. "Do you sense Roger returns this night?"

"I am not sure." Lady Mary pressed a hand to her temple. "I just have this sense that something will occur." She sipped her wine. "Tell me how you fare."

"I am well," Kathryn hid behind her goblet.

Lady Mary's laughter sounded a little rusty. "Kathryn, you are pacing the floor in the middle of the night. That does not say well to me."

"I would like Roger to return," she said, parceling out her truth carefully. Lady Mary already bore a heavy burden.

"I see Mathilda's husband is about still." Lady Mary stretched her slippered feet out to the fire. "He seems determined to see her."

"I will deal with him."

"We will deal with him." Lady Mary rested her head back, and closed her eyes. "The Lord knows we can do nothing about our situation. Do you still think he raised his hand to your sister?"

"I am not sure." Despite her loyalty to Matty, her doubts persisted. Matty's strange behavior did not ease them any either. "Matty is...different."

Lady Mary opened her eyes. "How different?"

Uncomfortable with speaking of what she had no answer for, Kathryn lightened her tone. "Matty will be fine."

"You may as well tell her all." Sir Arthur's hand landed on Kathryn's shoulder. For a big man, he crossed a hall like a wraith. "I have learned over the years to tell my lady what she wants to know."

"I do not want to burden you at this time." Kathryn took a sip of wine to ease her dry throat. Even speaking of Matty to another felt bad.

"Pfft!" Lady Mary waved her hand. "My own thoughts drive me near to screaming as it is. I welcome the distraction. Perhaps Mathilda is enjoying a taste of freedom for the first time?"

Lady Mary had missed nothing of Matty's cooing and flirting. That sharp gaze told Kathryn as much as clearly as if she spoke the words. "That is my hope."

"Have you any news of your mother? Do you know how she fares?"

The switch in conversation relieved Kathryn of having to go further down that road. "I had a brief message from her the other day. She said all was well."

"As she would." Lady Mary smiled. "She would not want to burden you."

A true strike, and Kathryn returned her smile.

"Sir Arthur?" A guard entered the hall. He removed his helm and bowed low. "There is a message from London."

Lady Mary stilled, and glanced at her.

"Give it here." Sir Arthur stalked the poor man.

The guard stepped back, the message out held in his shaking hand.

Kathryn dug her nails into her thighs as Sir Arthur read the message. It could not take so long to read the few lines the small parchment could hold.

Sir Arthur crumpled the parchment in his fist. He dropped his head.

"What is it?" Lady Mary rose, then sat again as if her legs could not hold it. "Is Henry...?"

"Nay." Striding to her, Sir Arthur flung the parchment from him. He crouched before her. "But the news is not good."

Kathryn swallowed the lump in her throat. "What is it?"

"The crown has received word that prisoners will no longer be ransomed."

"Dear God." Lady Mary's knuckles whitened on the arms of her chair. "But they have always ransomed their noble prisoners."

"The infidel want us gone," Sir Arthur said. "They want the pilgrims out of their land, and they act to ensure it."

No more ransoms, meant little to no hope Henry would survive if he had been captured.

Lady Mary slumped in her seat.

Kathryn crossed to her, but her clumsy tongue did not have the right words of comfort. She took Lady Mary's frigid hands in hers and chafed them. "It is bad," she said. "I know it looks bad but perhaps he escaped, or is hiding somewhere."

"Perhaps." Lady Mary drew a shuddering breath. "Does Roger say when he returns?"

"Soon." Sir Arthur rose and paced the hall. "He will spend a few more days to see if he can gather any more information."

Lady Mary's pallor concerned Kathryn, and she pressed her wine on the other woman until she took a sip.

"I must pray." Straightening her shoulders, Lady Mary pressed Kathryn back. "Will you send Nurse to me?"

"Aye."

Kathryn stood beside Sir Arthur as Lady Mary left the hall with her back straight.

Sir Arthur's stillness set the air between them alight. Tight-lipped, he watched his lady. His fists clenched. "No more."

Kathryn took a wary step back. This was a side of the man she had only glimpsed before. Here stood the fabled Sir Arthur of Anglesea.

"No more."

"What?" In his contained rage Kathryn could believe him capable of every wild story she had heard of his ruthlessness in battle.

"I am Arthur of Anglesea." His voice rose on a roar that bounced around the enormous hall. "I am not some puny, powerless runt to be dragged along in the wake of my fate."

"Sir Arthur." Kathryn dared not step closer.

Rage built in Sir Arthur until she feared it would burst from him. "I do not sit like an old woman in my hall when challenged."

"What can you do?" Kathryn tried to keep her tone calm and reasonable. He reminded her of Sir Royce, only far more frightening than her father had ever been. Even at his worst, kicking and punching her senseless, he had not held the raw power of Sir Arthur.

"What can I do?" Sir Arthur raised his fist. "I can act."

"What are—?"

"Heathens may have my son. I will raise the greatest army God or man has ever seen and I will break them until they give him back. For each drop of his blood spilled, I will spill a thousandfold more."

He was beyond reason, beyond control. Sick to her stomach, Kathryn knew she had to act. "Sir Arthur you cannot—"

"Do not tell me what I cannot do, Kathryn." He strode toward her. "I was barely old enough to shave and they told me I could not take control of my demesne. Yet here we stand." His voice dropped to a silky murmur. "Ask Garrett what happened when they told me I could not take his father's keep. Ask any of the misguided sods who have stood in the way of what I want."

He could not mean his words. Anger and pain had Sir Arthur in their grip. If Roger were here, or William even, she could run to them. "Let me get Gregory and Garrett."

"Tell them to fetch their swords or stay out of my path." Sir Arthur stormed for the entrance.

"Where are you going?" Kathryn trailed him as close as she dared.

"I am going to get my son," he said over his shoulder. "But first, I am going to get your mother back. Arthur of Anglesea fights." He threw back his head and bellowed, the sound echoing off the stone and swelling.

Kathryn covered her ears.

Dear God! She stood frozen as his boot heels rang against the stone. Then Kathryn ran.

Chapter Thirty

Making herself as small as possible beside a line of crossbows, Kathryn lingered in the armory and listened.

Garrett paced the room. Row upon row of lances stood to attention behind him on the wall.

Gregory leaned his hips against the table covered in maps, and watched him.

"He is beyond reason." Garret paced back to Gregory. "Nothing I say penetrates that thick skull."

"Sir Arthur is a man of war." Gregory folded his arms. "It is all he has known. It is all he knows now."

"Jesu." Garrett slammed his fist into the table. A pewter goblet clattered to the floor. "He will bring Anglesea to her knees if he persists with this."

Gregory put the goblet back. "He knows no other way."

"He gathers the men, right this minute, to march on Mandeville." Garrett strode to the casement, his back taut as he stared out.

Kathryn had caused all of this. Sir Arthur made war on Mandeville to get her mother back. King Henry would not tolerate it, and Anglesea would pay the price of his anger. All because of her. Thus stood the facts and she could not dance her way around them. She needed to fix this. Taking a small step closer, she raised her voice. "What if there was no reason for him to make war on Mandeville?"

Garrett whirled and glowered at her. "No matter what you say, he will launch this fool's errand. His grief over Henry renders him deaf to anything but his need to act."

Gregory cocked his head. He saw so much deeper than the average man. "My lady?"

"I mean, what if my mother was already at Anglesea. Then there would be no need for this war." Kathryn gripped her hands together. She could not show her nerves now. The audacity of her plan staggered her, but she saw no other way.

"Your father has already declared he will…" Garrett's tensed, his stare narrowed on her, sharper than the blades gleaming on the walls. "Whatever you are thinking, forget it."

"Nay." She could not falter now. "Sir Gregory is the calmest, most reasoned voice here. He must stay. You are needed by Beatrice's side." Garrett had to see her reasoning for the good sense it made. "Roger arrives any day now, but he might not arrive before the army marches."

"Lady Kathryn." Gregory shook his head. "Nay."

"Aye." Kathryn pressed forward. "I know the way better than anyone. I can be there and back long before anyone else. I have been sneaking in and out of Mandeville since I first walked." Her legs shook as she took a step closer to Gregory. She dared not look at Garrett. "All I ask is that you delay Sir Arthur. You can do that. He needs your men. Call them here. Persuade him to wait for them."

"You have lost your mind." He threw his hands in the air. "What is it with the air in this blasted castle? It makes all the women mad."

"I can do it." Kathryn held her ground as Garrett loomed over her. "Three days is all I need."

"Nay." Garrett's toes nudged hers. "You do not have three days because I am not letting you go."

"I agree with Garrett." Gregory's tone remained calm, but she could not ignore the implacable note in his voice.

"Three days," she said. "I can have my mother here in three days. By that time, Roger might have returned. Perhaps he can talk some sense into Sir Arthur."

"Nay." Garrett folded his arms.

Gregory shook his head.

Men! Kathryn nearly stamped her foot, but her case would receive no help from acting the petulant child. "I can be in and out before my father even suspects I am there. He will have no way of knowing I took her. We could hide my mother with Tom and Ivy."

"Nay," Garrett said, firmer this time.

Another headshake from Gregory.

"Aye." Kathryn squared her shoulders. "I am going."

"Not if I have to lock you up," Garret said.

Kathryn raised her chin. "You can try, but my father has never managed that yet."

Garrett growled and strode an agitated circle to the casement and back again. "Roger will wring your neck. We have a plan for your mother."

Kathryn stepped into his path. "Sir Arthur is not going to wait for your plan. He is not going to wait longer than three days at the most."

"Do not make me tie you to a chair." Garrett meant it, too. It poured out of every fiber and sinew of his tensed form.

A pity for him then, that Kathryn had never allowed a man to command her.

* * *

A day and a night of breakneck, but uneventful travel and Garrett still had not forgiven her. He had caught up with her the far side of Anglesea village as she made her ride for Mandeville. He had given it a spirited attempt to get her to change her mind, but Kathryn had stood firm. She had to do this.

Dagger saved her by vehemently objecting to her being tied to her horse and sent back to Anglesea.

Now, they skulked in the shadows beside Mandeville postern gate and argued, again.

Garrett had stubbornness to spare. He claimed it came from being married to Beatrice.

"I know the keep better." The wall sentry turned and marched away from them.

Garrett wrapped her fingers around a small stick. "Then draw me a map, because if anyone is going in there, it is me."

"She will never come with you willingly."

"I was not planning on asking her." Garrett pointed to the soft earth at their feet. "Now draw."

Dagger, the betrayer, dropped onto his belly and gazed at Garrett with adoration. Over the course of their headlong ride, he had decided to make Garrett his newest god.

"You are going to bundle her up and carry her off like a sack of grain?" Her mother would die of fright.

"Never you mind how I am going to get her here." Garrett jabbed his thumb at the ground. "All you need to know is that I am better at this than anyone you know. Now, show me where I must go."

"I am not explaining to Beatrice why you got killed in the middle of Mandeville," she said.

"You should have thought of that before you dragged us both on this crazed journey." He jerked his head. "Draw."

Already the sky to the east showed the first release of deep dark. So, Kathryn sketched out the interior of the castle for Garrett.

A flickering brazier from the walls provided barely enough light to see, but Garret must have absorbed it all, because with a nod he slipped through the postern gate.

No wait had ever felt longer. She divided her attention

between the pearly fingers of day creeping across the east, and the dark maw of the postern gate. She strained to hear any sound from within.

Dagger pricked his ears and stood.

Garrett appeared, a figure running at his side. She had not even heard a whisper.

"Kathryn?" Mother's voice rose from the cloaked form.

"Mother." Her mother. Safe at last. Kathryn steadied herself against the wall.

Garrett moved fast, staying to the shadows with her mother and already leaving her behind as they entered the trees where the horses were hidden.

Without allowing her a moment to greet her mother, he had her mother on Striker.

"She rides with you," he said, before leaping onto his horse.

Kathryn scrambled up behind her mother, and dug her heels into Striker.

Her heart still thumped against her chest. Her hands slid slick with sweat on the reins. She had barely recovered from Garrett appearing with Mother and they already headed deep into the woods, Mandeville growing further behind with each pound of hoof against earth.

Garrett certainly knew his way about an abduction.

She wanted to giggle all of a sudden.

"What is happening?" Mother's whisper cut into her thoughts. "He said I had to come. It was a matter of life and death."

So that is how he had done it. "It is. I will explain later." Kathryn tightened her arms about her mother. She should have thought of this weeks ago, but she had Mother now. "I promise."

Mother's forbearance lasted until midday, when they slowed the horses to a walk.

"Explain." She shifted in the saddle and pinned Kathryn with a stare.

"Your daughter thinks she is rescuing you," Garrett said without turning around.

"From your father?" Mother gaped, and then her shoulders slumped. "Oh, Kathryn, you must take me back."

Kathryn jerked on Striker's reins. This must be how Cecily lived day by day, without sensible thought in her head. Mother could not want to return to that animal. "I cannot."

"He is my husband." Mother straightened her shoulders. "I made vows to him that you cannot force me to break."

Garrett glanced over his shoulder. He shook his head and turned his attention back to the road. "Might I suggest you discuss this later," he said. "They will not be far behind us."

"Nay." Mother wriggled and nearly unseated both of them. "I belong with my husband."

"Well, you cannot go back now." Kathryn wanted to beat her fists against the ground. She had expected her mother to be shocked, but her anger completely wrong-footed her. "Garrett did not lie. This is a matter of life and death. If I do not get you back to Anglesea, there will be war."

Mother blanched. "Kathryn! What have you done?"

"Nothing." She could not hold her mother's accusing glare. "Sir Arthur is going to make war on Mandeville. To rescue you."

"Why would he think I needed rescuing?"

Kathryn had no words.

Fortunately, Garrett stepped in. "Sir Arthur is not himself. We thought if we could bring you to Anglesea, we might prevent the war."

"This conversation is not finished." Mother gave a regal wave. "We must make haste. I will not have war between our keeps over this."

* * *

Kathryn stood with her arm about Mother, as the noise in the armory threatened to shake the keep. They had barely stumbled off their horses before the fighting started. Any conversation between her and Mother would have to wait.

Angry enough to come to blows, Garrett and Sir Arthur stood nose-to-nose and bellowed at each other.

"Stop them," Mother whispered.

Kathryn shook her head. A woman could get crushed in the clash of two such large men.

Gregory pushed them apart, but the men came right back together.

"Get out of my way, boy." Sir Arthur shoved Garrett, hard enough it sent him stumbling back.

"Do not think I won't wipe my feet on you, old man." Garrett lunged.

Gregory caught him on a shout that rattled the rafters. "Enough!"

Everyone froze.

Gregory hardly ever raised his voice. Taller than Garrett and Sir Arthur, with a pair of barn-like shoulders, he loomed over them. "Neither of you is helping," he said. "We have enough trouble at our door without rushing out and grabbing more."

"Are they still fighting?" With a big sigh, Beatrice sidled up.

If her father and husband threatened to dismember each other, Kathryn would be doing more than sighing. Then again, if her husband threatened to dismember her father, Kathryn would cheer him on. Even hand him the gutting knife. "Gregory is keeping them apart."

Beatrice snorted. "Good luck to him. I have tried and failed to do that for years."

"Sit." Gregory pressed Garrett onto a bench. He kept one huge hand on his shoulder and glowered at Sir Arthur.

"Do not think to look at me like that." Sir Arthur stuck his chest out. "I answer to nobody."

"You answer to your wife," Gregory said. "And right now, she does not need you rushing around like an avenging angel.'

Sir Arthur grumbled but took the bench opposite Garrett. He

had not taken kindly to the news of their rescue. Not at all, and despite Kathryn's vehement protests, blamed Garrett for the entire thing. "I will make them tremble before the might of Anglesea."

Even worse, he remained resolved to march on the holy land. Once he and Garrett had finished trying to pummel each other. Just when had matters gone from bad to horrible?

Gregory beckoned a cowering Rob and his mead jug closer. "Let us discuss this calmly."

"I wish William were here." Beatrice tensed and ran a hand over her belly. "He has a way of calming my father down."

"Bugger calm!" Sir Arthur sprang to his feet.

Garrett leaped up.

"And here we go again." Beatrice flinched.

"Will they fight?" Matty arrived on Kathryn's other side.

Beatrice glared at Matty. "Why do you sound as if you would like that?"

"I would not." Matty squeaked and ducked behind Kathryn's shoulder. Kathryn applauded Matty's wisdom in staying clear of Beatrice.

"Mathilda!" Mother gaped. "Where have you been? What happened to you?"

Matty's mouth dropped open. Then she threw herself into their mother's arms. "Oh, Mother. I am so glad you are here. I have had the most terrible time."

Beatrice gasped and grabbed Kathryn's arm.

Kathryn glared at her sister. She agreed with Beatrice. Matty's need for attention could not surface at a worse time. "Not now, Matty. There are bigger things at work."

Sir Arthur thumped the table. "I will not sit idly by while—"

"You will do nothing." Garrett wrenched free of Gregory. "What you propose will bring war down on all of us."

"Scared, bastard?"

"Of you?"

Flushed with excitement, Matty peered over Mother's shoulder.

Beatrice grabbed Kathryn, and doubled over. "Oh, dear God!"

"You have upset Beatrice." Garrett yelled at Sir Arthur.

Sir Arthur grabbed Garrett by the tunic. "I would never upset my daughter."

Gregory sprang after him.

All three men went over in a crash of benches and tables.

Matty squealed.

"Stop it." Kathryn could not loosen Beatrice's grip on her arms. She jerked her head in Matty's direction. "Make her stop please, Mother. She is not helping."

The men disappeared in a tangle of grunts, arms, and legs.

Mayhem. Everywhere she looked.

A piercing whistle ripped through the hall.

Everything stopped. All gazes swung to the door.

Roger.

Her heart leaped. He stood in the doorway looking tired and travel strained but so beautiful she wanted to fling herself at him.

He surveyed the room. "What, in the name of God, is going on here?"

Where to start?

"They are fighting." Beatrice panted and squeezed Kathryn's arms. "And I am having a baby."

"Now." Garrett ran for Beatrice.

"Get her out of here." Sir Arthur bellowed.

Roger moved past her to Beatrice and Garrett. "Get her upstairs."

"Sir Roger." Matty wriggled out of Mother's arms. She threw herself against his chest. "Thank the Lord you are come. They have all gone quite mad."

Roger started, and glanced at Matty. To his credit he kept his arms at his sides.

"Sir Roger." Mother pried Matty off him. "It is good to see you."

"And you." Roger frowned. "When did you arrive?"

"You may very well ask." Sir Arthur strode forward. "Ask the bastard what he encouraged your wife to do."

Finally, Roger's gaze sought her. "My lady. Are you well?"

"Aye." Kathryn nodded. Tears misted her vision and she shook her head to clear them. She had missed him, like a huge piece of herself.

"Good." He nodded, and walked past her. "Now." Roger turned to the room at large. "We will all sit down and speak of this."

Gregory straightened his tunic. "Your father wanted to make war on Mandeville to get Lady Rose back." He indicated her mother. "In an effort to prevent war, Lady Kathryn and Garrett rode to Mandeville and...fetched her."

"Fetched?" Roger stared at her.

Kathryn fidgeted beneath his steady, ice-blue gaze. "Garrett came with me to keep me safe."

"I see." He put his hands behind his back. "And did Garrett see fit to explain to you, whilst you fetched your mother, that he and I already had the matter in hand?"

She nearly lied, but decided against it. "He did, but time was pressing and I..."

He nodded. "You decided not to trust me and to take matters into your own hands."

Nay, that was not it at all, but Roger had already turned his back, and approached his father.

"Come, Kathryn." Mother touched her arm. "This is not a place for women. Let the men talk."

Reluctantly, Kathryn followed her out. A cold, remote stranger stood in place of her husband.

* * *

As much as Roger wanted to follow Kathryn out of the armory and upstairs, his father had to be dealt with first. Dear God, exhaustion dwelled in his bones and made itself at home there. "So"—he took the bench beside his father—"war?"

"Aye." Sir Arthur clenched his fists in his lap. "Will you support me?"

"Nay." Roger laid his hand on his father's shoulder. "But not for the reasons you think. Let us talk first of Henry."

"You have more news." Up came Sir Arthur's head.

His father's hope sliced him clear to the bone. "No more." He shook his head. "But I spoke to a few people who are returned from pilgrimage. They say we should take heart that a body has not been found. Things work differently there, and Henry may very well be alive."

Sir Arthur nodded, his shoulders drooping.

"Newt found me in London." Roger poured his father a tankard of mead and handed it to him. "He is putting together the pieces of a plan Garrett devised."

"A fool's errand." Sir Arthur stood and straightened his back with a loud pop.

"I think not." Roger stretched out his stiff legs. He had ridden hard through the last two days to reach home.

Sir Arthur turned to him. "You trust Garrett?"

"With my sister." Roger kept his tone light. "And now with this thing with Mandeville."

"I cannot like it." Sir Arthur shook his head.

"That may be." Roger rose beside his father. "But you gave Anglesea into my care, and I must run it as I see fit."

"What is this plan?"

Roger pictured his father's reaction to Garrett's underhand machinations and for the first time in weeks, he wanted to smile. "You do not want to know," he said. "You are just going to have to trust us."

Sir Arthur stared at him for a long moment. At last he

nodded, and sank onto the bench. "This is a whole new world we live in now."

"Aye." It felt to Roger like he had not slept since he left Anglesea. "A world in which a man must think first, and then act."

Sir Arthur strode to the casement. Dawn broke across the sky in a vivid splash of scarlet over the sea. "Then it is a good thing that I have you as my heir."

Chapter Thirty-One

Kathryn entered the chamber Mother now shared with Matty. Facing the landward side of the castle, the casement overlooked the bailey and the fertile land beyond the castle wall. A pleasant chamber with rich furnishings that would have functioned as a lord's solar in a lesser keep than Anglesea.

Lady Rose sat by the casement, calm and serene on the bright, cheery cushions.

"Mother?"

"There you are, sweeting." Mother motioned her closer.

"Where is Matty?" She had parted from her mother and sister outside the armory, wanting to see if Roger would follow her out. Instead, Gregory had politely closed the door on her with a compassionate smile.

"Around." Mother breathed deep and folded her hands in her lap. "I thought we might talk alone first. We have had quite the adventure."

Kathryn sat on the bed, not sure she wanted to hear what her mother had to say. A brightly embroidered bed cover mocked her mood. She still struggled to make sense of their hasty words during their ride for Anglesea.

Mother rose and hugged her. The familiar scent of rosemary clung to her mother, the smell of childhood and brief snatches of happiness amidst the grim reality of Mandeville. Despite Father, they had managed to carve out moments of sweetness.

Kathryn clung to her mother, praying she could keep her alive and well at Anglesea.

"You have been worrying about me." Mother tilted her chin up. "All this time married and safe at Anglesea, and you have been fretting over me?"

"Aye." Kathryn nodded, not trusting her voice.

"And now you feel betrayed that I did not leap for joy at your rescue."

Kathryn's cheeks burned, because deep within, her mother's reaction smarted.

"Silly girl." Mother held her shoulders. "You were always thus, worrying about Matty and me."

A slight bruise marred her mother's cheek. Kathryn touched her fingertip to the place. "He hit you?"

"Only the once." Mother shrugged. "His pursuit of newer fields keeps him busy."

Kathryn did not know how her mother had stood it all these years. Now married, her father's treatment angered Kathryn even more. Now that she understood how a good man treated his wife. "How did you bear it?"

"Did I have a choice?" Mother returned to the casement. "I chose your father, you know."

"You did?" Kathryn found that impossible to believe. "I thought your father married you against your will."

"Nay." Mother sat and folded her hands on her lap. "My father let me choose from three or four suitors. Your father was my choice."

"Why?"

Mother shrugged. "He was not always as he is now. He came courting and said and did all the right things." She sighed. "I heard the stories about his broken heart because his true love died.

I believed I could be the one to heal him. I let my silly girl's heart make a bad choice." She cocked her head and smiled at Kathryn. "You chose much better for yourself."

"Aye, I did." If the old Roger remained buried beneath the stranger she had glimpsed in the armory.

Mother frowned. "Speaking of poor choices. I understand Matty has come running to you."

"Ah." Kathryn picked at the patterned thread on the bed cover as she tried to find a way to break the bad news to her mother.

"She tells me she married a farmer."

"Aye." Kathryn nodded. "She says he beats her."

"She would." Mother snorted.

She must have misheard. Kathryn stared at her mother, waiting for a clue.

"Kathryn." Mother glanced out the casement and back again. "What is the one thing she could say that would bring you armed and bustling to her defense?"

Well, there was that. "I am not sure she speaks the truth."

Mother stood and twitched her skirts. "You always did view Matty as you wanted her to be."

A few short weeks ago she might have scoffed at that, but Kathryn's faith in her judgment and Matty wavered. "She is changed."

"Nay." Mother shook her head. "It is not Matty who has changed, but you. You no longer see her with the same eyes."

"Perhaps."

Mother sat beside her, and took her hands. "This is your place now, Kathryn. Not Matty's and not mine."

"I just wanted to keep you safe." The words tore out of a deep place, so long hidden, that she ached as they came out.

"That was never your task." Mother smoothed Kathryn's hair back. "You always were such a fierce little thing. I believe I made the mistake of leaning too hard upon your strength."

"Nay." All that she had, she had given freely.

"This time apart has helped me see this more clearly." Mother placed an arm about her shoulder. "I have used your strength and not my own. That stops now, sweeting. You have a wonderful husband, a new family who loves you, all the things you deserve. I am not your responsibility. I never was."

A void opened within Kathryn, the place always filled with her love for Matty and Mother, her fierce desire to keep them safe. If she could not be that person anymore, then who was she? "You cannot mean to return to him."

"But I do."

Kathryn jerked in rejection of the idea

Mother tightened her hold. "I made my place at Mandeville. I have chosen my path, and made my vows before God. I will not break them."

Kathryn felt as if she stood on the edge of a cliff, and stared into a wide nothingness beyond. All her waking thoughts, all her plans and her determination, and now it came to naught. She could not accept this. "You will return to that monster?"

"I will return to my husband," Mother said. "And you will remain here with yours."

"Why?"

Mother sighed and rose. "I do not have much of the girl I was anymore, sweeting. I have my honor, still, and my pride, and I will not allow your father, or you, to take those from me."

Chapter Thirty-Two

Roger ached to take her in his arms and comfort his wife. "You have been to see your mother?"

"Aye." Kathryn had entered the chamber like a whipped dog, devoid of her usual fight and spirit.

He wanted to hold her, kiss her, make love to her. Find the smile and light buried in the uncertain girl before him. The absence from her had raked at him all through his time in London.

The strife befalling his family had brought matters into sharper detail for him. He felt scraped raw inside, fragile and easily broken. Blithely, he had entered this marriage and believed he could make her love him. Love him in the way he craved with every breath.

She went to their bed and sat, staring at him with those bottomless brown eyes that reached into the deepest part of him. He had chosen her. His heart fixed on her and no other would do. But neither would a pale ghost of Kathryn do.

"It seems I have erred," she said. "I sought to rescue my mother, but it transpires she does not want, or need, my rescue."

Before he gave in to his impulse to comfort her, he walked to the casement and stared blindly outside. "She intends to return to Mandeville?"

"Aye."

"Perhaps not for much longer." He could offer her this comfort at least. "As I said, Garrett and I have a plan in the works that might solve that."

She sat up straighter. "You do?"

"Aye," he said. "There was no reason for you to rush off with Garrett, as he well knew."

She fidgeted with her skirts. "I did not give him much choice."

"I suspected as much." Which Garrett could thank for still having a head on his shoulders. He struggled to believe Garrett had let Kathryn put herself in such danger. He near laughed at himself. Nobody let Kathryn do anything. She was her own woman through and through, which is why he knew what had to be done.

She stood and approached him, her hands knotted in her skirts as if she did not trust her reception.

Seeing Kathryn in a dress still took him by surprise. In his mind, she rode astride that great horse of hers, dressed in braies, her fist raised in defiant challenge to all comers.

"I am sorry for my actions," she said. "It is not that I do not trust you. I acted without thinking."

He nodded, because he did accept her apology. "We will need to find a solution to your sister as well."

She dropped her head and heaved a big sigh. "I know."

"If your father discovers her here, he will demand her back."

She nodded, then raised her head. "Roger?"

"Aye?" The uncertainty in her expression tore at him. With one move he could wipe it away.

"Are you not glad to see me?"

Dear God. The wrench within weakened his knees. Glad to see her? She brought the only light into his dark days at the moment. "I am always glad to see you."

"Then..." She frowned. "You seem...different."

He could not keep her in suspense any longer, but dread kept him silent for a few long moments more. This thing with Henry had made him think about many things. Life tossed surprises at a man all the time. Some of them good, some of them gut-wrenching and hard. In his contented life, most of those surprises had been good.

They had suffered their share of setbacks and difficulties at Anglesea, but they had always overcome. Henry's possible death brought their luck to a shattering end. This obstacle they could not fight their way through or negotiate their way around. Their options dwindled to two, wait and accept.

His father's inability to accept those options came from a lifetime of fighting to make his way in the world. Roger understood that sort of frustration to his marrow, but Father could raise the armies of hell and still not win this battle. He would speak with his father later, but first he had this matter to attend.

He had ridden out of Anglesea on a cloud of grief, resentment, and frustration. He had married Kathryn with all the arrogance of a man accustomed to getting his way in everything. A man who mastered his fate. He loved her, and he had seen no reason she would not come to love him.

"I lied to you, Kathryn."

She tensed. "How?"

Certainties did not exist in life. What if she never came to love him? Then, he and Kathryn would remain locked in a marriage of convenience. His love might fade and die, becoming bitter resentment. She might always look at him and see the person who stood between her and her heart's desire. The time had come for honesty between them. If they could not come to share a loving bond, then they would grow to be friends. Her rejection would score deep, for certain, but he could grow to accept it in time.

"I wanted to marry you, and I made my vow to protect your mother to get your agreement." The words came out with barbs attached, scouring him raw from the inside out. "I will do all I can to make good on that vow, but I offer no certainty."

She had gone paler than the sheeting on which she sat. "It no longer matters."

"But it does." Sweat trickled down his sides. He wanted to yank his hauberk off and fling it across the room. "I said many things, Kathryn. That day at Calder when I asked you to marry me."

"Roger." She pressed her hand to her throat.

He knew only one way to cover difficult ground, at a gallop. "I said I married you because of our situation. It was only partly true."

"Ah." She stood and walked away.

Speaking to her back was easier. "I married you because I loved you. I do love you."

Kathryn pressed her back against the wall. She clasped her hands in front of her until her knuckles whitened. "Nay."

"Aye, Kathryn." The distance yawned between them and he closed it. "I loved you then and I love you now."

"But—"

"I said what I needed to say to ensure you would marry me." His fingers twitched, desperate to touch her, but he gripped his hauberk instead. "I knew you did not love me, but I hoped you would come to love me in time. It seems that is no longer possible."

"Roger, I..."

Her inability to finish that sentence lanced through him. "I have failed you in this." Roger took a raw breath. "And you have held my vow up to me as proof of my failure."

She gasped, hurt flickering in her eyes.

Roger steeled himself. "Love is not dependent on whether a person proves themselves worthy or not. I do not love Henry because he is the best brother in the world. I find I miss the irksome parts of him as much as I miss the good."

"I do not understand." She gripped her skirts.

"If a man needed to be worthy of love to have it, my father would have been out on his ass years ago. My mother does not love him because he earned that love. Just as Bea does not love Garrett because there is no finer man in all the kingdom. Or William love Alice because she is the most beautiful woman he has seen. Love does not work that way."

He took a step closer, and she closed her eyes. So be it.

"So here we stand." He needed to get this said before he disgraced himself and bawled like a child. "Both of us caught in a trap of my making. You are married to a man you cannot love, and I am married to a woman who does not love me."

She raised her stubborn little chin. "So now what do we do?"

"We go forward." A bitter laugh escaped him. "Truthfully, I have no idea how we do that. I have a responsibility to my name and my title. I would ask that you give me an heir, but even that is your choice. I have brothers aplenty, and they breed sons to carry our name. You are free, Kathryn. For the first time in your life, you can choose where you go from here." He needed to get out of the chamber before the cost of his words overcame him. "Hell! If you want to sally forth as some modern day shield-maiden, I will provide the army at your back. Do what your heart desires."

The door closed behind him. Kathryn's legs crumpled beneath her, and she sank to the floor.

You are free, Kathryn. For the first time in your life, you can choose where you go from here.

Roger had granted her freedom, requesting only an heir in return and she could refuse him even that. Although, she might already be partway to fulfilling her end of that bargain.

She rubbed the tightness in her chest, but it did not ease.

All she had wanted and dreamed of handed to her in one

devastating conversation. Except her foolish heart ached to run after him and tell him... What? She thumped her head against the wall. She received a sore head for her trouble, but the ache in her chest throbbed unabated.

What did she know of love?

She loved her mother, and Matty. Her heart had never skipped a beat over a man, or even so much as fluttered at a handsome smile. Until Roger of Anglesea had put her atop Striker and told her to take up her sword and show him how she jousted. But what did that mean?

In times past she might have asked Matty, but a gap had opened between them and she did not have the strength to close it. Matty had married for love and now she slept at Anglesea, apart from the same husband she had risked everything for. Risked even Kathryn and their mother.

Digory professed to love Matty, and yet Kathryn had seen his flicker of doubt.

Mother had chosen Father, believing she loved him. Now she determinedly insisted on doing her duty by a man who treated her like a dog.

Garrett loved Bea, and yet they fought as if they could find no truce.

And Roger loved her.

Love.

Kathryn thunked her head a second time. She did not understand this love of which everyone spoke so much.

* * *

Roger bathed in the barracks and donned clean hose and tunic before he went to find his father. Not that Sir Arthur would give a rat's ass for his dirty state, but more to give himself time to gather up the tattered edges of his pride. His heart would take much longer to mend, but he did not mean to wear it seeping and exposed on his sleeve for all of Anglesea to view.

Rob directed him to his parents' chamber when he asked, and Roger knocked before entering.

His mother rose from beside the hearth, her expression soft with love. She enfolded him in a rose-scented hug that near brought him to his knees.

"What news of Beatrice?" He needed to move her attention off him.

"Another boy." Lady Mary smiled. "She was so sure it would be a girl this time."

"Four boys." Sir Arthur sneered. "You would think that would be enough for any man."

"Hush, Arthur." Lady Mary clucked her tongue. "It is not Garrett that keeps insisting on another child."

"Hmph!" Sir Arthur quaffed his wine.

"Mother is right." Roger stood in front of his father. "Beatrice always managed to get her way. She did with you as well."

"Well." Mother arranged her skirts and sat. "Beatrice and her new babe are both healthy and happy. I think they will name him Geoffrey."

"I am glad." The news lifted some of the heaviness from his heart. "I imagine she rests now."

"Indeed." Mother accepted a goblet from Father. "I caught a peek of my newest grandson earlier. He brings some much-needed joy to this old pile of stones. Say what you will about him, Garrett makes fine-looking children."

"I rather think you would say Beatrice makes fine children." Sir Arthur kicked the hearth surround.

"You would." Lady Mary snorted. She looked at Roger. "Your father shared the news from London. You look tired."

Trust his mother to see through any mask he might don. "The ride was long, and I did not sleep much at court."

"Have you seen Kathryn?" Her gaze could strip him to his flesh in a heartbeat.

"Aye."

She motioned him to take a seat. "I imagine you are also here to speak to this stubborn man about his disgraceful behavior."

Sir Arthur growled, but his silence spoke louder than any words.

Roger poured wine before taking his seat in the casement. "So"—he took a long sip—"what was your plan?"

"To get Lady Rose back." Sir Arthur hunkered elbows to knees and glared into the fire.

"You were going to make war on a man to steal his wife." Roger glanced at his mother.

Lady Mary hid a smile behind her goblet.

"All right, pup." Sir Arthur reared up. "Have at it! Mock and jeer all you like."

"I am not here for that." Roger well understood the demons on his father's back.

"Eh?"

"I thought you might like to know that Garrett has the matter in hand. I went to him a while back because he's a good man for seeing another man's weakness. He spotted yours like a hawk on a hare."

Sir Arthur barked a rusty laugh. "Aye, you have the truth of it there."

"He plans to offer Sir Royce what he values more than his wife."

Mother shook her head. "That should not be too hard, as he values his wife not at all."

* * *

Roger searched throughout Anglesea before running Garrett to ground in the kitchens.

"Congratulations." He clapped Garrett on the shoulder. "Another fine boy."

Garrett grinned. "Aye, another lusty one to be sure."

"Beatrice is well?"

"Tired, but well enough." Garrett motioned him to join him at the table. "I never thought I would say this, but I was never more glad to see anyone than you today."

"You were probably running a high fever." Roger dragged out a disused smile.

"I swear your sister's confinements are killing my brain." Garrett grew serious. "It will be the last baby for a while."

"I know." Roger nodded, because he did trust Garrett when it came to Bea. Nobody loved his wild little sister more than this poor sod. "I should not have stuck my oar in your stream."

"This is true." Garrett turned back to Cook. "I am attempting to wheedle some food for my starving belly."

"Come now, Cook." Roger smiled at the large, stern-faced woman who had ruled Anglesea's kitchens for longer than he had drawn breath. Cook never seemed to age, merely got larger with each passing year. "Have you nothing to feed the new father?"

Cook crossed her arms. "I might if the father had worked even a breath as hard as the new mother this day."

Roger shook his head. "I cannot help you there."

"It was worth the try." Garrett winked at Cook.

Cook rolled her eyes, then with a sigh stomped off into the larder.

Garrett studied him. "You look little better than a street cur."

"My thanks, I feel even worse." Roger rested his elbows on the large, scrubbed kitchen table. "You are my last call before I find my bed tonight."

Garrett smirked. "Newt found what I was looking for."

"Are you going to tell me what that was?"

"Do you really want to know?" Garrett placed his fists on the table.

Roger almost wept with gratitude as Cook stomped back in and thunked a jug and two beakers, a loaf of fresh bread, some butter and a jar of fresh honey on the table between them. "Marry me, Cook."

"You are already married, you daft sod." Cook smacked him

upside the head and whirled about. But not before she gave a tiny smile.

Garrett watched Cook until she left, banging the door behind her. "It is simple, really. I asked around about Sir Royce, dug into his past, and came up with the one thing he wants but could never have."

"That being?" Roger drank deep of the ale Cook had provided. Nowhere did they brew ale like here at Anglesea. It went down in a sharp bite of hops.

"His lost love." Garrett dipped a hunk of bread into honey and stuffed it in his mouth. "He lost the one woman he wanted to marry, married one he did not love and now chases every skirt he can as he tries to fill the gap."

Roger spread butter on his bread. God, he hoped he had not erred in leaving this in Garrett's hands "You gave Sir Royce a woman?"

"I gave him the woman he wants more than anything. Or the nearest thing to her I could lay my hands on." Garrett tore off another piece of bread.

Roger let that sink in as he ate his bread. His conscience twanged. As much as he wanted to honor his vow to Kathryn, he could not hand Sir Royce another whipping post. "You know how he treats women."

"I know how he treats women he does not value." Garrett went for more bread. "But, trust me, Sally is no innocent lamb being led to the slaughter. Given a choice between life managing one difficult man and a lifetime of spreading her legs for a host of sods and beaters, she made the best choice for her."

"How do you know he will want her?" Roger let Garrett finish off the loaf.

"I know Sally. She could draw a cockstand from a stone. She also happens to strongly resemble the dead girl, and she is not a woman to let a chance like this pass her by." Garrett stared at the breadcrumbs with a mournful expression. "Do you suppose there is more food?"

"In the larder. Cook also always keeps a cold joint in the box just inside the door." Roger sipped his ale and waited while Garrett made his foray and returned with a ham. "I am not sure I should have asked. You are sure this will work?"

"It is working." Garrett carved a slice and offered it to Roger. "Perhaps next time you will not ask."

Roger took the ham and ate it. "I suppose I should learn to trust your ability at finding another's soft spot."

"Eh?"

"Bea." Roger raised his brow at Garrett to let him know he saw right through the clever dissembling. "You studied my father, found his one weak spot and struck."

"Ah." Garrett looked at the table. "That did not turn out so well for me. I ended up tumbling into my own trap."

"Be that as it may," Roger said. "It was a good plan, even if I did beat your head in for it."

Garrett held up a finger. "As I recall, you got your own head beaten in for trying."

He did like Garrett, and Roger smirked at him. "Let us agree to differ on that. What made you come up with this crazed idea?"

"Ask yourself what Royce wants more than anything." Garrett ate three more slices of meat while Roger waited. "He needs money." Garrett ticked the first point off on his finger. "But he has that already. Having met the man, I would say losing his lady is more about losing command, and that stings his pride. Same thing with losing his daughter."

Roger had surmised about the same. "So?"

"So"—Garrett grinned—"we offer him a sop for his pride."

Roger let Garrett revel in his moment.

"What is the one reason a woman is ousted from a keep?"

The game grew wearisome, and Roger merely glared at Garrett.

"Another woman." Garrett slapped the table. "One woman is ousted from a keep because she stands in the way of another woman. We think men are possessive." Garrett snorted. "A vixen guarding her den is twice as vicious as her mate."

"What if you are wrong and he hurts this Sally?"

Garrett gave him a look of disdain. "You have spent too much of your life farting through silk. There are women who suffer worse." Garrett shrugged. "A man like Royce can be managed, if you understand what drives his fist."

"What drives his fist?"

"Power and command." Garrett thumped the table. "He needs to feel like the biggest hunter in the pack, all the time. Sally will have no trouble pandering to that, whilst making a tidy place for herself."

Roger tried to picture what sort of woman would willingly place herself in the power of a brute. "I am not sure..."

"Trust me." Garrett offered him another slice.

"I cannot save one woman at the cost of another." Roger took the ham. His belly tightened with unease.

"Roger." Garrett carved another slice of meat. "Not all women require rescuing. Some of them are a rather dab hand at doing it for themselves."

* * *

Roger bedded down in a small winter chamber his mother used for sewing. The deep casement made a reasonable bed, even if his feet did hang over the edge. If he went to his chamber this night, he would never be able to resist losing his sore heart in Kathryn's warmth. He wanted her love, freely given and not attached to a growing list of conditions.

A waxing moon rose above the ocean in a clear, star-strewn sky.

His weary body demanded sleep, but his mind refused to rest. His arrogance had brought him to this point. Arrogance and ridiculous boyish dreams of love and happiness. He had thought all he need do was find the girl who made his heart pound and the dream would be his.

Well, he had found the girl, and now he slept on a narrow casement seat and pined at the moon like a lone wolf.

A slipper slithered on stone. "Roger?" Matilda said.

Did he not have enough to worry about without Mathilda's midnight meanderings? He sat up and pulled the furs up. "Lady Mathilda."

She stood halfway between him and the door, her nightrail ghostly white. "I came to see if you needed aught."

"Nay, I thank you." Why did the girls in this family not see anything amiss with wandering into a man's bedchamber in the middle of the night?

Lady Mathilda glided closer, and stopped near his feet. She leaned her head against the stone casement. "It is lovely here."

"Aye." He did not want to discuss the view. If anyone came upon them this would be difficult to explain. "Lady Mathilda, I believe you should return to your chamber."

Silvery moonlight painted the delicate lines of her face. The difference between Mathilda and Kathryn were not that marked in the sparse light. "Do you?"

"It is not appropriate for you to be here."

"Appropriate?" Mathilda gave a musical tinkle of laughter. "Now you sound like your Nurse."

"Nurse often has the right of things." Roger stood and put some distance between them.

Mathilda followed. "You do not sleep with your wife, my lord."

"You should return to your chamber, my lady." It seemed a gross betrayal of Kathryn to have this conversation with anyone other than her.

"I thought you might be lonely." Lady Mathilda trailed her finger over his shoulder and down his arm. "I thought you might turn to me for comfort, as you did before. In the stable." She blew him a kiss, and then floated down the passage away from him.

He saw her damned game now. Tonight had confirmed his suspicions arising from her behavior before he left for London. That night in the stable, on the eve of his departure had been a mistake. He should never have allowed himself that moment of weakness. Never allowed her hands on him. Lady Mathilda had the morals of a cat. And, sadly, the unwavering loyalty of a sister who she in no way deserved.

Chapter Thirty-Three

Kathryn barely slept. The bed seemed too large and empty without Roger and she spent the night curled in a chair before the hearth. She woke with a stiff neck and a mood fouler than the rain clouds blocking out the morning sky.

Matty barreled through the door with a bright smile. "Good heavens, Kate. Do get up. The day is almost half gone."

"Kathryn." She eased the cricks in her back and stumbled to the washstand.

Matty stuck her hip out and huffed. "I do not know why you must insist on being called Kathryn. There is nothing wrong with being called Kate, and it sounds so much sweeter than Kathryn."

Matty knew why she hated the name Kate. Kathryn splashed icy water on her face and came up gasping. "Leave it, Matty."

She hobbled to her clothes tree and grabbed a bliaut.

"Will you wear that?" Matty grimaced.

The plain wool bliaut had come with her from Mandeville. Dark blue, serviceable and perfect for normal day activities. "Aye, I am."

"Well." Matty tossed her head and smoothed her blue silk

bliaut over her hips. "If I was married to a powerful lord, I would do a bit more to look the part."

"You had the chance to be married to a rich lord." Kathryn lost the reins on her temper. "You chose to marry a farmer."

"Kate." Matty drew a sharp breath. Her lip quivered and tears swam. "How can you be so cruel?"

Easy, when her entire world had been turned topsy-turvy. Kathryn dived into her chemise and laced it.

Matty slouched near the hearth, sniffling.

Normally, Kathryn would have rushed to comfort her, but she did not feel inclined to tolerate Matty's barbs this morning. "Have you eaten this morning?"

"I waited for you." Matty wiped her eyes with her sleeves.

Kathryn dragged her despised bliaut over her head. Unlike silk bliauts, this one laced at the side and she had no trouble fastening it. Who had been lacing Matty into her bliauts?

"I wanted to speak to you of Roger." With an arch look, Matty sidled closer to her. "He shuns your bed?"

Shuns! Who was Matty to speak of her marriage? Matty who sheltered here because of her own bad choices. "He does not shun my bed."

"Then why is he sleeping elsewhere?" Matty cocked her head, looking thrilled.

The notion twisted within Kathryn. Then again, Matty had always been thus with her. If Kathryn had a new toy, Matty wanted one just like it, if not better. But, God's teeth, they spoke of husbands now.

"That is between Roger and me." She mustered as much dignity as she could. "Let us break our fast."

During the meal, Kathryn studied Matty's behavior as she never had. Seated between Garrett and Roger, Matty smiled and giggled. Laying her hand first on one arm and then the other. Leaning too close to whichever man spoke.

Beatrice had stayed abed. Lucky for Matty she did, because Beatrice would not have tolerated the outright flirting. Dear God!

Had they not enough to deal with, without Matty stirring the coals?

With Matty, Roger managed a smile, but for her he had nothing but a cold, polite silence. She wanted to shove herself between them and push them apart.

Matty giggled and threw Roger a coy glance.

Kathryn surged to her feet. Her chair screeched against the flags. She would wring someone's neck if she stayed much longer.

Roger and Garrett hurried to rise but she waved them down. "Finish your meal."

She ran down the stairs and into the bailey. Reaching the stables, she slipped inside. The smell and sound of horses calmed her enough for a deep breath.

Peter nodded to her. "Shall I get Striker for you, my lady?"

Kathryn nodded, not calm enough to speak. Her morning mood had worsened, if that was even possible. She wanted to shake Matty until she shook that smirk off her. What had happened to them? They had always been the best of friends, closer than any two sisters. Now, everything had changed. She did not understand Matty, or—God forgive her—like her sister much.

Matty seemed to care for nobody but herself. Even her attempts to comfort the family were like shouts for all to look at Matty. Matty knew she and Roger had slept apart the night before. Instead of offering comfort or counsel, her sister had come to her chamber and gloated. Then sat at breakfast and made cow eyes at Roger.

Peter led Striker toward her, and helped her mount.

Kathryn waited until they had cleared the main gate before she let Striker have his head. Across the flower speckled meadow, they tore, and into the dappled shade of the beech thicket.

Striker took the path to the village and she let him.

Without having formed the conscious thought to do so, she stopped outside the small inn where Digory waited.

"My lady." Harrow, the innkeeper, bowed low as she entered.

He clasped his hands before him, his round face sorrowful. "Any news of Sir Henry?"

"Nay." These people had known Henry since his infancy. Of course they would be waiting for news. "Roger returned from London yesterday, but he had no more news. Until we find out differently, we continue to believe he found a way to escape the battlefield."

"We pray for that, Lady Kathryn." Harrow nodded, his cheeks jiggling. "We have kept a constant prayer vigil since we got word. How fares dear Lady Mary?"

"You know Lady Mary." The strongest woman Kathryn had met. "She bears it well, but it weighs on her."

"Aye, aye." Harrow nodded again, his head bowed. "Give her our best, would you, my lady. Let her know we keep all of you in our prayers.'

"I will." A lump formed in Kathryn's throat. Suddenly her sour mood seemed petulant and childlike in the face of Harrow's sincerity. The Anglesea family was well loved by the folk of their demesne. The same folk who had opened their arms and accepted her as one of them.

"We had some good news last night," she said.

Harrow straightened and rubbed his palms together. "We would all do with a touch of that. Do tell, Lady Kate."

She opened her mouth to correct him and shut it again. When Harrow called her Kate, he meant it with affection. A tiny bond he forged between them. "Lady Beatrice had another boy last night. A fine healthy lad they call Geoffrey."

Harrow pinkened and beamed. "Well, well!" He patted his belly. "That is the very best kind of news. Our Lady Bea a mother again. Such a treat she was as a child. Always tearing about hither and thither, laughing and smiling. Oh, that is fine news." Leaning forward, he gave her a broad wink. "I feel sure our Lady Kate will have some news of her own afore long."

Their Lady Kate. As if she belonged here. Strangely, the idea did not make her feel fettered. Instead, it warmed her within, in a cold, secret place she had not acknowledged in years. Anglesea was her home now. So, where did that leave her and Roger? She needed to think on it, but later when she could find some time alone. "I am here to see Digory," she said.

"He be in the common room." Harrow jerked his thumb. "Quiet lad. Does not say much, or drink and wench like a lot of the travelers we get here."

Digory looked up from the table where he broke his fast. He gaped at her for a long moment before scrambling to his feet. "Lady Kathryn. Is it Matty? Is she ill?"

"Nay, nothing like that." She took the seat opposite him and motioned him to continue his meal. "I came here to speak with you."

"Aye." Digory took his seat slowly.

"Tell me again." Kathryn needed to hear him, and this time with as open a mind as she could manage. "Tell me all of it. Start from when you met Matty."

Digory frowned. "Lady Kathryn I do not see—"

"Please." Her head felt heavy and she rested her chin on her palm. "Tell me everything."

She stayed with Digory through the morning. Harrow brought her tea and scones as she listened. And Kathryn really listened. Not as Matty's staunchest defender but how Roger or Sir Arthur would have heard the story when Digory spoke with them.

Her ride back took much longer, as she had much to think on. Digory's picture of life with Matty struck a chord of truth. Kathryn could not see Matty taking to domestic duties. When she and Roger had first found her, the state of the cottage spoke to that.

Had Matty grown tired of marriage, and decided to move on? Did she view it as an old, worn-out wimple that could be tossed in a corner for something finer or newer or shinier. Which brought up the state of her marriage. If Matty had tossed her old wimple aside, had Kathryn shoved hers to the bottom of the chest and tried to forget about it?

Roger loved her. Or at least he said he did. But how could she believe him? She was a wild, headstrong girl who rode better than she danced and would rather wield a sword than a needle. A woman so unsuited to be baroness it was laughable. And yet, Roger said he loved her.

She wished she knew what to do with that knowledge. What she could not do is stuff it to the bottom of the chest and leave it there. Something must be done about her marriage, but first, something must be done about Matty's marriage.

Matty sat in the hall with Mother. They had their heads together over a piece of sewing.

"Kathryn." Mother looked up with a smile. "I missed you this morning. Matty said you took a ride to clear your fidgets."

Matty said a lot of things to a lot of people. "Aye. I went to the village."

"The village?" Matty stiffened. "Is he still there?"

"Your husband is still there." Kathryn took the seat beside her mother. "I spent the morning with him."

Matty paled. "Why would you do that?"

"I needed to ask him about some things." Kathryn bent and pretended to examine the fine stitching. She could not tell you if they embroidered a dragon or a dandelion, her senses fixed on Matty as she let her absorb her statement. "I needed to ask him about the marks on you."

Mother dropped her embroidery to her lap. "What did he say?"

"I do not like to speak of it." Matty turned her head and stared out the casement.

"And yet you do speak of it." Kathryn took a shameful dose of satisfaction in her words. "All the time and to anyone who will listen."

Mother turned to stare at her. "Is this true, Mathilda?"

"Kathryn exaggerates." Matty sniffed and pressed her sleeves to her eyes. "She has become different now that she is a grand lady."

Mother frowned, looking from her to Matty and back again.

"Nay, Matty is right, Mother." Kathryn squeezed her mother's hand. "I have changed. Before I came here I would not have been able to listen to Digory's story with an open heart."

"I will not stay here and suffer this." Matty flung down her work.

"Sit down, Mathilda." Mother sighed and placed a perfect stitch in the fabric before setting her work aside. "I think this has gone on long enough."

"What did you do?" Matty glared at her.

Matty had a nerve even asking that. "I did nothing."

"You betrayed me."

Hot words in her defense bubbled inside Kathryn. She had always looked out for Matty, always.

Mother folded her hands before her and stood in front of them. "You have both made a fine mess of your marriages."

Kathryn winced as her mother's gaze fastened on her.

Matty looked smug.

"I will deal with you one at a time," Mother said. "First off, Kathryn. You are not my savior. I married your father of my own free will, and I made a promise before God to honor and obey him from that day forward." Her expression softened. "I know you acted out of love for me, but it was not your part to rescue me from your father."

Nay, Kathryn refused to believe that. "He is wrong to treat you so."

"Aye, but he is my husband, and I did make vows." Mother had her chin set at a stubborn angle. "Fight for your own marriage." Mother turned to Matty. "Which brings me to you. You will return to your husband."

Matty sprang to her feet. "I refuse."

"That is not an option." Mother drew her shoulders back. "You chose to run away from the marriage arranged for you. You chose that man, and now you belong to him in the eyes of the world and God."

"You cannot make me." Matty clenched her fists by her side. "Just because you are happy to let a man use you as a beating post, do not think I will allow it."

"If you force my hand, I will invoke the law," Mother said. "Pack your things. I am sending for your husband."

"I shall run away," Matty said.

"Again?" Mother shook her head. "That is your choice, but think about where you will go and whether it will be better than where you are running from."

* * *

Kathryn shivered in the stiff sea breeze battering the ramparts. Dagger pressed against her leg, endlessly patient and happy to be wherever she was.

Digory saw Matty for what she was, spoiled and willful, and still he loved her. It brought Roger's words back to her. Love is not earned or given to someone because they are worthy. If that were the case, she could think of only a handful of people who could possibly have love.

For that matter, what had she ever done to deserve Roger's love? Nothing. She had built her life and dreams on the notion that she would protect and save her mother and Matty. Now they had both chosen their own paths, and those paths put them beyond her shielding arm.

The idea of her mother going back to the grim reality of Mandeville still rankled. But her mother was a grown woman, and she made her own decisions.

Matty would be fine. Strange, she had spent so many years looking after her sister that she had not seen what was right before her. Matty could look after herself just fine. These past weeks at Anglesea had demonstrated that abundantly.

You could not rescue someone from themselves. No matter how much you desired to do so.

Below, people moved to and from Anglesea in a steady trickle. A cart filled with hay, the drover shouting out a greeting to a gaggle of girls, stopped before the gate. People moving about their lives, unaware of the crossroads now before her.

Roger had given her fate back to her. Funny, how she now no longer knew what path she should take. According to her mother, that path was clear. A woman stayed in her marriage, regardless.

One of the girls stood beside the drover's cart, twirling her hair and giggling. Kathryn had never courted the attention of men, because she had never wanted to be at any man's mercy. As a married woman, she had handed control of her life to Roger. Yet, he did not take that control. Instead he left it with her.

He said he loved her.

She kept coming back to that. He loved her despite her mannish ways and lack of feminine wiles. He loved her despite having lived rough with her while they searched for Matty. And he loved her even when she flung scornful words at his head.

An older woman bustled up the road, grabbed the flirting girl by the arm and marched her away from the drover. She harangued the girl until they disappeared into the beech thicket. The other girls trailed behind whispering and giggling.

The drover's cart rumbled through the gate beneath her.

On three sides of the castle spread the endless sea until it met the sky in a hard line. She could take a boat and see what happened when the sea ended.

On the approach to Anglesea a paved road led through the beech thickets to the village, and from there wherever she wanted to go.

Dagger stood and put his nose to the ground, investigating the interesting smells near the walls.

"There you are." Lady Mary's voice startled her. "I have been looking for you."

Dagger went to say hello and Lady Mary crouched and scratched beneath his ears.

"I like it up here," Kathryn said. "You can see to the end of the world."

"Aye." Lady Mary joined her, shivering in the stiff breeze. "I have often wondered what happens when the sea ends." She leaned against the stone crenellations. "Your mother came to see Sir Arthur and me. She says she would like to return to Mandeville."

"Ah." So this is why Lady Mary sought her. She had an uncanny knack for sensing when Kathryn needed to talk. "I was up here trying to make sense of it."

"Of course you were." Lady Mary turned her face to the sun and breathed deep. "It is not your way to calmly submit to the life your mother has."

"How can she even consider it?" The words burst from Kathryn.

Lady Mary shrugged. "I honestly have no answer for that. I can tell you that I would not return, but then I am not Rose. And neither are you."

"He will never stop beating her."

"Probably." Lady Mary looked at the ocean. "But she knows that. Perhaps she feels that is her place, or that she does not deserve more."

Hot, fiery denial rose in Kathryn. "She deserves so much more."

"I agree," Lady Mary said. "I tried to dissuade her from going, but she has her mind made up."

"She also insists Matty return with Digory."

"Aye." Lady Mary looked at her. "I think that is for the best."

"Aye." Because Matty's presence at Anglesea created more strife than anything else. "It seems neither of them needed my protection after all."

"Which leaves you with a bit of a puzzle," Lady Mary said. "I love my son, Kathryn, and it does not please me to see him so wounded. But if you cannot love him the way he deserves, then take the freedom he offers you. Release him to find someone who can return his love."

Nay! The word clattered around inside her.

Lady Mary left her there.

If she took her freedom, Roger would have his. Free to give his love to another woman. Free to smile at that woman, make that woman laugh, and give his huge heart to that woman. Not if Kathryn had strength enough to draw breath he would not. Roger's love belonged to her. Foolish she might be, and no doubt, unworthy, but she aimed to keep it.

Chapter Thirty-Four

Roger returned to his chamber to change before dinner. He had spent the day training with the men, and he stank of sweat. A bath sitting before the fire sent him a warm welcome. He had planned to have one brought up before he left the yards.

He stripped and dropped his dirty clothes in a pile by the door. His squire would be up shortly to take them to the laundry. The warm water wrapped around his aching muscles as he lowered himself into the bath. He rested his head on the bath lip and closed his eyes.

Lady Rose would return to Mandeville. He could not believe it, but Mother told him Lady Rose insisted. Garrett took the news with a shrug, and counseled they wait and see what happened next. Working with his brother by marriage had been an interesting diversion. The man had lived at Anglesea for years, and only now did Roger see his full value. With Henry missing, Garrett would make an excellent chatelaine. Slippery, sly, and with the ferocity of a rousted badger, Garrett made a valuable right hand.

The door opened.

"Rob, see to my clothes will you," he said. "And once you are done, could you take my practice sword to the smith? There is a nick in the blade."

"I see you found my gift," Lady Mathilda said.

Roger's eyes popped open. He jerked in the tub and turned.

Bold as brass, she sashayed into the room. "I watched you, and thought you would need a bath."

Suddenly the soothing water felt filled with nettles. He wanted to leap out of it. "What are you doing here?"

"I am here to see you." She drew her hands over her belly and hips. "I think it is time you and I speak honestly."

Speak honestly? Roger rather thought not, because in honesty he wanted to bellow at her to get out of his chamber and stay away from him. "If you wish to speak, let me dress and then we can have this conversation elsewhere."

Mathilda sauntered to the bed and draped herself across the foot. "I have seen a naked man you know."

"Aye, you are married. As am I, which is why you should not be here."

"Roger." She propped her head on her hand. "You are a good man, and I commend that, but the time for falsehoods between us has passed."

She spoke in pointless riddles. "What falsehoods?" Nudity be damned, he refused to sit here like a rabbit in the pot whilst she played out her little seduction. Roger rose. He snatched a drying cloth and tied it about his waist.

Mathilda took a long slow perusal of him. "You are a fine looking man, Roger."

"You need to go."

She threw back her head and laughed. "You do not really want that. I see how you look at me."

"I look at you like you have lost what wits God gave you." If she did not leave here, he might have to overlook a lifetime of scruples and toss her out on her ass. "You have no business here."

"I see how matters lie." She lay back on her elbows and

pressed her breasts forward. "You married Kathryn because you could not have me."

"I married Kathryn because I love her."

"Nay, you do not." She scowled. "And you do not suit. You forget I know where you spent last night, and I also know that she does not want to be married."

"Get out. Or I will put you out."

"Roger." She stood and slithered his way. "There is no need to fight this thing between us. You know you come to me for comfort. I am not like my sister. I would stay here with you at Anglesea, beside you always."

"Is that so?"

"Aye." She stopped within a breath of him. "I know a good man when I see one. I know how to make him happy." In one convenient stroke she had erased Digory, her sister, and the fact that he had been hers for the taking before she ran away.

Laughter overcame his outrage. "What of your husband?"

"Digory is a farmer. You are a lord." She put her hands on his chest.

Roger resisted the urge to shove her across the room. "So, I shall command him to leave here and leave you with me."

"Exactly." She caressed his shoulders. "Kathryn will leave and it will be just you and me."

"And a keep full of people," he said.

She made a face. "They will grow accustomed to us, and once you are lord here, nobody will question you."

"My father might."

"He will not live forever." She pressed her breasts against him, and draped her arms over his shoulders.

"Shall I shove him off the ramparts to quicken his demise?"

She started. "I did not—"

"And while I am at it, I may as well toss my mother with him." He pursed his lips as if thinking. "That would still leave the problem of Garrett and Bea. Oh, well." He shrugged. "Over the walls and into the sea with them as well."

Her arms slid from his shoulders.

"By that stage, Faye and Gregory will probably take the hint and skulk off to Calder and leave us in peace. And if not...well, there is a lot of space in the sea."

The chamber door swung wide. "Roger, Rob said you were —" Kathryn stood in the doorway.

Roger leaped away from Matty. "Kathryn, I can explain."

"I am eager to hear that." Kathryn straightened and stared at Matty.

Matty raised her chin. "Roger and I are in love. We want to be together."

"What?" Horrified, he turned to Kathryn. "Nay, we are not. I do not even like your sister."

"Really?" Kathryn strolled into the chamber. Her expression reminded him of his mother, cool and aloof. Kathryn stopped in front of Mathilda. "How long has this been going on?"

"A while." Matty faltered and dropped her gaze.

"Kath—"

She raised her hand.

Roger adjusted his drying cloth about his hips. He shivered in the sudden chill of the room. He wished he had full armor on for this encounter.

"Matty?" Kathryn cocked her head. "I want to hear you explain this."

Dear God, nay. Mathilda's version of the truth in no way matched his. Roger stepped forward. A frigid glance from Kathryn halted him. The situation drifted into ridiculous.

"I am the right woman for Roger." Mathilda set her shoulders back. "I always was. You never wanted to be married, never wanted any of this." She nodded. "Well, now you can walk away from it. I shall take your place."

They had this conversation as if he was not standing right there, as if he had no opinion to offer on the matter. "For the—"

"I will get to you, Roger." Kathryn kept her attention on Mathilda. "But I wish to hear from Matty first."

"You want to hear me say you told me so." Matty's cheeks flushed. She waved about. "All right, then. You were right. I should have married Roger when we first came here. You were right. He is perfect for me."

Nay, he sodding well was not. Roger stepped forward.

Kathryn heaved a huge sigh. "Matty, I love you. You are my sister and I will always love you." The loss in her voice made him want to wrap his arms about her. Then, up came that Kathryn-stubborn chin. "But if you think I am going to step aside and let you have my husband, you have lost the meager wits God gave you in the first place."

Roger shook his head, not sure he had heard that right.

Kathryn put her shoulders back. "Roger loves me," she said. "Only me, and you standing here in his chamber while he is naked does not change that. It just makes you a very foolish woman. You have your own man. You cannot have mine."

He almost yelled for joy.

"You do not even want him." Matty sniffled. "You only want him because I have him."

"Of course I want him, you henwit." Kathryn's voice rose with each word. "I love him, and not because I think he would make a good addition to my collection of men and can give me a comfortable life. I love him because he is good, noble, kind, funny, and wonderful."

Roger glowed from within. She loved him. God, he could scarcely believe it.

"He takes care of me, even when I do not think I need it. He watches over me, and he wants more than anything for me to be happy." Kathryn's expression softened. "I am sorry you feel that you do not have the same, but that does not mean you can have what I have."

"He loves me." Matty stamped her foot.

"Nay." Roger judged it a good time to step in. "I really do not. I love Kathryn."

Matty gaped at him. "You cannot mean that."

"Aye, I can." Roger tugged his fiery wife into his arms. "What man would not?"

"Roger." Kathryn pressed her forehead into his chest. "How can you say such things?"

"Very easily." He tightened his arms about her. With Kathryn in his arms he could do anything, conquer the world if need be. "I love you, Kathryn. From the first moment I saw you waving your sword around like a jester."

She stiffened. "You said I was a good swordsman."

"You are now." He smirked. "After I had the training of you."

"You will pay for that." She grinned at him.

"I look forward to it."

Matty harrumphed. "I am standing right here."

Kathryn stared at him, all her heart on view for him, and he almost disgraced himself with a few happy tears. Fortunately, standing in a bathing towel with her sister throwing a fit three feet away helped maintain his manly decorum.

"Go away, Matty." Kathryn kissed him.

* * *

Kathryn stood beside Roger as Digory entered the hall. Roger had sent for him, but only after he spent the night making up for time lost between them.

Digory ran his hands over his slicked back hair, and adjusted his stiff new tunic. Stopping a good distance away from her and Roger, he executed a bow. "You sent for me, Sir Roger?"

"Aye." Roger waved the man to take a seat. "Relax, man, let us share a goblet together and talk about your future."

Digory rubbed his hands on his thighs. "Begging your pardon, Sir Roger, but I would prefer to hear your decision." He swallowed. "Not that it will make any difference, mind. I mean to get my wife back."

"And I mean to make sure you get her back." Roger sat and motioned Rob to bring the flagon and goblets. "Now sit."

Digory collapsed into the nearest chair. "You do?"

"Aye."

He took the goblet from Rob. His hand shook and wine dribbled onto his clean chausses, but Digory barely noticed. "Matty is coming home with me?"

"If you want her." Roger shrugged.

Kathryn discreetly trod on his toe as she took her seat beside him. There was no need to torture the man so.

"I do." Digory gulped his wine. "I really do."

Roger shook his head. "You are certain of that?"

"Aye."

Kathryn ground her heel down.

"Very well." Roger shifted his foot. "But I have a piece of land, not too far from the keep that needs a good farmer. It is a large piece and requires a man of experience whom I can trust."

Digory glanced behind him, and then gaped at Roger. "You mean me?"

"Aye he means you." Kathryn could not leave the poor man dangling any longer. "And we would see to it that you had help on the land."

Digory's goblet clattered to the ground. Wine spilled across the fresh rushes.

"If you would, Rob." Roger glowered at the squire.

Rob huffed and bent to repair the damage.

"I..." Digory stood and sat again. "I...aye. I could...aye." He broke into a wide grin. "Aye, my lord, that would be perfect."

"My bailiff stands ready to show you the place," Roger said. "Matty waits with him."

"Thank you." Digory lunged and grabbed Roger's hand. "Thank you, Lord, I mean, Sir Roger. I will not fail you." He spun about and ran from the hall.

"Poor bastard," Roger murmured. "He is going to need all the help he can get to deal with your sister."

Kathryn wished she could disagree, but Roger spoke true. Matty had ranted and raged most of the night against returning to

Digory. Finally, Sir Arthur had stepped in and with a bellow to frighten bears, told her in no uncertain terms she would return to her husband and remain there. Or she could return to Mandeville.

Lady Mary had added that Mathilda was welcome to visit Anglesea, on occasion, but she was no longer resident of the keep. Lady Rose had added her support.

Resigned, with the air of a true martyr Matty had prepared herself for her departure. Barely recovering herself enough to thank Sir Arthur for the plate, cookware, and pewter he sent with her.

Kathryn had tucked the bliauts Matty had worn into the chest with bed and bath linens.

Garrett strolled into the hall wearing a smug grin. "I see you have dealt with that problem."

"Aye." Roger stretched his legs. "Have you come to lay a new problem before me?"

"Me? Would I do that?" Garrett pressed a fist to his chest. "Nay, I have come to hear your praise on a job excellently done."

Roger raised his brow.

"Ask me what I have in my hand?" Garrett waved a piece of parchment at them.

When Roger stayed silent, Kathryn leaped in. She really did want to know what made Garrett smirk. "What do you have in your hand?"

"I have a letter from Sir Royce's priest." Garrett smoothed the parchment. "In it he states that it would be best if your mother remains at Anglesea for the foreseeable future. Matters, and he does not elaborate, but matters make it impossible for her to return to Mandeville. Sir Royce commands that Lady Rose remain here."

Roger snatched the parchment from Garrett.

Kathryn sensed the air thick with secrets between the two of them, but she cared only for the news Garrett brought. "My mother is to stay here?"

"It looks that way." Garrett chuckled.

"Huh!" Roger lounged in his chair. "I suppose you are taking full credit for this."

"Indeed." Garrett grabbed a goblet from Rob. He raised it to Roger. "To a job well done."

Roger raised his goblet, his gaze warm as it found hers. "To a perfect ending."

Roger left Kathryn fast asleep in their bed, and met with Newt and Garrett in the armory. The watch called the hour well past midnight.

Newt stood dressed for travel.

Garrett counted out gold coins and slid them into a bag. "Send for more if you need it."

"Generous with my money, are you not?" Roger clapped Garrett on the shoulder.

Garrett chuckled. "Better yours than mine."

Newt had grown so much since they had sent him to squire for Henry, but he still appeared hopelessly young for the task on his shoulders. When Newt first suggested this, Roger had laughed. But the boy—man—wanted to do this. He still felt responsible for what had happened to Henry.

Garrett had persuaded Roger to let him go. At times, a man needed to do what he must to set matters right. Garrett understood that better than most.

"You are sure you want to do this?" Roger needed to hear him say it one more time.

"I am." Newt nodded. "I can find my way around any back alley anywhere. I have spent my life surviving on my wits, and now I will use that in the best way I can." He shrugged. "I know the language and I know what to look for." He weighed the gold bag in his hand before sliding it beneath his tunic. "I will try to get word back to you, but it may not be possible."

The holy land lay a long way away.

"Go with God." Roger gripped his shoulder.

Newt met his stare. "If Sir Henry is to be found, I will find him. Or discover what has happened to him."

Roger stood beside Garrett as Newt strode out of the armory. "Do you think he can do it?"

Garrett shrugged. "If anyone can, Newt can."

"Pray God you are right." Roger had not told his parents of this venture. He did not want to spread false hope and break their hearts further. Beside Garrett, only he and Newt knew of the plan.

Mother and Father would leave in the morning and go north to William and Alice. They left him and Kathryn in charge of Anglesea. Father even seemed a little excited to be going. Mother had lost her sparkle, and Roger dearly wished for her, that somewhere between her remaining children and her grandchildren she would find some part of it again.

Nurse refused to accompany them, stating vehemently that she would remain at Anglesea and raise the next generation. Roger applied himself diligently to the task of providing Nurse with some charges.

Bea had already started her campaign against Garrett for a daughter. Thus far, Garrett held firm. Not for a year or two and then they would revisit.

Roger pitied the poor sod. He was clay in Bea's hands. He knew of what he spoke. Kathryn could ask him for the moon and he would get it for her.

Matty visited occasionally, and his respect for Digory grew with each visit. He knew not how the man tolerated such an insistent nag.

Together he and Garrett strolled up the stairs.

"It strikes me that I am in need of a chamberlain," Roger said.

Garrett glanced at him. "You have one in Henry."

"If Newt can find him, and if he returns."

"When." Garrett drew him to a halt. "When Newt finds him, Henry will be your chamberlain." He climbed the stairs. "But until then, I would be happy to keep you from making a dog's ballocks of your demesne."

* * *

Sir Arthur's Legacy is a completed five-book series. It begins with **Sweet Bea** and then **My Lady Faye,** before **Conquering William** and **Defying Roger**. All books in the series can be read standalone, but reading them in order gives you extra insight into the characters. If you want to know what happened to Henry, read book 5, **Henry's Honor** (previously published as Releasing Henry).

* * *

Two worlds unite

Idealistic, honor-bound Henry has lost his way. Alone and enslaved in a foreign land, he has surrendered his hope, his faith, and his belief in love. The only light in his darkness is the daughter of his captor, the mysterious and beguiling Alya.

The only child of a Genovese merchant and a daughter of Cairo, Alya's world is shattered when her father forces her to leave her home and everything she knows to save her life. As her guide in the new world she must enter is Henry—a blue-eyed, golden-haired stranger who fascinates and intrigues her.

Together they embark on a perilous journey to reach safety, but their growing bond must face tests neither is prepared for.

Ignorance and intolerance threaten their hasty marriage of convenience and, eventually, Alya's life. Amidst a clash of cultures, they must find a way to survive and for their love to grow.

* * *

Read Henry's Honor

* * *

Chapter 1

A mix of dust, goat, and the spices of a hundred evening cook fires infused the air. Cumin, coriander, and cinnamon twined together and made English's mouth water. Sunset splashed the sky above Cairo in burnt orange, growing brighter closer to the fiery ball sinking behind the soaring minaret. He tried to remember the name of that mosque, but his head didn't work like it used to.

After herding a small flock of goats into their pens for the night, he ended his working day with the soft click of the latch.

From the city beyond the walls came the wail of a *muezzin* calling the faithful to prayer. "Allah is great; Allah is great."

The inner courtyard emptied as people sought their prayer matts.

"I bear witness that there is no divinity but Allah."

English bore witness to no divinity, and he did not pray. At one time, in another land and to another god, he might have.

Drawn to the heat the stones gathered during the day, he pressed his aching back to the wall and waited.

Like him, she did not pray. The girl on the wall. He knew her name as Alya, had heard it called often enough, but to him she remained the girl on the wall.

Curtains fluttered at the open doorway on the roof balcony. Here she came. For certain, she remained unaware of him concealed in the deepening shadows and watching. To be caught with his eyes on her now would mean Bahir and his whip. Still he waited, would not move from this spot until he saw her.

There. A slim figure shrouded by her *hijab*.

The girl on the wall stopped at the parapet and faced the street. She pushed aside the *niqab*, which concealed all but her eyes. Then, she lifted her hijab and shook her hair free. It spilled down her back as she raised her face in a silent blessing to the day that passed. Dying sunlight rushed to pay tribute to her loveliness. Her hair dark and lustrous as the wood of the wild cherry that grew in a thicket he had once walked, her skin like crushed almonds.

Not that he could see from this distance, but her eyes above her niqab were lighter than he would have expected. A mix of green and brown that he had only glimpsed in passing before she hastily lowered her head. He wouldn't call her beautiful in the way of other women now hazy in his mind. Her chin held too firm a jut, her nose slightly hawk-like. The strong slash of her cheekbones bore testament to her mixed blood. She had a strong face, fascinating, and in her private moment on the rooftop her elemental fire drew him like a starving man to a feast. Her very essence called to that barely living part of him that remembered life in abundance.

In her evening ritual, she discarded the modesty she showed during the day. She believed the rest of the household to be at prayer and in these forbidden moments before she would be called in, or admonished by the older woman who always accompanied her.

And in this stolen moment, English became a man again.

* * *

For first dibs on news, deals, and giveaways, and so much more, join the @Home Collective

Or if Facebook is more your thing, join the Sarah Hegger Collective

Anything and everything you need to know on my website http://sarahhegger.com

About the Author

Sarah Edwards is also published under the name Sarah Hegger

Born British and raised in South Africa, Sarah Hegger suffers from an incurable case of wanderlust. Her match? A hot Canadian engineer, whose marriage proposal she accepted six short weeks after they first met. Together they've made homes in seven different cities across three different continents (and back again once or twice). If only it made her multilingual, but the best she can manage is idiosyncratic English, fluent Afrikaans, conversant Russian, pigeon Portuguese, even worse Zulu and enough French to get herself into trouble.

Mimicking her globe trotting adventures, Sarah's career path began as a gainfully employed actress, drifted into public relations, settled a moment in advertising, and eventually took root in the fertile soil of her first love, writing. She also moonlights as a wife and mother. She currently lives in Ottawa, Canada, filling her empty nest with fur babies. Part footloose buccaneer, part quixotic observer of life, Sarah's restless heart is most content when reading or writing books.

Drove All Night
"The classic romance plot is elevated to a modern-day, wholly accessible real-life fairy tale with an excellent mix of romantic elements and spicy sensuality."
Booklife Prize, Critic's Report

Positively Pippa
"This is the type of romance that makes readers fall in love not just with characters, but with authors as well."
Kirkus Review (Starred Review)

"What begins as a simple second-chance romance quickly transforms into a beautiful, frank examination of love, family dynamics, and following one's dreams. Hegger's unflinching, candid portrayal of interpersonal and generational communication elevates the story to the sublime. Shunning clichés and contrived circumstances, she uses realistic, relatable situations to create a world that readers will want to visit time and again."
Publisher's Weekly, Starred Review

Hegger's utterly delightful first Ghost Falls contemporary is what other romance novels want to grow up to be." – Publisher's Weekly, Best Books of 2017

"The very talented Hegger kicks off an enjoyable new series set in the small Utah town of Ghost Falls. This charming and fun-filled book has everything from passion and humor to betrayal and revenge." –
Jill M Smith, RT Books Reviews 2017 – Contemporary Love and Laughter Nominee

Becoming Bella
"Hegger excels at depicting familial relationships and friendships of all kinds, including purely platonic friendships between women and men. Tears, laughter, and a dollop of suspense make a memorable story that readers will want to revisit time and again."
Publisher's Weekly, Starred Review

"...you have a terrific new romance that Hegger fans are going to love. Don't miss out!"
Jill M. Smith – RT Book Reviews

Blatantly Blythe
"Ms. Hegger has delivered another captivating read for this series in this book that was packed with emotion..." Bec, Bookmagic Review, Harlequin Junkie, HJ Recommends.

Nobody's Fool
"Hegger offers a breath of fresh air in the romance genre." – Terri Dukes, RT Book Reviews

Nobody's Princess
"Hegger continues to live up to her rapidly growing reputation for breathing fresh air into the romance genre." – Terri Dukes, RT Book Reviews

"I have read the entire Willow Park Series. I have loved each of the books ... Nobody's Princess is my favorite of all time." Harlequin Junkie, Top Pick

Also by Sarah Edwards

Sarah Edwards also writes as Sarah Hegger

Urban Fantasy

The Cré-Witch Chronicles

Prequel: Cast In Stone

Vol l: Born In Water

Vol ll: Purged In Fire

Vol III: Raised In Air

Vol IV: Cradled In Earth

Vol V: Joined In Spirit

Sports Romance

Ottawa Titans Series

Roughing

Contemporary Romance

Passing Through Series

Drove All Night

Ticket To Ride

Walk On By

Ghost Falls Series

Positively Pippa

Becoming Bella

Blatantly Blythe

Loving Laura

Willow Park Romances

Nobody's Angel

Nobody's Fool

Nobody's Princess

Medieval Romance

Sir Arthur's Legacy Series

Sweet Bea

My Lady Faye

Conquering William

Defying Roger

Henry's Honor

Love & War Series

The Marriage Parley

The Betrothal Melee

Western Historical Romance

The Soiled Dove Series

Sugar Ellie

Standalone

The Bride Gift

Bad Wolfe On The Rise

Wild Honey